THE
RIPPER
AFFAIR

"*Bastarde!*" A familiar cr⋯⋯⋯⋯⋯⋯ce catching halfway, and the ⋯⋯⋯⋯⋯⋯m the crowd, his pox-pocked ⋯⋯⋯⋯⋯⋯air still plastered down from ⋯⋯⋯⋯⋯⋯.

Clare had enough time to think *oh, dear* before the Eirean rebel in the dock screamed something in his ancient Isle's equally ancient tongue. The crowd, not realising what was afoot, was busy shouting its own discontent, for the judge had reached another pitch in his denunciation.

A simple twist of the Spencewail brother's wrist, and not only would the nitrou-glycerine soaked into sawdust and pressed into sticks tear its bearer to shreds, but also everyone around him.

Including the mentath who had brought the accused to this pass.

Clare's hand slapped the flimsy wooden barrier behind which a witness gave evidence, and his legs tensed. A single leap would bring him to Valentinelli's aid.

It was a leap he did not have time to make. A great ruddy light bloomed as the Eirean student's ink- and chalk-stained fingers found what they sought and twisted, and they *had* solved the problem of the stuttering fuse.

A soundless sound filled the courtroom, and a great painless blow hammered all along Archibald Clare's body.

His last thought was that death had come while he still had his facul⋯⋯⋯⋯⋯ did not hurt.

By Lilith Saintcrow

Dante Valentine novels
Working for the Devil
Dead Man Rising
The Devil's Right Hand
Saint City Sinners
To Hell and Back

Dante Valentine (omnibus)

Jill Kismet novels
Night Shift
Hunter's Prayer
Redemption Alley
Flesh Circus
Heaven's Spite
Angel Town

Bannon and Clare novels
The Iron Wyrm Affair
The Red Plague Affair
The Ripper Affair

THE RIPPER AFFAIR

Bannon & Clare: Book Three

LILITH SAINTCROW

www.orbitbooks.net

ORBIT

First published in Great Britain in 2014 by Orbit

Copyright © 2014 by Lilith Saintcrow

Excerpt from *Full Blooded* by Amanda Carlson
Copyright © 2012 by Amanda Carlson

A CIP catalogue record for this book is available from the British Library.

ISBN 978-0-356-50094-2

Typeset in Times by Palimpsest Book Production Limited,
Falkirk, Stirlingshire
Printed and bound in Great Britain by
Clays Ltd, St Ives plc

Papers used by Orbit are from well-managed forests
and other responsible sources.

MIX
Paper from
responsible sources
FSC
www.fsc.org   FSC® C104740

Orbit
An imprint of
Little, Brown Book Group
100 Victoria Embankment
London EC4Y 0DY

An Hachette UK Company

www.hachette.co.uk

www.orbitbooks.net

Alone in a crowd

Chapter One

A Messy Method

The trouble with dynamitards, Clare had remarked to Valentinelli that very morning, was the inherent *messiness* of their methods.

Of course, the Neapolitan had snorted most ungraciously. Anyone who killed with such a broad brush was a bit of a coward in his estimation – a curious view for one who named himself an assassin, certainly. Still, Clare had not meant merely their means of murder, but everything else as well. It was just so dashed *untidy*.

This Clerkenwell courtroom was packed as a slaughter-yard's pens, and the lowing crowd stank of rotting teeth and stewed potatoes, violet or peppermint cachous and sweat, wet wool and the pervasive breath of Londinium's yellow fog. It had been a rainy summer, and even those venturing into the countryside to pick hops had been heard to grumble. The weather did not fully explain the crush; there were hangings elsewhere in the city that served the lower classes as better amusement.

However, the public – or at least, a certain portion of that great beast – expressed *quite* an interest in these proceedings. It did not take a mentath's faculties of Deduction or Logic to answer why – the Eastron End of Londinium's great sprawl was slopping over with both foreigners and Eireans; Southwark crammed to the gunnels with Eireans as well. Twenty or more to a stinking room and their blood-pricked fingers, Altered or not, largely responsible for the gleaming, expensive mechanisterum shipped out each Tideturn.

It was no wonder they were restless, given the ravages of the Red, cholera and tuberculosis as well – and the rampant starvation on their Emerald Isle, where their over-lords, most of supposedly healthy Englene stock, behaved more like petty feudal *seigneurs* than benevolent citizens entrusted with the task of dragging Papist potato-crunchers from their ancient green mire.

That was, however, not in the purview of a lone mentath to speak against. He was merely present to give evidence. He could not allow Feeling to intervene with Logic *or* Truth.

Sometimes, even a mentath could wish it were otherwise.

"The device you refer to is unquestionably the work of the accused," he said, clearly and distinctly, and ignored the rustle that went through the courtroom. Whispers and hisses rose. "For one thing, the manner of twisting the fuse is very particular, as is the signature of the *chemica vitistera* used to make the bomb itself. Had it not been defused, it would have been rather deadly for anyone visiting Parliament that day."

"A modern Gunpowder Plot, then, sir?" the judge enquired, his cheeks flush with pride at his own wit.

Archibald Clare did not let his lip curl. Such a display would be unworthy of a soul dedicated to pure Logic. Still, the temptation arose. Under the powdered wig and above the robes of Justice, the man's petty chuckling and drink-thickened face was a florid insult to the very ideal he had theoretically been called to serve.

Still, one could not have shaggy brutes blowing up Parliament. Once that was allowed, what on earth was *next*? He had no choice but to send the young Eirean, shackled in the Accused's box and guarded by two sour-faced bailiffs, to the gallows. There would be a crowd of murdered souls waiting for the lad in whatever afterlife he professed, since he had already been twice successful – the explosion on Picksdowne, and another at the Bailey. Now *that* had been a horrific event.

The question of how these events could be traced to the Great Blight wracking the young man's homeland was an open one. There were whispers of the Eirean spirit of rule struggling to manifest itself – a blasphemous notion, to be sure, but even such blasphemy found a ready hearing when the staple crop rotted in the ground and the tribes of Eire found themselves starving as well as browbeaten and outright terrorised. Could such a thing excuse this young man, or mitigate his murders?

When, Clare was forced to wonder in some of his private moments, could a man, even a mentath, cease unravelling Causes and concern himself only with Effects?

The young Mr Spencewail was accused of treachery to the Crown, both as a dynamitard and as a member of a particular Eirean brotherhood that called its members Young Wolves. Eireans were subjects of Britannia; but the Englene's privilege of a trial by jury did not apply to them as a whole, and the Crown had not seen fit to intervene or offer a pardon.

Distaste for the whole affair, finished or not, was a sourness against Clare's palate. "Perhaps," he said, carefully. "That is outside my concern, sir. I may only speak to what I witnessed, and what may be deduced."

As a sop to his conscience, it was not quite all Clare could have hoped for. As Emma Bannon sometimes remarked, conscience was a luxury those in service to Crown and Empire did not often possess.

"Quite so, quite so," the judge bugled, and fetched a handkerchief from some deep recess of his robe. He sniffed loudly, affected to dab a patriotic tear from his deep-set eyes, and launched into upbraiding the young Eirean.

Clare turned his attention away. He was not given leave to go *quite* yet, but experience told him this particular judge would not ask anything resembling a question for a long while. Mr Spencewail had no solicitor: he might as well have been a sullen lump, voiceless and inert.

Miss Bannon would have been watching him with bright

interest, though, ever unwilling to let a potential danger go unobserved.

Upon Clare's thinking of her, the small crystal and silver pendant tucked under his shirt on its hair-fine chain – a Bocannon's Nut, meant to warn the sorceress when Clare was in dire danger – chilled sharply. Wearing it while engaged upon investigations of a somewhat dangerous nature had become routine, even if the thing seemed to have some variance of temperature even when he was not in any difficult strait. He had not yet had a private moment to take the necklace off, *or* sleep. It was a bloody miracle he had possessed a few spare moments to wash his face and shave said countenance before appearing here, and once he was excused there was more work to be done.

As far as the authorities were concerned, the culprit was caught and further danger averted, but Clare was not so certain. He would not rest until he *was*. His faculties – and his quality of thoroughness, however inconvenient – would not allow it.

The courtroom, packed to the gunwales as it was, positively wallowed every time a fresh piece of evidence was introduced or a rise in the judge's voice denoted something of interest. Somewhere in the high, narrow, stone-walled room – a leftover from the Wifekiller's time with the rose of his royal dynasty worked into chipped, cracked carvings near the ceiling – was Valentinelli, who had flatly refused to cool his heels in Mayefair or at Clare's often-neglected Baker Street quarters. Mrs Ginn, redoubtable landlady that she was, sometimes complained that Mr Clare kept the rooms so as to gather dust, but allowed that a gentleman was sometimes allowed to live as and where he pleased, even if he was one of her blessed lodgers.

Another ripple ran through the crowd. Were they bored with the lord justice, as he was? Did they think his refusal to speak outside his purview as a sign of support for their Cause? Did they have anything so concrete as a Cause, or was their dissatisfaction that of the mute beast?

What is this? Feeling, in place of Logic? It was not merely the press of the crowd; for a moment Clare's collar was far too tight. He did not lift a finger to loosen it; the Bocannon was a chip of burning ice. The curious internal doubling a mentath was capable of held the crowd in a bubble of perception, while his faculties raced under the surface of his skull to pinpoint the discomfort.

What is amiss?

Observe.

Sweat. Beads of sweat, a slick brow under the brim of a wool hat; far too flush even for a man caught in this press. High colour on scrape-shaven cheeks, but a pale upper lip told Clare the young man had possessed a moustache just this morning, and the line of his jaw was very familiar. His cloth was wrong as well – the coat was ill fitting, and too rough for the shoulders of a clerk unaccustomed to a drover's work. Besides, there were traces on the sleeves, smears of familiar blue chalk, and the connection blazed into life.

Ah. So Spencewail does *have a brother!* The satisfaction of having his deduction proved correct was immense, but at the moment Clare could not luxuriate in it, for the man in the chalk-smeared coat undoubtedly had explosive sticks strapped to his torso.

The man ripped his coat open with blistered fingers, a single horn button describing an arc as it fell. A familiar brass dial attached to strips of leather gleamed against his sunken chest and the stained cloth of his workman's shirt.

Spencewail, standing in the dock, had not yet realised what was afoot. He still glared at Clare, who had already begun to shift his weight. The blast would be quite vicious if they had solved the problem of sputtering in the catch-dial—

"*Bastarde!*" A familiar cry, Ludovico Valentinelli's voice catching halfway, and the Neapolitan assassin appeared from the crowd, his pox-pocked face alight with fury, his lank hair still plastered down from his morning's hurried ablutions.

Clare had enough time to think *oh, dear* before the Eirean rebel in the dock screamed something in his ancient Isle's equally ancient tongue. The crowd, not realising what was afoot, was busy shouting its own discontent, for the judge had reached another pitch in his denunciation.

A simple twist of the Spencewail brother's wrist, and not only would the nitrou-glycerine soaked into sawdust and pressed into sticks tear its bearer to shreds, but also everyone around him.

Including the mentath who had brought the accused to this pass.

Clare's hand slapped the flimsy wooden barrier behind

which a witness gave evidence, and his legs tensed. A single leap would bring him to Valentinelli's aid.

It was a leap he did not have time to make. A great ruddy light bloomed as the Eirean student's ink- and chalk-stained fingers found what they sought and twisted, and they *had* solved the problem of the stuttering fuse.

A soundless sound filled the courtroom, and a great painless blow hammered all along Archibald Clare's body.

His last thought was that death had come while he still had his faculties intact, and that, strangely enough, it did not hurt.

Chapter Two

A Remedy For Concern

Morning at 34½ Brooke Street thrummed with orderly activity. The kitchen bubbled with preparations for luncheon, tea, and the evening's dinner; footmen hurried to and fro in preparation to accompany a maid or two a-marketing; a bath had been drained; and the mistress of the house, in a morning dress of amber silk, stood in her conservatory, her fingers infinitely gentle as she parted a tinkling climate-globe of golden ætheric force over a struggling hellebore.

The experiment was not going well, and Emma Bannon probed delicately at the plant with several nonphysical senses, seeking to find the trouble. She hummed softly, finding the proper series of notes, and winced internally at the dissonance in the plant's response.

A slight cough near the door informed her that her lean,

yellow-eyed Shield was not finished with his own troubleseeking. He had already ruined breakfast by almost quarrelling with her.

Or, perhaps not quarrelling. Perhaps he really did believe her in need of coddling, or maybe he was truly anxious that his mistress was sinking too deeply into eccentricity. Primes were notorious for their oddities, which grew more pronounced over the course of a very long life. In some instances, the peculiarities turned deadly.

In any case, he chose exactly the wrong way to express said anxiety, phrased as a command. "Sooner or later you must face the world."

If she were charitable, she would concede that it was not *quite* a command, and most probably intended as a statement of fact. Her skirts rustled – this morning dress, with relatively loose corseting and an unfashionably small bustle, had the advantage of being almost comfortable. "I will," she replied, absently. "Not while *she* reigns, though. At the moment I am very busy with events occurring under my own roof."

Mikal subsided, but not for long. "You are unhappy."

Why on earth should that matter? She untangled an ætheric knot, her concentration firming and the pleasure of sinking herself into a task almost enough to soothe her irritation. "I am *quite* content, except my Shield continues yammering while I am engaged upon an experiment. You were trained to act more appropriately, Mikal."

She sensed the flare of unphysical heat from him, denoting his own irritation and further sensed a tightness in his limbs. Did he perhaps wish to strike her?

It was a novel idea. It would certainly save them both from boredom.

If he wishes to, that is all very well. As long as he does not attempt it in fact.

Boredom, too, could drive a Prime to experiment too rashly with certain facets of the irrational arts. She was not yet at the point of seeing certain necessary precautions as mind-numbingly time-wasting, but she was perhaps very close.

"Now, what are you about?" she murmured to the hellebore. The plant was carrying on gamely, but traceries of virulent yellow and twisting black ran up its stems, down the central spine of each drooping leaf. Leprous green sorcery sought ineffectually to contain it, but the yellow would not be halted. Even loosening the invisible knots did not help.

Bloody hell. The ætheric tangle was growing worse, and strangling the life out of the hellebore's tissues. *I wonder why it does that. Hmm.*

Unravelling the sorcerous threads required a light touch and considerable patience. The problem was a resonance; she caught herself worrying at her upper lip with her teeth. *A lady's face should not make such a display*, Prima Grinaud would have said, and the thought of the wasp-waisted teacher and her whispering black, watered-silk skirts was enough to smooth Emma's expression while she hummed a descant, seeking to find the vibration responsible.

Ah, there. Her humming shifted. A tiny thread of ætheric

force spun down, the ring on her left index finger – a confection of marcasite and chrysoprase – glowing sullenly. Yellow veining retreated as the hellebore lifted its drooping leaves, the stems firming and the sudden *rightness* of a correct bit of sorcery sending a delightful thrill all the way down to Emma's toes, encased in dainty button-up boots that also were unfashionable, but reasonably comfortable.

"Very satisfying." She brushed her fingers quickly against her skirt, flicking away a tiny crackling of excess force. The climate-globe sealed itself, singing its soft muted bell-tone; the plant would survive. Not only that, it would downright thrive, and the manner of its cure gave her a fascinating new vista to experiment upon.

Clare would approve. Chartersymbols flashed along the globe's shimmer, naming its confines and its function; a spatter of rain touched the conservatory's windows.

Mikal, tall in his usual olive velvet jacket, the knives worn openly at his hips and his dark hair freshly trimmed, stood to one side of the door. Perhaps inevitably, he was boiling with carefully reined irritation: a lemon-yellow tinge to Sight. "You have not left the house in months, Prima."

Which was true enough, she supposed. At least he was not asking *why*. "I have seen no need to go gadding about. Should you wish to visit the Zoo or perhaps take a turn in Hidepark, you are more than welcome to." She clasped her hands, tilted her head and felt the reassuring weight of her lapis earrings as they swung gently.

"The Palace sends you dispatches."

She decided the familiar tone he currently employed could be borne only so far. "Which I return unopened, Shield." *The Empire has not crumbled without my help to prop it up. I cannot tell whether to be pleased or vexed.* "And," she continued, "no doubt you are relieved I am no longer in any possible danger, feeling no urge to step outside. It must be wondrous calming for a Shield when his charge behaves so."

"I am . . . concerned." The thundercloud knitting upon his brow might have cheered her own darkening mood, had she let it.

"Ah. I believe there is a remedy for your concern." Her tone dripped with sweet solicitude. "You may leave the worrying to me, Mikal. Your head is simply not fit for it."

"Your temper, Prima, is as sharp as your tongue."

She took a firmer hold on said temper. "And you are speaking out of turn."

"Emma." His hands spread slightly, and she wished he would not look so . . . downcast, or so pained. His presumption she could easily parry.

His affection was another matter entirely. It took a long while to undermine a citadel with kindness, but it could be done.

She was saved the trouble of responding by a sharp, almost painful internal *twitch*.

The sorceress stilled, her attention turning inward, and her Shield's sudden tense silence was a familiar comfort. *What on earth is that?*

It had been a long while since she had felt that

particular sensation; she flashed through and discarded several invisible threads before finding the one that sang like a viola's string. Plucked by a long, bony finger . . . he had marvellously expressive hands for such a rigid logician, though Emma had never told him so.

Clare. In danger. But he has the . . . The string yanked sharply again, a fishhook in her vitals, and Emma almost gasped, training clamping down upon her fleshly body's responses to free a Prime's will to work unhindered.

She returned to herself with a rush, the walls of her house vibrating soundlessly. Her indentured servants, well accustomed to such a sensation, would be calmly pursuing their duties.

Mikal leaned forward, his weight braced, ready to move in any direction. "Prima?" Carefully, quietly – no matter how he might test her temper, it was best not to do so when there was sorcery to accomplish.

She supposed it was a small mercy that he was, at least, willing to cease his questioning when an emergency threatened.

"It is Clare," she heard herself say, distantly. "To the stables, saddle two horses. *Now*."

Chapter Three

Stillness Descending

Moans and cries, an acrid reek, blood crusting or fresh, the throat-coating nastiness of scorched stone. There was no ventilation, and the crush of the crowd had only worsened.

"Move *back*!" Clare coughed violently, a painful retch bringing up a dry thick gobbet of something he spat to the side with little ado. "He cannot *breathe*, give him space!" The Bocannon was a cicatrice of frost upon his chest; his shirt and jacket were in tatters. His bare knees grated against shards of smoking wood, and somewhere a woman screamed, high-pitched repeating cries piercing Clare's aching skull. "And for God's sake clear the doors!"

"*Bastarde*," the wreck of a body in his arms muttered. "Cold."

"All will be well," Clare lied numbly. "Ludo—"

Whistles sounded, shrill and useless. Help had arrived outside, perhaps, but the shouts and curses amid the struggling mass at the door sought to bring a deduction to surface amid the porridge his brain had become.

Ludovico . . . The struggle to think clearly stung his eyes, or was it the thick smoke? Blood, hot and slippery over his hands, and the foul stench of a battlefield. He knew what it meant, knew he should gaze dispassionately at the shredded flesh and shattered bone he clasped, so heavy.

So, so heavy.

Deadweight.

Do not think such things. "All will be well," he repeated. "Help is coming."

Half the assassin's face was a scorched ruin. Well, he had never been pretty, even on the best of days.

Why had he thrown himself upon the dynamitard?

He thought to do his duty. As always. Quite remarkable sense of honour, for an assassin.

The body in his arms stiffened. Ludo's dark eyes dimmed, blood bubbling at the corners of his shredded mouth. There were spots of soot on his pitted cheeks, and dewdrops.

Do not be an idiot. There is no dew. His eyes were burning, blurring. It had to be the smoke.

The crowd screamed and surged for the doors again. Ludo's lips moved, but Clare could not hear through the din. Trampling and thrashing, the courtroom had become a seething creature with its own panicked mind. The pressure against the inward-opening doors would preclude those outside from offering aid.

Nevertheless, a great stillness descended. Clare stared down, into the face he knew as well as his own, horribly battered now. A shudder heaved through the floor – no, the body he held? Or was it his own frame, stiffening against the onrush of irrational emotion?

The Bocannon gleamed, clearly visible now that Clare's shirt and jacket were in tatters. Ludo's gaze fastened on that spark, and his lips moved again. The pendant gave a last flare of fiery ice, and Clare's nerves were alight all through his skin.

His whole, unbroken skin. He had survived, fantastically, unbelievably, suffering only rent clothing and the stinging of smoke. "Ludo—"

"*Stregaaaaa . . .*" the Neapolitan sighed, and Clare bent forward over him, unheeding the illogicality of his own broken sobs.

No. No, no no—

No protest would avail; no exercise of deduction would halt this. The mentath closed his eyes.

He did not wish to see.

There was a sound. Low and vicious as a blade cleaving wet air. The noise of the crowd was pulled away, a curtain swept aside by an invisible hand. The Bocannon gave out a high tinkling rill of notes, and a breath of sweeter scent cut through the reek.

Clare could not look. He crouched over the body,

even heavier now that its occupant had fled. The quiet was immense, crushing, the blackness between stars, and when they found him he was no longer weeping.

Chapter Four

Some Order Here

It was, as a Colonial might say, a bloody horrific *hell* of a mess.

By the time Emma half fell out of the bay clockhorse's saddle – her morning dress was never going to be the same – into Mikal's hands, the narrow street leading to the Clerkewold was jammed with a milling crowd, straining carriages and a great deal of nasty smoke, as well as policemen blowing their damnable silverwhistles and clacking blocks together instead of doing anything *useful*.

In short, it was a situation only a sorceress could remedy, and Emma Bannon stalked forward. The tugging of the Bocannon had crested and subsided, and why it should lead her *here* she had no idea, except that Clare was somewhere in this disorder and needed her aid. She had not seen him for a week or two, but that was normal, when he had an affair engaging his attention.

The fog was not bad this afternoon, pale yellow and merely unpleasant instead of choking. Still, Londinium's great bowl seethed differently, as if potent yeast had been added during her absence. Or perhaps it was merely that she had lost the habit of familiarity with crowded, odiferous streets and high-pitched cries.

First, a bit of quiet. A half-measure of chant slid from her lips, spiked with ætheric force, every inch of jewellery on her flaming as she drew upon its accumulated charge. The screaming, both human and equine, cut off sharply. It was a moment's worth of work to clear a path to the Clerkewold's set of high narrow double doors, but three of the four were fastened shut and the stream of people fleeing whatever disaster had taken place had dammed itself to a mere trickle.

Emma paused, the crowd exploding away as it realised one of sorcery's children was present and quite likely irritated. Mikal was at her shoulder, having no doubt attended to the clockhorses in some fashion; she set her heels, her hands coming forward, fingers curled around empty air.

She *pulled*, a second rill of notes issuing from her throat, and expended a little more sorcerous force than she strictly had to. The doors exploded outwards, shards of wood whickering as they sliced the air, and smoking bits peppered the crowd.

A torrent of persons issued forth, stumbling down the

stairs, their cries shrill and tinny as they met the blanket of silence Emma had laid over the street. She unknotted a single strand of the first spell with a discordant note; it would unravel on its own and slowly return clamour to this part of Londinium.

She picked up her skirts, suddenly acutely aware of being outside her domicile with nothing even approximating gloves, a shawl, or a hat. Her hair was likely disarranged from the ride here as well, and familiar irritation at being dishevelled rose inside her.

At least the escapees, singed and shrouded in foul smoke – had Clare been conducting experiments in a courtroom? – had the wit to give her space as she climbed the worn stone steps; dividing around her much as a river embraces a stone.

The Bocannon's tugging was faint now; whatever had occurred was now largely finished. Its bearer was still alive; beyond that, she could sense nothing.

He has Ludo to guard him. And he has . . . it. The Stone.

She discarded the thought as useless. Besides, why would she wish to be reminded of that nasty affair? It had cost them all dearly.

The vapour was foul, and there was a sick-sweet odour of roasting. What manner of disaster had he embroiled himself in *now*? She should have paid closer attention to the affairs he was engaging himself upon.

It was no use to scold herself now.

Mikal's hand touched her shoulder. He pointed, and there was another set of doors, old wood rubbed with so much oil it had turned black. The walls teemed with the rose of Henry the Wifekiller's family crest, worked over and over again, an explosion of arrogance. Of course, the man had been an apotheosis of pride, almost rivalling a Prime's traditionally large self-regard. It was a very good thing a reigning spirit would not deign to inhabit a vessel with sorcerous talent. A double measure of such over-weening vanity might well leave whatever Empire it graced a smoking ruin.

It was another moment's work to shatter the blackened wood, widening the aperture through which more smoke-maddened human beasts poured. She was spending force recklessly, and found she did not care one whit.

Where is he?

Some manner of legal proceeding had been in session; paper fluttered, blackened and torn. The stink of a battle-field roiled out with the smoke, but she could spare no attention for an air-cleansing charm.

Because there, amid the shattered bodies, knelt Archibald Clare, a lean man past his youth whose sandy, greying hair was flame-crisped at the ends. His shirt and jacket had been blown away, ribbons hanging from the cuffs, and his trousers were just short of indecent.

He hunched over a horribly burnt and battered form.

Emma, who had seen many a death in her day from illness or . . . other events, halted. The sorcery she had been gathering to restore some order and breathable air to the room died unformed, her rings sparking and sizzling, the bronze torc at her throat warming dangerously as ætheric strings snarled, tangling against each other just as the fleeing crowd had.

No. Oh, no.

There was nothing to be done for the shattered body; no spark of life left to seal into the violated flesh. Even had she been a Mender, there was no help for Ludovico Valentinelli now, and Emma let out a shaking breath.

"Clare?" She sounded very young, even to herself. Firmed her expression and strode briskly through the wreckage. In the remnants of the judge's bench another well-built man torn by the force of some ungodly explosion – though there was no trace of fiery sorcery lingering in the room, merely the quivering shreds of truthtelling and inkwell charms unravelling as their physical bases lay broken – bubbled and croaked, probably close to dying. She paid him little mind. "Archibald. Dear God."

He did not move. Muscle under the flour-pale skin of his narrow back did not flicker, and for a moment something black lodged in her throat. Was he . . . despite the Stone's gift, was he . . .?

"I hear his heartbeat," Mikal murmured. "But not . . . the other's."

Ludovico. It was unquestionably the assassin she had blood-bound to Clare, the most intelligent and reliable of his ilk she had ever come across during her erstwhile service to the Crown. One of his hands was whole and uninjured, slack against the stone pavers lining the floor. His fingernails, of course, were filthy, and for some reason that detail caused a great calm to descend upon her.

Who did this?

For the moment, it did not matter. First things must be tidied, Clare must be made safe, and . . . Ludo. There were arrangements to be made for his eternal rest. She owed him as much, at least.

Then, she told Clare silently, *I shall visit vengeance upon whoever did this.*

Mikal's hand had tensed, fingers digging painfully into her shoulder. Did he think she would buckle? Swoon, like some idiot woman? Or was he relieved at the fact that it was the assassin who lay dead, and not the mentath? Who knew?

"Turn loose of me," she managed, and her tone was ice. The words echoed in the suddenly empty room, and the wreckage quivered. She rearranged the ætheric strings that had become tangle-frayed, and the air-cleansing charm crackled as she set it free. "Help Clare. And for God's sake let us have some order here."

Chapter Five

Quite Possibly Your Regard

There was a sense of motion, and jolting.

A carriage? For a moment the protective blankness his faculties were swathed in threatened to thin – or worse, shatter completely.

So he withdrew, and for a long while there was nothing, until he heard her voice again. Cultured and soft, and yet brisk as ever. "Yes, there . . . Carry him to his room. Mr Finch, there are arrangements to be made. Alice, please tell Madame Noyon I require her – I shall be wearing mourning. Horace, fetch wax and parlieu, I shall be sealing a room. Mikal – oh, yes, thank you. Quite."

More motion, outside the cotton-muffling. Sadly, his flesh would not allow him to retreat much longer. Certain pressures were building, not the least the urge to avail himself of a commode or its equivalent. Even a stinking alley would do.

Memory rose – Valentinelli, his eyes a-glimmer in the dark of a filthy dockside lane, amused at Clare's distaste for such quarters. *When you are done pissing, mentale, there is work to be done*.

The choking sensation must have been leftover smoke. For a moment his brain shivered inside its hard bone casing and the edifice of Logic a mentath built to house the constant influx of perception and deduction threatened to crumble. If it failed him, he would be lost – his fine faculties a useless mix of porridge and ash, the irrelevance every mentath feared even more than the loss of mental acuity descending upon him.

Mentaths did not go mad, but they could retreat into phantasies of logic, building a rational inward castle that bore no relevance to the outside world at all. A comfortable room in some asylum would be the rotting end of such an event. He would no doubt have every manner of care – *she* would do no less – but still, it was a fate to be feared.

Softness about his frame, and familiar smells. Leather, dust scorched away by cleansing-charms; linen and paper, and a breath of Londinium's acrid yellow fog. His body was demanding to be heard. He turned away, into the blackness. It was his friend, that mothering dark, and something in him shivered once more.

Impossible. It is impossible, irrational, miraculous —

On that road, however, lay something very close to madness.

"Archibald?" Quite unwontedly tender, now. Miss Bannon sounded weary, and breathless. "If you can hear me . . . I am attending to matters. You are quite safe. I . . ."

Tell me it is a dream. A nightmare.

But mentaths did not dream. There was no room for it in their capacious skulls. Or if they did, such a thing was not remembered. It seemed a small price to pay for a rational, orderly world that performed as expected.

You suspect the world is not rational at all, Clare. Therein lies your greatest fear.

A rustle of silk, a breath of spiced pear. She had worn this particular perfume for quite some time now, and it suited her well. The smoky indefinable odour of sorcery, adding complexity. Another scent, too – the mix of flesh and breath that was a living woman.

Living. As he was.

Everyone about me was injured fatally. Perhaps I am grievously hurt and I cannot tell? Shock?

Yet he could feel his fingers and toes, the flesh he was doing his best to ignore. There were cases of those who had lost a limb reporting phantom pain; were there also other sensations? A ghost-limb . . . perhaps the nerves, enduring a shock, struggled to re-create the lost wholeness?

The horrible bubbling of Valentinelli's tortured body struggling against the inevitable refused to recede into memory. Paired with the utter gruesome silence of death, the two set up an echo that threatened to tear him asunder.

"I am attending to everything," she finally repeated. Had she paused, or had he simply lost track of Time, that great semi-fluid that could stretch at will? No matter how a clock sought to cage it, that flow did as it pleased.

"Mum?" A discreet cough, and printed on the back of Clare's eyelids came the cavernous face of Mr Finch, the indentured butler's balding pate reflecting mellow light from the sorcerous globe depending from the ceiling. He could tell from the slight lift at the end of the word that Finch considered the situation rather uncomfortable but certainly not dire. "Carriage, from Windsor. Requesting the honour of your presence."

A short, crackling silence. There was a soft touch to the back of Clare's hand – he shut it away, Feeling warring with Logic again. If he allowed any quarter in that battle, he would be defeated into sludge-brained uselessness in short order.

Her reply, measured and thoughtful. "Give the coachman a dram and send him on his way. Say that I am indisposed."

"Yesmum?" It was all the question Finch would allow himself.

"Thank you, Finch." In other words, she was *quite* sure she did not wish to be transported to Windsor. Inferences began to tick under the surface of Clare's faculties, but he did not dare give them free rein. "Archibald, if you can hear me . . . simply rest. You are safe."

A whisper of silk, the sound of bustling, and no doubt one of the footmen would be sent to sit with him and make certain of his continued breathing. Murmurs and hurrying feet, and Clare finally let himself face the unavoidable conclusion.

Miss Bannon performed some miracle long ago, while I was ill with the Red and expected to die. She has not spoken of it since, and neither have I. But now . . .

Now I rather think we must.

As a means of wrenching his attention from the memory of blood and dying, it was not enough. The tide of Feeling arose again, and this time he could not contain it. His body locked against itself, and a scream was caught in his stone-blocked throat.

Nobody heard. For he did not let it loose.

He woke to dim light, and for a long while stared at the ceiling. Dark wood, familiar stains and carven scroll-work. He heard the breath moving, in, and out. In, and out, the sough of respiration less than a cricket's whisper. Just one pair of lungs, small and dainty as the rest of her.

Her Shield was not standing inside his door, which was not normal but by no means completely unusual. It could mean she was cautious, or disposed to privacy.

Whatever she wished to say, she wanted no witnesses. It suited him as well.

Start with a bare fact. "I was untouched," Archibald Clare heard himself state, dully. The ceiling did not move, and he did not look away from its curves and hollows. "I should have died."

Her dress made a sweet silken sliding as she shifted. "That would distress me most awfully, Archibald."

"And Valentinelli?"

A long silence, broken only by a single syllable. "Yes."

It was, he decided, not quite an answer. Was he likely to receive more from her?

This room was part of the suite he used while availing himself of Miss Bannon's hospitality. Dark wood wainscoting and worn red velvet, the shelves of books and the two heavy wooden tables littered with papers and glassware for small experiments, both like and unlike the larger tables in the workroom she made available for him.

It had taken him some time to enter that stone-walled rectangle again, though. After the affair with the Red, it had taken him a long while to look through a spæctroscope, too. Flesh remembering the nearness of its own mortality, despite Reason and Logic pointing out that at least he was still alive – the inward flinch when he heard a wracking cough, or the sick-sweet smell of some spun-sugar confections, were also troublesome.

He wrenched his attention away from that line of thought. This bed was as familiar as an old pair of slippers. Wide and comfortable, and his weary, aching body sank into it with little trouble.

Questions boiled up. He attempted to set them in some approximation of order, failed, tried again. When he had the most important one, he finally set it loose. "What did you do,

Miss Bannon? What manner of miracle did you perform upon me?" Stated twice, so she could not possibly misunderstand.

"Are you certain you wish to know?" It was the first time he had ever heard her sound . . . well, *sad*. Not merely downcast, but weary and heart-wrung. She was altogether too brisk and practical at any other moment to sound so . . . female?

No, Archibald. The word you are seeking is human. *Instead of* sorceress.

"I think I have some small right. I should have died, and I have not so much as a scratch upon me."

She did not demur. "And you have no doubt noticed you are far more vigorous than your age should permit. Even your hair is thicker than it was, though no less grey." A slight sound – her curls moving, she had nodded. "I thought you would remark upon that. I am amazed you did not press for an explanation sooner."

He held his tongue with difficulty. Long acquaintance with her had accustomed him to the fact that such was the best policy, and that she was on the verge of solving the mystery for him. She very much disliked being compelled, or harried. The best way of inducing her to speak was simply to be attentive and patient, no matter how time or need pressed.

"Do you remember when we met?" Her little fingers had crept upon his hand now, and the intimacy of the touch surprised him. They rested, those gentle fingertips, upon his palm, just below the wrist. "The affair with the mecha, and the dragon."

How on earth could I forget? He permitted himself a slight nod. His scorched hair moved against the pillow, crisp white linen charm-washed and smelling of freshness. His throat moved as he swallowed, dryly.

Her words came slowly and with some difficulty. "There was . . . during that rather trying episode, a certain artefact came into my possession. I bore it for a while afterward, but when the plague . . . Archibald." Her tone dropped to a whisper. "I could not bear to lose you. And the weight of the artefact . . . the method of its acquisition . . . it wore upon me. I sought to expiate a measure of my sins, such as they are, by ensuring your survival. You are proof against Time's wearing now, and your faculties will suffer no diminishing. You are immune to disease, and to all but the most extraordinary violence."

He waited, but apparently she had finished.

His most immediate objection was at once the most pressing *and* the most illogical. "You should have *told* me."

"I said I would."

"In twenty years' time. Had I known, Miss Bannon, I would have taken better care with Ludovico's slightly more tender person."

"No doubt." Her hand retreated from his, stealing away. A thief in the night. "It is my doing, Clare. Perhaps I all but murdered him."

What must it cost her, to admit as much? The tide of Feeling still threatened to crack him in two. "You should have told me." Querulous, a whining child.

"I feared your reception of such news."

Rightly so, madam. "Can it be reversed?"

"Perhaps."

"Would you reverse it?"

"No." Quickly, definitively. "I am loath to lose you, Archibald."

"But Ludovico is expendable?" For a moment he could not believe he had said such a thing. It was brutish, ill mannered, illogical.

"We are all expendable, sir. Have I not often remarked as much?" She stood, and it was the brisk Miss Bannon again. "No doubt you are quite angry."

I am a mentath. I do not anger. He closed his lips over the words. His body informed him that it had been held passive long enough, and it had a rather large desire to attend to some of its eliminatory needs. *Anger is Feeling, it is illogical. It is beneath me.* "Your Shield performed a miracle upon you as well, Miss Bannon. You lost nothing in that transaction."

She became so still even his sharp ears could not find the sound of her breathing.

There was no crackle of live sorcery, no shuddering in the walls of her house as he had sometimes witnessed, her domicile responding to her mood as a dog responds to its master's tension.

Finally, she let the pent breath out. "Nothing but Ludovico." Each word polished, precise. "And, I suspect, your regard. I shall leave you to your rest, sir."

Hot salt fluid dripped down Clare's temples, soaked into

the pillow and his scorched hair. He lay until she closed the door with a small deadly click; he slowly pushed back the covers and shuffled to the incongruously modern privy. There was a mirror above the sink-stand, but he did not glance into its watery clarity.

He did not wish to see the wetness upon his cheeks.

Chapter Six

Too Winsome And Winning A Place

She had never thought to be glad there were still Papists left in Londinium. As always, where there was Religion there was also a man whose palm was amenable to greasing. Consequently, even a wayward son of a Church such as Ludovico Valentinelli could be laid to rest in Rome-approved fashion. Emma paid for masses to be sung for his soul, too, though it was her private opinion that Heaven would bore him to a second death and Hell was entirely too winsome and winning a place to hold him for long, did he seek amusement elsewhere.

Yellow fog wreathed the gates of Kinsalgreene, elbowing uneasily with the incense puffing in clouds from swinging censors. There was a choir of small urchins, and the roly-poly Papist in his black cloth, scarlet-crossed stole, and long supercilious nose looked askance at her as she stood, clearly not willing to leave as a woman traditionally did before the coffin – the most comfortable that could be obtained, for he would not rest in a beggar's box – was lowered and covered.

The Papist muttered something and glanced at Clare, who stood leaning upon Horace the footman's proffered arm. Finch was there too, in his dusty black – appropriate despite himself, it seemed – and her housekeeper, Madame Noyon as well, dropping tears into a small, exquisitely wrought lace handkerchief. Even broad genial Cook, whom Ludo had tormented shamelessly, stood solemn and sedate. The footmen wore their best, indenture collars glowing softly, and the maids, both lady's and common, scullery and all-work, sniffed and dabbed.

Of course he had been at the maids too, but they seemed to have forgiven him.

The hearse and attendants, not to mention the pallbearers, constituted quite a crowd. Pages, feathermen, coachmen, mutes, how he would have hated the attention.

If she raised his shade through the lead sleeve and oak covering, he would sneer and spit.

Or perhaps he would not. That was the trouble – how could one ever be sure what someone would do, could you restore them to a manner of breathing? Memory was an imperfect guide, and Ludo in all his changefulness could not be compassed.

It was, she suspected, why she had kept him so close.

Mikal was at her shoulder, and she denied herself the faint comfort of leaning against him. There was a toll exacted here, and she paid it as Madame Noyon and the maids retreated, as the coffin was lowered and the footmen clustered around Clare. She paid double when Clare did not so much as glance at her, staring at the coffin's mellow polished gleam with his bright blue eyes narrowed and intent.

You should have told *me*. Of course, even a machine of logic trapped in flesh would feel disturbed, or even outright betrayed, at such a secret. Sometimes she wondered if other mentaths were as thin-skinned as her own. They had alarmingly sharp faculties of Perception and Deduction, and were said to have no Feeling whatsoever. Indeed, it was supposed to discommode them quite roundly.

Sometimes, though, she suspected that a *lack* of Feeling was not quite the condition Clare suffered.

Her mourning-cloth was not quite appropriate, for what proper lady would feel the need to mark the passing of a man who was, strictly speaking, a hireling?

Yet she chose to wear something close to a widow's weeds for him, if only to silently tell Clare . . . what?

Black henrietta cloth, an unfashionably small bustle, a crêpe band holding tiny diamonds to her throat, long silver and jet earrings thrumming with Tideturn's stored charge, matched silver cuff-bracelets ice-burning under her sleeves and gloves. She had not worn these earrings for years, not since the last time she had been in grief. .

Thrent. Harry. Jourdain. Namal. Eli. Now another name to add to the list. *Ludovico.* A *rosario*, perhaps, like the one the Papist clutched as he mumbled his prayers, sealing the baptised body of one of his God's children into eternity.

There were other matters to worry over, chief among them the richly appointed carriage that had lurked behind the cortège and even now squatted, toadlike, outside Kinsalgreene's high, flung-open iron gates, their spikes wreathed with anti-corruption charms and deterrents most – but certainly not all – grave-robbers would hesitate to cross. She had paid to have the Neapolitan well armoured against the theft of his shed mortal cloak. Time and rot she could do little against now, but she could make certain nothing else interfered with his resting.

Whoever was in the carriage, well, she would deal with them after this ceremony.

Clare's paper-paleness. The thin bitter line of his mouth, drawn tight. Tiny tremors running through him, as well as the haphazard haircut – he had trimmed the burnt bits himself, shrugging aside Gilburn, who would have been more than happy to perform a valet's duty.

Ludovico's duty.

Though the bowl of the sky was a blind eye of cloud, the rain held itself in abeyance. It had been a cold, damp summer even for Londinium, and some whispered Britannia was unhappy.

Had Emma not been so painfully aware of her surroundings, she might have made a restless movement.

If she is unhappy, it is no concern of mine. Not now.

The thump of the oaken cask settling sent a shudder

through her, one she quelled even as Clare's face crumpled and smoothed itself, soundlessly.

Yes, I should have told you. I was afraid of the illogic unsettling your mind. I was afraid of . . .

Such an admission could not be borne. A Prime did not *fear*.

"Prima?" Barely a whisper, Mikal sounding not quite happy with her movement.

She had taken a step forward.

Hushed greenery and glowing marble mausoleums, their cargoes of quiet rotting hidden behind the gleaming façade and held safe in nets of ancient barrowcharm, to ensure they slept soundly.

Her Discipline roused slightly within her, and even the weak sunlight stung her sensitive eyes. She was glad of the veil's obscurity, and still miserably compelled forward.

Wet earth full of mouldering, the open grave and the stone sleeve within it, nestling the coffin and its inner lining of charmed lead. A box within a box, within another, and inside them all a kernel that had once been . . . what, to her?

More than an acquaintance, more than a hireling, not quite a friend, caught in some space for which there was no proper word.

The first time she had ever engaged his services, he had played, catlike, as if she were a mouse under his paw. When the mouse turned out to be a lioness, the cat had merely blinked once, and afterwards still practised a cool disdain. There had been another woman involved, and sorcery, and plenty of blood. The sounds he made as he almost choked on the gallows, before she cut him down.

Strega. Whispered, like a curse, afterwards. She had paid him double, though he had sought to refuse her. *You should have let me die*.

Her own reply – *That, sir, would not please me at all* – greeted merely with a knife driven into the wall beside her head, and a muttered curse. Mikal had come very close to killing the Neapolitan, the first great test of his obedience to her will as her Shield . . . and the first moment she had begun to think that perhaps she might not have erred in accepting his service and sheltering him from the consequences of murdering his previous master.

She blinked, rapidly, grateful again for the veil. Later, glowing marble would rise above the nested boxes, and the stonewrights would chip a farewell into its gleaming face. Building a house for a dead man required time, even if one could pay double or triple for the best.

Her throat closed as she stared at the polished oak.

I am of the Endor. Did I will it, he would rise even from this . . . but it would bring no comfort.

The dead did not grant absolution. They merely answered simple questions of fact, and to ask them of Feeling was a waste. Once, one of her Discipline had brought a spirit fully to flesh to answer a king's questioning, but such a feat was beyond Emma, Prime or no.

Or is it? There was little comfort in finding, at last, an act of sorcery that she did not dare attempt. It had merely taken her entire life so far to discover it.

Ludovico. Her back held iron-straight, Emma Bannon extended her hand. A sharp flicker of sorcery, the fabric of tangled æther that condensed into physical matter shivering, and her glove was sliced neatly open.

The black glove – and the flesh underneath.

"*Madam!*" The priest, scandalised. She ignored him. The barrowmancer, standing ready at the periphery, stepped back nervously.

Ludo. I am sorry. Blood dripped, and her housekeeper, as the women obeyed custom and retreated, let out another sob. Emma did not move.

Mikal hissed in a breath as a spatter of scarlet drummed on the polished lid. Its pattern trembled for a moment, the sensitised fabric of reality rippling. Here was not a place for one of sorcery's children to shed blood.

It mattered little. For this, nothing but blood would do. There was no vengeance to be had: Ludo's killer had vaporised himself with the explosive as well. Were she to hunt down every last one of his accomplices, or even take her rage to Eire's green shores, the scales still would not balance.

After all, hers was the hidden thumb upon one side. A cheat so accustomed to thievery it becomes habit, a partial judge. A sorceress who chose one life over another.

I am sorry, and I shall pay penance. She stared down at the bright scarlet spots. Mikal snatched her hand, and she let him. His fingers folded around hers, and she resisted only when he sought to draw her away from the graveside.

"Fill it in," she said, each word a dry stone in her throat. "For God's sake, as you cherish your lives, *fill it in*."

There was a soft commotion. Clare had faltered, Horace and Gilburn caught him. There was a tingle up her arm as Mikal applied healing sorcery, a Shield's capability. Part of a Shield's *function*.

That was worrisome, too. *Your Shield worked a miracle . . . you lost nothing in the transaction . . .*

All this time, she had thought her survival stemmed from a different source; from the sorcery worked by the greatest Mender of his age while the city lay wracked under the lash of a plague let loose on the world by the very Crown Emma had sworn to serve. If her recovery had not been of Thomas Coldfaith's making . . .

Troubles thick and fast, and she could do nothing but stand and watch the open mouth of the grave as the diggers bent their backs to the work, the lone barrowmancer in his long black gown and traditional red stripes still eyeing her nervously as he felt the disturbance spreading from her.

A Prime was a storm-front of ætheric force, sorcerous Will that brooked precious little bridle exercised and fed until it became monstrous.

A woman with a Prime's will and corresponding ætheric talent, monstrous indeed. If she lost control of herself here, in this place of the dead, what could she set loose? If she opened the gates of her Discipline in this place, she could well shatter every stone and coffin. She could hold the door wide for a long while, and fuelled by this, what could it bring forth?

A spatter of earth hit the lid with a hollow noise, each shovelful another barrier between her and . . . what?

She could not name what he was to her, even now.

Ludo, Ludovico, I am . . . sorry.

It was not enough.

Chapter Seven

Not Well At All, At All

The carriage ride to Mayefair was silent and extremely jolting. Clare, marginally restored by an application of salts and a mouthful of brandy from Cook's surreptitious flask, held grimly to consciousness despite the roaring in his ears. Across from him, Miss Bannon sat, her childlike face composed and wan under the veil's obscuring net, the sliced, bloody glove on her left hand wrinkling slightly as her fingers twitched.

A fraction of coja would help, perhaps. He had not availed himself of its sweet burn since the plague incident, seeing no need to sharpen his faculties against that whetstone. And, truthfully, he had not felt the craving to do so. Was it a function of whatever illogical feat she had performed?

A certain artefact, she said. Did he dare ask further questions?

She might very well answer. In that case, was he a coward not to enquire?

The coffin, lowering into the earth. The bright spatter of blood, and Miss Bannon not even glancing in his direction. Had he thought her indifferent to Ludovico's . . . passing?

Call it what it is. Death.

The roaring in his ears intensified. It took actual physical effort to think through the wall of sound.

"Clare?" Where had Miss Bannon acquired this new, tentative tone? "Are you well?"

I am not at all well, thank you. "Quite," he managed, through gritted teeth. "You made certain of that, did you not?"

It was unjustified, and the slight stiffening of Miss Bannon's shoulders told him the dart had hit true. She turned her head slightly, as if to gaze out the carriage window. Her left hand had become a fist.

"Yes." Softly. "I did."

Nothing else was said as they inched homeward, and when the familiar clatter of iron-shod mechanical hooves on the echoing cobbled lane leading into the carriageyard resounded she began gathering her skirts. She wore very deep mourning, and if she did not weep and wail as a woman might be expected to, perhaps it was because she was not inclined to such a display.

Or perhaps she felt a loss too profoundly to risk making any further comment upon it.

He was given no time to remark upon this observation, for as soon as the carriage halted she reached for the door, and it flung itself open as if kicked. There was Mikal, his lean dark face set, breathing deeply but with no difficulty. Whatever method he used to move as quickly as a carriage – granted, Londinium's streets were usually congested enough to render that no great trick, but still – Clare had not yet deciphered, even after all this time.

She accepted the Shield's hand as she left the carriage, and Clare found himself in the position of having behaved in a most ungentlemanlike manner, again.

What is the matter *with me?* Feeling or no, there was hardly any excuse for treating a lady so.

Of course, if what he suspected of Miss Bannon's origins was correct, she was not of a quality to feel the lack of such treatment.

She is of a quality of character you have witnessed several times, and you are behaving abominably.

Clare climbed from the carriage as an old man would, despite the fact that he did not feel in the least physically decrepit. No, the problem lay within the confines of his skull.

She had assured him there would be no dimming of his mental abilities. Very kind of her.

Cease this nonsense. His shoes struck the cobbles, swept twice daily by the disfigured stable-boy, and the jarring all through him dislodged the roaring in his ears for a moment.

Miss Bannon swept ahead, her head bowed as if walking into a heavy wind. Mikal had not followed. Instead, the Shield paused, watching the black-veiled figure whose faltering steps clicked softly.

Then his head turned, with slow terrible grace, and he examined Clare from top to toe. Weak sunlight picked out the nap of the black velvet he wore instead of his usual olive-green – perhaps because Miss Bannon had insisted. The Shield's opinion of Valentinelli had always seemed to hover about the edges of condescension mixed with outright distrust, and Clare had finally decided it was Miss Bannon's fondness for the assassin that . . .

The chain of logic drifted away, for Mikal's tone was quiet, pleasant, and chilling. "Mentath." A slight pause, during which Miss Bannon disappeared through the side-door. "I do not know what has passed between you and my Prima."

I suspect that is a very good thing. "No?"

A ghost of a smile curled up one corner of the Shield's mouth, and for an instant it seemed – no, it *was*. His pupils flickered into a different shape.

Clare all but reeled back against the carriage's side. The edge of his calf struck the step, a deep bruising blow. *No more irrational wonders for today, please. I am quite finished.*

"No, sir, I do not." The honorific escaped on a long hiss of air. "Pray I do not discover it."

"Do you *threaten* me, sir?" He meant it to sound less fearful.

"Not a threat, little man." Mikal's smile twisted further, a hideous drooping movement. "A warning."

With that, he was gone, striding across the carriageyard. Harthell the coachman cooed at the gleaming black clockhorses, and the stable-boy, his wide, black eyes gleaming as his hunched and corkscrewed body twitched out from the shadow of the stable, scurried to help. The beasts snorted and champed, gleaming flanks married to delicate metal legs, their hooves chiming almost bell-like as sparks struck from the cobbles.

Clare leaned against the carriage's mud-spattered side. A thin misting rain began to fall, and the low venomous smell of Londinium's fog filled his nose. His calf throbbed, his head was full of noise, and he began to suspect he was not very well at all, at all.

A fraction of coja would set him right in a heartbeat. First he must change his clothes, then tell Ludo to hurry . . .

But Ludo was gone, closed in cold earth with a sorceress's blood spattering his coffin. It was perhaps what the Neapolitan would have wanted. The only thing better would be a burning boat, as the pagans of old in cold countries had sent warriors into the beyond.

Clare's eyes were full of hot liquid. He hurried into the house, creepingly thankful few of the servants had returned from the graveside yet, to see him in such disarray.

Chapter Eight

I Shall Enlighten You

"Person to see you, mum." Finch's face had squeezed in on itself in a most dreadful fashion. Rather as if he had sucked a lemon, which could either mean he was impressed by the visitor's status, or *quite* the opposite.

Emma lowered the chill, damp handkerchief over her eyes. Her study was very dimly lit, and the leather sopha she had collapsed upon was a trifle too hard. Still, it was not the floor, and if furniture witnessed her *déshabillé*, or behaving not quite as a lady should, it would not speak of the matter.

Nor would Finch, and she took care to answer kindly, "I am not receiving, Finch. Thank you." The shelves of leather spines – each book useful in some fashion, if only for a single line – frowned down upon her, and the banked coal fire in the grate gave a welcome warmth without the glare of open flame.

Finch cleared his throat. Delicately.

I see. "A rather fine carriage, following us from the graveyard," she murmured. "Yes. Did they, perchance, present a card?"

"No mum."

Of course not. "Mikal?"

"Is aware, mum."

I certainly hope he is. "And what do you make of the carriage, Mr Finch?" For though her butler appeared a gaunt dusty nonentity, he most certainly was not thick-headed. *Or* easy to ruffle.

His lemon-sucking face intensified, his collar pressing papery neck-flesh. The indenture collar would grant him a longer lease aboveground, but he was ageing. "Not so much the carriage as the guards about it. All of Brooke Street's under their eye, mum."

"Indeed." They were all aging. Severine Noyon sometimes limped, old injuries stiffening her thickened body. Isobel and Catherine, once bonny young maids, were past the first flush of youth now, and would perhaps marry if she settled a dowry upon them. Bridget and Alice as well. She should attend to that, and soon.

A Prime's life was long, and enough of a burden without a Philosopher's Stone taken from a dead lover's wrack and ruin to weigh upon one. She had intended to make Clare proof against time, and also to assuage her damnable conscience in the matter.

And yet.

Finch brought her back to the matter at hand. "The watchers arrived just as Cook and the girls did."

In other words, they did not wish to be remarked by a sorceress or a Shield, knowing one or both of us would sense a watch upon the house as we returned. I should feel insulted. An involuntary sigh worked its way past her lips. "The servants?"

"All accounted for, mum. The carriage is a fine bit of work, but without design. Clockhorses worth a pretty penny. Black as . . . well, black, mum."

Black as death. "How very interesting." She crushed the scrap of lace and cambric between her fingers and her sweating brow. "Very well, send word I shall receive *one* person, and one only."

"Shall I bring tea?"

A cuppa would do me a world of good. "No. Rum. And *vitae*."

"Yesmum." He sounded relieved, even though he would know the very thought of violet-scented *vitae* would unsettle his employer's stomach most roundly.

"Thank you, Finch." If the carriage held what she suspected, the drink would come in handy.

For *both* of them.

"Yesmum," he repeated, and shuffled out. The set of his thin shoulders was profoundly relieved, no doubt eased by this intimation that his mistress knew exactly what she was about. As usual, her own steadiness provoked calm and assurance in her servants.

Emma allowed herself one more deep, pained sigh.

Of course Clare was . . . upset. The wonder was that he had not bethought himself to ask such questions before. For a logic machine trapped in distracting flesh, he certainly seemed a bit . . . well, naïve.

She rose, slowly, her hands accomplishing the familiar motions of setting her dress to rights. She lowered the veil – a tear-stained face and dishevelled curls was not how she wished to face whatever manner of unpleasantness this was likely to be.

Blinking furiously, Emma Bannon lowered her head and strode for the door.

Pale birch furniture, indigo cushions, the wallpaper soft silken blue as a summer sky. The mirrors glowed faintly, though the curtains were drawn – a strip of garden before a stone wall was not the *best* view, though sometimes Emma thought of a Minor Seeming – a lakeside, perhaps? The trouble with such a fancy was that it weakened any ætheric defence, though glass was wondrous when it came to building illusion upon a physical matrix.

She stood by the cold fireplace – no flame had been laid, and the room was chill. It reflected her feelings toward the entire day, she supposed, and cast a longing glance at the settee. But, no – standing, and the presumed advantage of being afoot, was called for.

The air vibrated uneasily, and the door opened. "Mum," Finch murmured, showing the visitor inside.

Another heavily veiled figure in black, and for a

moment the sensation was of falling into a reflective surface. Or the past, that great dark well. But this woman, while slightly taller than Emma, was considerably rounder. Her black was very proper widow's weeds, and jewels flashed as she smoothed the veil aside with plump fingers.

There was another soundless flashing, the light that preceded thunder, and Emma's mouth turned itself to a thin, bitter line before she smoothed her features.

But she did not make a courtesy. Pride, a sorceress's besetting sin.

Perhaps I have simply learned to value myself.

The face behind the veil's screen was rounder too, and beginning to exhibit the ravages of time, care, and rich food. The girl she had once been had vanished. Pressures of rule had hammered that girl into this woman – weak-chinned, yes, but the eyes were piercing, as well as black from lid to lid, and spangled with dry constellations not even a sorcerer could name. Her cheeks were coarser, and slightly flushed, and perhaps it was a blessing that Alexandrine Victrix, Queen of the Isles and Empress of the Indus, bearer of the spirit of rule, did not know how much she resembled her deceased mother.

The drawing room trembled like oil on the surface of a wind-ruffled pond. A Prime's temper could tear this entire house – and a good portion of Mayefair, did it become necessary – asunder, leaving only a smoking hole of chaos and irrationality. The scar would be long in healing.

Why stop there? Londinium itself could bear some cleansing. Perhaps if stone was pulled from stone, the trees blasted and the birds silenced Emma Bannon might find some peace.

Is peace my aim, then?

Victrix's lip twitched, perhaps a sign of disdain. Certainly it was not amusement, as it might have been once. "Emma."

As the first blow of a duel, it left rather something to be desired. "Your Majesty." *Do you see your mother's face in the mirror? Gossip holds that you were reconciled to her on her deathbed, even though you found certain proof in Conroy's papers of some terrible guilt.*

What was it like, she wondered, to host the spirit of rule, to be the law and will of the Isles incarnate . . . and to find your own mother had plotted against you? Then there was the matter of the Consort, whose health had never been fine after the Red had swept Londinium. Emma would have thought the widow's weeds a silent rebuke, but for the fact that a queen would feel no need to *rebuke*, certainly . . . and the ancillary fact that it was Victrix's own government that had loosed that particular scourge on the world.

The method of making a cure was known far and wide now, and Emma had held her tongue.

For after all, Clare had survived, even if Emma's Shield, Eli, had not. He had rendered faithful service, and she had failed to protect him.

I am not calm at all. Harsh training sank its claws into her vitals, a vice about her forehead as well. A tiny tremor rippled through her skirts, making a soft sweet sound.

That was all.

Victrix's chin rose slightly. "We are here to speak with you."

"Obviously." Emma did not have to search for asperity. She was slightly gratified to see the woman's chin wobble: a very small, betraying movement.

The queen's face shifted, like clay in cold running water. Emma watched through the veil as Britannia woke, Her fleshly vessel filling like the Themis in its stony bed during the autumn torrents that would soon start and drown Londinium as the summer had failed to do.

The spirit of rule peered out of Her chosen bearer, and Victrix's jewels flashed again, with a power different than sorcery.

"Arrogant witchling." The voice was different, too, and Victrix's expression a stony wall. "Is it a grudge you bear?"

"What good would that do?" Emma lifted one shoulder, dropped it in an approximation of a shrug. An unladylike movement, but it expressed her feelings perfectly. "What is it the spirit of Empire requires?"

For a long moment Britannia studied her, the spirit's gaze sharpening further. "Do you still obey My vessel, witchling?"

I return every communication either of you see fit to send me unopened, and have for a long while now. "Does she still see fit to insult me?"

"Petty." Britannia narrowed her eyes, the glow above Her veiled, grey-threaded head the most evanescent crown of all, a sign of the spirit fully inhabiting its vessel, all its attention brought to bear. "Who are you, to take *insult*?"

I am Prime. You should know better, Britannia, even if Victrix does not. She simply gazed through her heavy veil, willing the wine-red fury within her to retreat.

"We are weakened," the spirit finally said, its cold lipless voice somehow faintly obscene, issuing from a stout woman's throat. "We have . . . there is a draining of Our vital energy. A threat."

A draining? Weakened? Emma frankly stared. The world seemed to shift a bit beneath her. "Ah," she managed, finally. "I see."

"No." Britannia drew Victrix's mouth back, into a rictus. "You do not. But We shall enlighten you."

❁ Chapter Nine

How Many Acquaintances

A few effects stuffed higgledy-piggledy into his trusty Gladstone, and Clare halted to stare at the bed. It was neatly made, the linens snow-white and the red velvet counterpane as familiar as the worn quilt covering his narrow Baker Street bed. Here the furniture was heavy and dark, of a quality to last; his flat seemed rather shabby in comparison.

How many times had he slept here, though? Contemplated a case at Miss Bannon's dinner table, had a companionable tea in the solarium – both of them silent except for a *Pass the marmalade, if you please* or a *How droll, this article claims thus-and-such*? How many times had Miss Bannon quietly arranged matters to suit him, or anticipated his need for a particular item? *A woman's sorcery*, she would remark, brushing aside his thanks.

He was behaving most shabbily. The voice of Logic demanded he halt and consider, and he would heed *that* dictate before pausing to even consider the voice of Manners.

His breathing came heavily. His heart thundered in his chest, the heart she had repaired – Valentinelli had dragged him here, spattered with ordure and in the throes of a severe angina. Miss Bannon had not questioned or demurred in the slightest. Instead, she had thrown her considerable, if illogical, resources into working a miracle to keep Clare alive. It was Miss Bannon who had brought him to Ludovico in the first instance, during the affair with the army of mecha. Protection for Clare's tender person, indeed.

He would not, if he understood her correctly, have to fear a repeat occurrence of the angina, or the slow clouding of old age. His faculties would remain undimmed. The greatest fear a mentath could suffer, set aside with breathtaking speed.

The fear of physical harm, never overwhelming for a mentath used to calculating probability and setting aside Feeling, was now non-existent.

The possibilities for experimentation were utterly boggling.

He could, no doubt, find a fraction of coja at an apothecary's, and begin there. Clare snapped the Gladstone closed. He glanced at the door, opening his mouth to tell Valentinelli . . .

. . . absolutely nothing. The Neapolitan's place was empty, and would remain so.

Now *there* was an avenue of thought best left unexplored: dealing with how many acquaintances Clare would outlast.

If I had known, I would not have allowed him to attend the trial. The danger was clear.

How could he have halted the Neapolitan, though? Stubborn as a brick, that man. And why had Miss Bannon not inflicted this burden on *him*? They were two cats, the sorceress and the assassin, disdainful but never far from each other, sidelong glances and mincing steps. Valentinelli had been married once, but the name of his wife was a mystery, just as so much else about him.

His last word, *strega*, whispered the way another might take a lover's name into the dark.

The dark Clare would not experience for a long, long while. How long? Was there any way to tell? Questions! Questions that required answers.

He sank his sweating fists into the velvet counterpane. Bent over until his forehead touched the bag's use-blackened handles, and attempted to impose some order on his scattered thoughts.

It came slowly. The rest of him was wet with sweat by the time he braced his arms and straightened, his knees creaking.

"I should apologise." It was not quite the thing for a mentath to speak to himself. It was rather a sign of uncertain faculties, wasn't it? "I treated her most dreadfully. Yes."

He found himself at his chamber door, clutching the bag with a sopping hand. A great undifferentiated mass of

Feeling rose again, swamping him, and he dropped the Gladstone with a solid, meaty thump that unseated his usually excellent digestion.

He could not remember breakfast, but he bolted for the water closet and evacuated it in a most decided fashion, pausing to suck in deep breaths between the heaves and wincing at the taste of his own bile.

Chapter Ten

And Nothing Came Of It

Emma sighed and indicated the settee, faintly surprised when Britannia did not take offence. The ruling spirit settled her vessel carefully, and for a long moment her face became Victrix's as she arranged her voluminous skirts. Drawn despite the doughiness, careworn as well, Emma could not find the young queen she had known in the matron's features.

Did it disturb Victrix, to find her former servant so unchanged?

If it did, she did not show it, merely pursed her lips with distaste. When she spoke, there was only a faint shadow of Britannia under her words, a chill wind mouthing the syllables. "There have been . . . events. In the Eastron End of Londinium. Whitchapel."

"Events." The blood crusted on Emma's left glove was

irritating. "In Whitchapel." The thought of that filthy sinkhole, the Scab covering its floors and cobbles with thick green caustic sludge, was unpleasant, to say the least.

"We *felt* these events, Lady Sellwyth. In Our very core." One plump hand waved, diamonds flashing. "And now there are . . . disturbing signs. A weakness, such as We have not felt since . . ."

Since when? But the practice of holding her tongue in the presence of royalty had always stood Emma in marvellous good stead, and she found it easy to adhere to at the moment. And *Lady Sellwyth*, as if Victrix sought to remind her of the fanged gift of a title set as a seal upon Emma's faithful service, and the Sellwyth ancestral lands held in Emma's fist, guarding its secret.

Victrix's mouth barely opened far enough to let the words loose. "Since those ingrates sought to disturb the taproot of Our power."

Which ingrates? History is full to the brim of those who would supplant a vessel. Perhaps it was Cramwelle's reign she referred to – the shock of Charles the First's execution must have been a nasty one. Or perhaps she meant Mad Georgeth's reign, though Britannia had held fast to even that ailing container.

She could even have meant the affair with the dragon, given her mention of Sellwyth.

Interesting as that avenue of questioning might prove, the issue of what the taproot of a ruling spirit's power consisted of was even *more* intriguing.

A heavy sigh, and Britannia retreated from Victrix's features. Her shoulders rounded, a flicker of expression crossed her broad face — what was it?

Almost *haunted*, Emma decided. "Your Majesty." She aimed for a soft, conciliatory tone, and perhaps did not succeed. Still, the effort had been made. "This seems to trouble you greatly."

"Can you imagine, sorceress, what it would be to lose your powers?"

I do not have to imagine. "Yes." Memory rose – dripping water, smell of stone, the manacles clanking and her own despairing noises as she struggled fruitlessly – and Mikal's steady breathing as he throttled and eviscerated the Prime who had trapped her and sought to tear her ætheric talent out by the roots. His *own* Prime, the one he had sworn to serve . . . a vow broken for what?

He hurt you, was all Mikal would say of the matter. She had never sorely pressed him on that point, for a variety of reasons. Clare's accusations rose before her again, unwelcome guests indeed, in the crowded room her brain had momentarily become.

"Yes," she repeated. "I can imagine it very well."

"Then you know how difficult it may be to speak of." Then, a crowning absurdity. "We ask your patience."

There was a tap at the door, and Mikal ghosted in. He held a silver tray – the rum, and a small fluted bottle of *vitae*. Just the sight of the glowing-purple glass was enough to unseat Emma's stomach a little.

His irises flared yellow in the dim light, and, for the

first time in a long while, she found herself slightly worried about her Shield.

Victrix studied him closely; her gaze had lost none of its human acuity. "We remember your face. You were with Us during the affair with the metal soldiers."

He glanced at Emma, who nodded slightly but perceptibly. Which freed him to answer – and also made a subtle point.

"I was." Two brief, dismissive words, and he set the tray down with a small click on the tiny, exquisite Chinois dresser, the three other decanters and crystal glasses already perched atop its gleaming mellowness.

"So long ago." Victrix sighed. "Emma."

She found her shoulders tight as canvas sail under a full gale. Took care to speak softly. "Your Majesty."

"We ask you to investigate. These . . . events have caused disturbance and threaten to rob Britannia of strength. What may We offer you for your service?"

"I am not in trade, Your Majesty." Stiffly. *You could offer an apology, but I think it unlikely indeed.*

"Did We treat so ill with you? You are still of the Isle, witchling."

"Perhaps I dislike travel, Your Majesty." *And consequently have not left.*

"Impertinent hussy. Do you think I do not know your origins? Your pretence at Quality is merely that."

And your pretence at graciousness, Victrix? This house is clearly in mourning. As you still are, mourning that petty Saxe-Koburg you married.

She held her tongue, and accepted a tumbler with an inch of rum from Mikal. One of his eyebrows lifted fractionally. The meaning was plain – whatever else lay between them in private, he was her Shield, and no onlooker would be allowed a glimpse of any tension. A burst of relief filled her chest so strongly she almost rocked back upon her heels.

Such a betraying movement could not be allowed. So she composed her features, tucked aside her veil with her free hand, and tossed the rum far, far back without waiting for Victrix to be served a thimbleful of *vitae* by a ghost-silent Mikal.

"And who are you, to treat with Us so?" Victrix's lip actually curled. "We are your sovereign."

You were *my sovereign, and I would have done much more for you, had you not used me as you did.* The comforting, soothing heat of a drink most ladies would not dare bolstered her. *I did not mind being a glove for your hand, my Queen, but a Prime does not brook being* insulted.

Emma chose the next few words carefully. An outright refusal would not do. "There must be other Primes in your service."

"None with your . . . efficiency." Her face twisted as if the admission hurt.

I hope it does. "Quite a compliment." *Now will you tell me of the other Prime, the one dogging my steps after the plague was released? The one leaving me posies and presents?*

Even now, there were secrets to keep.

"Sorceress." Britannia's voice filled Victrix's mouth, the sibilants long and cold. "You try Our patience."

"What would you have of me, spirit?" Deliberately hard, each word pronounced with the crispest of accents. Her Discipline sent a heatless pang through her. Those of the Endor were held in some caution, even among the Black. Even a Prime could not hope to strike down a ruling spirit . . . but she could certainly inconvenience one.

And do so mightily. If only by inaction.

"Someone in Whitchapel has committed murder." Victrix, now, using her own voice.

"That is hardly an event," Emma observed.

Mikal had gone very still, standing by the Chinois dresser in a Shield's habitual attitude, hands clasped loosely and the readiness clearly visible on him.

Carrying weapons in the queen's presence.

Victrix had come inside, alone, though the street was watched.

The realisation was a slap of cold water, stinging Emma into functioning properly. She continued, with great deliberation. "Starvation, Crime and Vice walk the Eastron End every night." *Every morning, too.* "Someone is always violently shuffling off a mortal coil there, with assistance and without."

"We are aware of such things."

Emma let silence cover that remarkable statement. Her gaze met Mikal's. It would be so easy to cross the room, open the door and step into the hall, consigning this whole conversation to the realms of *Such a thing occurred, and nothing came of it*.

She weighed the idea and found much to recommend it.

When Victrix finally spoke again, her tone was no more than a weary mortal woman's – middle-aged, a desert of hopes lost and the knowledge of grief. "We – *I* – witnessed a brace of murders. It is unspeakable. They have been savaged, Emma. We *felt* it. It was done with intent, and it tapped the source of Our power in some fashion. The weakness is . . . horrid. We do not know how or why. *You* must discover this, and quickly."

For a moment, Emma simply stared. Who knew what she might have said had the door not been thrown open and Clare staggered through, his hair wildly disarranged and his jacket askew?

"Emma, I must apolo – Dear God in Heaven, Your Majesty, what are *you* doing here?"

✤ Chapter Eleven

Complete His Cowardice

"Dear heavens," Clare repeated, vainly trying to smooth his wild, greying hair down. His blue eyes were blood-shot – he knew as much – and he was in no fit state to be before royalty. "I had no – mum, I mean, Your Majesty—"

"Sit down." Miss Bannon was at his elbow. She all but dragged him across the drawing room and pushed him firmly into his wonted chair, a walnut affair with high curved arms he tapped thoughtfully when a complex case had his undivided attention.

"In front of the *Queen*?" He sounded genuinely horrified, even to himself.

"I care little who is present, sir, *sit down* before you collapse."

She held an empty glass, and his sensitive nose discerned the odour of rum.

Her nerves must be frayed, indeed.

The remarkable fact that the Queen of the Isles was on the settee, without a guard or a minister anywhere in evidence, impinged upon his consciousness as well. It did not bode well at all, and thankfully gave him something new to busy his faculties with. "What dire news is it this time? The dynamitards, have they struck again?"

"No, indeed." Victrix essayed a pale smile. "It is quite a different danger, and I am begging our redoubtable sorceress's aid with it."

"Begging? Nonsense. Miss Bannon is always more than happy to . . ." He blinked up at the lady in question, whose expression had shifted a few critical degrees. "I say, Emma, I am well enough. Do tell me, how may I be of service?"

"You may sit where I place you, and cease being ridiculous. Mikal – yes, thank you." She pressed a snifter of brandy into Clare's willing hands, and the amber liquid suddenly seemed the best remedy in the world for his pounding head. "And – yes, very good." She lifted her replenished glass of rum, and tapped it against his. "Come now, sir. Chin up, buckle down."

"And devil take the hindmost." The familiar refrain, usually uttered when an affair they were pursuing had reached a breaking point of urgency and strain, comforted him. "I am sorry, Emma. I was dashed brutal about Valen—"

"Let us not speak of that." She eyed him for a long moment before straightening and glancing at Mikal. The Shield's face was a bland, closed book; he did not even spare a moment's worth of attention on Clare. "Now, stay there." She turned, regarding the Queen with a level, dark-eyed gaze.

It was odd to see such a childlike face so set and pale, the tiny diamonds on the crêpe band about her slim throat ringing with sorcerous light. The Queen, round and stiff in her mourning – the Widow of Windsor's sorrow was rather a mark, Clare thought, of a certain calcification of character – wore more jewels, and certainly more costly, but they did not seem as expressive as Miss Bannon's oddly matched adornments.

He noted the tremor in Queen Victrix, the hectic colour of her cheeks and a fresh scratch on the outside edge of her laced boot. Gravel, meaning she had hurried into a carriage, most likely on a wide walkway. And there, behind the careful mask of a middle-aged matron's face, was a flash of Feeling.

He peered more closely, disregarding the rudeness of staring, to verify the extraordinary evidence of his senses. Yes, he was certain he could identify that flash.

Fear.

"I shall investigate these occurrences," Miss Bannon said, formally. "If possible, I shall remove the danger to Britannia. I shall require every scrap of information there is to date; running after every murder in Whitchapel will only muddy the issue."

Whitchapel? Murder? Clare's faculties seized upon the extraordinary words with quite unseemly relief.

Victrix's mouth compressed. "The first body was buried

a-pottersfeld, the second is at Chanselmorgue. Her name was Nickol, I am told. More I cannot speak upon here."

How very odd. It galls her to request Miss Bannon's services. Miss Bannon has not stepped forth on the Crown's business for . . . quite a long while now, really. He had become accustomed to such a state of affairs, he supposed; Accustomed was a set of blinders where Logic and Reason were concerned. Just as befogging as Assumption and Comfort, and just as dangerous.

The tastes of bile and brandy commingled were not pleasant, and his head still ached abominably. But the storm seemed to have passed for the moment, and Clare had a rich vista of distracting new deduction before him to embark upon.

It would serve quite handily to push the distressing news, distressing *events*, firmly away.

"Did you view the bodies yourself, Your Majesty?"

Miss Bannon . . . was that a flicker of a *smile* hiding behind her steely expression? Had he not been so thoroughly acquainted with her features, he most certainly would have missed it.

She was enjoying Victrix's discomfiture, it seemed. Highly unusual. His estimation of the relationship between queen and the sorceress was incorrect. Perhaps said relationship had shifted by degrees, and he had missed it? For Miss Bannon did not speak upon the Queen much, if at all. Especially since the Red affair.

How very intriguing.

"We did, witchling." Soft and cold. "And now *you* shall.

Do not fail Us." The Queen rose on a whisper of black silk and colourless anger, and Clare scrambled to his feet. Neither woman acknowledged him. Victrix stalked through the drawing-room door, which opened itself silently to accommodate her passage. Miss Bannon's fingers did not twitch, but Clare was suddenly very sure that she had invisibly caused the door to swing itself wide. Mikal slid through after the Queen's black-skirted, sailing bulk.

The sound of the front door, shut with a thunderous snap, was a whip's cracking over a clockhorse's heaving back.

Miss Bannon turned to the mentath, and she wore a most peculiar smile. Tight and unamused, her dark eyes wide and sparkling, colour rising in her soft cheeks.

He downed the remainder of his brandy in one fell gulp, and grimaced. Medicinal it might have been, but it mixed afresh with the bile to remind him that he was not *quite* himself at the moment.

That is ridiculous. Who else would you be?

"Emma." He wet his lips, swallowed harshly. "I am sorry. I should thank you for your pains, and apologise for my behaviour."

The sorceress shook her head, and her little fingers came up, loosened her veil. "It is of little account, Clare. I expected you would be angry. But you are alive to feel such anger, which is what I wished."

"And Ludo?"

"Do you think he would have thanked me for such a gift?" Another shake, settling the veil firmly. Her features blurred behind its weave, yet Clare's quick eye discerned the tremor that passed through her. Only one: a ripple as subtle and dangerous as the shifting of rocks heralding an ice-freighted avalanche. "No. Death was Ludovico's only love, Clare; he would not have been happy to have her snatched away."

Yours was the name he spoke when she came calling, Miss Bannon.

There was no purpose in telling her so. If a sorceress could keep secrets, so could a mentath. Were he a lesser creature, he might feel a certain satisfaction in the act of doing so. As it was, well . . . "I deduce your torpor has been shaken, Miss Bannon."

"Certainly my leisure has been disrupted. Would you care to accompany me? I am to view a body, it seems, for our liege."

What was the sudden loosening in his chest? He decided not to enquire too closely. "Certainly. Do I have a moment to change my cloth? I am a trifle disarranged."

"Yes." She paused. "I rather require another glove, I should think."

"I shall make haste, then." And, to complete his cowardice, Clare escaped while he could.

❂ *Chapter Twelve*

Corpses Rarely Are

C hanselmorgue's spires pierced the waning daylight, thick ochre fog gathering about its walls as it was wont to do in the afternoons. It had been a Papist church long before, one of the many taken by force in the Wifekiller's time and pressed into service in the most secular ways possible. There was rumour of scenes within its walls during that uncertain time that verged upon the blasphemous, but the Sisters of Chansel kept their archives locked. They still had a convent or two tucked in an inhospitable locale, moors and unhealthful swamps where children and young women of a certain regrettable condition were sent to meditate upon their sins – usually of resistance in some fashion to their disappointed elders. Or, truth be told, if there was an inconvenience in the matter of their drawing breath while an inheritance was in question.

A Chansel Sister was a formidable creature, if only for the chainmail she was suspected of wearing under her habit. Not to mention their particular set of charter symbols. Of all Papist orders, only they and the Templis openly and regularly admitted sorcery's children. Oh, some of them made it clear they would not turn away a sorcerer or above possessed of the requisite wealth and connections. The Domenici and the Jesuiri were remarkably accepting where filthy lucre or influence was involved, and the Franciscis and Clairias made it a practice to accept the sorriest wretches they could. For most of them, though, the workers of wonders and their defenders were *quite* beyond the pale.

Feared, respected, allowed to survive in most countries . . . but beyond.

Chanselmorgue was a four-spired hulk now, with sheds sprouting from its backside in the manner of the huge bustle fashionable some few years ago, like a ridiculous growth. One could still remark the *tau*, with a writhing corpse nailed to it, worked in the stone over the front doors, and also see the chisel marks where blasphemers had taken advantage of the Wifekiller's feud with the Papacy to wrench bits of coloured glass and other shiny objects from the facing.

Apparently Emma was expected – perhaps Victrix had been certain of tempting her into action, or had she thought Emma would crumble in the face of a personal visit? Did Victrix have that high an opinion of her own persuasiveness, or of her erstwhile sorceress's pride?

Do I care? Whatever she thought, I did not agree to more than "If possible". I wonder if she noted as much.

In any case, it took very little time for a narrow-eyed barrowmancer and a hunched, scuttling morguerat to guide them to the shed containing the body in question, as well as five others.

As soon as she stepped inside the enclosure – waiting for Mikal's nod, and followed by a pale Clare holding a handkerchief under his long, sensitive nose – she had no difficulty discerning which one was Nickol.

The barrowmancer – a milk-cheeked young man with greasy dark hair and long fingers, the traditional red stripe on his trousers and his slouched hat pulled low – nodded as she halted, her eyes no doubt widening.

"Aye," he said, a broad nasal Cocklea accent reverberating around the shed's flimsy walls. "Enough to put a sour in ye belly, ennit? Doctor co'nae feel it, but he the skullblind. Wasn't til I saw 'er that anyone realised muckie'd been æther'd aboot."

"Indeed." Emma stepped past Mikal, who examined the body of what appeared to be a costermonger laid on a chipped, traditional marble slab, hands and feet pierced with true iron and the gashes scorched with charter symbols to ensure the corpse's peace. The heavyset man's mouth was pried open, the funnel for pouring salt or wine into the cavity laid aside. No flatscraper for pitch to seal the spirit away, so the barrowmancer judged him unlikely to have died by violence. "The report?"

"Ah, yes, will fetchit. Ye're nae gon swoon?"

"I think I may be able to avoid swooning, thank you. In any case, I have plenty of assistance."

"Aye." He paused, studying Clare, then shot a dark glance at Mikal. "Ye're nae gon turn a fillian?"

"I most likely will not be calling her spirit forth to answer questions, never fear." She tried not to sound amused. "And in any case, I would not do such a thing *here*. I am not so irresponsible."

"Well, tha's mun fair." He nodded, and touched his hat. "Will fetch tha report, then. Mind you, she's not decent."

"Corpses rarely are, sir. Thank you."

He hurried out, followed by the morguelrat, whose filmed gaze betrayed precious little excitement. Of course, morguels were taken from the workhouse's lowest strata, since a self-respecting beggar would hesitate to spend his days with the dead. For all that, they had room and board, if they did not mind sharing it with said corpses, and the peculiar blindness that struck after a few years of such work did not seem to bother most of them. Perhaps by then they had seen enough that sightlessness was a blessing.

Odd, how barrowmancers were not feared, though their Discipline was only slightly less Black than Emma's own. To shake hands with morguelrats was considered just slightly less lucky than with chimneysweeps.

"I do not think I shall ever become accustomed to that," Clare muttered darkly.

"To what, sir?" There was much in the current situation she herself did not wish to become accustomed to.

"To how casually you speak of bringing a shade forth to answer questions."

"I have never done it in your presence for a reason, Clare."

"And I appreciate your restraint." He all but shuddered, smoothing his jacket sleeves. The black armband, secured with a pin-charm, was a mute reproach.

As if she needed more than the weight of her own mourning-cloth. She did not fully indulge in a widow's bleakness; perhaps she should the next time she was forced to see the Queen. Although perhaps Victrix would likely take little notice of whatever Emma chose to wear.

"Are you quite well, Clare?" It was not like him to show such discomfort.

"Quite. I . . ." He shook his head, arranged his hat more firmly upon his head. Mikal, giving the costermonger's body a thorough appraisal, appeared to ignore them both. "It has been rather a trying . . . yes, rather a trying week."

She was about to reply, but her attention fastened afresh on the body she had come to view. *How very curious*.

The æther trembled around it, not the quiver of a living being producing disturbance and energy or the low foxfire of soul-residue. She stood, head cocked to the side, and took in what she could with every sense, physical or otherwise, she possessed.

Mikal appeared at her shoulder, his hand closing about her upper arm. He had noted her sudden stillness, and was ready to act as anchor or defence.

The corpse in question was a middle-aged woman, heavy and inert on a discoloured marble slab. Her mouth was open, and one could see the stubs of rotten teeth, as well as the searing from the preparatory mixture of hot caustic salts that preceded sour pitch.

Clare stepped to the side, his head cocked at a familiar angle. When he had gained all he could from observing the corpse's face, he reached for the ragged sheet covering her and glanced at Emma.

She nodded, a fractional movement, but one his eyes were sharp enough to discern. They had examined other bodies; it was, still, not quite *routine*. Ritual, certainly, though neither of them stood overmuch on ceremony when bodies were involved in an affair such as this.

She closed away *that* distracting line of thought. Attention was called for.

What is that? There, and there, it moves very peculiarly. And there. Most interesting. I wonder . . . She extended a tendril of non-physical awareness, delicately, and recoiled swiftly when the æther over the body trembled.

Mikal said nothing, but his awareness sharpened.

Clare twitched the sheet down to the woman's hips. The marks of a brutal life were clearly visible and the sewn-up gashes from autopsy – and the attack that had killed her – were livid. He folded the sheet with prissy carefulness, then took its edge and uncovered the rest of her, tucking the neat package of cloth at her feet. Her knees turned outward, and the ragged aperture between her legs oozed dark, brackish corpsefluid.

"*Most* peculiar," he murmured. "And she was Respectable once, or at least well-fed. Hrm."

Though the skin hung loosely, and one could see the marks of violence and hard living upon her, there were none of the deformities associated with childhood want or neglect.

She had afterwards fallen far, as Emma could clearly see from the wooden box containing the deceased's effects. Workhouse cloth, though mended neatly, her boots sprung-sided, and even through the varied reeks of a charnel-house Emma could discern a faint thread of gin. The woman's round face had begun to blur with drink during life, and a shiver worked its way down Emma's spine.

A horrid gash in the throat. The marks of frenzied stabbing over the entire torso were vicious too, but the cluster of open, gaping wounds about her parts of privacy were the most worrisome.

That is where the attack was centred, and that is where the disturbance issues from. Her womb.

Emma's entire body went cold.

This was gruesome news indeed.

Chapter Thirteen

Wholly Unguarded Sentiments

"Marian Nickol, called Polly, though the inquest will legally ascertain her identity." Clare blinked owlishly at the scrawls upon the thin paper as the carriage jolted. "Found by a carter on Bucksrow, near the Hospital. Slashed throat. Abdominal injuries . . . Omentum, uterus . . . sharp object . . . peculiar, most peculiar."

"Indeed," Miss Bannon murmured. She had a queer look upon her soft little face: distant, as if listening to faraway music.

A copy of the particulars of this and another murder had been prepared in advance of their arrival, and Clare had noticed Miss Bannon's tiny *moue* of distaste when *that* was discovered. Perhaps she resented the Queen's easy assumption of her pet sorceress's service? How could Her Majesty be certain, though, given how Miss Bannon had scrupulously avoided such service for . . . how long now?

When the Consort had died of a fever perhaps typhoid in origin – his health never having been very strong after the Red Plague had wracked Londinium – Miss Bannon had not worn mourning, as many of Britannia's subjects affected. Indeed, she had merely drunk a little more rum than was her wont at supper, and retreated to her study instead of to the smoking room, where Clare was habituated to sit and discuss various and sundry with her afterwards, as if she were a man at a dinner party.

The particulars were an easily solved conundrum. Britannia had more than one sorcerer or mentath in Her service, and the pages could easily have served another. He brought his attention back to the report, which held the details of the body's discovery as well. "The first – Marta Tebrem – was found in Whitchapel, too. Georgeyard Building. Stairs – first-floor landing. Dashed odd, that."

"Not if she was an unfortunate." Her gloved hands were clasped together a trifle too tightly. "I would be surprised if she did not bring a customer to that place more than once. Or if she sheltered there, to sleep."

"Ah." He coughed slightly. "Yes. I see."

She sat bolt upright, as usual, and had tucked the veil aside for the nonce. Two spots of hectic colour burned high up on her soft cheeks, and he was struck by how impossibly *vital* she appeared. Primes had long lives, certainly . . . he had taken it for granted that she would outlast him.

What an unpleasant thought. And followed by others equally unprepossessing, much like a steam-locomotive dragging carriage after carriage.

Even steam-locomotives possessed charmed whistles, and sorcerous reinforcement upon their boilers. A triumph of Science, yes, but larded with irrational sorcery.

One would have to go far, Clare had found, to escape such things.

"Out of the rain, and dark," Miss Bannon continued, "though I would chance a guess that the first victim was also much under the influence of gin the night of her misfortune. We cannot rule the choice of venue as hers until we examine it. The murderer may have taken her to the building while she was not quite of right mind, impersonating a client for her bodily services."

Of course, they would start with the first murder, and take the chain of deduction from there. It was how they began an affair such as this if time permitted, seeking the site of the first event they could distinguish. There was a certain comfort in the habit, Clare supposed. "She was last seen with a Guardsman, it says."

"Of course that may have been . . ." When she did not continue, he looked up from the papers. She stared out the window, and her fierce gaze was not ameliorated by matted eyelashes and reddened, brimming eyes. Her left hand had clenched, and she had sunk her pearly teeth into her lower lip, cruelly.

For the first time since he had met her, Clare was witnessing her wholly unguarded sentiments. The moment was so novel he almost crushed the papers as the carriage rocked itself, and his mouth had gone dry.

It took another cough before he could speak, and the sound served to alert her to his scrutiny. She smoothed her expression with amazing rapidity, and reached up to free the veil from its fastening. Her rings flashed, a heatless fire.

"Miss Bannon—"

"The morning has disarranged me." Her face was swallowed by darkness again. "Please, continue. I shall be better shortly."

"Miss Bannon, I—"

"The report, Clare. Please do continue."

He swallowed dryly, and forced himself to concentrate. "The medical examiner, in both cases, was quite thorough. There seems nothing missing from the notes. The most recent gentleman performing that duty – Killeen? Yes, that is his name – shall no doubt be at the Nickol inquest."

"Which you shall attend."

"Should time permit. Will you?"

"No." A slight shake of her veiled head. "I think I shall be hunting for clews in other quarters. There was a great deal of . . . disturbance about the body. I am uncertain what to make of it, and I think I shall be *quite* occupied in ferreting out the source."

"Hm." He digested this, and halted before he could make the quick glance aside that would ascertain whether or not Valentinelli had anything to add. The rattling of pebbles against a coffin's lid rolled inside his skull, deafening like the roar of traffic and crowd noise outside. "You are expecting further unpleasantness, sooner rather than later."

"Oh, yes. The first murder appears, if I may make a ghastly observation, merely a rehearsal. First we shall view the scene of Tebrem's discovery."

Did he imagine the slight unsteadiness of her tone? It could be blamed upon the carriage ride – Clare steadied himself as the conveyance rattled again. "And then?"

"Then we shall view the second, and return home for dinner – I am quite sorry, but we shall likely miss tea. Tomorrow, you shall visit quite another Yard." She returned her now-loosened hands to her black-clad lap, and Clare found himself wondering if her face was contorting again behind the veil. "If I may presume to suggest as much."

"Of course." He looked back at the paper. "I was dashed brutal to you, Emma. I apologise."

"Unnecessary, sir." Yet the words remained thoughtful, rather than dismissive. "I understand a temperament such as yours would find such a revelation quite a shock. Pray set yourself at ease."

He was not quite ready, he decided, to be treated with such cool politeness. He had seen her employ such a tone before, to set an overly familiar interlocutor back on his heels, so to speak. Were he not a mentath, Clare acknowledged, such a realisation might sting. Nevertheless, he soldiered on. "No reason to act so ungentlemanly, indeed. I am . . . I was fond of Ludovico, but—"

"As was I," she said, colourlessly. "Do continue with the recitation of facts from these papers, sir. There is a mystery at hand, and I wish it unravelled as soon as possible, so I may return to my accustomed habits."

✵ Chapter Fourteen

For Want Of A Pause

The Georgeyard Building had been new a decade ago, and clung to shabby respectability by teeth and toenails. Of course, it was off Whitchapel High Street, so the question of its respectability was an exceeding open one.

The day had brightened enough that the Scab's vile green, velvety organic ooze had retreated under muffled sunlight's lash, leaving an evil oily steam instead of its usual thick rancid coating over the cobbles.

Not to worry, though. It will return with darkness. So would Emma, if she gained nothing with this visit. For now, though, she followed Clare, their treads echoing in the dark.

She was glad of the stairwell's dimness; her eyes were burning from even the cloudy sunshine outside.

Or from something else.

Nothing you need take account of, Emma. Do what duty demands here, and retreat as soon as you may.

Why had she agreed to this? Merely because Clare had immediately assumed she would, or because she had felt some twinge of fading . . . what, for Victrix? Because she feared eccentricity was pressing in upon her too soon, her mental faculties becoming brittle? Perhaps because if she had not, she would have had to solve the questions gathering about her Shield?

Mikal followed her, taking care not to crowd too closely. The first floor came quickly, and she all but staggered when the disturbance in the æther pulsed sharply. All other considerations fled. "There," she managed, through numb lips, and pointed with a rigid arm. "*Right* there."

Mikal leapt up the last two stairs, caught her other arm. "Prima?"

"I am well enough. It is simply . . . I have never . . ." *I have not ever seen this before. I have never even* heard *of such a disturbance.* A Prime's memory was excellent, her education the best the Collegia could provide, and there was precious little sorcery she had not witnessed or read of. "What *is* this? It is still echoing. And she was discovered last *month*!"

"Miss Bannon?" Clare sounded nervous, for once. "There is a rather definite drop in physical temperature here. Remarkable. And . . ." He bent rapidly, and plucked something from the floor. "How very odd. Look."

It was a small pebble, no doubt carried in from outside, on a shoe or in a cuff. He turned it in his long capable fingers, then flicked it into the corner where the disturbance was greatest.

She stepped forward as well, Mikal moving with her. The Shield's grasp was a welcome anchor as she felt the chill difference in temperature, sharp as a falling knife-blade.

The stone hung, turning, in midair. A simple piece of cracked gravel, rough and clotted with dirt that unravelled in fine twisting threads. Now she could see the canvas-covered floor quivering through a curtain of disturbed, snarling æther. A stained piece of wooden wall, heavily scarred with use, was bleached as its physical matrices warped.

"Mr Clare," she heard herself say, as if from a great distance, "it would be very well if you were to retreat from that spot. Quickly."

"Prima?" Mikal's single word, shaded with a different question.

Her free arm, rigidly pointing at the floating pebble, trembled. "Take Clare halfway down the stairs." Mikal hesitated, and her temper almost snapped. "*Now*, Shield."

He turned loose of her with less alacrity than she would have liked, but he obeyed. At least Clare knew better than to question at this juncture. For a moment it was as if Time itself had turned back and it was one of the many investigations or intrigues between their inauspicious first meeting and the crushing denouement of the Plague affair. The only thing missing was Ludovico's silent sneer as he hustled Clare to safety or took up a guard post down the hall, which he might have done if he could have moved more quickly than Mikal.

Do not think upon that, Emma.

Instead, she *focused*, tucking the irritating veil aside as her jewellery flamed with heat, its ætheric charge responding to the spreading disturbance. The pebble still hung in midair, and she wondered if any of those who sheltered here noticed the spot, or if they simply felt the chill and avoided even glancing at something inimical. Even a lowly charter with barely the ability to trace a symbol in quivering air could have sensed the disturbance, and probably found other accommodations forthwith.

If there were any to be had; shelter of any kind was expensive in Whitchapel.

She extended a few thread-delicate tendrils of awareness to discern the true shape of the tangle. It throbbed, an abscess under the surface of the visible, a monstrous root driven deep through the real and almost-real. Emma risked another light touch, as a woman would pass her hand down a pinned dress-fold to discern if it would hang true. Intuition plucked at the knot, finding its shape and the likely directions it would bulge upon being observed.

She could have patiently unpicked it, inch by careful inch. It would have been better to refuse Victrix outright than to hurry now, and yet the sooner she found precisely what manner of disturbance this was, she could leave the entire displeasing mess behind her.

The solution, as ever, was to simply cast her net and see what rose with it to the surface. Training clamped its iron grasp about her body and she exhaled smoothly, stepping deliberately forward into the small pond of concentrated irrationality.

The gin, false friend, hung thick and close inside her head, veils of welcome warmth. A rancid burp, the simmering smell of her own clothes, as familiar-strange as this wide-hipped body, loose and sagging with despair. Stumbling, falling against the wall, she turned to see him, his hat pulled low and only the suggestion of a chin under its shade.

Twas not his features she was interested in, but the pence burning in her hot palm. A man paid before he received, that was the best way of business, even for one as curst as old Marta. He had not demurred.

"Le's ha'at thee, then," she slurred, and that was when a jet of light cleaved the gloom.

She did not feel the first blow. It was the warm gush down her front that warned her, but her throat was full of that darkness, the same covering his face. It crawled down as if it wished to inhabit her stomach, and the knife came up again.

He fell upon her, and her fist clenched, but only because she thought, "Not m'pence, needs it for a doss I do", before the void swelled obscenely past her stomach, clawing at her vitals, and she knew no more.

Emma staggered, the shock of her knees hitting the filthy floor only slightly cushioned by her skirts. Her spine stiffened, bending backward as if on a medieval spikehoop, and she was not conscious of her own voice: a high curlew cry that punched a perfect, circular hole in the bleached, sagging wall. Her jewellery blazed, diamonds at her throat emitting shrieking stress-screams, and the jet earrings shattered, their shards driven outwards as if propelled by burning gunpowder. Later, she would find the silver cuffs heat-rippled and all but useless for carrying ætheric force.

Still, they had performed another service: keeping her from being overwhelmed.

Tension snapped and she was thrown back, hitting something almost-soft and tumbling, a brief moment of merciful unconsciousness before the pain swallowed her whole. Even then training did not fail her, but behaved even more mercilessly, shunting the force of the blow aside as the entire building – and the street outside – shivered like a whipped cur. Her own shrieks rattled the walls, plaster dust falling fine and thin, Mikal's answering curse lost under a wall of rushing noise as he lowered her, his fingers biting cruelly as he sought to stop the wild thrashing.

He had left Clare to see to her, and she did not even recognise the fact.

One of a Shield's functions was to conduct such an overflow away from her, but this was too immense. A high ringing noise, a wet snapping, peeling sound, and the world settled into its accustomed dimensions again with a thump. Emma sagged, vicious-toothed trembling all through her as hot pain pounded between her temples.

Silence filled the dark stairwell. Soon there would be

shouts, and running feet. Even in Whitchapel, such an event as this would not go unremarked.

"Prima?" Mikal, raggedly. "*Emma?*"

One last pang, ripping through her, phantom blade cleaving flesh and breastbone. She curled around the blow, blind and witless, and Mikal held her down. It passed, and the shuddering, great gripping waves of it, began anew.

"*Saw* it," she managed. "*I saw it!*" Which meant the sorcery performed here, driving itself through the physical and ætheric, had found some resonance within *her*, and jolted home with explosive force.

The pebble completed its fall, and pinged against the floor. It did not sound right; the entire area bounded by the cold had been changed smoothly and seamlessly to glass. One could peer down into a dim, narrow hallway underneath, and the circular hole punched in the wall had thin, knife-sharp crystalline edges. A nasty smell boiled through, whistling darkness loaded with the breath of the privy-closet that had hidden behind.

At the moment, the crushing ache in her skull and the savage pain all through her body somewhat precluded examining the damage further. Now she was well and truly involved in this affair – all for the want of a pause before leaping in. "I . . ." She coughed, retching, her stomach threatening to unseat itself. "*Hurts.*"

"*Pax*, Prima. I am here." Was Mikal shaking too, or was it merely her own shivering?

"Dreadful," she managed, in a colourless little voice. "Home. Shield . . . *home.*"

"Yes."

With that assurance she let go of consciousness again, retreating to the deepest parts of herself as her violated mind sought to compass what had happened.

Two ideas followed her, both equally chilling.

The first was *He had no face*.

The second? *But he had a knife*.

✸ *Chapter Fifteen*

Unremembering Such A Thing

The return to Mayefair proved long and tense, the streets clogged with shouting, heaving traffic. It was also cramped, for Mikal cradled the sorceress's small form and ignored Clare entirely, studying her wan, slack face as if it held a secret and feeling for her throat- or wrist-pulse at intervals.

Clare did not feel it quite proper to venture forth again that day, even though Miss Bannon was in no condition to attend dinner and would consequently care little about his absence. He was to visit another Yard, and he had an inkling of which, yet he could not leave while the sorceress, pale and so unconscious she represented quite a dead-weight, was abed. Mikal carried her upstairs, and Madame Noyon fluttered about fussing at the lady's maids to help tend their mistress.

Clare himself went straight for the smoking room and its heavy walnut sideboard. His hand shook slightly as he poured himself a *very* healthy measure of brandy, and he downed it with quite unseemly haste. It left a burning in its wake, and he had to suppress a rumbling of the rudest sort from his scorched throat.

So much illogic could unsettle even the finest mind, he told himself, and his, while acceptable indeed, was not of *that* calibre. He could have Finch send out to an apothecary's for coja, and yet the thought of its deadly stinging did not soothe as much as it could.

No, the brandy was far better. He eyed the sideboard. This being Miss Bannon's house, there was no stinting in quantity *or* quality. Should he be so unfortunate as to feel a lack, no doubt any of the other liquids in crystal decanters would do, even the *vitae*. He had never drunk to excess – the consequent blunting of a mentath's faculties was unacceptable – but he could at this moment bloody well see the attraction.

A rather awful day, all told. The sounds Miss Bannon had made – terrifying, wrenching cries, loaded with horrifying, illogical force. No doubt there would be a great deal of speculation over the burst of sorcery, and her carriage may have been remarked.

Dreadful indeed. The sound of earth hitting a coffin lid again, rattling through his skull vehemently, over a spatter of blood. Even *he* knew that for a sorceress to spill that most precious of vital fluids in such a place was dangerous.

"*Eh*, mentale. *Drinking to death now?*"

Clare whirled. The room was empty, its heavy dark wainscoting and fancifully painted ceiling – cavorting satyrs and nymphs, perhaps Miss Bannon's comment on a man's ideas – just the same as they always had been. The billiard table, where sometimes the clack of heavy striking reverberated as he cogitated upon a particular matter and Miss Bannon sipped her rum, was just the same, covered with its loose canvas because he had not availed himself of its geometric soothing for quite some time.

His sensitive nostrils flared. A breath of dirt, the smoke of a snuffed candle. And the strong oiled-metal smell of a man who lived by violence, his wits sharp and his pock-marked cheeks sallow.

Impossible. The silver globe-lights were not flickering. It was his eyelids, falling and rising with extraordinary rapidity as his faculties sought to discern the evidence of the real from heated phantasy. *Simply impossible*.

There was no Neapolitan lounging near the door, where he was wont to pause before edging in to select a cigar from the silver-chased humidor – long, slender, floral in taste, and utterly strange in his blunt, dirty fingers.

"Merely the strain," Clare muttered, the words falling into dead, heavy air. He had never noticed before how close it was in this particular room without a woman's light laughing questions, a muttered reply in Calabrian when a man forgot himself and the tone of his youth wore through his careful mask. Or the clack of the heavy billiard-spheres providing their own music, smoke hanging in the air before being whisked toward the fireplace with a charm-crackle. "A dreadful day. A dreadful *week*. A touch more brandy, and some rest. For my nerves."

As if a mentath was prey to such a thing as shattered nerves. It was ridiculous to even *suggest*.

And yet.

He wiped at his mouth with the back of his hand, turned back to the sideboard and poured another generous measure. No, not rest. Rest would not do him any good at all. Only work would cure this uneasiness, the feeling that the earth itself would cease obeying its laws of proper quiescence or motion and begin behaving as irrationally as sorcery itself.

"Experiments." He gazed at the hand holding the tumbler of brandy, amber liquid trembling. Familiar as his own breath, that fleshly appendage, and the possibilities began to swirl inside his skull.

He did not realise, as he swilled the brandy and poured himself another, that he had left the crushed papers detailing Marta Tebrem's injuries, and statements given by witnesses, in Miss Bannon's carriage, where Harthell would find them and hand them to Finch without comment, to be placed upon Miss Bannon's study desk. It was a shocking sign of absent-mindedness in so normally precise a man.

Indeed, had Clare even an inkling of unremembering such a thing as said papers, he might have thought his condition warranted no little concern. As it was, he simply poured and swallowed until the decanter was empty, and left the smoking room and its shrouded table with a hurried, slightly rolling gait.

He did not feel inebriated in the least.

❀ Chapter Sixteen

Rare And Wondrous

Waking after such an atrociously uncomfortable event could not possibly put one in a cheerful mood. Especially when said waking was triggered by an amazing, thumping bang from the depths of her house, and Mikal's muttered curse as he flung her bedroom door open.

Without knocking.

"He will kill himself, Prima." The Shield's eyes were alight and his dark hair disarranged, as if he had run his hands back through it. "Or one of the servants. Or he may even bring the house down around our ears."

Emma sighed, turning over and burying her face in the pillow. Even though the room was dark, her head ached abominably, and any hint of light scored her irritated eyes. "Unlikely," she muttered, "on all three accounts. Go *away*."

He reached her bedside, touched her shoulder with two

careful fingers. "I hesitated to wake you. But he will harm someone, perhaps even himself."

The last thing I remember . . . She shuddered as the recollection rose. Yet unconsciousness had blunted its sharp edges, and training had drained the venom. At least, enough for her to consider the vision calmly.

She had experienced Tebrem's death, stroke for stroke.

She had also, more to the point, disrupted whatever that death had been meant to achieve or cement. A spreading, deepening stain, with all the febrile tension of Whitchapel's poverty and violence – even in that semi-respectable building – to feed it. Now began the difficult but less dangerous work of deducing what she could of the murderer's method and intention – then descending upon said murderer with the force of law, and the more considerable force of Emma's irritation.

Speaking of deduction, she finally emerged from the haze of restorative slumber as another thump rattled the house. It was not a sorcerous sound, for the defences on her abode rippled only in response to her attention. "What on earth is he doing?"

"He is locked in the workroom, and since Tideturn all manner of noises have issued forth. The door is solid, and in any case . . ."

"Yes." She blinked, yawned daintily, pushing the pillow and his fingers away with a measure of regret. An attempt to force the workroom door would trigger certain protections and a Prime's will might strike before she was fully conscious. "Very well. Send up Severine and the maids. I shall sally forth and find out what he is about. But only *after* I've a bath and perhaps some *chocolat* – I feel dreadful."

"No doubt. Dare I ask what that was?" He all but glared at her, as if she were an errant child.

She decided she did not wish to have such a conversation with Mikal just at the moment, and so feigned to misunderstand his meaning. "I gather he was chasing a set of mad political dynamitards; no doubt they opened up a fascinating and explosive line of enquiry for his active little brain. You are dismissed, Shield."

For a long moment he stayed precisely where he was, waiting. When it became clear she would not speak further, he sank back on his heels. "Prima?"

"If you are not promising to bring me *chocolat* as quickly as possible, *or* informing me of a sudden disaster levelling the whole of Londinium, I do not think I am disposed to hear you." A stretch informed her of her body's protest over yesterday's – at least, she hoped it was yesterday and that she had not been abed for more than a Tideturn or two – events, and she took stock. Stiffness in the lower back, her arms ached, and her head throbbed as if she had been at the rum a bit too much.

"Then I shall not speak." His face closed in on itself; he spun on one heel, stalking for the door. A bright tang of lemon-yellow irritation was clearly visible to Sight.

Emma exhaled sharply, returning her focus fully to the physical world.

When we do have a conversation, Shield, it will be on my terms, and mine alone.

She finished her stretch, tasted morning in her mouth, and allowed herself a grimace. Her eyes were sandy and her hair was a bird's nest, like a witch's tangled mane. All in all, though, she felt surprisingly hale.

That was odd, wasn't it? She had grown accustomed to a feeling of well-being, since she had awakened from the Red with none of the scarring or other ill effects that disease normally entailed. It was similar to the Philosopher Stone's heavy warm weight, but without the crushing burden of . . . guilt? Her accursed conscience had weighed on her more and more, the longer she bore the Stone plucked from Llewellyn Gwynfudd's . . . body?

Perhaps it had not been ejected from his corpse. Had it been clasped in his hand as he performed the movements to aid him in remembering the cantos of his brilliant, earthshaking, and utterly insane act of sorcery?

Her return to the site of his demise had gathered no proof: only hole-eaten, anonymous bones, gryphon as well as human, drained even of the ætheric traces of their living. The shock of such a Major Work unravelling had bleached the environs into a sorcerous null-point; truth be told, she had not wished to find a distinguishing mark that proved some of the bones were *his*. She had seen his corpus shred as his interrupted Work tore him apart; it was enough.

She had privately thought, for a very long while, that his talk of a second Stone had been merely a ploy to cause her some hesitation. In the end, she had always been disposable to him.

Emma settled back among the pillows as another rattling

thud from downstairs rocked the house. *Oh, for God's sake*. A moment's worth of attention informed her that the stone walls of Clare's workroom were as solid as ever, and the door – reinforced with sorcery and iron, just to be certain – was likewise. There was precious little he could *do* to himself, with that single Stone safely wedded to his lean, no-longer-aging body. And just at the moment, she was . . . a trifle peeved.

Did she wish to think upon such a thing now?

Well, at least she had a few precious moments of solitude to pause in reflection.

Clare could not fail to grasp the immensity of her gift. He might have some trouble with the illogical nature of near-immortality, of course – and there was another possibility, that the shredding of Llew's physical substance as his wonderful, completely mad Work had unravelled had not been too much for even a wyrm's-heart Stone to soothe.

Concentrate upon Clare, and let Llew rest. He is, after all, dead. How would she appease the mentath?

She did a great deal of smoothing-over when it came to Archibald Clare. He had *some* manners, but a mentath was not an easy companion. She did not grudge him the time and attention, but she very much grudged cavalier treatment.

It was, after all, the reason she had quitted Victrix's service. Not openly, of course. But in the secret chambers of a Prime sorceress's heart, a measure had been taken . . . and a queen found wanting.

Clare was not quite found wanting. He was a most

logical, yet fragile, being, and seeing his limitations went far toward the forgiveness of certain of his regrettable tendencies. Still, it irked her. How could it not?

To be a woman was to be a creature most put-upon and taken for granted, and even those among the opposite sex who meant one well had their moments of treating one otherwise.

Yes, she had to admit, she was outright piqued.

And . . . Ludo.

She shut her eyes again. A precious few minutes of consciousness without the scrutiny of servants or Shield, and all she could think of was . . . what was Ludovico, quite, to her?

What had he been?

Simply a tool, an instrument to be played with fine attention and no little respect.

Oh, Emma, lying to yourself is still bad form. That much, at least, has not changed.

She had grown . . . *accustomed* . . . to the Neapolitan, much as she had grown accustomed to Clare. To Mikal, and Severine, and Isobel and Cook and Harthell. They were under her aegis, they were her responsibility, and if she cared for them as hothouse plants, had not such care acquired her certain rights as well as responsibilities? Watering, pruning, adjusting the climate-globes and their charmed tinkles . . .

They are not plants, Emma. A Prime's arrogance was a weakness, and one to be reined firmly lest it blind her to real dangers.

Like yesterday. A bad bit of business, wouldn't you say?

She exhaled sharply, turned her attention to a more productive avenue. Had Victrix seen and felt what *she* had? It flew in the face of much of what was accepted about sorcery, but Sympathy was an ancient art. What could have made a drab in Whitchapel – because Emma Bannon knew a frail when she saw one, thank you very much – possess enough resonance to cause a reaction in the ruling spirit of the Isle, the Empress of Indus, the queen of an empire grander than even the Pax Latium?

Viewing the location of the second body's discovery should be done, but not until she had taken certain precautions.

She stretched again, tapped her lips with a finger, and sighed. For the moment, enough to accept that a resonance indubitably *had* existed. The murders were not unconnected events, and they had some aim in mind.

Why had Britannia bothered to move Victrix to Emma's door? Why had Victrix come *alone*? Cold reflection would perhaps have assured the Queen that Emma Bannon was, perhaps, not likely to bruit the news of a ruling spirit's weakness about high and low. Even if Victrix disliked her methods and person, Britannia was wise enough not to doubt Emma's loyalty to Crown and Empire, no matter that the first rested on a wanting head and the second had not needed a certain sorceress's efforts to continue widening its sway.

Why had Victrix come to her?

That is the wrong question, Emma. The correct question

is: what is she hoping to gain? From the lowest sinks of the Eastron End to the Crown itself, that is the great secret that moves the world. Finding a man – or a woman – who does not obey its dictates is the rarity.

And *that* was precisely why Clare could continue to treat her abominably if it so pleased him, and why she had allowed both Ludovico's informality and his pride. It was why she allowed Severine's nervousness and Mikal's secrets and silences. It was why she had paid for Gilburn's Altered leg and retained Finch's services, why she had taken in Isobel and the half-crippled stableboy, not to mention Cook. Those who did not play the great game of living solely for their own profit were rare and wondrous, and it pleased her to have a collection of them.

Since she was, most definitely, *not* one of their number. Yet it was through her grace and under her protection they could thrive. If one had to bloody and muck oneself in the service of Empire, or even in the business of living in such an imperfect world as this one, sheltering such castaways could take some of the sting from the wound.

"I have grown philosophical," Emma Bannon murmured, with a wry smile, for she heard Severine Noyon's step on the stairs, and further heard the housekeeper fussing at Catherine to *step lively, the mistress waits!*

She arranged her expression into one most suited to a lady's rising, and allowed herself one more luxurious stretch before pushing the covers away and sliding one small foot free of their encumbrance.

It was at that moment a curious thought struck her. She supposed, had she been Clare, it would have already done so.

This first murder was rather sloppily performed – it was a trial. There have been other trials, no doubt; perhaps the second was as well? Impossible to know without viewing the scene. What is it Clare says – experiment requires small steps? Britannia waited for a repeat of the event before moving Victrix to my door.

She was still abed, staring across her bedroom at the lovely blue wallpaper, when the housekeeper and lady's maids bustled in to begin their tending.

For the logical extension of her ruminations was chilling indeed.

There is likely to be another death, and very soon.

⚙ *Chapter Seventeen*

Find The Limits

Clare coughed, wrackingly, and set the knife against his forearm. He was interrupted by a sound not of his own creation, and he blinked rapidly as he watched the last shallow slice slowly congeal. The more he practised, the faster the superficial wounds seemed to seal themselves.

The ramifications were quite fascinating. What had interrupted him?

One step inside his workroom, despite the locked door – this was, to be sure, *her* house, and should she require entry into a portion of it, well, he could not grudge or gainsay her – and Emma's dark eyes widened dangerously. Of course, the blood spattering the smooth stone walls, the chaos of tools on one of the sturdy wooden tables, and the shattered glass upon the floor – he had swept a few alembics from its surface in his irritation – were not comforting in the least.

"What on earth are you *doing*?" Emma Bannon demanded, her earrings of shivering cascades of silver wire and splinters of jet trembling as she halted just over the threshold.

She was in black again today, and looked none the worse for wear. In fact, with her eyes so wide and her expression so shocked, she looked more childlike than ever.

Clare, blinking furiously through veils of acrid smoke, actually goggled at her for a few moments before finding his tongue. "Experiments! Must find the limits, you see. This is quite interesting." He waved the knife absently. "It will make shallow cuts, but no matter how I try, I cannot so much as lop a fingertip off. Controlled explosives merely toss me about a bit. This is very—"

"You've gone mad. *S – x'v!*" The collection of sounds she uttered shivered the walls, refusing to stay in Clare's memory for more than a moment. When the echoes died, he found he could not move. The knife clattered from his nerveless fingers, and she made a short, sharp gesture that gathered up the thick white and grey smoke, compressing it into an ashen sphere that bumbled over her head and drifted out of sight up the stairs, seeking a chimney. "Good heavens. *Look* at all this."

Mikal appeared behind her, one eyebrow fractionally raised. "Is that . . . what is it?"

"Dynamite." She lifted her heavy skirts, stepping briskly through the litter of glass and splinters. "Nitrou-glycerine and sawdust; it tends to be volatile. Do take care. Clare, what on *earth*?"

He could breathe well enough, but his limbs refused to budge. Invisible bands circled him, gently but firmly, and he had the sudden, quite thought-provoking realisation that she was being rather delicate with him. "Experiments," he wheezed. "Interfering . . . damn nuisance."

"Quite." She examined the walls, wrinkling her small nose. "What are you hoping to discover, sir?"

"What the . . . the limits of . . ." The words fled from him as he stared at her throat. Her pulse beat, a fraction too swiftly. "I say, you are quite agitated. And your dress is fashionable even for mourning, despite the tiny bustle, which means you did not deny what Isobel first proffered. She quite thinks you need a bit more *mode* lately, you have not been yourself. And Madame Noyon is becoming forgetful as she grows older—"

"Clare." She shook her head, the curls over her ears a bit old-fashioned, but she could simply have been a well-bred young miss with a hidebound guardian or *duenna* choosing her cloth. An observer who did not note the fact of her sorcery would perhaps draw such a conclusion. "You will refrain."

But I do not wish to. "I must know what the limits are. What the logical . . . what I can extrapolate . . ."

"Did it occur to you to simply *ask*?"

His reply was loosed before he considered its weight or its edge. "Would you answer honestly if I had?"

She made a small spitting noise, expressing very

unladylike irritation. Yet she did not deign to answer more fully, and Clare could hardly blame her. He strained against the invisible ropes holding him fast, and reflected that it was no wonder a woman with her abilities was held in such caution.

It was downright *unnatural* for a female to possess such power.

Miss Bannon examined the workroom once more, turning in a complete circle so as to leave nothing unseen. "You have not slept at all," she remarked.

"No." *There is too much to discern, too much to do.*

"You will likely continue in this fashion until you find some means of harming yourself."

"My dear lady, I cannot—" His struggles increased, and his voice rose. "Turn loose. I *demand* you release me, Emma."

"Have I been in any way unclear? I am *quite* unwilling to see you harmed, Archibald. I shall take steps to prevent it."

"You are not my nursemaid!" Why was he *shouting*? A mentath did not lose his temper. It was unheard of. It could not be borne.

Neither could the restraints, and she watched him curiously as he continued to writhe without moving. Could she feel it? Her expression gave no indication. It was frankly maddening to see a slip of a girl, her head cocked slightly, regard a grown man much as a child might a specimen pinned to a board.

"No. I am most definitely not your nursemaid." She nodded once, briskly, her curls swinging. "But you do need one at this juncture. And I think it best you sleep now, dear Clare."

He was about to protest even more hotly, but a rumbling passed through him. More of those damnable unremembered words, her lips shaping incomprehensible, *inhuman* sounds, and blackness swallowed him whole.

⚙ *Chapter Eighteen*

⚙ *Even If I Do Not Grant*

L onging thoughts of rum floated through her head.
Emma pressed her fingers delicately against the bridge
of her nose. "I cannot keep him in a cocoon."

"No," Mikal agreed. He was maddeningly calm, but the
high colour in his lean cheeks told her it was mere seeming.
"Prima . . ."

"I know. *You* cannot look after him, I need you
elsewhere." She decided to overlook his very plain
sigh of relief, and turned the question over in her mind
again.

The workroom was a shambles. Clare was propped
upright, trapped in sorcerous restraints she kept steady
with threads of ætheric force trickling from the chalcedony pendant at her throat. The blood on the walls
troubled her, and the wild-eyed man who had outright

screamed at her troubled her even more. It was so unlike him, and doubly unlike what she knew of mentath temperament.

"Perhaps . . ." But Mikal shook his sleek, dark head as she glanced at him. Whatever idea he had, perhaps he had discovered a great many holes in it as soon as he gave it voice.

"Finch." She twitched a slender ætheric thread, and the call bloomed subtly through the house. It took less than a half-minute for the familiar light step to be heard on the stairs outside the workroom – he must have suspected she would summon him.

When he stepped through the flung-open door, his cadaverous face betrayed no surprise or irritation at all. It was a distinct relief to find him as imperturbable as ever. His indenture collar flashed once before subsiding to a steady glow.

Her sigh was only partly theatrical. "I've a bit of a quandary, Mr Finch."

"So it seems, mum." There was a hint of a curve to his thin mouth, and Emma allowed herself a rueful smile in return.

"I need a minder for Mr Clare. Someone singularly . . . *useful*. And loyal, though I shall of course require a blood-binding."

Finch absorbed this, his thin shoulders stooped. He did not immediately answer, which gave her cause for hope. Which was roundly justified when he finally nodded, slowly. Sharp as a knife when he first entered her service, he had lost none of that edge in the ensuing years. Age sometimes brought a man more fully into dangerousness, and he had experienced enough of treachery to know even its hidden faces.

He was no longer youthful-quick, but he was exceedingly *subtle*.

To prove it, he produced an impossible necessity once more. "I've a . . . cousin, mum. He might do."

"A cousin?" Her eyebrows rose dangerously high. She could hardly help herself.

"Well, after a fashion. He's, well—"

Was he *blushing*? She forged onward, twitching her skirts absently as she turned to regard the somnolent, propped-up figure of Clare. Who looked rather peaceful, d—n him, while she was required to solve this problem. "If you think he would suit, Finch, it is enough to set my mind at ease."

"He's . . . well, he's a molly, mum. If you catch my meaning."

It was a mark of her distraction that she did not take his meaning immediately. Perhaps Finch was right to blush, though he could hardly think her intolerant of such a thing, considering her acquaintance with, for example, the infamous Prime Dorian Childe, and others of his ilk. Society might very well frown upon the men of Sodom, but Emma had found no few of them bright and above all, *useful*.

If Finch recommended a certain man, it mattered not a whit what that man liked to sport with. Unless said sport could lead him to treachery, but Finch's recommendation would mitigate that danger somewhat. "I see. Well, I care little what he buggers, as long as he does his duty. Do we understand each other?"

"Yesmum." Finch bobbed his head, and she caught a slight movement – as if he would tug his forelock, as he used to before he studied a butler's manners. "I shall go myself and fetch him."

"You are a treasure, Finch. Be about your business, then." *Do hurry. There is much to be done*. She did not add the last, it was unnecessary.

"Yesmum." And he glided out the door.

"A molly?" Mikal sounded amused, at least. He could not fail to be familiar with the term.

She gathered herself, leashed her temper, and paused once more to determine what should be done and what was the most efficient way to accomplish it. "Perhaps he will feel affectionate toward Clare. Heaven knows our mentath seems to need it, and I rather think he would not receive *my* affection gratefully at the moment."

"Then he is a fool, Prima." The warmth of Mikal's tone was somewhat indecent, but they were alone. Or close to alone, as Clare was unconscious. He would rest until Tideturn, and by then she hoped to have made *some* arrangement for his comfort.

And, incidentally, for her own.

"Perhaps. But he is *our* fool." She sighed, set her shoulders, and brushed at her skirts, though there was no need to set them to rights. "I had rather hoped to view the second site today, but that is of little account. Come, help me get him to bed."

The cousin was a lean foxlike youth, a measure of rust touching his dark curls and no shame in his wide dark eyes. His cloth was indeed flash: a waistcoat very fine but the coat a trifle ill fitting, no doubt bought secondhand. His shoes were not quite fashionable but they were brushed very neatly, and the half-resentful courtesy he afforded the visibly relieved Finch was telling. A watch-chain that had certainly started life in a gentleman's pocket before being deprived of such surroundings by quick fingers, the dove-grey gloves, and the pomade in his curls all shouted *rough lad*. The only question was whether he paid for his buggering – or was paid for it.

Just where the line was drawn between an Æsthete (or Decadent, for that matter) and a slightly circumspect Merry-Ann was difficult to tell, since those who affected to live for Arte and Beauty often dressed in imitation of the panthers of St Jemes or Jermyn Street. Often in finer fabric, though the end result was the same.

He passed the first inspection, and Emma motioned them further into the room.

"Mum." Finch inclined slightly from the waist. "May I present my cousin, Mr Philip Pico?"

The drawing room was not the best setting for this lad. He belonged in one of the taverns the Merry-Anns frequented, or along the docks in the darkness wreathed by yellow greasy fog . . .

. . . or in some dark corner of Whitchapel, where the trade was less merry and far more rough. Where a gentleman might go to seek danger to spice his buggery, where the panthers, both of Sodom and murder, prowled.

"Mum." The young man made the same motion Finch almost had that morning – as if to tug his forelock. He caught himself, and offered her a very proper half-bow.

"How do you do," Emma murmured, not deigning to offer her hand, and examined him closely.

It was in the feet, she decided. Placed just so, his weight balanced nicely, one slightly forward. The fact that his shoulders were broad – though he was at pains to appear slender – was another indicator. He was not averse to violence, and he was alert.

"Your cousin has no doubt informed you of my requirements." She nodded slightly, and Finch shuffled away to the sideboard. If she found the lad did not suit, she would give him a drink and send him on his way, with a guinea or two for his trouble.

"Discretion, loyalty, efficiency, so on, so forth." He chanted it sing-song, and she almost missed the flicker of his gaze towards the door as Mikal entered, noiseless. She did not miss the sudden tension in his left hand.

That is where the knife will be, then. "Yes. You may be amusing, but I do not countenance impoliteness."

"Your countenance is set very politely, madam." Quick as a whip, and with a winning smile to boot.

She found herself measuring him against a Neapolitan with a sneer and dirty fingernails, and had to eye him afresh, so she would not find him wanting without reason. "I take pains to preserve it so," she replied, dryly. "You have no objection to a blood-binding?"

He paled slightly, but set his shoulders. "None at all, mum. He—" A slight tip of his head took in the attentive Finch. "—tells me you do right by those in your service, and that I'm getting too old to molly much more. The gentlemen prefer younger, even with the rough." A defiant tilt to his chin, watching to see if he could shock her.

Her estimation of his intelligence rose, even though he seemed very young indeed to her. "And just how old are you, Philip?"

"Old 'nough. I don't enjoy the molly, mum. It's just easy."

Ah. She allowed herself to feel cautiously hopeful. "Your enjoyment of such things, or not, holds no interest for me. I wish to know if you are capable of discharging the duties of a minder for my mentath. He requires a companion of a certain . . . durability, discretion, and capability to deal with Londinium's nastier areas. *I* require that you keep his skin whole and your mouth closed on the subject his affairs, and my own, to anyone outside this room. Mr Finch has no doubt negotiated your wages, should you be accepted for the position, and has also given you to understand certain . . . peculiarities . . . of said position."

He waited. Mute and stubborn, giving nothing away.

Very good. "Mikal?"

The Shield was suddenly across the room, locking the

young man's wrist and striking the knife from his grasp. Finch did not move, a curious expression – part distaste, part amusement – flickering over his graven features. The youth actually almost managed to strike Mikal once, but the Shield finished by holding him by his scruff and shaking lightly, before dropping him to hands and knees and stalking away.

Her Shield retook his place by the door. "Amateur."

Which was high praise indeed, coming from a fully trained Shield. At least he hadn't said *useless*.

Emma found herself suddenly weary, and a sour taste had crept into her mouth. "Very well. You shall do, Mr Philip Pico. Do you wish the hire?"

The youth looked up. With his curls tumbled and high colour in his shaven cheeks, his true age was a little more visible. Yes, he was rather a shade too old for mollying to gentlemen, and a swift pang passed through her. Mikal must be out of sorts, to embarrass the lad so.

He climbed swiftly to his feet, scooping up the knife and slipping it back into its hiding-place behind his left hip. "One condition."

After that display, I suppose you might be allowed to ask, even if I do not grant. "Which is?"

He pointed at Mikal. "He's a fair boxer. He teaches me that. I'll not shirk, I'll not talk, and I'll keep your mentath safe as a babe in cradle."

She found herself smiling, and Finch's relief visibly mounted. Of course, she supposed he had to have been very sure of the boy to bring him, and who knew what their true relationship was? "Cousin" was as good a word as any, and it mattered little, if the youth was dependable.

"I think that is quite possible, and even acceptable, though Mikal is a much harsher taskmaster than myself. As long as his tutelage does not distract from your other duties, you shall do very nicely, Philip. While Finch arranges for your effects to be brought, we shall settle you in a room and you shall see your charge immediately." *Clare will not like this. But I cannot watch him day and night, and this young enigma will at least keep him occupied while I seek to discern what nastiness is afoot.*

"Yesmum." Pico bent to retrieve his hat, as well, and darted a venomous look past her, at Mikal. Who would, of course, be entirely unaffected.

The little molly seemed to completely discount her as a threat.

Which was very much how Emma preferred it at the moment. She nodded once again, more to herself than to any man present. "Very well."

❀ *Chapter Nineteen*

Like A Weathervane

Archibald Clare woke from a sound, sorcery-induced sleep and sat straight up in the bed's familiar embrace. "Who the devil are you?"

The young man in the high-backed chair cocked his head. "Shh. Listen."

What now? He opened his mouth to take this stranger to task, before he noted that the youth's shirt and waistcoat were tailored with familiar, tiny stitches – Catherine's work, beyond a doubt – and the way his hair was plastered down bespoke a good scrubbing. Whoever he was, he had the blessing of the mistress of the house, and had been given attention so his clothing did not offend her sensibilities. His boots were well brushed and sturdy, but their age shouted quite plainly that they were his own, instead of Miss Bannon's largesse.

"Tideturn," the young man breathed, and the vowels placed him as one of Londinium's native sons, born within a few yards of Lincoln Inn unless Clare missed his guess. Or perhaps he had merely been a child in such a place, for Clare's sensitive nose caught traces of . . . pomade? And ash, and old blood.

What on earth can this be? "Does she think . . . ?" Words failed him.

The youth gave him a scorching, contemptuous look – and the entire house, from cellar Clare had never seen to whatever attic Miss Bannon saw fit to keep under its trim roof, shook like the coat of a dog shedding itself of water.

Clare did not halt to consider the fascinating conundrum of the lad at his bedside. Instead, he scrambled from the covers, hopping as he found he was barefoot on cold wooden flooring, and hurled himself for the door.

It was not locked, which was a mercy, for he would have bruised himself on its heavy wooden carapace had it been. He scrambled up the corridor, booted steps behind him too heavy to be Valentinelli's, the stairs at the end of the hall heaved, creaking and crackling. Screams came from the depths – the servants, of course – and there was a single hissing curse as he slipped.

The youth's fingers clamped around his upper arm like a vice, and he was hauled to his feet as the house shook again. Up the stairs, the other familiar hall shuddering as its very walls warped.

What is she doing?

Her dressing-room door ran with foxfire light, leprous

green, and for a moment Clare was caught in a net of memory: Emma Bannon dying of the Red Plague and his own monstrous, helpless uselessness in the face of that event. But then it had only been the lights dimming and the sobbing of the maids—

A blow, and he was spinning. His elbow hit the hall floor, but he was on his feet again and striking with a bladed hand, just as Ludo had taught him, *strike for throat, mentale, if a man no breathe, he no trouble you—*

"*Stop!*" Mikal hissed, and bent back with impossible grace, out of the path of Clare's strike. His fingers clamped Clare's wrist and he twisted, one foot flicking out to double the youth, who was hard on Clare's heels. A chiming clatter – *someone has a knife* – then a keening scream rose behind Miss Bannon's dressing-room door, turning the air frigid and shivering. Clare's breath became a white cloud as he fell once more, twisting to lash out at the Shield's legs with his own. It was an instinctive move, which somehow Mikal evaded as a final grating shock ran through the house, wood groaning and plaster cracking, the floor rippling in incomprehensible, *impossible* ways.

The Shield did not fall. Instead, he leapt backward, fishlike, his own bare feet thudding on the heaving boards. He flung himself at the dressing-room door, carried it down in a tide of exploding shards and splinters. He was gone into the darkness then, and the house settled against itself with an audible *thump*.

"*Pax!*" Mikal screamed, beyond the door. "*Pax, Prima! Emma! Emmaaaaaa!*"

Clare pushed himself up, staggered after him.

Miss Bannon's dressing room was pale-carpeted, strewn with broken wood, and he thought, quite calmly, that she was going to be extremely put out by the mess.

The youth caught at his arm, but Clare evaded him easily enough. There was a very real danger of skewering his feet; when he reached Miss Bannon's bedroom door he was gratified that he had not done so. "Emma?" he called tentatively, into the dimness. It smelled, powerfully, of a foreign, feminine country – perfume, and long hair, and silk. The rustle of dresses and the slightly oily healthiness of a dark-haired woman, the smoky overlay of sorcery, pear-spiced perfume, and a hint of rosewater from her morning ablutions. The impressions whirled through him and away, and he had stepped over the threshold before he knew it, blindly. "Emma, please, say something."

"Clare?" She sounded very young, and breathless. "And . . . Mikal." A huskiness – of course, that throat-scouring scream. Was it merely a nightmare?

Somehow, no matter how given the fairer sex was to vapours, he did not think so.

"Here." The Shield sounded even more sober than usual. "What is it?"

"I am not dead." Wondering, a half-disbelieving laugh. "I . . . Mikal. Clare."

"Yes." Mikal's eyes were a yellow glimmer; Clare's adapted to the darkness. He saw Miss Bannon's bed, the dressing table and its beautifully clear oval mirror, the bulk of an armoire, other shapes he could not quite infer just yet. Mikal's glare was a pair of yellow lamps in the dimness. "Come no closer, sir."

"Mikal." She sounded much more like herself now. "Do *not* be impolite. I am well enough. It was . . . simply a shock. Clare, have you been introduced to—"

"—the young man who was at my bedside? Quite an odd choice for a nanny, madam."

"I suppose I am to let you lock yourself in the workroom and attempt to bring down my house with explosives?" Did she sound irritated? It was, he decided, a very good sign. "Yes, Mr Clare. That sounds *ever so helpful*. Kindly remove yourself from my bedroom, sir, I have little time to quarrel with you."

"You do not need explosives to level your domicile, Miss Bannon. Which is why I am here."

"The damage is temporary. *Get out*. No—" This was no doubt directed at Mikal, for there was a flicker of movement in the darkness near her bed. Light glinting from metal, and Clare's skin chilled. "Mikal. Absolutely *not*."

"Little thief," the Shield said, softly. "Come closer, and lose a limb."

"Just looking after me investment, squire," came the cheeky reply – from right next to Clare, and he was hard-pressed to suppress a start. *How very curious*.

"Investment?" he enquired, blithely. "Did you think to replace Ludovico, Miss Bannon?"

"No." Sharp and curt, material sliding, and a bloom of silvery light from the sconces near the door. A globe of malachite on her bedside table, next to a stack of novels – her taste in bed-reading was shockingly salacious, really – made a soft slithering sound as it turned in its stand, and a shiver ran through the house again. "I thought to ensure your safety, sir. A rather onerous duty, but one I have undertaken. Now leave me in peace, I must dress."

She inhaled sharply, and Clare was confronted with the exotic sight of Miss Bannon shrugging herself into a wine-red dressing gown over her nightgown, lace and satin scratching against plain, high-necked white linen. Her small, well-formed feet were bare as his and Mikal's, and her unbound hair was a river down her back. With her tumbled curls and the high colour in her cheeks, she looked every inch a child up too late on a holiday night. "Mikal, send Severine up and rouse Harthell, have the carriage prepared. We are bound for Whitchapel." She strode for her dressing table, sliding past the Shield with a determined air.

"Whitchapel?" *How extraordinary*. Clare's rebellious faculties strained, turning sharply in a most unwelcome direction. "There has been another murder." *And you have sensed it in some sorcerous fashion. Very extraordinary indeed*.

She glanced over her shoulder, and he stepped back, almost into the nameless youth, who was observing this scene with a great deal of interest. "Yes. There has. And I must go."

* * *

"Philip Pico." The youth offered his hand, a firm shake, and settled into the carriage's upholstery just where Ludovico had been wont to sit.

Clare suppressed a protest. It was illogical; the seat was there, he had to sit *somewhere*, and—

"Absolutely not," Miss Bannon said. Her mourning today was wool, and her hair was in place again. There was no trace of the dishevelled, just-wakened child she had appeared, except for a slight puffiness about her eyes. "Archibald, I do not have *time*—"

"You – and *she* – asked for my aid in untangling this affair." He quite enjoyed her discomfiture. "Which I am determined to provide. And this young man, no replacement for our dear Valentinelli indeed, is nevertheless bound to be quite handy."

The door slammed, Harthell cracked the whip and the carriage jolted into motion.

Miss Bannon closed her eyes, the cameo at her throat flashing once. It was a familiar sight, and he knew a silvery ball of strange witchlight would now coalesce before the gleaming clockhorses, directing the coachman to whatever incident had drawn his mistress's attention – and telling the rest of Londinium a sorcerer was impatient with delay.

So much irrationality he had learned to live with as merely part of his acquaintance with this most *logical* of sorceresses. Had he not often thought that if only all practitioners of the arts of æther were as practical as she, mentaths would have little difficulty with their number?

Now he cast a fresh eye upon her as the carriage jolted, and found she was pale, her veil tucked aside, her gloved fingers entirely too tense, and her chin set.

She met his gaze directly. How had he never noticed before that her manner was of a man facing a duel? So much of Miss Bannon only made sense if one ceased to think of her as a proper woman.

And yet. Her little attentions, her gracefulness, her arranging of matters to suit those about her, her collection of castaway servants – none of those graces bore a masculine stamp.

The woman in question remained silent, still gazing at him with that odd expression. As if she expected trouble from his quarter, and soon.

He drummed his fingers upon his knee. It was past baker's-morn but still grey-dark, Londinium's yellow fog choke-wreathing wrought-iron lamps both sputtering with gasflame and, in the better quarters, held to steadier life by carefully applied wick-charms. Hooves sounded and carriage wheels thrummed, even at this hour. The city did not sleep, and a vision of it as a gigantic coal-fed, sorcery-stroked beast had no room in a mentath's logic-ordered brain.

Still, even mentaths had passing fancies. He leaned forward slightly. "Are you . . . are you quite well, Miss Bannon?"

"I was a-study all afternoon, seeking to discern a clew, ætheric or not, to the identity of our killer, and had absolutely *no* success. I did not wish to view the site of the second murder after a day spent so unprofitably, so I retired."

She took a deep breath. "Then I felt a woman die within my own *corpus*, sir. I am a trifle unsettled." She did not look it. "And do forgive my manners. Mr Clare, meet Philip Pico; he is a cousin to Mr Finch and I have engaged him to perform a valet's duty for you, as well as other small tasks you may require of him. Philip, this is your charge, Mr Archibald Clare. Esquire, I believe. *Do* behave appropriately."

"'Ave no fear, mum." The youth gave her a toothy grin, and stretched his legs out most disagreeably in the carriage's close confines.

Clare suppressed the urge to poke the lad in the ribs. Such uncharitable Feeling could not be tolerated. He told himself firmly not to mind its prodding. "You are not in a tavern, sir."

"No, there'd be drink if I were." A twist of a half-grin, and the attention he paid to paring his fingernails impinged on Clare's consciousness like a silent thunderbolt.

A quite extraordinary further deduction occurred to Clare. He tested it thoroughly, and found it not wanting at all. *A Sodom boy? In Miss Bannon's employ?* "Your taste in domestics, as usual, is most curious."

"So I am told." She tilted her head, slightly, perhaps listening to some sorcerous noise. "Now do be quiet, if you can. I am rather occupied."

Nettled, he sank back into the seat and felt a most uncharacteristic desire to curse, roundly and loudly. This was the deadliness of Feeling: it swung one about like a weathervane, and made Reason so very difficult.

I was merely seeking to find the limits of this extraordinary thing you have inflicted on me, Emma. But he realised, as Harthell cracked his whip and Miss Bannon's paleness took on another, more worrisome cast, that was not quite accurate.

He had, for a short while, lost his bloody mind. The longer this state of affairs endured, the more likely it was he would do so again. Unless he found some method of making rational the fact of his unwanted, unwholesome . . .

. . . and, likely to be very *useful*, immortality.

❀ Chapter Twenty

Founded Upon Much Less

Emma freed her hand from Mikal's and took in the grey light of predawn, the fog sallow and the Scab underfoot slippery enough that she had to take care with her balance.

"What the *devil* are you about here?"

It was a greeting from a direction she would *not* have preferred, but at least the hailer's presence would solve a number of problems. She used her sweetest smile. "Mr Aberline. My, you've grown."

Frederick had thickened since she last saw him, and acquired a very fine moustache and side-whiskers. At the moment he was scowling, and it did not improve his knife-beak of a nose *or* his slightly choleric cast. He had been a very promising lad, a watchmaker's son who rose through the ranks of the Metropoleans by dint of ability and persistence.

It must be something extraordinary to set him a-glower, for normally he was rather . . . sedate. Many of his suspects had learned too late that his solicitor's mien did not make him stupid *or* placid.

And many of his quarries, in his younger days, had learned that a broken head in the service of Justice did not trouble Aberline overmuch. He was rightly feared among the more intelligent flashboys in Londinium's seamier quarters.

"Is it . . . Bannon? Yes. A pleasure." But his mouth turned down, and she rather thought not. "How's our lad Geoffrey?"

"Mr Finch is still in my employ, sir." *If that changes, he will be in another country before* you *get wind of it.* "How is your wife?" *I seem to recall she was perennially sickly.*

"Which one? And, Miss Bannon, what is the occasion that honours us with your presence here?" His sharp gaze drifted over her shoulder, took in Pico and Clare just alighting from the carriage, and he looked even more unhappy – if that were possible. "Sightseeing on the Scab's not for gentlefolk this morning."

As if you think me an excitement-seeker. How very insulting. She had never given him reason to think his attempts to be offensive were even noticed, and she saw no need to alter her course now. "The gentle are no doubt still abed. We are left to our own devices in this affair."

"I should have known," he muttered. "He said someone else from the Crown would be along."

Now *that* was interesting. "Who?"

"Oh, Gull. He's become Her Majesty's hangman now, like Conroy was her mother's, God rest that poor woman's soul."

He jammed his bowler hat more firmly atop his dark, slicked-down hair, and she saw, even in the dimness, grey beginning at his temples. His boots splorched and slid through the Scab crusting the cobbles, and she did not have to glance about to know she was upon Hanbury Street.

The smell alone would have told her so, and she wondered if Peggy Razor still door-watched a dosshouse a few doors up; if Trout Jack still ran the child-thieves in this slice of Whitchapel; if the Scab still made fine delicate whorls up every wooden wall before sunlight scorched it away, leaving a filigree of caustic char . . .

Gull. Her well-trained memory returned a face to go with the name. Physicker to the Queen, and a singularly bloodless and dedicated man. Rumour had him as one who had always wished he were among sorcery's children, but *educated* rumour simply said he liked a bit of secrecy, and so had joined a certain "Brotherhood of Stone". They played at Ritual and Initiation, with a certain degree of ridiculousness, and, like any gentlemen's club, membership was skewed toward the wealthy, or those who wished influence.

Nothing about said brotherhood interested Emma overmuch, but if there was gossip linking Gull and Victrix as her mother and Conroy had been linked, it was a trifle worrisome.

She set the consideration aside; Victrix's troubles, except

in this one small matter, were no longer hers. This affair was to be laid to rest quickly, so she could return to her studies and other concerns.

Chief among those concerns was Clare, who sniffed the soup passing for air in Whitchapel with bright interest. He glanced down, toyed with the Scab's green organic sludge with one boot-toe, and nodded slightly. "Most interesting."

Would you find it so, if you saw what it does to bodies? Or to rats, on particularly active nights? Emma turned back to Aberline. "I am gratified to find my coming was foretold," she remarked, drily. "There is a body, sir."

"Yes." The inspector – because he was no doubt one of that august brotherhood now, being neither encased in a bobby's blue cloth nor bearing the ubiquitous whistle – furrowed his brow mightily as he took in the mentath. "There is quite a crowd already—"

"Be a dear and clear them away, so we may examine the premises." She put on her most winning smile again, and saw his flinch with a great deal of satisfaction. "My companion is a mentath, and quite useful. As you shall no doubt be. The Yard's taking an active interest in this?" *Not just at the Queen's bidding, if you are here.*

"Third's a charm. This will be in the broadsheets and dreadfuls before long." The man's face was positively mournful. "I don't suppose you could . . ."

"Mitigate somewhat?" Her sigh took her by surprise, and Mikal's comforting warmth at her shoulder was the only thing on Hanbury Street that did not appear worrisome. "My days of mitigation are somewhat past, Inspector. But I shall do what I can." *Mostly to suit myself, for I do not wish to be bruited about in print.*

"Well, good. Come along then." He did not further insult her, which was a very good sign – or a very bad one. He halted, and she noted the breadth of his shoulders under his jacket. Inspector Aberline had not let the iron go cold, as the saying went. "I don't suppose this is merely a social visit?"

From me? Now there is an amusing thought. "Of course not, sir. I shall, however, see whatever unpleasantness this is to its conclusion, and as quickly as possible."

"Good. Because the Eastron End's about to explode."

Is this a new state of affairs? "Is that so?"

"Foreigners." His lip actually twisted. He moved through the Scab with a distinctive sliding step. You could always tell Whitchapel flashboys and the like from that step, rolling and settling the weight only after they were sure something under the thick, resilient slime wasn't going to shift. "Have you still a strong stomach, Miss Bannon?"

"You ask *me*?" She shook her head, glad Mikal was following step for step. He had not the trick of moving in the Scab's deep cover, and she could actually *hear* him.

Her skirts dragged in the caustic sludge, and she let them. Scab would eat at the fabric, but there was no use in holding them high; she might need her hands. No doubt this affair would ruin a frock or two by the end. *You can tell a Whitchapel drab by her ankles,* the saying went. Or, if you were raised in the argot, *A nav'Whit slit shews gam, sh'doon.*

She might have let herself consider sending the Crown a bill for whatever cloth was ruined before said end. While amusing, it did not have the savour such thoughts usually did.

Aberline was speaking again. "We've mancers now. At the Yard, and in the station houses." He did not sound pleased by the notion. "I doubt any of them would want to see *this*."

And you sensitive to sorcery, but unable to hold a charter symbol in free air. How that must grate upon your pride. "Indeed."

She followed him to a dark cleft, a passage leading to the back of the building. Mikal's attention sharpened. The Scab became much thicker, giving reluctantly under her heeled boots and still coating the cobbles at the bottom of every step. Her ankles ached – she had not lost the trick of easing through the mire, but her legs had grown unused to it. Her skin chilled, remembering slipping barefoot and barelegged through the sludge, dodging cuffs and curses, a stolen apple clutched to her flat child's chest.

Clare's voice, indistinct behind her. Philip Pico's murmured reply. And Mikal's hand at her shoulder, fingers slightly digging in as if he felt her . . . uncertainty?

The passageway ended, and Aberline pointed. He needn't have, for Emma could feel the plucking in the æther all along her body, down into her core. There was no question it was a corpse, and not a drunkard in stupor-sleep.

"No name yet." Aberline's expression was set. He pointed to the far end of the yard. "There is the Yudic

Workingman's Club, though. Which will no doubt prove a deadly coincidence."

"Yudic?" The ætheric disturbance pulsed as if sensing her nearness. *Twice now he's mentioned the Foreigners.*

"Coming from the east and taking jobs from poor honest Englene, the story goes. And socialist to boot. Bloody anarchists. The End's full of them, and trouble every time one's accused of anything from following a pretty girl to murdering a thief." He shook his head. "Now this."

"Has it truly grown so dire?" *Well, of course. Why else would a full-blown detective inspector from the hallowed Yard be here at this hour?* "Yes. I see. Three corpses and a workingman's club – there have been unwholesome incidents founded upon much less."

"Examiner's been sent for. I hope you've some idea of what to do, Bannon. Can we move the body?"

I have no desire to endure another vision of murder. "It should be safe enough." *The Tebrem woman's corpse was moved, after all.* She stared at the mangled corpse, took two steps past the inspector and examined it more thoroughly. Yes, there was the head turned to the side, the ripping-open of the abdomen, entrails flung over the unfortunate's shoulder. Thick legs in striped stockings, the legs obscenely splayed. Two dull farthings lay on a blood-soaked handkerchief by her curled right hand, and her pocket had been slit. The throat was cut, and there was a quantity of blood . . .

. . . but not nearly enough.

She decided it was perhaps time to remind the detective

inspector just who held the whip hand in this particular situation. "Curious," she murmured, and heard Philip Pico's sharp, indrawn breath as he caught sight of the body. "Tell me, Inspector, do you still have dreams?"

He was silent for a long moment. Finally, he shook out his left hand, which had tightened into a fist. "Curse you." Softly, conversationally. "Bloody sorceress."

Yes. And you have, though not in the way you might think. I merely need to remind you to mind your duty, and your place. "Indeed. Tell me something else, Inspector. Where did the blood *go*?"

"I know where some went. See that?" He pointed, and she stared for a few moments. Even with her sensitive eyes, it took time for what she saw to become comprehensible.

"Leather. Cobbler's apron?"

"Or slaughterer's. Could have been there already. Soaked in the claret, Bannon, though still not enough. And you don't need to be a mancer to know something's amiss here. Look." He jabbed two fingers at the shimmering over the corpse. It was akin to the heat-haze over a fire, or a slate roof on a hot day. "And underneath."

"Yes." Under the body, the Scab's venomous green had been scorched. *Where blood falls, the Scab greens*, that was the proverb. Here, the blood – or something else – had burned down to ancient, slime-scarred cobbles and blackened, sour dirt that hadn't seen free air in longer than Emma had been alive. "Yet she was not murdered elsewhere."

"I'd ask how you know that."

"And I would tell you I know, and that is enough."

"Bloody sorceress." No heat to it, he merely sounded weary. He scrubbed one flat-bladed hand over his face, precisely once, a familiar mannerism. "I happen to think you're right."

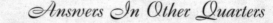 Chapter Twenty-One

Answers In Other Quarters

The poor woman had perhaps never been as much a subject of attention in life as she was now. The surgeon – a round, jolly little physicker in a dark suit, his hands quick and deft as he performed incisions – muttered to a thin boy in a transcriber's gown, while behind them a sour-faced barrowmancer tended to a charm-heated bowl of pitch, eyeing the body warily as if he expected it to perform some feat.

Which was much the way Miss Bannon regarded said corpse, too, when she glanced at it at all. Most of her attention seemed taken by rumination; certainly there was much in this turn of events to cogitate upon.

It was not like her to seem so . . . distracted, though.

The dank little stone room in this morguelrat warren was noisome enough, but it was also crowded. Clare stood at the periphery of a group clustered near the door, comprised of Miss Bannon, the ever-present Shield, the lad Pico, and the stout detective inspector who addressed Miss Bannon with quite amazing familiarity. The hall outside was packed as well, for the murder had attracted no little attention, and the broadsheets were already crying out its details. A small army of scruffy newsboys were having a fine time selling the sheets as quickly as they could be printed.

Clare leaned a little closer, using his height to advantage as he peered over the examiner's shoulder. "Most curious," he said. "The viscera . . . where has the uterus gone?"

"Don't know," Physicker Bagswell said, cheerily, hunched over the scarred granite slab. "There's a rumour some scraper in Stepney is paying in guineas for them. The ovaries are missing too. Look there, a very sharp blade."

"Yes, and handled with some skill." Clare did not hold a handkerchief to his sensitive nose, but he was tempted indeed. "Scraping the underside of the diaphragm, even. And the kidneys . . ."

"The Tebrem woman." Aberline aimed the words in Miss Bannon's general direction, though his posture shouted that he would rather not speak to her. "And Nickol. Yes, the similarities are striking. Both did work as . . . well, unfortunates. This one, no doubt, did too."

"I know a frail when I see one, sir." Miss Bannon's tone held a great deal of asperity. "Yet this one's farthings were left upon her corpse. *Most* troubling."

"When *you* say such a thing, it fills me with dread." The

inspector sighed, his breath making a cloud. It was unhealthily damp here, and the coolness no doubt kept the bodies from becoming *too* fragrant. Still, it was nasty enough. The victim's entrails – what was left of them – were in a bucket, sending up a stink of their own, and her slack face was nowhere near as peaceful as those who called Death a tranquil state would credit.

"Her fingers are abraded." Clare pointed. "I wonder . . ."

"Rings? And look there, the nicks in the cervical vertebrae." Bagswell tutted over the the steady dripping from the slab into the drain, its black eye exhaling its own foulness up through rusty metal grating. "Note that, Edric."

"Yes, sir." The boy was slated to become a physicker himself, and was remarkably unmoved by the spectacle. "Shall I list them separately?"

"Do, please. There are three. Take care with the locations, sketch if you must. Hm."

"Right-handed," Clare prompted. "And her throat slashed from behind. Now why would that be?"

"She would face the wall and raise her skirts." Miss Bannon, archly. "Much easier than couching upon cold ground."

"Must you?" The inspector was crimson.

Clare noted this, turned his attention back to the body.

"You would prefer me not to speak of something so indelicate?" Her tone could best be described as *icy*. "My mentath works best when given what information is necessary, clearly and dispassionately. Now, you mentioned another attack? Before Tebrem?"

"Might not be related. Name of Woad, seamstress and occasional frail. She was assaulted, said it was two men with no faces, or a single man with no face."

"*Really*." Bagswell found this most interesting. He turned, his arms splattered elbow-deep with gore. "I saw the body. Collapsed in the workhouse, ruptured perineum. Infection. Faceless, she said?"

Aberline's expression could not sour further. "Quite insistent upon that point."

Clare glanced at Miss Bannon, who had gone deathly pale. He doubted it was the setting, for she had gazed upon much more unsettling *tableaux* with complete calm on more than one previous occasion. *Interesting*. Again, he filed the observation away, returned his attention to the body. "Half the liver missing. No doubt an error."

"Do you think so? He has some skill—"

Clare pointed. "Oh yes, but look there, and there. The marks are quite clear. He was aiming otherwise and slipped."

"Detective Inspector." Miss Bannon had evidently heard enough. "I require you to shepherd Mr Clare to the Yard, and give him every answer he seeks, access to *anything* he might require."

"McNaughton's not going to be fond of this," Aberline muttered, darkly. "Nor will Swanley. *Or* Waring."

"That is beyond my control. You shall give them to understand the Crown's wishes in this matter. I am bound to seek answers in other quarters. Pico? You know your duty."

"Yesmum." The lad had sobered immensely, which was a relief.

"Mr Clare? Try to be home for dinner, and *try* not to experiment too rashly." She smoothed her gloves, and her quick fingers were at her veil fastening. "I shall leave you the carriage and Harthell. Mikal, fetch a hansom."

"Bannon—" Clare had to tear his attention from the body before him. "I say, I rather think—"

"Archibald. Please."

You misunderstand me. I suppose it cannot be helped, now. "Oh, certainly. I simply wish to remind you to . . . to take care."

"As much as I am able. Good day, gentlemen." And she was gone, the crowd in the passageway no doubt drawing back from Mikal's set grimace preceding her slight, black-clad form. Did they think her a relation of the deceased? Who knew?

"You might as well tell a viper to take care where it stings," the inspector muttered, his face set sourly.

Clare cleared his throat. "I shall thank you, sir, to speak no ill of that lady." *How odd. Only I may do so? To her face, no less.*

Thankfully, the man did not reply, and Clare turned back to the body and the physicker, who had watched this with bright interest.

The barrowmancer crossed his arms, as if he had felt a chill.

Perhaps he had.

* * *

The detective inspector was an interesting case. A proud nose and side-whiskers that did not disguise the childish attractiveness he must have once possessed, but purple shadows bloomed under his sharp dark eyes. His distinctive sliding step would have told Clare he was accustomed to the Scab's fascinating resilience underfoot, even if the fraying along his trouser-cuffs hadn't. Aberline moved with precision and economy, though he took care to appear more a clerk than one of Commissioner Waring's boot-leather bulldogs.

Added to his familiarity in addressing Miss Bannon, and the evident caution he held her in, as well as the fact that he was rather young to have achieved such an exalted rank as detective inspector . . . well. It bespoke some manner of *history*, and would have served to keep Clare's faculties most admirably occupied, if they had not been so already.

Now Aberline looked rather mournful, planting his feet and staring at the flayed, opened body. "Throat cut from behind, right-handed, and then he gutted her."

Clare's collar was uncomfortably tight. He made no move to loosen it. "Could sorcery account for the vanished blood?"

"Oh, aye, it could. *She* said as much. And she's never about but there's nasty work going." He sighed heavily, from the very soles of his sturdy, Scab-scarred shoes. "Whitchapel's in a fine stew. We'll be lucky to avoid more unpleasantness."

"So I overheard." Clare's brow knitted itself rather

fiercely. Something teased at the edge of his deductions, a nagging thought that would not *quite* coalesce. "We shall do our best. Those are her effects? I wonder . . . why take the rings and leave the coin?"

Aberline nodded. His nose was reddened from the chill. "I've seen men murdered for less, and women too."

The examiner let out a gusty breath of disgust. "He needn't have hurried her along. Lungs, heart, all raddled like the rest of her. Prime example of drink and dissolution."

"The question becomes, why *her*?"

"There are thousands of unfortunates prowling the End, sir." Aberline's mouth was a grim line, only opening barely enough to spit the words free. "Perhaps she was merely unlucky."

I am not so certain. What in this unfortunate – or in the other members of Londinium's almost-lowest dregs – would have concerned Queen Victrix so? And the organs of generation removed with a very sharp knife. It was unthinkably crude. "Perhaps. Poor thing."

Aberline's eyebrows rather nested under his bowler-brim at that, for Clare had uttered the words softly. A mentath generally did not speak so.

"Well. Gentlemen, should I stitch the bag up?" The physicker's good humour was almost shocking, but Clare took a renewed grasp upon himself. "Or is there more to be seen?"

Aberline's expression grew even more troubled, if such a thing were possible. "Can you tell if she had, ah, *relations*? Before, ahem, the event?"

"Well, that's rather a curious thing." The doctor scratched his cheek, leaving a trace of gore in his whiskers. "What little remains of her organs of generation seems . . . scorched."

Clare blinked, and leaned closer. "Yes, indeed. How very curious. It seems to follow the blood channels and nerves."

The barrowmancer coughed, nervously. Clare's attention fastened on him. "Well?"

"Nothing, sir." But the man was much paler than he had been when Clare had arrived. "Just . . . well, sorcery follows blood and nerve, mostly. But to sear it . . . nasty stuff, that is. Especially *there*."

"Miss Bannon shall be informed." Clare nodded. "Very well, then. Detective Inspector, I believe we are to endure each other's company for some little while longer."

❋ *Chapter Twenty-Two*

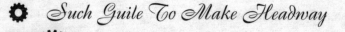

Such Guile To Make Headway

The hansom rattled along, and Emma's chin dipped as her attention turned inward.

Outside the carriage's shell, Londinium seethed, and she felt the drag of the Scab along the wheels lessen. Passing out of Whitchapel might improve her mood, but she rather doubted it.

In any case, the hansom was merely a gesture to misdirect a pursuer, albeit an exceedingly lazy one. Still, it was a matter of habit not to approach some things too directly.

Also, it gave her a small increment of badly needed time to think.

The bodies bore the marks of the blackest of sorcery – not of Emma's Discipline, thank the heavens, but the marks of ætheric force harnessed to an intent so foul even those of the Endor would fain avoid it. The only major

Discipline deeper of the Black than Emma's own was the Diabolic itself, but this held no smoky, addicting incense-ghost of *that* art.

Those of the Endor had once been murdered as soon as certain . . . disturbing signs . . . were noticed during their schooling. Those of the Diabolic still were. Not in civilised Englene, of course, but elsewhere. Especially where the Papists still held sway. Any of sorcery's children unfortunate enough to have a Discipline darker than Diabolic most often became a malformed monstrosity, ending their short lives dead in the womb. At least, that was the current understanding. She could safely rule out such a hapless monstrosity, and likely rule out the Diabolic as well.

And yet. The bodies were merely instruments; it was the *locations* that showed deeper marks. *The taproot of Our power*, Britannia had said.

Which seemed to imply that the power of a ruling spirit was a force that renewed itself, as Tideturn's flow filled sorcery's Englene children twice a day. Or was it otherwise, and the draining Britannia was experiencing more . . . permanent? Was it a longed-for result, or merely a symptom?

I do not know nearly enough. Frustration boiled inside her; the rock in her throat refused to be dislodged. And there was the unwelcome chain of thoughts again, rising inside her skull's few inches of private space.

Had Clare expected her to let him die of the plague? What had he expected her to do to ensure Ludovico's survival? Did he think she would wrench the Stone from her mentath and return him to fragility?

For good or for ill, she had chosen Clare. At that moment he had been the one in direst need. Had he not been . . . would she have married her conscience-heavy burden with Ludovico's flesh?

Another question I do not require an answer for at this moment. Or that I will not answer, even to myself.

The driver *huphup*ed to his clockhorse, and she took stock of her surroundings. She had precious little time before she alighted and Mikal appeared again.

The bodies are torn; the womb is the locus. A root is driven down in the location; it is a matrix . . . A root, more likely. Into what? How does it echo with Britannia? Can it be Sympathy? How to target it so effectively, though . . . it makes little sense.

Of course, Clare would likely chide her for assuming it was so, and Britannia's weakness simply incidental. What proof did she have otherwise?

Britannia's word. Besides, the need would have to be pressing indeed for Victrix to come to Emma's door alone, and lower herself by asking, instead of merely commanding, a sorceress's aid.

It was small comfort that perhaps even Britannia thought Emma Bannon unlikely to simply *obey*.

Clare, now there was another worry to be had – that Pico would not be able to effectively restrain him from descending into another fit. It was all she could do, barring keeping watch on the mentath herself. Finch was reliable, and there was the blood-binding as well – which she had performed on an unconscious mentath, and not spoken of.

Clare would no doubt be quite put out by that, too. When he realised she had done so, or when he questioned Pico closely on the matter, or . . .

The driver chirruped, and the hansom jolted again, slowing. Her moments of precious peace were disappearing. Continuing on too scattered to even *think* properly, she told herself sternly, would only result in more deaths.

Will it? Unfortunates die every night in Londinium. If their deaths weaken Britannia . . . is that acceptable?

The woman she had been before the Red Plague exploded into the world would have retreated from such a thought, shelving it as absurd. Now she considered, quite calmly, something absolutely treasonous, as well as repugnant.

Clare assumed she would throw herself upon this mystery and seek a solution as a matter of course.

There was also the little matter of the most recent murder intruding upon her in a most rude fashion. She was sensitised to whatever Work was being performed now, due to her tampering with the site of Tebrem's misfortune. Which could have unpleasant symptoms – yet the work she had done yesterday in her study should have insulated her from such effects.

Obviously, it had failed to do so properly.

The hansom halted. A bare few moments later, the door was released and Mikal's hand was as steady as ever as she alighted. The driver, well satisfied with an easy fare, tipped his hat and was off with a clatter and a crack.

Londinium's soup-thick fog, lit with morning sun to a nauseous glow, walled a busy street-corner, shapes moving in its depths. Mikal did not let go, and she was forced to look up at her Shield.

A Prime normally kept a half-dozen of the brotherhood in service, for physical defence and as a guard against an overflow of ætheric force. There were also other . . . uses . . . for them, quite obviously. She had not seen the need for more than Mikal in a very long while. And Eli—

Do not think upon that. The dead shall wait; we are concerned with the living at the moment.

Mikal waited. Of course he would betray no sign of impatience.

The fog was choking-close this morning. For all the sound of traffic, they might have been alone, just outside the north-eastron edge of the Scab's furthest creep. Pedestrians hurried by, almost faceless, for Mikal had drawn her aside, the brick wall next to her scarred and pitted with age.

For a moment, his face was a stranger's, too. Emma gave herself a severe mental shake. "Mikal."

"Prima."

"We are bound for Bucksrow." *I might as well tell you.*

"Just inside Whitchapel again." He nodded. "The site of the second murder?"

"Yes. I wished no witnesses."

He nodded, but still paused, in case she wished to add anything further.

What did you do, Mikal, when I lay dying? Clare said you performed a wonder. I survived, and you have not mentioned a price for any feat you performed.

The question bubbled up inside her, was forced back, and she was suddenly aware of the weight of her mourning-cloth; the heaviness of her jewellery; her hair braided, piled and pinned by Isobel's quick fingers; the constriction of her shoes; and her stays – she had never followed the fashion of extraordinarily tight corseting, but they were tight enough – compressing her.

Other pressures crowding upon her flesh, as well. Ludovico. Clare. Victrix. This faceless man with his shining knife. Mikal himself, and all those of her household. Her collection of drifting souls, each one an anchor.

Without those weights, would she rise from the surface of the earth?

And where would she float *to*? There was no escape. The only solution was to arrange her immediate surroundings as comfortably as possible, which meant dealing with this affair quickly, directly and ruthlessly.

She swallowed, her throat obeying with a dry click. "Come along then." She reclaimed her hand, and his expression did not change.

It was not as comforting as she might have wished, but at least it freed her for other worries. Chief among them was what, precisely, she might endure on Bucksrow, at the site of the second murder.

"A cart driver found her." Soft, thoughtfully. Strengthening cloud-filtered sunlight had scorched Bucksrow clean of its thin coating of Scab, but the cobbles and pavers held thin whorls and traceries of its green, burrowing into the cracks between to wait for darkness. "The Hospital is *there*." She pointed at its distant, looming bulk, more sensed than seen through the fog. Her forehead furrowed in a most unlady-like manner. "But there is little trace of disturbance. How very curious."

Cracked and missing cobbles, crumbling paving, timbers blackened with age and paint peeling – where the Scab had not eaten it – from whatever it coated.

Mikal took in the surroundings. "*She* was certain this . . ." It was eminently clear who he meant, both by the stress on the *she* and the suggestion of a lip-curl.

"Was an act by our quarry, yes." Emma drew her fur-lined mantle closer. Its surface glimmered with moisture, and it did nothing to stave off the cold that descended upon her. Autumn had arrived. *Soon after, winter*. A further chill coursed down her back. "I am quite certain this is the place."

"Bloodstain." He pointed, a swiftly elegant gesture, tendons standing out on the back of his hand. "Right before the stable doors."

He did not mention that the Scab had been scorched away there too, and no thin traces of green remained even in the crevices.

Emma glanced at the street again. Something about the angle of the stain was not quite *right*. "Locked after dark, one presumes." A steady, warm exhalation enfolded them both – the dryness of hide and mane, the sharp mechanical tang of oil for clockhorse gears. She extended a tendril of awareness, probed ever so gently. "I wonder . . ."

She stepped forward, directly onto the darkened paving stones. Her *corpus* had braced itself for an uncomfortable experience, and the complete lack of one demanded a response. Her training dug its clawed fingers in her vitals, and she shook the sensation away. "Hm. Mikal?"

"I am here, Prima."

Of course you are. But it was the response she had wanted. She closed her eyes, tugging on invisible threads in the tangled snarl of the fleshly world.

There. A raw, aching space inside her throbbed in response and she leaned forward, barely conscious of Mikal's fingers closing about her arm. He braced her, and she gave up outward consciousness, plunging *in*.

One string, a spider's thread of *wrong* amid all the myriad twisted, tangled knots.

Salt against abraded flesh, copper terror flooding a mouth not her own, a rocking motion and the crack *of a whip*.

Her head snapped aside. Reflex let the blow slide away, her body stiffening only slightly. Impressions flashed through her, a tide of hot sourness and deep-driving pain, a warm gush down her front.

"*Carriage*," she gasped.

Another rehearsal. It did not go as well as the preceding, I should think.

"Here now! What are you aboot?"

It was a florid, stocky man with a coachman's cap, massive side-whiskers and shoulders giving him the appearance of a walrus. He had barrelled from the stable's stinking depths, and as Emma thudded home into her own flesh she was aware of high shrills of equine fright and loud crunching bangs.

Mikal barely glanced at the man. He steadied her, and the faint smile on his lean face would have been chilling even had she not understood its meaning. *No*. She shook her head, fractionally, and his free hand fell away from a knife hilt.

"I say, what are you—?" The worthy took in the quality of her dress and Mikal's coat, and the Shield's knives. The noise from inside mounted another notch, and Emma dispelled a shudder. "Miss, are you quite well?"

A cough to clear her desert-dry throat, and she found her voice. "Yes. Quite. Thank you. The horses seem . . . upset."

He tipped his cap back, scratched under its brim. "Been sparky ever since the bad doins, Miss. Did you come to see that'un? Blood was right there. I says to my mate, I says, *What is this coming to?* Even a frail shouldna be done a' that."

"Was there anything surpassing strange about . . . it?" Her head felt too large for her neck, but the words must have come out naturally, for he considered them, his work-hardened hands dropping to his sides. "Other than, oh—!" A helpless movement, she fell into playing the part of a too-gently-bred idiot with the usual effortlessness. Such a persona would make the man facing her much more at ease, and for a moment she wondered what the world would be if it did not require such guile to make headway in.

"Wellnow." He stuck his thumbs in his braces and took up a widespread stance as the banging and clattering inside mitigated somewhat. "I told the leather bulls, I did. I locked up nice and proper, and came i' the morn to find the nasty had been left here. Paid a pretty penny to get rid of any bad mancy, too. But the one who came out, he said there weren't nothing more than a tangle there, took my coin and off he went."

"Indeed," she murmured. "Was he a fair hand with sorcery, then?" *Since you obviously did not dare refuse payment.*

He shrugged, made as if to spit aside, and visibly reconsidered in the face of her quality. "I'm no magicker. Fellow from two streets over, name of Kendall." He visibly enjoyed telling the story of the body on the doorstep, though it became clear he had *not* been the one to find it, only coming across it while the first on the scene – a rather unfortunately-named chandler – had been running to fetch assistance.

She managed to elicit the sorcerer Kendall's address and soothed the stablemaster as well as she was able with her head pounding badly enough to cloud her vision. He took her welling eyes as a sign that she was affected by the poor unfortunate's fate, and waxed rhapsodic about the quantity of blood, and how the belly had been opened just as a fish's. How the horses still shied coming out, and how his trade had been disrupted by the crowds come to see, of which she was presumably a late member. She appeared to hang on his every word and finally made a subtle gesture, whereupon Mikal stepped forward with a few pence for the man's pains.

The stable had returned to its former quiet, but Emma could taste the high brassy tang of horse-fear.

She could also taste the sourness of her own, as well. Her stays cut most abominably, and her dress was soaked under her arms and at the small of her back.

Mikal turned as the stableman shuffled back into his dark domain, his broad back vanishing like a spirit's. "Prima?"

"This Kendall. Two streets away. It might be profitable to visit him."

"Indeed. You're . . . pale."

No doubt. Her mantle, drawn close, could not ease the shudders seeking to grip her. She denied them outright, her jewellery warming comfortingly. "I suspect I shall be much more so before this affair is over. I have a rather curious thought."

"Which is?"

"First, that the body found here was thrown from a carriage. And second . . ."

"Second?" He visibly braced himself, for he knew she would put the more pleasant – or less dangerous – of two tasks first, if only to gather herself for the last.

"I believe it's time to visit Thin Meg."

Chapter Twenty-Three

From The Hind End

Whitehell Street had become a rather brooding organism, having been taken over by the Metropoleans. Robertson Peal's vision of a castle of Order and Detection had spread like a mushroom colony, and his knights were now "Bobbies", an affectionate diminutive of the man who made Bow Street famous. The Yard now consisted of several buildings, with the official entrance – through what used to be a back street – granting the entire sprawl its name. It was perhaps a measure of Londinium's intransigence that it was named for the back street instead of Whitehell; Justice, as it were, always approached its prey from the hind end.

Or was often approached from such by those wishing to enact it.

The detective inspector's office, shared with another

inspector, was a curious place. He was of the few Yard occupants fortunate enough to have a window, but all that could be seen was shifting yellow fog and the base of a street lamp, for the room was half underground. Feet passed by, their owners hurrying or ambling as they pleased, or as they felt the eyes of the Yard upon them. There were windows above as well, blank eyes that often as not held flickering gaslight on dim evenings as the knights of boot-leather and order kept the great beast of Law fed with paper and deduction.

In this cave, the shelves were crammed with redrope files, as a solicitor's office might be, but there were also . . . other things. A scrap of calico, bloodstained from the look of it; a cracked globe of crystal with a tiny point of light in its depths; a curved knife in a tooled leather sheath – its provenance was uncertain, and Clare longed to study it further, but other items cried for his attention as well. A red velvet pillow held a heavy, tarnished brass ring; next to it a small brass dish held a parson's collar buttons; and they were kept companion by a small silver candle-snuffer. There was a wealth of inference to be drawn.

"You have a sentimental nature, sir." Clare turned from the shelves to find the inspector standing behind his desk, his mouth slightly ajar as if thunderstruck. He relished the expression. "Mementos from your cases, I take it."

However, the inspector's next words put matters in a different light entirely. "Clare," the man replied, in a wondering tone. "*Archibald* Clare. I *knew* the name was familiar. If you look to the right and down, sir, you shall find your monograph."

"Is that so?" He glanced down, and there was a familiar blue-marbled cover. "Ah. Well." It looked well thumbed, too, and he felt the pinch of Pride. Another instance of Feeling seeking to lead him astray. "I am . . . yes, quite touched. Who would have thought?"

"I *have* actually read it." Aberline now sounded a trifle defensive. "I perform the recommended Exercizes at dawn and dusk, unless I am in dire emergency. They have been of inestimable value, sir. Had I known it was you, I would not have treated you so coolly. Miss Bannon's acquaintances, while . . . effective . . . are also usually somewhat troublesome."

"I have discovered as much," Clare allowed. *Myself among them.* He glanced at Philip Pico, who leaned against the wall near the door – just where Valentinelli might have placed himself, though without such an insouciant sneer. "She is a singular lady, Miss Bannon. I am glad you have found my poor scribblings of some use. This is, however, not why you brought me here. I gather that even Miss Bannon's threats of the Crown's displeasure would not induce you to bring a stranger into this hallowed sanctum – because you do sleep often at that desk, sir, there is a mark just where your forehead or cheek would rest upon the blotter – without some other pressing reason to do so?"

"Just as I imagined you." Aberline's face lit with a grin that showed the youth he had been perhaps a good ten years ago. Sharp as a blade, Clare fancied, and with a hot, easily touched pride kept under a mask of diffidence. "I say, sir, you are remarkable."

"I am merely a mentath." Clare straightened his cuffs. A sudden thought drew him up short. "You were aware these murders were committed by the same hand long before now."

The man sank into his chair, indicating the other one with a wave. "Yes. Lestraid and I – he shares this office, but right now he's chasing some damn fool in Devon – had an inkling of trouble to come when the Tebrem creature was found. There are . . . I say, do sit. And you too, sir."

"Why?" Philip Pico wanted to know. "I'm just a sodding nursery maid."

"A nursery maid wouldn't have half your long face, and wouldn't be eyeing the exits, and wouldn't be sweating at the thought of the Yard." Aberline cast a small, satisfied glance Clare's way, and the mentath found himself agreeably surprised by the inspector's capability at deduction. "You're of St Georgeth's, or Jermyn Street, but you're too old for the play there. And that blasted sorceress obviously entrusted this gentleman – who she seems rather attached to, since I've never seen her take such an interest in keeping someone's skin whole – to you, so you must be at least halfway dangerous." Aberline nodded, smartly. "You've naught to fear from me, little lad. I know better than to set foot where *my lady* chooses to engage a service."

There it was again: the tantalising hint of a History between Miss Bannon and this man.

It was merely a distraction at this juncture; Clare returned his attention to the matter at hand with an almost physical effort. "As soon as Tebrem was found, you say?"

"Do come and sit down, old chap." Aberline's mouth had compressed itself into a tight line again. He had an inkstain on his right middle finger, Clare noticed, and a thin line of Whitchapel grime had worked its way under his wedding ring.

He was suddenly certain the man had been up very late last night.

Quite possibly, he had not been to bed at all. The deduction caused a sinking feeling in Clare's stomach, which he told sternly to cease being idiotic. His normally excellent digestion choosing this particular time to misbehave was a most unwelcome development.

Clare lowered himself into the appointed chair, a monstrous leather thing with sprung stuffing crouching behind a hunched ottoman which bore the marks of another's boots – perhaps the missing inspector, chasing fools in Devon?

He arranged himself, steepling his fingers before his face, and nodded fractionally. "Proceed, sir."

"Are you familiar with *lustmorden*?"

Clare frowned. *What a curious portmanteau of a word. German?* He thought of his friend Sigmund, who would no doubt be brightly interested in this, as he was in anything that involved Miss Bannon. Dear old Sig was growing visibly older; Clare had not availed himself of the man's company in months. Now, Clare had the uncomfortable sensation of wondering precisely why. Of course, Sig was still tinkering with that bloody mechanical spider of his. "I am uncertain. Do explain."

"There are several cases. The Beast of Dusseldorf, for example, or the Florentine Monster. A man so maddened by uncontrolled—" Aberline shifted uncomfortably. His cheeks pinkened slightly. "Or *uncontrollable* desire, committing murders, each with a distinguishing mark springing from the obsession."

Clare's eyelids dropped to half-mast. "I see. A remarkable theory. Could it not be that some criminals simply desire to murder? That it is in their nature?"

"Of course. But these monsters, when caught – I say, Mr Clare, I am not distressing you by speaking so?"

If only you knew. "By no means."

"And it will not distress you if I have . . . unorthodox methods of detecting?"

"My own are rather strange, sir." Clare blinked. "Do go on."

"Very well." Yet Aberline still seemed uncomfortable. "The obsession dictates the murder. I shall now tell you what I have ascertained, Mr Clare. The murderer has practised his deadly art. He will be extremely difficult to catch. He is possessed of a coach or some other conveyance, and he has some aim in mind." He drew a deep breath. "And he is nowhere near finished."

Clare nodded, slowly. "I see. You are certain he has a conveyance? A personal chariot of some sort to travel from one nightmarish deed to the next?"

"I am."

"How are you so certain?"

"I . . ." Aberline coughed, looking even more uncomfortable. "I cannot say."

"*Quite* interesting." Clare nodded again. "Tell me what you *can* say, then."

"The very idea of *lustmorden* is so repulsive, it is difficult to even convince our superiors of its existence. To them, Murder is a product of Insanity and Criminal Character alone, and no room is granted for . . . for lack of a better word, no room is granted for sheer evil." Aberline coughed slightly. "I am of the opinion that those who rise in the world's estimation do not often make the best detective inspectors, but they do make excellent commissioners and mayors and lord justices." A cloud passed over his features, but he waved a hand, dismissing it.

This had all the character of a speech polished over long, sleepless nights, and Clare settled himself to the peculiar state of absorbed attention he often practised when Miss Bannon could be induced to speak at length on a subject she found interesting.

It was the interest – or the outright obsession – of an intelligent subject that often led to the most fruitful lines of enquiry and deduction, even if the subject was blind to them as a consequence of said obsession.

Oh, so Miss Bannon is a subject now? She is not present; do not think upon her. He brought his attention back to the matter at hand, and nodded, since Aberline had given him an enquiring glance.

"Proceed," he said, and a prickle of . . . irritation? . . . furrowed his brow.

If it had been Miss Bannon speaking, she would not have needed the glance to ascertain his attention.

"You have rather a listening air, sir, and it is most welcome. Do tell me if I—"

Let us move on, and quickly, too. "These murders – *lust-morden* is a very evocative name indeed – are of a variety and species your superiors, if we can call them that, are not equipped to effectively halt. By virtue of your almost daily experience of the effects and settings of Vice and Crime, you have acquired a body of knowledge which grants you certain . . . feelings, if you will, for the causes and prevention of both. Which leads you to conflict within the Yard, for though you have many other fine qualities, you do not have the necessary oil to smooth bureaucratic waters."

The silence greeting his observation might have been uncomfortable if Aberline had not been smiling broadly.

"Quite so," he finally said. "Quite so. Lestraid is much better at it, and without him, I confess, I am somewhat at the mercy of my own temperament. It does not help that my methods are . . . In some cases, I have been accused of being little better than a criminal myself."

Ah. Now there is a frank admission. The mementos on the shelves were either tokens of cases where Aberline had known the criminal and mucked himself in order to bring him or her to justice . . . or tokens of victims he had been unable to avenge, even by behaving in a not-so-noble fashion.

Or both. So little separated a bootleather knight from a criminal.

You have grown philosophical, Clare.

He turned to another avenue of thought. The man's mien was so sober and exacting, it was difficult to conceive of him as one willing to turn the law so that the spirit instead of the letter was fulfilled.

Which meant Clare must look more closely at him. Appearances deceived, and such a valuable clew into a man's character was not to be taken lightly. Especially when Clare himself was . . . *was he?*

Yes. He was distracted. It boded rather ill.

Aberline shrugged. "The fact that I have some small ætheric talent – not enough to charm," he added hurriedly, "no, not enough to be apprenticed, to be sure! And yet I am viewed with a certain trepidation by every hemisphere of the Yard."

"Sorcerous or not," Clare clarified, "bootleather or bonnet."

"Indeed." Aberline looked gratified to be so comprehended. He settled himself more deeply in his chair, and his gaze focused on the shelves of mementoes and files, leatherbound books and bundles of paper. "Yet I digress. *Lustmorden* all share certain characteristics, which Lestraid and I have isolated by poring through bloodcurdling accounts of deeds unfit for print. These murders share such characteristics—"

"Which include?" Clare prodded.

"Savagery, for one. But that is not enough. A certain

method – the progression is quite clear. The murderer begins with experimentation, though one may see the, ahem, you could call it the marks of his obsession—"

"His?"

"Oh, a woman may drink, and a woman may poison, and there may even be the rare woman like Miss Bannon, who is more a viper in frail flesh than a proper *female*. But a woman does not commit *lustmorden*. It is simply unthinkable."

Clare's silence was taken for agreement, and Aberline continued. He had quite warmed to his theme.

"For one thing, the violence of the attacks is anathema to a woman. For another, the driving force is . . . well, the name says it quite clearly. The driving force is the prerogative of the male."

"I see," Clare murmured.

"The marks of the obsession are very particular, and unique to each criminal. Rather as the Anthropometric school of thought holds that the ridges on each man's hands are unique – are you familiar with Faulds, and Bertillon, dactyloscopy? Very good. *Lustmorden* is merely an outgrowth of the principle that a criminal's chosen vice is an expression of their *personality* . . . the theory is complex," Aberline acknowledged, and pushed himself to his feet. He paced to the window, looking up at the gleam of strengthening daylight piercing layers of fog and falling on his face, shadowing the traces of sleeplessness and care. Driving them deeper.

How frail flesh is. Yet Clare's own, now . . . not so at

all. He found the logical consequence to Aberline's pause. "The initial attack, the one that came to such attention recently, was not the first? Is that what you mean?"

"There are plenty that bear the same marks; the avocation of drink and prostitution is a hazardous one. But the site of the Tebrem murder . . . there were troubling . . . would you believe me, sir, if I said I possessed what a colonist might call 'an intuition'? A . . . *feeling*, one sharpened by my . . . experiences."

"I would believe you." Clare sought for the right tone. "You are saying that there may have been others, but the Tebrem murder was successful enough to propel the murderer forward? It stoked the fire of his obsession past the critical point, and we are now—"

"—facing what may become an explosion. Especially since the Eastron End bears a distressing resemblance to a powder-keg recently. The influx of Yudics, the Eirean troubles, the Red, sheer laziness and ill character finding its level, so to speak, and the dreadfuls and broadsheets irresponsibly striking sparks against a very short fuse." He turned on his heel, striding for the shelf, and reached for a redrope folder.

Holding it, he looked even more solicitor-like, and Clare had to quash a moment of amusement. The situation most certainly did *not* call for a smile, and his expression might be misinterpreted.

Had he not spent so long watching Miss Bannon smooth over misinterpretations, he might have unwittingly made the situation precarious.

Aberline took no notice of his expression either way. "And the Crown has now seen fit to muddy the waters by bringing pressure to bear on the Yard. I confess I am rather disheartened by the fact, since said pressure will inevitably make it more difficult to pursue a single murderer through the worst sinks of Londinium. Disturbed silt does not permit clarity in a pond, so to speak."

"Ah." Clare cogitated upon this set of statements for a few moments. "I say, Detective Inspector, you very much seem to view these deaths as a personal affront."

The man had the grace to cough slightly, and redden a bit. "Some cases, Mr Clare, become so."

"Indeed they do." Clare settled himself more firmly in the chair. "I believe the file you hold contains the information you deem particularly worthwhile, and also particularly damaging to public order. I further believe you have every reason to be as cautious as you are. This has all the marks of an affair that could end very badly. And Mr Pico, do come and have a seat. I believe you may be of some use to us."

"Glad to become so, squire," was the cheeky reply, and Clare found, much to his surprise, that he was almost agreeably irritated with the lad.

Perhaps Miss Bannon had not been so wrong to engage him.

No doubt there was a sorcerous component to this case, but vanquishing it with pure logic – and the resources of the Yard, no matter how muddied the waters had become – might indeed be possible.

The question of why such a prospect could warm him so agreeably was one he decided to set aside for the nonce.

"These are murders Lestraid and I believe fit the pattern." The redrope was distressingly thick, and the small table dragged to suit Clare's perusal of it was rather overwhelmed by its bulk. "Tea, while you read?"

"Quite welcome, thank you." Clare's brow furrowed as he opened the file, and his faculties woke even further.

He settled himself for a long afternoon's work.

Chapter Twenty-Four

Thin Meg

Kendall, two streets over, turned out to be somewhat misleading. Perhaps the man hadn't meant to be deceptive, but the fog was thickening and Emma's thoughts were of a similarly impenetrable nature. She rather wished Clare was about, for he had the most wonderful way of clarifying matters. At least, he did when those matters did not involve his own tender sensibilities.

In any case, it was the rank narrow reeking of Blightallen, the Scab thick and resilient underfoot – sunlight didn't reach past the sloping overhead tenements, leaning together to confer on business best kept low-voiced – that held their quarry. Or, more precisely, his stinking domicile, which was one low-ceilinged room, with a door that had been shivered to pieces.

There had been more than one murder in Whitchapel

last night. The closet was thick with an ætheric tangle of violence. A small, blood-soaked bed, a strongbox that had been rifled – by murderer or by neighbours was an open question – and torn, faded wallpaper; one sad, frameless painting of a woman with dark eyes and a decided down-turn to her mouth, dressed in the fashion of the Mad Georgeth's early reign, powdered curls and a plaid beauty-mark high on her left cheek. The painting was varnished to the wall at least twice, which solved one mystery, while a round of questioning the foul-haired, slattern of a landlady solved another.

"I runs a respectable house, I does," she repeated, tightening her dirty shawl about her consumptive-thin shoulders. Her skirts were patched, and two of her corset stays were missing; it could have produced unsightly bulges had she not been so wraithlike. "Owner's a Westron End gent, high and mighty as yourself, Missy."

"No doubt." Emma pointed at the bed. "And where was his body removed to?"

"Body? Warnt no body, Miss. This morning there's an uproar, our sorcerer gone and his bed all drenched. Nobody heard a thing but, says I, we're Blightallen, of course nobody hears a sodding thing. Still, he's a magicker, and who can tell? His idearn'a joke, p'raps."

Not likely. Emma absorbed this. "Is he much of a prankster, this Kendall?"

"Dour as the Widow, Miss." The slattern's mouth pulled against itself, a tight compressed line. Emma nodded, and Mikal produced a shilling. He offered it, and the landlady reached . . . but his fingers twitched and it vanished.

"Are you certain nothing was heard?" Emma enquired, sweetly.

The woman drew herself up, wrapping the shawl even more tightly. She darted a glance back down the darkened hall, and Emma was suddenly aware of the confining space. There was no window, and with the door shut it must have been oppressive. There was no space for even a Minor Work, and the walls held little trace of ætheric defences. Of course, the reverberations were so complicated and snarled, there was little she could tell without adding to the problem.

To compound the oddness, there was not a single fly to be found on the mangled, shredded, blood-soaked bedding. With no window for them to find their way in, it was not *quite* out of the ordinary . . . but still.

"Nuffink." But the landlady's voice had dropped. "I ent had time to come up and change the sheets neither – none of the drabs'll touch it even for forgiving their doss-money. *None heard a thing*, mum, and first I knows of it was that sot Will Emerich come down to kitchen rubbing his eyes and complaining on the splinters in the hall. I'd've said he was dead drunk only Black Poll Backstearn's room is next door, and she don't sleep well. She ent been on gin for a month, and it shows. Whatever happened, was silent as . . ." She made the *avert* gesture with her left hand, tiny eyes almost lost in their pouches of darkened flesh narrowing further. "An' that puts us all fair off our mettle, mum. Silent it was, and Kendall gone."

Emma nodded again, and Mikal handed over the shilling. The woman bit it with her rotting teeth to test its truth, then glanced back over her shoulder again. "And now you visit," she continued, "lady high and mighty, go straight for his room. It's bad business, it is. Bad business all way round."

"You may tell anyone you like that I appeared as a bird of ill fortune, madam." Emma lowered her veil. A snap of her fingers, more for effect than for actual utility, and her jewellery warmed as she drew on its stored force. The blood-soaked bedding leapt into thin blue witchflame, spitting and hissing like a cat as the landlady shrank back against the shivered door.

"As a matter of fact," Emma added dryly, "I would take it as a kindness if you would tell everyone that a woman in mourning was here, and what she did."

With that, she brushed through the door as a burning wind, speaking the minor Word that would confine the flames to the traces of blood – and not so incidentally, sensitise her to the remainder of that vital fluid, wherever it might have been shed or come to rest.

Several unphysical strings tugged at her attention, most of them probably attached to a trap.

She was beginning to have a healthy respect for the canny nature of her quarry.

Mikal's hand was at her elbow to guide her in the sudden gloom of the rickety hallway, and Emma realised she was shaking.

*   *   *

The Chapelease Leper was now a peeling crumble, clotted with whitewash applied indifferently every so often. Around it, the busy thoroughfare of Whitchapel Road throbbed, the Scab sucking at cart wheels, verdant even under the lash of fogbound sunlight as it crawled up pale walls.

Some held that it was here the Scab had been birthed, but not too loudly.

You never knew what *she* might take offence at, or catch wind of.

It wasn't the peeling or the scabrous clots on the walls that made all give the Chapelease as wide a berth as possible, and had made the road divide around it as a rock divides a river. It wasn't even the way the gaslamps that had been erected near it were warped and blasted by some unimaginable fury – or simply by a slow steady exhalation of malice.

No, those who could avoided the place largely because of its washed-clean, gleaming stairs.

Those stairs were wide and sharp-edged, capacious and sturdy, but they were rarely seen. They were, instead, crowded with huddled bundles of rags with fever-bright eyes ranked upon them shoulder to shoulder, with only a narrow ribbon of scrubbed brightness leading to the rotting-cream doors.

These were Thin Meg's brood, and none dared touch them or move them along until there was a soft thud, and a stick-light body was rolled down into the road to be collected. None pointed at, jeered at, or spoke to them.

They sat in their rags and watched Whitchapel Road go by, and only in the dead of night could a sound be heard from them.

A thin sound, a low sound. A soft, hissing, draining mumble.

Emma walked briskly, her eyes stinging even under the veil's protection. The din of traffic was incredible, and were it not for Mikal she might have been accosted, or worse. He drifted at her shoulder, between her and the gutter, and even the alley-side cutpurses retreated. Shouts and curses from coachmen and carters, the crack of a whip, children screaming as they ran past engaged upon some game or another – or intent on relieving pockets of their contents, for theirs were nimble and desperate fingers.

The drabs had mostly retired to sleep off their work and the gin they deadened its rigors with, but the public houses were open and brawling, flashboys crowding the doors and displaying their Alterations: shiny metal, oiled leather, bits of glass, sellsongs from the wheelbarrows jammed wherever they could elbow a niche and pay the "protection" fee levelled from whoever controlled that slice of paving or wooden-slat walk this week, footsteps, hoofbeats, conversation and cries. Crackles of ætheric disturbance, spat charms, lightfinger wards and oil-charms popping blue or yellow sparks as they reacted to the eddies and swirls of the crowd.

The noise drew away when she stepped over the invisible border between the rest of the world and Thin Meg's domicile.

She had to hold her skirts close to pass through the hunched rag bundles as they leaned away from her. A spill of cold slid down her skin as she stepped up, and up again, Mikal behind her.

The Endor in her woke, and the starvelings' bony hands appeared, fingers of bleached anemone blindly seeking for the disturbance in their cold, silent suffering.

A Prime could not pass unnoticed; there was simply too much ætheric force in them to do so. And any of the Black who braved these stairs would feel a certain . . . trepidation. Still, she lifted her chin and twitched her skirts away from the seeking fingers.

The crop of starvelings was dense at the top of the stairs, where those not yet whittled to apathy hunched, swaying slightly as a wheatfield rippled by a cool wind. The Chapelease doors – massive, oaken things not yet Scabrotted perhaps because of the rancid renderings poured over them every Twelfthnight – hung ajar, quivering.

They never closed.

Mikal was suddenly before her, and he pushed the left-hand door wide, its hinges giving that same faint hissing noise. Emma quelled a shudder, took a very tight grasp on her temper, and continued on.

The sudden dimness was a balm, lit only by shuddering candleflames atop thick tallow columns, their smoke greasing the painted roof. If one looked up, cripplewing angels and spinning saints could be seen leering through the scrim of rippling soot.

Emma did not. Instead, she passed her gaze smoothly

over the ranks of broken pews marching up the narrow interior, the alcoves on either side full of deeper shadows. Nothing amiss, though thick whitish gauze-mist peeped above the slumping wooden backs, moving cold-sluggish.

"And what is this," a deep voice rasped and slipped between chipped and blackened columns, "come to my doorstep now? A little tiny witchling, already slight as a sparrow." A thick, burping chuckle. "More meat on her companion, and a pretty leg he shows too."

Emma's pace did not falter. She continued down the central aisle, and the air grew heavier. Satin and rotting silk shifted, fabric rubbing against itself, and the massive bulk slithering in the well-hole where an altar had once stood resolved into a shape. Just what *kind* of shape it was difficult to say, for there were huge folds and bulges, bright blinking eyes and ivory teeth, yards and yards of cloth piled, buttoned, and stretched about peeping sickly white flesh.

"Marimat the Fallen." Emma put her gloved palms together, halting, and bowed slightly. "I greet you."

"Oh, she *greets* me." Several long, chubby, oddly flexible fingers crawled over the blasted altar-wreckage, and there was a heaving. The many eyes blinked, flashing in their preferred dimness, and the sliding and scraping in the pews were those who had offered her more than just their physical weight in exchange for the starving peace she granted. "Did you come here to trade, wee witchling?" A thick, groaning laugh, cold as leftover black pudding.

Emma cocked her head. Mikal was tense and silent. The

pews behind her would be full of gauzy movement by now, phosphorescent suggestions of cheek and hand and shoulder, supple smoky coils. "Careful," she said, mildly enough. "Your starvelings appear restless."

"Do they?" A long groaning noise, and the gauzy whispers retreated. More bits of her bulk bubbled up, winking with jewels, both paste and real. A hen's-egg sapphire in tarnished silver – probably real – chimed as it boiled over the edge of the stone cup and rolled away.

Emma ignored it, and therefore Mikal did as well.

"I think," the thing in the well continued, hauling and shifting even more bits of herself, "*you* are the restless one. Or is the word 'troubled'? An ill wind brings you here."

"That should delight you." The next few moments were very delicate, so Emma gave herself a pause. "Ill wind and misfortune usually does."

A great rolling, rippling shrug. "*They* seek me out, little witchling. I do not stir one foot to seek *them*."

And you fatten on their despair, a little at a time. "Yet all Whitchapel feels your fingers, Thin Meg." Very quietly. "Every dark corner, and every crevice between cobbles."

Stillness filled Chapelease. The walls groaned a little as the creature's attention constricted.

The eyes narrowed, their gleams intensifying. Finally, the creature shifted again, heaving still more of her bulk up toward the lip of the depression where the shattered altar had once stood tall and proud. More fingers splatted dully in dust and splinters, grinding against stone.

They were plump, and they looked soft, but those tiny appendages could find the smallest crack and slide in. Stone crumbled before their persistent fingering. It was ever thus with those of her ilk – they had all the time in the world to poke and prod, to cajole and wear away.

"State your business," Thin Meg finally said, and now Emma could see her actual mouth, the V-shaped orifice peeling open to show serried rows of sharp white teeth. "With no riddles, witchling."

How very interesting. "Something new has been added to Whitchapel."

More stillness. Mikal's arm lifted, and he gently, slowly, pushed Emma back a step. His other hand lingered at a knife hilt, and Emma's pulse sought to speed itself, was repressed.

"Oh, aye, and not with my leave." Thin Meg laughed, and this time the heavy, ugly sound was truly amused. Still cold, though, a razor's edge cutting the gloom, sparking against creeping fingers made of fine-woven smoke as they inched closer, pressing against Emma's skirts. "What do you know of it? One of your kind, little hands prodding and poking where they shouldn't. Take care lest the lid snap on those fingers!"

"I suppose if the odd bit of information comes to your lovely ears . . ."

Meg found this funny as well. At least, she shook with jollity, bits of her heaving and slopping, flashing dead-white flesh and pinging creaks as the building itself shuddered. Material split, shredding; the tortured souls in the chapel's shadows shrank back from Emma, Mikal, and the stew of flesh and tawdry finery bubbling before them.

Mikal's shoulders were rigid under black velvet; Emma's throat ached to cut the din with a sharp Word, but she did not.

Finally, the heaving ended. Meg's bulk receded, the sucking and shifting quieting as she eased back.

"It suits me to send you a starveling, should I have news." Her mouth was still plainly visible, that stark, sharp smile causing candleflames to shudder and gutter *en masse*. A breath of rank foulness now slid between the columns, disturbing the fluttering smoke-hangings, which had quieted as they pressed back against the door, half-seen faces writhing with dismay. "You shall pay me by stopping *him*."

"Him." Emma nodded. "The faceless one."

"He has no need of a face," the creature crooned. "He's a sharp canny jack, that one."

Mikal stamped sharply, and there was a wet splattering. Thin Meg hissed, a long indrawn sound of pain, and Emma found herself pushed back further, blinking and shaking her head.

Her Shield shook the green, sticky sludge from his boot, and the pale, wriggling tendril retreated into the cauldron. "Prima?" Soft, but the edge of leashed deadliness under the word made each flame straighten and dance.

"Can't fault me for trying." The creature bubble-hissed, chuckling thickly. "But sparrow-slight she is. Now you, *you* are a finer morsel."

"Not for your dining, madam," he returned, equably enough.

Emma found her tongue. "Very well." She turned, despite the fact that her skin was alive with revulsion – imagine feeling one of Meg's grasping little fingers curling around one's ankle, nudging upward, and the lassitude that would follow . . .

Her footsteps tapped with their usual authority as she set off down the central aisle. "Thank you, Maharimat of the Third Host. We shall be on our way."

"He knows your name, sparrow-witch." There was no laughter now, and the foul breath of a fallen creature that had once sung of and to holiness in other spheres was darker than sewage. It was difficult not to gag, and Emma took her air in tiny sips as she made for the doors. "You have more enemies than you know."

"Pray you do not find yourself among them, bonny Meg," she returned over her shoulder, finding she had enough breath for a parting sting. "For I might decide to let him finish his work, and weaken *you* as well."

The doors creaked open, and she might have tumbled into the ranks of starvelings if Mikal had not caught her again.

Their clutching, brushing fingers were feeble, easily pushed aside, but she did not halt until they were a good distance from both the Chapelease *and* the creeping, cringing, venomous green tendrils of Scab.

Chapter Twenty-Five

Beyond Your Ken

"I am no donkey, sir." Philip Pico bridled, as Alice took his gloves and hat with a sniff.

The other maid, Bridget of the slightly lame left leg and the engaging gapped-tooth smile, took Clare's, and he held his peace until they had both vanished into the depths of 34½ Brooke Street. "You bear a suspicious resemblance to a stubborn ass. And yet it is *me* saddled with *you*."

"Keep him in one piece, she said. Welladay, I will, sir."

"Oh? And what else did she say?"

"Naught that would interest you."

"Oh, I think it would. Did she mention your predecessor?"

"The one you were in love with, sir? No. She said nothing to me about *him*."

Clare halted, and the heat in his cheeks was new and

unwelcome. "His name was Ludovico, and I was not *in love* with him. Mentaths do not—"

"Good evening, gentlemen." A rustle of black silk, a breath of smoky sorcery laced with spiced-pear perfume, and Emma Bannon halted on the stairs, eyeing them both with arch amusement. "A drink before dinner?"

"Rid me of this *encumbrance*, madam," Clare managed, stiffly. "This is insupportable!"

"Oh?" One eyebrow, elegantly arched. "Philip?"

"About to go slumming with the detective inspector, he was." The bratling straightened his sleeves much as a gentleman would, and matched Clare glare for glare. "And on such short acquaintance. I thought it best we come home for dinner."

"It is not *slumming*, it is searching for clews! And, had you not rudely objected, *Philip*, we would have had Aberline here for questioning during dinner, and added his considerable talents to our—"

"Inspector Aberline is not welcome at my table, Clare." Very softly. "Philip, you did well. Go and dress for dinner, if you please. Mr Clare and I have a few matters to settle."

"Oh, I shall say we do." Clare straightened as the youth made that same abortive gesture – as if to tug his forelock – and made for the safety of the stairs. He passed Miss Bannon, giving her as wide a berth as possible, and Clare almost did not note that she did not bother to twitch her skirts back as if he suffered something contagious.

As she always had with Ludovico. Did this young annoyance have Valentinelli's room as well?

Why, Clare asked himself, should he care?

Miss Bannon rested one hand on the banister, the curve of her wrist just delicate enough to make a man think of snapping it.

The idea was a dash of icy water, and Clare inhaled, tensing fruitlessly. He had spent the entire afternoon sifting through papers holding bloodless information about singularly bloody acts, and they had not nettled him one whit. Now, just a few moments in Miss Bannon's company, and he was boiling.

This is Feeling. It is illogical. It did not help that the murders Aberline had so painstakingly gathered were clearly not the work of the current madman – except for two, and those two offered frustratingly little in the way of fresh insight.

"Do go on." She was maddeningly calm, but her fingers were tense. A girl who could snap a word that immobilised a grown man, and yet she appeared so fragile.

Clare had seen this woman perform illogical miracles, and they had left no mark on her youthful face. Was this what the churches of the world, both Popish and Englene, meant when they raved of Woman's diabolical nature?

He gathered what he could of his dignity. It was a thin cloak indeed. "I am not a pet, nor am I your ward."

"I agree." She nodded once, her dark curls swinging. "Were you one, I would cosset you, and were you the other I would not allow you to step forth into the dangers outside for a good long while. You are not well, Clare, and this affair, I am beginning to think, is beyond your ken."

For a moment he could not quite believe his ears. "I am *perfectly* well." He was aware of the lie even as he spoke it. "I have endured a succession of shocks to my faculties, true. And I had some . . . difficulty . . . with the notion of . . . but *dash* it all, Emma, this case is fascinating, and work is the best cure for a completely natural . . . loss."

"Except you do not consider your loss natural at all, sir, on either account. This is a matter best left to sorcery. I have discovered much today, and it quite disturbs me."

He could have fastened on *that* little tidbit, but the tide of Anger had him now. "So, I am to be set upon a shelf? I think not. Aberline and I do get on very well, and he is the best man to investigate—"

"He is a slightly useful tool, nothing more, and will serve to distract my quarry quite handily with his bumbling about." Her tone cooled, and the movement on the stairs above her was Mikal, a gleam in darkness. "You would do well to be cautious of the good inspector, Archibald. If he may do me a disservice through you, he shall no doubt try."

"And what did you do to earn such treatment from a gentleman?" Unjustified, perhaps, but the way she rocked slightly back onto her heels, paling a shade or two – though she was already much whiter than her wont, almost drained-looking – made a certain hot bubble rise under his breastbone.

No trace of paleness in her tone, however. "I saved a somewhat-soiled innocent from his clutches, and consequently he bears me a grudge. It nettles a certain type of petty man to be denied something by a woman."

Did she mean it as a return cut? Clare's head had begun to pound as he struggled to lower his voice. "What baseness you attribute to a gentleman who—"

Her chin lifted, and her eyes were flashing dangerously now. "On what do you build your assessment of his good character, mentath? Let me hear your logic."

"I would grant you a full explanation, if I could be certain of your understanding it." Was he actually *sneering*? Clare had the exquisitely odd sensation of falling into a hole, watching himself from its bottom as his face twisted and took on a rather ugly cast.

"Likewise, sir." A dot of crimson had appeared on each soft cheek, yet she was iron-straight. "You are relieved of the need to give any further attention to this matter. *Do* try to stay out of trouble while I attend to the Crown's business."

With that, she swept down the stairs, turning so sharply at the foot her skirt flared and almost touched his knee.

Mikal drifted in her wake, but her pace was such that he had no time to do anything but glower in Clare's general direction, the flame in the Shield's yellow irises waking.

She goes to her study, instead of to the drawing room. Angry? Perhaps. Nettled? Hurt?

What on earth had *possessed* him? A mentath did not behave so. Nor did a proper gentleman.

He found he was wringing his hands, and forced himself to stop. To let them hang loosely, fingers throbbing and the appendages afire because he had driven his nails deep into palmflesh. His shoulders loosened, and he cast about for something, anything, to distract his aching head.

Nothing was to be found. He made it to the stairs before sinking down, dropping said tender head into his hands, elbows on knees, and there he stayed until Philip Pico found him an hour later, to bring him to the dining room, where Miss Bannon – and Mikal – were both absent during a long, exquisite, and tortuously silent dinner.

Chapter Twenty-Six

With Whatever Means Are To Hand

"Prima?"

"Hm?" She glanced up from the large leatherbound tome, her eyes for a moment refusing to focus as she was pulled away from creaking ropes and singing sails. The book – *Marina Invicta* – which her well-trained memory had dragged forth the remembrance of from a dusty room, contained several passages about Britannia.

Nothing of any real use, however. Just as every other blasted book she had pulled from the shelves was useless in the current situation.

Mikal closed the door: a soft snick of the latch catching and the lock thrown. "Shall you be attending dinner? Or shall Finch bring you a plate?"

"Neither." She waved a hand, her gaze already straying back to the pages. "Rum, perhaps. Thank you."

"Emma." He had approached her desk, soundlessly, and the study came back into focus around her. The shelves were arranged as they should be, though holes had been created by her rummaging, and a stack of tomes large and small lay heaped upon the table she had pulled from its place behind a leather chair she was wont to sink into on certain nights, watching the coal in the grate shed heat and ætheric force while it built its white jacket. Bits of paper covered in her handwriting – sketches of charter symbols and Name-glyphs shifting uneasily as their ink shivered – littered the entire room, but the sopha was bare. It was perhaps where she would sleep tonight, did her researches take her in any promising direction.

She was being rather untidy. And there was a line between Mikal's eyebrows, though his expression was just the same as usual in every other regard. Trouble was brewing in that quarter.

Of course, she had ordered him to cool his heels outside the door and vanished; normally, she did not mind his company while she worked. But she had not wished him to see her discomfiture. Or the tears that had blistered a spare page of notes, tossed unceremoniously into the grate and lit with a hissed imprecation.

To add to her displeasure, every single ætheric strand leading to the fate of the unfortunate Keller *had* been trapped, closing off each avenue of possibly safe enquiry. It took a great deal of power, and a great deal of care, to hide the distinct stamp of one's personality on one's sorcery so completely. Whoever this murderer was, he was thorough, and wickedly intelligent to boot.

She grimaced at the thought, but only inwardly. A lady's face did not twist so. "You have my attention, Shield. Is there some new manner of disaster?"

"Not so much. I merely thought . . . you seem distressed."

"I have undertaken what is likely to be a thankless task. And my library, while normally more than adequate, is of very little use." She blew a vagrant curl out of her face; it irritated her mightily to be so disarranged. "I am distressed only by the bloody *inconvenience* of this entire affair."

"The mentath—"

Oh, is that what you wish to speak of? "—is none of your concern, Shield."

"He *distresses* you."

"So do you. Now, if you will not leave, at least be quiet." *Though I have little hope of you doing either. It seems every single blessed thing on the Isle is conspiring to try my temper today, from Marimat to a simple hansom ride.*

"How do I distress you, Emma?"

"Shall I list the ways? And yet, I am very busy right now. *Do* be quiet."

"How long will you ignore—"

"As long as I please, Shield. If you do not cease, I shall force you to do so."

"And how shall you do that, Prima?"

She set the book down carefully, brushing her hands together as if to rid them of dust, and rose. The chair legs squeaked slightly against the wooden floor, and she reminded herself again that a lady did not shout. Then, and only then, she met Mikal's gaze, and the room chilled slightly. Every piece of paper ruffled itself, brushed by an unphysical current.

When she was certain she could keep a civil tone, she spoke. "With whatever means are to hand. Are you weary of my employ, Mikal?"

"Of course not." His hands were loose, and he seemed relaxed. She did not trust the seeming. "You are my Prima."

Miles Crawford was your Prime; you strangled him as I watched, then mutilated his corpse. Because he hurt me. The contradiction – trusting her life to a Shield who had done the unthinkable and murdered his charge – was as sharp as it had ever been. Yet he had earned that trust, times beyond counting. Whatever danger he represented, it was not mere murder. "Then why do you take me up in such an unseemly manner?"

"He causes you pain." His chin jutted slightly, and how he managed to look like the defiant, almost-ugly boy he must have been on the Collegia's training grounds could have been mildly entertaining, if she had been inclined to amusement. "Much of it, and I am helpless to stop him. As long as you continue to let him, he will pain you."

"Yes." Anger, tightly reined, suddenly evaporated. Her stays dug into her flesh, and she wondered if she would ever see a day such appurtenances were no longer fashionable or expected.

Of course, Fashion being the beast she was, something equally uncomfortable and ridiculous would likely take its place.

"Yes," she repeated. "He pains me. I am told this is an occasional consequence of having friends. Which is no doubt why so many of my colleagues have so few they use that word to describe. At least, to describe seriously and with meaning."

"And I distress you."

"That is a consequence of having . . . you."

"What am I, to you? If I may ask, Prima."

"You may not." She found her head was aching again, and longed for vinegar and brown paper to soothe the pounding. "We shall have a reckoning, as they say, at some moment. But not *now*, Mikal." She found herself almost willing to utter an absurdity.

Please.

A Prime did not *ask*. A Prime *commanded*. But with Clare chasing will o'wisps with the bumbling idiot inspector – and he was too sharp an idiot to give any lee to, indeed – she had lost . . . what? Certainly a resource, and possibly Clare's regard as well.

"I believe a Prime may be behind this series of murders," she said, carefully. Almost, dare she think it, *logically*. "If so, I believe this Prime's aim is no less than the toppling of Victrix, which may please me to some small extent, and the uprooting of Britannia, which may or may not. In any case, *I* am now entangled in this affair, and I may suffer an unpleasant consequence or two if it is not tidily arranged in some fashion." *Which means you – and the rest of my household – may be cast adrift*.

"Ah." A slight nod, and his gaze had grown sharp. "A Sympathy has been created?"

"Perhaps." Yet she was uneasy even as she admitted the possibility. The oldest branch of sorcery, while powerful, was not enough to cause these effects on a ruling spirit's vessel – and if a Sympathy to Victrix had been in effect, Emma herself would not have become attuned to whatever work was being performed.

If it was indeed a *work*, and not a symptom of some other series of events at play. Uncomfortable thoughts were crowding her fast and thick now; Emma returned her attention to the present situation with an effort. "In any case, there is another . . . aspect . . . to this matter."

"Which is?"

At least he did not seek to *guess*.

Emma turned, took two irresolute steps toward the coal grate. Halted. "If not for an accident, I could have been one of them." *Who can tell what makes a sorcerer? Had the Collegia childcatchers not found me, I could have been dead, laid out on a marble slab with a doctor rummaging through me*.

Or worse. A shudder passed through her.

"Ah." Thankfully, he added no more. He merely let her know she was heard, perhaps understood. Though *understanding* was much to ask of any man.

She swung back to face him, her jewellery running with

crackling sparks as tension made itself visible. "I need your help, Mikal."

The Shield cocked his sleek dark head. He actually looked thunderstruck, and well he might. Two slow blinks – his yellow irises quenched for a moment – then another.

"You have it without asking, Prima." Formal, and very soft.

Do I? But she merely nodded, her face a mask. "Good. Fetch me some rum, and leave Clare to himself for a while. I cannot spare attention to keep him from trouble, I only hope Finch's cousin can."

"He seems capable of that much, at least." A half-bow, a Shield's traditional obeisance, he turned on his heel and was gone in a heartbeat.

The door closed behind him, and she let out a pent breath.

If he sought to reassure her, he had succeeded halfway. She gazed over the wrack and ruin of her study, and brought her hands together, sharply.

The resultant *crack*, freighted with a sharp-edged Word that left her with the sensation of a weight lifting through her spine, echoed for far longer than it should have. The books flew, snapping shut, arranging themselves in their appointed places. A slight lift at the end of the sound shuffled the paper together in a neat pile, stacking it on her desk; ink hissed free of the blotter in venomous little puffs of steam.

What had she not told him?

She held up one hand, counted said and unsaid reasons as if teaching a child-rhyme.

One finger. *I am alone*.

Two. *I suspect I am not drawn into this dance by mere chance*.

Three. *I am matched against another Prime*.

Four. *One I do not recognise*.

And fifth, last but not least, the most galling of all, counted upon her dexterous thumb, the digit that separated man from beast.

I am afraid.

Chapter Twenty-Seven

A Legitimate Concern

The night passed without incident, and so did the next
day, save for the broadsheets screaming of murder in
the Eastron End. Those were carried immediately to Miss
Bannon's study. Clare was, of course, supplied with his
own.

The *without incident* disturbed Clare mightily, for
Miss Bannon did not appear. She did not take breakfast
in the breakfast room or the solarium; she did not lunch;
she did not take tea with him. Trays were taken to her
study, and Finch's lean face was grave. The butler gave
no information about his mistress's mood, and Madame
Noyon attended to Clare's tea with a sombre air that was
quite unwonted.

The house was in mourning, and Philip appeared every
morning wearing a black armband. *Just to be mannerly, sir.*

His bland good nature was irritating in the extreme, but Clare did not take him to task. He also did not gather his effects and retreat to his own Baker Street flat, for some reason he could not quite name.

The fact that reminders of Valentinelli's presence would fill the rooms there as well was certainly not a consideration, was it?

Late in the evening, Finch tapped at the door of the workroom. Clare had been a trifle surprised at the mess left in that stone-walled room, but Philip had not even blinked at scrubbing the blood off the walls. Tidying the place had taken a day's worth of work, and he was cogitating upon the advisability of a series of experiments involving his own blood and a spæctroscope.

Philip tossed the door open. "Morning, guv! Come to visit the peasants?"

"You are an annoyance, boy," Finch replied, quite unperturbed. "Telegram, sir."

"Telegram?" Clare straightened his sleeves and viewed one of the large wooden tables with satisfaction. A tidy workroom meant a tidy mind, indeed.

"Yes, sir." Finch's tone betrayed nothing but neutrality. However, there was a fine sheen of sweat on the butler's forehead, and there was a slight tremor in the hand that proffered the slip of paper.

It was from Aberline, and the satisfaction of deduction burned through Clare's skull.

Ah. So it is Finch the inspector would like to pry from Miss Bannon's grip. It made sense, now – the butler, as one of Miss Bannon's oddities, had a chequered past. He affected a laborious upper-crust wheeze and a slow, stately walk, but his movements often betrayed a knife-fighters's awareness of space and familiarity with tight corners. Several interlocking deductions filled Clare's faculties for a moment – a sweet burn, rather like coja.

The telegram itself was almost an afterthought.

SEARCHING FOR CLEWS STOP REQUEST YOUR PRESENCE STOP

"How very interesting," Clare murmured. "Is the boy waiting?"

"Yes, sir."

"Give him tuppence, please. And send for a hansom, there's a good man."

"Yes, sir." Finch retreated, Philip watched with bright interest. His hand twitched, and Finch's fingers tightened slightly, but the young man merely offered a wide grin.

"Finch?"

"Yes, sir?"

For a moment, he wished to utter an absurdity – *Worry not, good man, I shan't bring the inspector home*. Then the likely consequences of such a statement became apparent, bringing him up short. Not to mention the thought of calling Miss Bannon's house *home*. He had a flat of his own, did he not?

Then why am I still here? "Do make certain Miss Bannon knows my whereabouts. I do not quite trust the good inspector's intentions."

Finch hesitated. He glided for the door, and Clare

detected a smidgen of relief on his gaunt face. "*Yes*, sir," he said, finally, with a peculiar emphasis on the first word.

So. It was *Finch, and I have reassured him*. It would not do to remark upon it, but Clare permitted himself a small smile and a tiny warm glow of satisfaction.

He turned in a slow circle, taking in the view of the workroom, and was struck by the shocking idea that he had been wasting time. Waiting for Miss Bannon to descend from her tower, so to speak, and pass commerce with his mere mortal self again.

Though how mere a mortal I am remains to be seen.

"Well now," he murmured, staring at the racks of beakers and alembics, each one shining-clean. "I say, Lud – ah, Philip, I have been imposing on Miss Bannon's hospitality rather much lately."

The lad made a short sound, whether of approbation or complaint Clare could not tell.

Clare forged onward. "You are rather an odd sort, but you are quick and know when to stay silent. I think you may do very well as an assistant."

Philip's nose wrinkled slightly. "A fine compliment, sir."

"And heartily meant. Fetch what you need, we may not return."

"*She* won't like that, sir."

"Nonsense. She has every faith in your capability, or she would not have engaged you to follow me about." He felt, he realised, extremely *lucid*, and the prospect of another tangle to test his faculties against was comforting in the extreme.

He also felt quite calm. Having a course of action to pursue helped to no end.

Philip had no witticism to answer with, so Clare set forth at a little faster than a walk but still short of a run, to fetch his hat and pack a few necessaries.

Perhaps Miss Bannon did worry for his well-being; perhaps this was an affair sorcery alone could untangle. Perhaps she was correct, and perhaps it was dangerous for Clare to accompany the detective inspector into the murderous knots that sprang up thick and rank as weeds wherever illogical sorcery was found.

Yes, Clare admitted to himself as he hopped up the stairs and turned for his rooms. She had quite a legitimate concern, had the lady in question.

Nevertheless, my dear Emma, I cannot wait to prove you wrong.

"I say, I wasn't sure you'd come," Aberline said grimly, rising to shake Clare's hand. His desk was littered with piles of paper, his inkstand had seen heavy use of late, and the shelves in his office were disarranged somewhat. The place was full of dust occasioning from that rearranging, and there was a betraying tickle in Clare's nose.

He suppressed the incipient sneeze and cleared his throat instead. "Whyever not? I am quite happy to be of service. This shall keep my faculties tolerably exercised, I should think. Besides, we cannot have murderers running loose. It is an affront to good order."

"Indeed." The inspector's hand trembled slightly, and

there were still dark circles under his eyes. "Many of the public agree. In fact, we are inundated with well-meaning letters, telegrams, notes, scribbles, and opinions. They are certain someone they know has acted suspiciously, or they tell us how we may go about doing our duty and catching the damned man. He seems to have rather caught the public interest."

"Gruesomely so. The broadsheets are full of *Leather Apron* this and *Murder* that." *The less responsible are blaming the Yudics in all but name*. Clare cast about for a place to perch, but there was none. The chair he had settled in last time overflowed with paper – no doubt there was a rich trove of deduction to unearth there. "Do tell me how I may help, sir."

"I would set you to weeding through these, but I rather think it a waste of time and of your magnificent talents. If you can believe it, these are the missives that have been judged to have some merit in other quarters, and are thus passed to me."

But there must be hundreds! "Good heavens. Surely there is a better use of your own resources than *this*."

"I rather think so." Aberline tugged on his gloves, of a little higher quality than a mere inspector's, but by no means reprehensibly Æsthete.

Clare noted his walking-stick – Malacca, with a curious brass head that looked rather too heavy – and the overcoat hanging behind the inspector's desk, on a wrought-iron contraption. "I deduce we are going walking."

"Rather healthful, at our age." Aberline shrugged into the overcoat with quick movements.

A flash of amusement passed through Clare, a swift pang, over quickly. He did his best to ignore it. "I further deduce our destination is an unsavoury part of Londinium."

"Will he take cold, our young lad?" The inspector scooped up his walking-stick and thrust his chin at Philip Pico, who held a mutinous peace.

The youth merely let his lip curl slightly, and Clare thought the russet touches to his hair were perhaps natural. Even his eyebrows held a tinge of burning.

"I doubt it. He has overcome his reluctance to accompany me on such salubrious excursions." *There are some advantages to logic, indeed.*

"Very well. He may even be useful." The detective inspector cast a final glance over the room, and an extraordinary flash of Feeling surfaced on his features.

Observe, analyse. Clare's faculties seized on the unguarded expression. Longing, disgust, a heavy recognition of futility.

Detective Inspector Aberline was a man who loathed his employment, and yet he would continue in it for as long as possible, devoting his energies faithfully and completely, with little regard for his health or happiness.

Perhaps his dislike of Miss Bannon sprang from the fact that they were, on that level, very much the same. There was no antipathy like that of the familiar. "Mr Pico is singularly useful, sir. I deduce we are bound for Whitchapel?"

Aberline's broad, sudden smile was a marvel of cheerfulness, showing another flash of the youth he must have been. "Incorrect, sir!" He drew himself up, settled his bowler, tested the heft of his walking-stick, and strode lively for the door. "We are bound for Limhoss, and for an explanation."

"Oh, *blast* it all." Emma's temper frayed still further, and Finch's head drew back between his thin, hunching shoulders, rather in the manner of a tortoise.

A telegram from Aberline, and Clare was out of the door like a shot. At least Philip had gone with him, and she could safely consign the mentath's welfare to the list of problems not to be solved at the moment.

She took a deep breath. "Never mind. They shall distract my quarry admirably for the time being. Thank you, Finch."

"Mum." He paused, ready if she wished to add anything more.

Fortunately, she did. "I am closing the house. Pray let the other servants know, and take care none of the deliveries are allowed to step inside. I do not have time for the bother that would ensue." Not to mention it might drive the prices of some goods up, and while she had a good head for business – a Collegia education rather instilled such a thing – there was no reason to be *flagrant* with what she had accumulated. A second thought occurred to her. "I do rather hope Clare does not bring his new acquaintance to my door. The result would be singularly unappealing."

Finch's posture did not change one whit. "Mr Clare said he did not quite trust the inspector's motives regarding yourself, mum."

"Did he now." A thin thread of amusement bloomed, very much against her will. "Well, Mr Clare is wise to do so." She halted, one foot on the first stair. "Finch . . . *Geoffrey*."

He blinked, and the mild surprise on his thin face might have been amusing as well, except for the sudden flare of fear underneath it. Lime-green to Sight, bitter and acrid, it stung her far more sharply than she dared admit.

"I have not forgotten my promise," she continued. "The inspector may go elsewhere to satisfy the grudges he bears both of us. Should you leave my service or retire, you shall be safely ensconced in a lovely warm foreign country with a comfortable independence before *he* receives a whisper of such an event."

"I would not leave your service, mum." Finch had drawn himself up. "Not willingly, God strike me down if I don't mean it."

Her smile was unguarded, and for once Emma was content to have it so. "Thank you, Finch." She found her gloved hand had rested on his forearm, and her own shock at her familiarity was matched by Finch's sudden thunder-struck expression. "I would be saddened to see you go."

"Erm. Shall you be needing the carriage, mum?"

"No, thank you. I shall most likely return very late, possibly not before dawn. You may all go to bed early, I should think."

"Yesmum." And he glided away, suddenly very small and slight against the foyer's restrained elegance. How Severine had clucked and fussed when Emma brought him home, how the housekeeper had expressed her disdain in every possible way until Emma had informed her tartly that *she* was the resident sorceress and Severine Noyon, treasured and valued as she was, did not have the final say in what or whom Emma pleased to employ.

If I bring home a dozen cutthroat syphilitic Dutch mercenaries, Madame Noyon, you will be gracious and greet them kindly, and have some little faith in your mistress.

Her smile faded, remembering how poor Severine had quailed, going cheese-pale, her plump hands waving help-lessly. Emma had gentled her, of course – *You must trust me as you did before, Madame. Have I ever led you astray?*

Still, it was . . . unworthy. Frightening the soft and broken held no joy. Given the habits of Severine's previous employer, it was no wonder the woman still cowered.

"Prima?" Mikal appeared, striding from the drawing room.

"I am closing the house." She shook herself into full alertness, and set aside memory. "Finch shall warn the servants; I hope Clare will not bring his new friend home like a street-found cur."

"If he does, the result will no doubt be satisfying."

"Very. And yet, messy, and no end of inconvenience." She breathed out, softly, and drew her mantle closer.

The scrap of cloth in her skirt pocket was an unwelcome weight, no matter that it was merely a small strip soaked with *vitae* and sealed in a ball of virgin wax cooled with a sketched charter symbol. *Vitae*, no matter how unwholesome for one of Emma's Discipline, was still a most useful fluid, which could be imprinted with the sympathetic qualities of *other* fluids.

As in a sorcerer's blood, shed in a Blightallen doss.

The Sympathy would be weak, but that weakness would insulate her from another overwhelming vision of murder. Or at least, so she hoped. She further hoped it would not sensitise her further to whatever damnable Work was occurring. Her careful, delicate probing of the æther over the last two days had crushed whatever lingering hope she had held of it being simply a mistake, or of the effects upon Victrix and herself being simply coincidental.

"You could merely stay here." The Shield's irises were lambent in the foyer's dimness, and he was a solidly comforting shadow, at least. "Let *her* taste the fruits of her sowing."

If those fruits did not echo so loudly inside my own body, I might consider it. "I could. However, Clare expects me to take a hand in this affair."

He nodded. And, thankfully, did not take issue with the statement.

"Come." *I should do this quickly, before I find another reason to avoid doing it at all.* "And Mikal?"

"Yes?"

"Tonight, strike to kill."

A gleam of white teeth, shown in a smile. "Yes, Prima."

The edge of Whitchapel was already showing thin traceries of virulent green, and the fog had thickened to a soup best strained through a kerchief. Emma found she could push her veil aside without her eyes stinging, but chose not to. She was merely a darker shadow hurrying along, Mikal in his black a blot beside her.

The fog lipped every surface, turning passers-by into shades risen from some underworld described in one of the Greater Texts, strangling the gaslamps' tiny circles of illumination.

The alleys were muffled by Scab already, and there were choked sounds from some of them. A soft cry ahead resolved into a confused flurry of shadows, but when they reached the corner there was only a splash of bright smoking blood on the cobbles, Scab threading busily through its warm nutrition in delicate filigreed whorls.

Emma continued, stepping briskly along, the digging of her stays as well as the stricture of her point-toe boots both welcome reminders that she was *not* a child.

Mikal's presence was noted, of course. There were gleams in the darkness: altered limbs, cautious eyes with no more humanity than a Nile crocodile's, a jet of shivering gaslamp glow reflecting from a knife blade. She was not approached, though once Mikal touched her elbow, drifting a few steps away towards an alley-mouth as she stood, bolt upright and breathing calmly, her training sinking its claws deep in her rebellious vitals as her body recognised the heatless scent of danger.

The gleams retreated, but Mikal still stood, the set of his shoulders somehow expressing reluctance to move further, but equal unwillingness to back away. A silent language, one the knives of Whitchapel understood.

Finally he relaxed a trifle, and paced back to her side. She continued without a word.

Blightallen, where the vanished Kendall had met with such misfortune, was of a different character after nightfall. Her ankles ached with the step-glide that was necessary to keep her footing, for the Scab had thickened. The darkness was a living thing, almost impenetrable, and Emma could not decide whether to be grateful she could discern the shapes around her or nauseous at the filth underfoot. For one whom even candlelight could glare-blind during the deeper use of her ætheric talents, it was an unexpected . . . well, not a gift, but it certainly made visiting this hole *easier*.

For a certain value of "easy", she supposed.

Her gloved hand dug for the wax ball; she drew it out securely caged in her fist. Mikal, his fingers quick and deft, knotted a hank of silk about her closed hand, and glanced at her face. Could he see in this reproduction of Stygia?

"Are you . . ."

Was he about to ask her if she was certain? Or ready? Emma shook her head, acutely aware of curls brushing her mantle's shoulder, the fog making its own whisper-sound as it crept uneasily above the Scab. Occasionally it dipped its fingers down to almost touch the thick coating, then recoiled as the surface of Whitchapel's greediest resident twitched.

She opened her mouth to speak the minor Word that would unleash the Sympathy.

It died unuttered, ætheric force tangling and snarling under the surface of the world as Mikal clapped his free hand over her mouth, his head coming up with a quick, fluid, somehow *wrong* movement.

Footsteps, light and quick. *What is that?* She braced herself, and when Mikal took his hand away they shared a look of silent accord – visible because the cameo at her throat had lit with leprous green brightening as the sound grew closer. There was no *splorch* of the ooze releasing a running foot, nor was there the sliding of an accomplished flashboy who had learned the trick of not breaking the Scab's surface in order to move quickly along.

What on earth—

It burst from the gloom at the end of Blightallen, and Mikal was there to meet it, his knives out and flashing dully.

Flickers of motion, a whip-crack of sound – and her Shield was driven back, sliding on the uncertain footing.

It *did* have a whip. Emma's eyes narrowed as she flashed

through and discarded invisible threads. The æther reso-
nated oddly, curdling; she had time to take a deep breath
before Mikal was flung aside and hit a dosshouse door
with a sickening crack.

Scab curled and smoked, oily steam rising as it cringed
away from the tall, square-headed figure – it had a coachman's hat, and the whip was a heavy one meant to sound
over several heaving clockhorse backs at once.

She had fractions of a moment to decide what manner
of creature it was as it leapt skimble-legged for her. A
glamour could kill if she believed in its truth; a bound
spirit or a Construct could injure her grievously if its binder
or creator had entrusted it with enough ætheric force; a
dollsome or Horst's Mannequin could *only* strike physically; a Seeming could not injure her unduly; and there
were so many other categories to consider she was almost,
almost too late.

Mikal let out a choked cry, but Emma had set herself
squarely, the cameo sparking and two rings on her left
hand – one a bloody garnet set in heavy gold, the other
cheap brass with a glass stone that nevertheless held a
fascinating twinkle and a heavy charge – flaming with
ætheric force.

A violet flower bloomed between her and the thing in
a coachman's form: sorcerous force widening like a painted
Chinois fan. The Word she spoke, sliding harsh and whole
from her throat with a harsh pang, was not of Mending or
Breaking or even of Binding. No, she chose a different
Language entirely, and one not of her Discipline.

Strictly speaking, Naming belonged to neither the White nor the Black, nor the Grey besides. Its only function was to *describe*, but such was a law of sorcery: *the Will makes the Name*.

Had she not been Prime, she perhaps could not have forced the creature's dubious reality to temporarily take the form most suited to her purposes. The Word warped as the thing fought her humming definition of its corporeality, and that very twisting and bulging gave her indications of its nature.

But only indications.

A tricksome beast you are, indeed.

It hit the shield of violet shimmering and Emma was driven back, her heels scraping long furrows through crisping, peeling Scab. Her gloved hands flew, describing a complex pattern, and the violet light snapped sideways and forward, again fanlike. The edge slashed up, sharply, and the thing's howl blew her hair back, cracked the folds of her mantle, stung her watering eyes.

She ignored the irritation. It *was* a coachman, its yellow and red striped muffler wrapped high to conceal a void where the face should be and its high collar doing its best to shade the face as well, its coat flapping open, worn and patched in places with tiny needle-charmer's stitches; its boots caked with manure and street-scum. The hat was of fine quality, a jaunty black feather affixed, the waistcoat of embroidered purple and gold a proud bit of flash. It was not liveried, but the boots and the hat said *servant* instead of *hire*, and who would send a creature like this in a livery which could be identified? The clothes were no doubt pawnshop acquisitions, probably corpsepicker gains.

It fell, splatting dully onto the Scab-covered cobbles. More vile steam rose. Its fingers had torn through the ragged woollen gloves, being far too long and corpse-pallid, each sporting an extra joint that no doubt helped the thing wield a knife.

Or its whip, which clattered on the cobbles beside it.

Emma set her chin, bringing the fan-shield back smoothly. The creature's advantage of surprise was lost, and she had successfully driven it down. But where was Mikal, and what precisely *was* this unholy thing?

It hissed, scrabbling at age-blackened cobbles with malformed hands to find its weapon, and she had a moment to be grateful Clare was not further involved in this matter before it twisted upright with inhuman speed and flung itself at her again.

Chapter Twenty-Nine

A Babe In Woods

The saying *Foul as Limhoss breath* was marvellous apt. Whitchapel had its own stench, and Limhoss no Scab, but in Archibald Clare's considered judgment there were few places in Londinium to outdo the latter in matters of fragrance. Perhaps it was the Basin, or maybe the mariners who congregated in its dens and dosses, the tar of the ropes or the tight-packed press of alien flesh – for the Chinois population of the Isle was concentrated here, and their suffusion of odours was foreign as well as rank.

Ginger and spices, the starch of their rice and boiling of their odd oils, different fish than an Englene would eat, the dry rough note of raw silk, and an acrid smoke enfolded them. Even the fog was a different shade here, its billows assuming the shapes of their odd writing, their crouching, painted charter stones near the doors alive with weak saffron light so they could practise their native arts of minor charming without the risk of nasty side-consequences.

Aberline knocked twice at a collection of splinters masquerading as a door, which shivered and opened immediately. Perhaps he was expected, or perhaps, Clare thought as he ducked to pass through the tiny opening, *anyone* was expected after dark.

Down a close, reeking passageway and into a womblike dimness, the light turned red by the paper lampshades it passed through, and Clare realised it was a poppy den.

Long shapes reclined on bunks built into the wall, giving a rather nautical flavour to the room. A brown fug rose from winking scarlet eyes as Morpheus's chosen flower carried its devotees into fantastic languor. The eyes were the bowls of the pipes, a beast with a thousand gazes.

"Your methods are indeed unusual," he remarked, breaking the hush. Coughs rose in protest, weakly; he had not adjusted his tone for the confined quarters.

The bent, blue-garbed Chinoise who had bobbed ahead of them into the room made a *shush* sound, but not very loudly. Clare could not quite decide what age the crooked stick of a woman had attained, for her thinning hair was still lacquer-black – as were the few teeth she still possessed – and the skin of her face had drawn tight. She scuffed along in embroidered slippers, threading through those on the floor gathered around the long poppy-pipes, beckoning them along and bowing repeatedly to Aberline, who appeared a giant in a toy shop next to her.

"Nodders all," Philip Pico muttered behind Clare. "Ripe for rolling."

"Not here," Aberline whispered. "*Do* be a good sport, little lad."

Of course, the prickly little russet took offence. "I'm no nodder. Not with the filthy Chin—"

"Silence is good for your health." Aberline cut him off, and Clare observed him handing the Chinoise a handful of coins. He received a key and a packet in return, and she pointed them up a rickety staircase.

"Surely there are more wholesome dens than this." Clare found himself walking stiffly, avoiding the chance of the surfaces of this place brushing against his clothes.

"But here, dear sir, I am certain we will not be overheard."

Is that a danger? "Are we plotting, then?"

"We are engaging in a method, Clare. Have you ever ridden the dragon?"

Philip caught at Clare's arm. "*She* won't like this, sir."

Was it Annoyance Clare felt? He shelved it, stepping to avoid a limp hand lain along the floor. "It is a good thing she is not about, then. And really, this is no place for a lady."

A slight cough from Aberline, but thankfully, the man restrained himself. He murmured to the Chinoise crone in what seemed a dialect of their strange tonal language, and she retreated past them, her loose trousers under a long, high-collared shirt fluttering forlornly. She gave Clare a wide obsequious smile, blackened stumps on display, and was gone into the red-drenched gloom below.

The heavy iron key fit a door in a high narrow hallway, which led into an equally high but not very spacious room. Still, it was quiet, the soughing of Londinium outside merely a suggestion of pressure against the eardrums.

Two low sopha-like things heaped with tattered bolsters, rather more in the style of the Indus than the Chinois, a wretched oil lamp Aberline put a lucifer to and turned down as low as possible, and four poppy-pipes on a small round table of glowing mellow brass and mahogany.

Clare took in the dust upon the table, the marks about the rim of one pipe, the dents in the upholstery and pillows on the far side, set where the smoker could recline and watch the door.

"You come here often, Inspector."

"As often as necessary." Aberline indicated the other sopha, and Clare found himself sharing a look of silent accord with Philip. It was a moment's work to move the other divan to a more salubrious position, which manoeuvre Aberline watched with a tolerant smile. "I am afraid, little man, that there is only enough here for two."

Philip bristled. "I am no nodder. I'll take my laudanum like a civilised gent, thank you." He rattled the door. "This wouldn't stand a good beating."

"It doesn't have to with you standing watch, now does it?" Aberline settled himself on the sad wreck of furniture that was, Clare saw, a broken-backed chesterfield that could not even be salvaged for Eastcheap's sorry hawking. Its just-moved companion was sturdier, but much dirtier. "Do sit, Mr Clare. You are about to view a marvel."

It was not at all like smoking tabac.

A small amount to start, Aberline had said. _We are not here to enjoy but to learn. To plumb the depths._

Perhaps the man fancied himself a poet.

A blurring across the nerves. A deep hacking cough. What did it smell like? Acrid, certainly, resinous. A faint amount of spice. Was he already . . .

The couch was quite dirty, but it was also comfortable. Clare leaned back, and the problem burst in upon him in all its dizzying complexity.

Some manner of sorcery, making me proof against an explosion. Proof against knives, and Time. My faculties will stay sharp. Yet the poppy had a distinct effect upon him. What would coja do? He had lost the taste for it, but he could experiment.

Later.

The walls, their dingy paper peeling, suddenly took on new breath and interest. Each rip and fleck, each bit of plaster showing, gave rise to a host of deductions. They split and re-formed, the history of this sad little room unreeling in a gorgeous play of light and shadow, logic and meaning.

Why, this is marvellous! The urge to laugh rose from his navel, but he set it aside. Irrational, messy, uncertain Feeling had no place here . . .

. . . but, still, the poppy blunted the painful edges and the outright *sloppiness* of Feeling, and he could consider the entire situation rather calmly.

Ludovico.

It was grief, of course, and the world became a mist of rose shot through with crimson. He had read of this, the welter of contradictory emotion when death struck; he had not felt it as a young man when his parents had succumbed to mortality. Had it been a blessing, that numbness? What was different now?

No, Clare. You felt it. He remembered the nights of working straight through, studying for the Examinations in his draughty, cramped student lodgings. Burying the Feeling, because it was a distraction, and after all, he was young and just coming into his faculties' full bloom. After a long while the ache had retreated, because he was a mentath and Feeling was an enemy to logic.

Yet one must account for it, in all one's dealings. How odd.

Aberline was speaking, but Clare could not distinguish the words through thick rosy fog. It was like Londinium's vaporous breath, except it smelled of some sweetness. Spiced pear, smoke . . .

Emma. His faculties painted her image against the inside of his eyelids. Her soft face, steely with the force of her character or slack in sleep as he had seen it once. Her small hands, and the fire in her dark eyes. The way her footsteps echoed, and the brush of her skirts.

The images came one after another, tumbling in their rapidity. Emma bloody and battered at the end of some

dangerous bit of business, her mouth set tight and determination burning in her gaze. Tucking a stray curl up into
the rest of her complex hairstyle; she did so hate to be
dishevelled. Poring over a broadsheet or two in the morning,
making quite serviceable deductions, writing in her firm,
clear hand at her morning desk in the solarium.

And finally, Emma at his bedside. *I am loath to lose
you, Archibald*.

Grief for Ludovico, and the sweet sting that was Emma
Bannon. It was the sting that wrapped crimson threads
through the fog and pulled it tight.

Here, with the poppy smoke burning his lungs and rest
of his flesh a loose soup, he could admit the waves of
Feeling. He could let them slide through him and away,
and when the poppy dream ended he would be whole – and
rational – again.

Or so he hoped. His eyelids lifted, and Aberline was
speaking again.

The inspector, instead of relaxing into languor, had
leaned forward. He was still speaking, and Clare sought
to grasp the words, but they slid away as well. There was
a reply – Philip Pico, near the door, a light amused tone.
Why had she bothered to engage such a person to look
after him? If he was immortal now – but perhaps she feared
not for Clare's physical frame. Perhaps she feared for Clare
himself, and what the double blow of grief and irrationality
would do to him.

This is ridiculous. Preposterous.

Yet the idea had some merit. It was, he decided, a

deduction taking into account a weight of Feeling, and not sinking in the process.

The glow was leaving, draining away too quickly. The crimson threads gave one last painless twitch and were gone, the rosy fog evaporating, and he became aware of a hammering sound.

Aberline had reached his feet. He swayed slightly, and Clare realised the man had been speaking of the murders. He blinked several times as Philip gave a curt command, *None of that now*, and Clare found himself on a broken sopha in the middle of a Limhoss poppy den, the world a sudden vivid assault after the rosy fog.

"Inspector Aberline, sir." A whip-thin young man in a brown jacket, but his hair cut too short for a labourer's. From the Yard, then, judging by his shoes, and out of breath. "There's another one."

Clare's stomach turned over, queerly.

"Another murder." Aberline nodded. "Yes, Browne. Hail a hansom, there's a good man."

The brown-jacketed Browne gasped, red blotches of effort on his sweating cheeks. There was a fog of smoke in here – how much had Aberline produced? The inspector was not only standing, but moving about. Clare gathered himself, an odd burning in the region of his chest.

Philip Pico's face was a fox's for a moment as he bent down over the mentath. The sharp black nose wrinkled, and his ears were perked, alert. "Come on, nodder."

"You, sir, are a fox." Clare's flesh moved when he told it to. It was an odd feeling, thinking of himself inside an imperishable corporeal glove, his faculties simply observing the passage of time. There was a certain comfort in the notion.

"And you're a babe in woods, sir, for all your bright-penny talk. Come along."

Aberline glanced over his shoulder; it really was quite irritating that the man seemed so unmoved by whatever quantity of poppy he had smoked. Instead, he was merely haggard, drawn, the dark shadows under his eyes ever more pronounced. Soon they might swallow his gaze whole . . .

Wait. Clare searched through memory, grasping for whatever the inspector had said into the smoke-fog. *He did something, something quite alarming. He spoke of . . . what?*

The tantalising memory receded, and Clare's head began to ache.

I suspect this was a very irrational event.

Chapter Thirty

Profit In Reminding

The coachman-thing darted forward. Violet light flashed as Emma brought the fan-shield up smartly, slashing it across the chest. Blightallen was alive with cries and running feet, yellow fog thickening and swirling in a most peculiar manner as the residents of this sorry street realised an extraordinary event was occurring in their midst.

She snapped the shield sideways again, her throat swelling with a rill of notes. Her rings were fading as their stored ætheric charge drained, and the end of the street was fast approaching. She could not give much more ground before she was forced to think of an alternate method for dealing with this creature. She had forced it into precisely the correct proportion of physicality, so it could be hurt, but confining it thus was taking *far* more of her resources than she liked, and it was only a matter of time before its creator noticed her refusal to politely die and perhaps took steps to free the thing from her strictures.

Where was Mikal? How badly was he wounded?

Tend to him later. Right now content yourself with not dying, for this thing wishes to kill.

It made no noise now, save whip-cracks and the stamping of its feet. The whip flickered, the fan-shield snapped closed as she trilled a descant, turning on itself to force the flying tip aside. The whip wrapped around a teetering wrought-iron lamppost, its cupola dark since the lighters rarely came to a street so thickly padded with Scab. Emma skipped forward, bringing the shield low and snapping it open again, its edge sharpening as her concentration firmed.

It fell back, and under its curved hat brim were two coals that had not been there before. The whip twitched, iron shrieking as the lamppost bent, and she knew she would not be able to bring the shield up in time. The notes curdled in her throat, breath failing her.

Oh dear.

It shrieked, the sound tearing both æther and air, as Mikal's face rose over its shoulder, his eyes yellow lamps. A knifepoint, dripping, protruded from its narrow chest and the Shield wrenched the blade away, his other hand coming up to seek purchase in its muffler. If he could tear the thing's head loose—

Emma spun, the whip's sharp end tangling in her skirt as the fan-shield blurred, becoming a conduit to bleed away the force of the strike.

A vast noise filled Blightallen, Scab-steam flooding up to mix with cringing yellow fog.

She fell, *hard*, knees striking cobble and her teeth clicking together jarringly. Folded over as silence fell, the inhabitants of the street temporarily stunned into mouth-gaping wonder. What could they see through the fog? Anything?

Through the sudden quiet, the thing's receding footsteps were light and unholy, and Mikal's hands were at her shoulders.

"Prima? *Emma?*"

Hot blood against her fingers. Emma winced, drew in a sharp breath, and brought her fist up sharply.

It was barbed, so it tore even further on its way free of her thigh and her skirts. A small, betraying sound wrung itself from her as she finished wrenching it loose and found she had not lost the wax ball either. *Oh, good.* The traces of Keller's shed blood would serve a useful purpose now, giving her a chance at triangulation rather than mere fumbling direction-seeking.

She looked up to find Mikal's face inches from hers, striped with blood. He was filthy – no doubt he had rolled in the Scab – and there were splinters and brick dust liberally coating him. Her hair had come loose, falling in her face; he brushed away a curl and his fingertips found her cheekbone.

How comforting. A cough caught her unawares, then her voice decided it would perform its accustomed function. Scraped into a shadow of itself, it nevertheless was tolerably steady. "Are you hurt?"

His expression went through several small changes she could not decipher, before settling on relief. "Only slightly. My apologies. I was . . . briefly stunned."

"Quite a stunning experience." She caught her breath. Looked down again, found herself holding a sharp, barbed metal weight from the end of the coachman's whip, torn free. Catching it in her own leg had not been the best of ideas, she had to admit, even if it had served its purpose. "But still, educational, and *so* entertaining."

"If you say so, Prima. Can you stand?"

"I think—"

He took further stock of her. "You're bleeding."

"Yes. Mikal, I rather think I cannot stand without help."

"You never do anything halfway, Prima. Lean on me."

"Mikal . . ." The words she had meant to say died unuttered, for in the distance there was a bell-clear cry cutting Londinium's yellow fog.

"*Murder!*"

And Whitchapel . . . erupted.

The crowd was a beast of a thousand heads, and its mood scraped against every ache in Emma's tired body. She leaned upon Mikal, letting the press wash about her, and listened.

Cut her throat . . . side to side, a sight, found in a yard . . . no doubt it's him, it's him! A leather apron . . . Leather Apron . . . foreigner . . . drinking our blood, they are . . .

If the bloodied apron outside the Yudic workingman's club had been a ruse, it was a clever one. If it had been merely a bit of refuse, it was still serving the author of all this unpleasantness tolerably well.

Her left thigh throbbed, the healing sorcery Mikal had applied sinking its own barbs in. "This will not do," she murmured. "Is the entire Eastron End mad now?"

"Another murder, they say."

"I felt nothing." She clutched at his shoulder, jostled and buffeted. The churchbells were speaking, Tideturn was soon; she could feel it like approaching thunder.

Half past one, of course not a single hansom in sight, and the crowd, spilling out into the streets as word leapt from doss to doss. "Mikal. *I did not feel it.*"

"I know." He steadied her. "Prima . . . that thing—"

"It was a coachman. And it had a knife." *What manner of creature was it, though? I shall know soon enough.*

"Yes." He pushed aside the rags of his bloodied black velvet coat, irritably. Underneath, his skin was whole but flushed in vivid stripes. "A very sharp blade. I hardly felt it."

"I shall wish to . . ." The world tried to spin away underneath her. She had expended far more sorcerous force than was wise, and lost *quite* a bit of blood. The Scab was probably growing over it now, green and lush, not scorched away as it had been under the coachman-thing's feet. "I shall wish to examine the exact pattern of the cuts."

"Yes." He propped her against a wall. Peered into her face, uncertain gaslight flickers turning his eyes to shadowed holes. "You're pale."

"I am well enough." She even managed to say it firmly.

Across the street, a flashboy tumbled out of a ginhouse, his right hand a mass of clicking, whirring metal. He was greeted by derisive laughter as a gaptooth drab with her skirts hiked around her knees shouted, "*Leather Apron's aboot tonight, watch yerself!*"

The crowd gathered itself, and Emma shivered, suddenly very cold. Her breath was a cloud, and she stared into Mikal's familiar-unfamiliar face. "There is about to be some unpleasantness," she whispered.

"I understand. Here." He ducked under her arm, his own arm circling her waist. Her stays dug most uncomfortably, but at least she was alive and drawing breath to feel them. "Close your eyes."

She did, and Mikal coiled himself. He leapt, and below them the street boiled afresh. More screams, and the high tinkle of breaking glass.

The riot bloomed, a poisonous flower, but Mikal held her, slate and other tiles crunching under his feet as the rooftops of Londinium spun underneath them. This was a Shield's sorcery, and very peculiar in its own way, managing to unseat the stomach of those without the talents and training of that ancient brotherhood.

Which explained why, when he finally set her on her feet in a Tosselside alley, the riot merely a rumble in the distance, she leaned over and heaved most indelicately.

Londinium turned grey around her, and she surfaced from an almost-swoon to find Mikal holding her upright again.

Her mouth was incredibly sour, and she repressed an urge to spit to clear it.

A lady does not do such things. "The unrest will spread. And likely foul any trace of where that thing went."

"Yes. You are very pale, Prima. Perhaps we should—"

She discovered she did not wish to know what he would advance as the next advisable action. "The decent and sane thing to do would be to go home, bar my doors and wait for this affair to reach its conclusion without me. The Coachman was set upon my trail, just as a bloodhound."

"I thought as much." Did he sound resigned? "I rather think you will not retreat, though."

Indecision, a new and hateful feeling. The temptation to retreat was well-nigh irresistible. Her left leg trembled, and she felt rather . . . well, not quite up to her usual temper.

In the end, though, there was quite simply no one else who could arrange this affair satisfactorily. It was not for Victrix, nor for Britannia, and not even for Clare so high and mighty, looking down upon her for daring to give him a gift sorcerers would use every means they could beg, borrow, or steal to acquire.

No, the reason she could not retreat just yet was far simpler.

The Coachman-thing had made her afraid.

For a Prime, that could not be borne.

"No," she said, and took a deep breath, wishing her stays did not cut so and that her skirts were not draggled with blood and Scab-muck. "I shall not retreat. I require a hansom."

"Where are we bound?"

"The Yard, Mikal. They will not venture into Whitchapel until the riot burns itself out, and there may be certain profit in *reminding* one or two of Aberline's superiors of certain facts."

Chief among them that I am acting for the Crown – but I am not particularly choosey about how I finish this bloody business.

❀ Chapter Thirty-One

𝒜 Somewhat Durable Cast

A thickset man in bobby's blue, his whistle dangling from a silver chain, put up both hands to halt the detective inspector's headlong rush. "Whitchapel's ablaze, sir. We're not to go in. Orders."

"Oh, for the love of . . ." Aberline looked almost ready to tear out handfuls of his own hair. "Clare?"

Clare blinked, cocked his head and sought to untangle the various cries and crashes rending the night air. "Who would order—"

"Commissioner Waring, no doubt." Aberline all but bounced up on his toes to peer between two other broad, beefy bootleather knights, who were viewing the traceries of Scab on the cobbles with studied disinterest. "*Candleson!* Over here!"

The bobby who glanced up and sauntered to join them

was a mutton-chopped and gin-nosed bulk with an oddly mincing gait. His knees no doubt gave him trouble, judging by how gingerly he stepped, but Clare caught a steely twinkle in the man's deep-set eyes and the calluses on his beefy paws. Candleson carried a knotty stick, much in the manner of an Eirean shillelagh, dark with use and oil. A leather loop on his broad, creaking belt was its home on the few occasions, Clare thought, that it was not in his hands.

No doubt it had cracked many a criminal's skull in its time, too.

"Evenin', sir. There's a bit of the restless tonight." His accent was a surprise – reasonably educated, though with a lilt to the consonants that bespoke a childhood on a farm, most probably in Somerset.

"Your understatement, dear Candleson, is superb as always. Let me guess, Waring says to wait for morning?"

"Bit dark in there," was the laconic reply. But Candleson's mouth turned down briefly, and the crease under his chin flushed.

"Another murder." Aberline's eyebrows rose.

"Still bleeding when she was found. Dunfeld's, Berner Street. There's another of those clubs there. Workingmen, foreigners." He looked even more sour at the notion.

"Good God." Aberline did not pale, but it might have been close. "They will kill each other in droves over this."

The noise intensified. Whitchapel buzzed as a poked wasps' nest might. The entire Eastron End might well catch fire, figuratively *or* literally. Clare twitched at his cuffs, bringing them down, and took stock of his person. He did not even have his pepperbox pistol or its replacement, and no doubt the quality of his cloth would attract unwanted attention. He glanced at Philip Pico, who stood with his arms folded and feet braced, watching him with a peculiar expression.

"Well." Clare drew himself up. "There is nothing for it, then."

Aberline rounded on him. "Sir, I—"

Clare set off for the line of venom-green Scab. The onlookers did not expect trouble from his quarter, so he was through the line and marching onwards when Aberline caught at his arm. "What in God's name—"

"I must examine the site of this new event before it is trampled by a mob, and daylight will only bring more of them. Stay here, if you—"

"You shall not go alone. I should warn you, there is tremendous risk to your person."

"I rather think there is." The noise had intensified, and he had to raise his voice to be heard. "I am sure you will find it reassuring that I am of a somewhat durable cast, though. Philip?"

"Oh, she's not going to like this," the lad said, but he seemed willing enough. High spots of colour burned in his beardless cheeks, and there was a definite hard merriment to his tone. Rather as Valentinelli had sported a fey grin, when they were about to plunge into danger.

"She has other matters to attend to," Clare said shortly,

and set out afresh. Aberline followed, with a muttered word that might have been a curse.

Behind them, the line of bobbies and a growing mass of curiosity-seekers murmured and rustled. Ahead, there was a cacophony, the fog billowing in veils as if it, too, sought to misbehave tonight.

Clare did not consult his pocket-watch, but he thought it very likely they had been in a Limhoss daze for quite some hours.

The question of just *what* Inspector Aberline had been saying in the midst of that daze would have to wait. For they rounded a slight bend in the cobbled road, and the fog became garishly underlit with flame. Cries and running feet, piercing screams, and a high sweet tinkle of breaking glass.

The poor, crowded together here, needed little enough reason to strain against the bonds of decency and public order.

The wonder, Clare reflected, was that they did not do so more often.

Underfoot was slick and treacherous. Clare kept to the building side, but gave alley entrances a polite amount of space nonetheless. Darker shapes began to coalesce through the fog.

Between that vapour and the choking slickness under his soles, there was precious little for his faculties to fasten on except the noise.

Slip-sliding footsteps, scurrying tip-taps. Excited babble, and rougher exclamations as some took advantage of the confusion to perform a deed or two best attempted in such circumstances. A seashore muttering, another crack of breaking glass. The fogbound shadows became more distinct, and a clockhorse's excited neigh cut through the cacophony. A hansom drawn by a weary roan nag lumbered past, its driver perhaps thinking to escape the unpleasantness brewing behind him as metal-shod hooves struck the Scab with muffled splorching sounds. To be plying his custom so early, the driver was probably a gin-headed muddle, desperate for—

"Watch yourself, squire." Pico jostled him, not roughly. Clare returned to himself with a jolt, and found that they were now in the fringes of a crowd. Hike-skirted slatterns with frowsty hair, gin-breathing flashboys with their Alterations gleaming dully, barely respectable workingmen in braces and heavy boots, a kaleidoscope of sensation and deduction pouring into his hungry faculties.

The entire population of Whitchapel seemed to be awake and moving. Rumour and catcall bounced through the mass of people, and the going quickly became difficult.

Aberline shouldered through, brushing off no few enticing offers from the ladies – if one could call them such – and rough *Watch yerself*s from flashboy and workingman alike. Clare followed in his wake, more than once pushing away fingers questing for his pocket-valuables. Pico shoved through after him, and it was probably the lad's care and quickness that kept Clare from being *more* troubled by said pickpockets and thieves.

If Miss Bannon were present, she would no doubt find some more efficient way of working through the crowd. Clare winced inwardly. Could he not keep the damn woman out of his head for more than an hour?

"*Leather Apron!*" someone bawled, and the crowd stilled for a breath before . . .

Chaos, screams, Clare was lifted bodily as the mass surged forward. Pico's fingers dug into his shoulder once, painfully, before being ripped away, and Aberline vanished.

Oh, dear.

His jacket was torn and his foot throbbed where a heavy hobnail boot had done its best to break every bone in said appendage. Somewhere in the distance a clockhorse was screaming, equine fear and pain grating across the rolling roar. Clare slid along the wall, a splatter of warm blood already traced with thin green tendrils of Scab splashed high against the rotting bricks.

He coughed at the reek, consulted a mental map, and edged forward. Cast at the edges of the crowd like flotsam, Pico and Aberline nowhere in sight, he found the Scab underfoot thinning and eyed the buildings about him once again.

Logic informed him that he was near the ancient boundaries of the City, its oldest municipal heart. Under the Pax Latium, Londinium had been merely a trading village burned to the ground by one of Britannia's early incarnations.

The spirit of the Isle's rule had not looked kindly upon the Latiums. Still, the legions of the Pax could not be denied, and they rebuilt the town to make a replacement for Colchestre. Londinium's sprawl since then had been sometimes slow – and at other times marked by fire, not to mention rapine and plunder – but, on the whole, inexorable.

One could call the green filth that hugged Whitchapel's cobbles a similar inexorable creeping. For it seemed to be spreading, thin curling threads digging into the valleys between the stones, hauling hoods of slippery green film over the tiny hills. He followed in its wake, leaving the noise and crush behind, meaning to skirt its edges. Between here and Berner Street lay the bulk of the crowd. There was no penetrating its raging at the moment, but perhaps he could hurry along and come at the site from another angle.

As Clare was comparing his internal map and compass to the fogbound glimpses he could gather, he found that he had come too far, though there was a passage likely to take him in the direction he needed to—

A wet, scraping sound intruded upon his ruminations. He turned, peering through the damp blanket of Londinium's yellow exhalation, a raw green edge to its scent that reminded him of mossy sewage, if such a thing were possible. He supposed it was, in a dark place – what botanical wonder might grow from such rich, if foul, nutrition?

Crunch. Slurp. A humming, married to a crackling Clare

had heard many times before, during his acquaintance with Emma Bannon.

Live sorcery.

The fog drew back, for he was approaching, impelled by curiosity and a nasty, dark suspicion. There was another edge to the fog-vapour now, brass-copper and hot, that Clare recognised as well.

Blood.

He realised he was moving as silently as Valentinelli had taught him to, a flood of bright bitterness threatened to overwhelm him. The poppy, lingering false friend, opened a gallery of Memory and Recollection he could not afford to pay attention to, for a shape crouched before him, in a darkened corner of a square.

The gaslamp overhead was dark, burnt out or simply cloaked by the shame of witnessing what Clare now viewed.

A small, dirty, blood-freckled woman's hand, cupped but empty, fallen at her side. The rest of her was an empty sack, her head tipped away and a black bonnet tangled in its greying mass. Dead-white thighs, spattered with dark feculence, flung wide. A section of greyish intestine, poked by long thin spidery fingers. Those fingers returned to the abdominal cavity, plunged and wrenched, and brought a dripping handful up.

Wet slurping sounds underscored by a hum of contentment, like a child or a dog face-deep in melon on a scorching summer day. The figure – a coachman's cap tilted back at a jaunty angle on its blurred head, a red and yellow muffler wound around its throat more than once

– bent over again, the mending on its coat small, skilled needle-charmer's stitches. Its arm came up again, there was the bright flash of a knife, and the blade cut deep into soft flesh. It wrenched the resultant mass free as well and gobbled it.

A rushing filled Clare's ears.

The fingers were gloved, but no trace of blood or matter seemed to adhere to the material. They unravelled at each fingertip, for the thing had extra joints on each phalange. It rooted in the mass of the woman's belly again, and found what it sought. Still smacking its unseen lips, it lifted a clot-like handful – rubbery, pear-shaped, Clare knew there was no way he should be able to discern such a thing, but he knew what it was.

It is eating her womb. Dear God.

The crackling of sorcery intensified. The thing hunched, and its figure blurred more. Cloth rippled as the shape underneath it swelled in impossible ways.

Observe, Clare. Observe. Miss Bannon must know of this. You must give her every particular.

Blackness rippled at the edges of his vision. He was holding his breath, he realised, for the figure's head had come up, a quick enquiring movement. He was just barely in the range of its peripheral vision – assuming it had human eyes, which, he realised, was not at all a supportable assumption.

It was dark, and he was utterly still, hoping such immobility would hide his presence. Yellow fog swirled uneasily, a tendril sliding between Clare and the . . . *creature* – for nothing human could crouch like that, its knees obscenely high and its head drooping so low, its spidery extra-jointed fingers spasming as it twirled the knife in a brief flashing circle.

The Scab had arrived behind Clare, its wet greenness creeping forward. Tiny tendrils, their sliding almost inaudible under the wet smacking sounds of enjoyment. The quite illogical idea that perhaps some feral, inhuman intelligence was *guiding* the nasty green sludge occurred to Clare, the poppy still blurring the edges of rationality.

Now, when he needed sharp clarity most, it had deserted him.

Fascinating that the drug would linger, even in the face of whatever miracle Miss Bannon had performed upon him.

A rasping, as of a scabrous tongue over chapped, scraped lips. The creature's head made another quick, enquiring movement. The woman – the *corpse* – had worn, sprung-sided boots, and her stockings were soaked with foul matter. Her petticoats were mismatched, and torn to bits. Those white, white thighs, spattered, and the *smell*, dear God.

Had she suffered?

Does it matter at this particular moment? Stay still, Clare.

Valentinelli's sneer, echoing through dim memory. *Stay where Ludo put you, mentale, and watch.*

His lungs cried for air, even though the soup around the creature became foul enough to see. Or perhaps it was the blackness crowding his vision as his flesh, even if functionally immortal, reminded him that it did still require respiration and all its attendant processes.

A wet sliding. The Scab darted forward, and the creature tumbled aside, fluidly. Steam rose, and Clare caught a glimpse of the thing *under* its clothes. Cracked hide runnelled with scars, terribly burnt as if acid had been flung upon it, and two glowing coals for eyes.

One pale hand came up, the knife blade a star in the dimness, and Clare stumbled back. He felt the slight *whoosh* as the sharp metal cleaved air an inch from his face, fell with a tooth-rattling jolt on a thick carpet of oozing green. A hiss, a whipcrack, Clare's arm instinctively flung up to shield his eyes and suddenly a stinging, a patter of warm blood.

The thing fled, light unnatural footsteps tapping on cobbles, a grating sound, roof tiles shattering as they were dislodged and hit the ground.

Clare scrabbled for purchase, thick resilient slime dragging him as it retreated. It carried him a good ten feet before reluctantly releasing him, his jacket smoking against its caustic kiss and the wound along his forearm smarting as it sealed itself.

The gaslamp above the body burst afresh into feeble flame, and when he gained his feet, Archibald Clare bolted for its circle of glow, telling himself it was merely so he could examine the body in its uncertain light. Certainly not because he felt anything irrational, though his mouth tasted of copper and his sorcerously repaired heart laboured in his chest. It was merely the sudden activity, he told himself, not anything so illogical as *fear*.

And certainly not because as the Scab retreated, it made a low, thick noise, somewhat like a chuckle from a sharp-toothed mouth.

Chapter Thirty-Two

Error Of Provocation

Even if one could *find* a hansom when one required conveyance, there was always the chance of said hansom being as slow as a newlywed's knitting.

Since Mikal was loath to leave her alone, even though with her safely inside a hansom he could watch over from the rooftop road, she did not even have the luxury of a few moments of solitude to collect her scattered thoughts.

It was ridiculous; a Shield was not the same as *company*, the ancient brotherhood had been trained to discretion and a certain abnegation. And yet . . . it was Mikal.

His hand was on her wrist, perhaps to anchor her. Yet she was attempting no sorcery at all. Perhaps it was the odd, trembling feeling in her legs, the clawed healing sorcery working its way into deep layers of muscle, that made his gaze so worried and disconcerting at the same moment.

She freed her wrist and took the opportunity, in the small, jolting carriage, to push aside sliced black velvet and examine the bright red marks upon his torso. Not claw-marks, which was interesting, and yet the creature had to have been inordinately quick to strike so many times with a single blade. Those long, spidery fingers could wield such a blade, she thought, with amazing delicacy. Very sharp, curved just enough, possibly a physical focus for the creature? Knife and whip.

For a moment, an idea teased at the back of her consciousness. She waited, but it was not yet fully formed, and it retreated into shadow. "How very intriguing," she murmured, and settled back into the dingy seat-cushion. *I suspect I shall never look upon coachmen in the same fashion again.*

The hansom jolted, and the hunched, well-wrapped man holding the reins chirruped to the worn-down clockhorse. Emma's vision blurred for a moment, and she breathed out, sharply, dispelling the weakness.

She had lost quite a bit of blood, but so had Mikal. A Shield was exceedingly hard to kill, and yet if the Coachman had stopped to actually fully eviscerate him instead of simply slashing to bleed him out she might be adding his name to the list of her failures.

Obviously she had been judged the larger threat. Or the creature – though she had forced it into exactly the proper proportion of physicality, she still was not entirely certain what it *was* – had not judged her *enough* of a threat to warrant more than incapacitating Mikal for a few crucial moments.

Either way, it had been set upon her by the Prime she faced.

She knew the Primes resident in Londinium, of course; this bore none of their particular stamps.

At least, as far as she could tell.

Not *every* Prime on the Isle was known to her, she allowed. Yet this was indubitably native work. A sorcerer would not risk the possibly calamitous side effects of performing so major a Work in a country not his own.

Even if a foreign sorcerer wished to attempt such a thing, he would have to find a space enclosed by charter stones, and any Major Work, if it did not shatter said stones and make a very public noise, would be bounded by the charter boundary. No, a foreigner would not do such a thing.

Unless, of course, he was insane. She could not rule out that possibility. Still, even the most lunatic of Primes would baulk at performing such a Work in a foreign land and accepting the double risk of side effects and failure. True, one could spin the irrationality of such a Major Work away and evade the confines of charter stones, but there was always the chance of the flow returning, filling the one who cast it to the brim with warping irrationality, with all that would entail. A Shield could handle some overflow, certainly, but still, the risk was enough to send a shudder down any Prime's spine.

She was so sunk in her own reflections she almost missed Mikal's fingers closing about her wrist again. Irritation rasped under her skin, she reined it, sharply. "I am well enough."

"No doubt." His reply was maddeningly equable. "I am merely reassuring myself."

Of what? "I am not likely to expire at any moment. Unless it is with sheer pique."

"Comforting." He tilted his dark head, the gleam of his irises a peculiar comfort in the enclosed space. "There is unrest."

On many fronts. "Where, precisely?"

"Behind us, and before." He tipped his chin towards the hansom's front, but a glance out the night-fogged window told her very little. The d—d thing was slower than cold pudding.

Just as she was about to knock for exit – she could, she thought, at least have the benefit of moving her limbs freely if she were to be baulked at every turn tonight – the hansom slowed, and she gathered they had reached their destination.

Mikal's tension warned her, and as she alighted, she sensed the disturbance. A glaring note against the low brassy thunder of approaching Tideturn, and several of her nonphysical senses quivered under the lash of fresh tugging on already sensitised ætheric strings.

Whitehell Street was alive with much more activity than it should have been, and Emma sighed, squaring her shoulders. It would be too much to hope for that Aberline and Clare were about, ideally in Aberline's office – perhaps Clare had even returned to Mayefair, though no doubt if he thought she would be relieved at the notion he might well stay away. Of course Aberline should have been at his own home at this hour, or, more likely, trawling Whitchapel in search of trouble.

Perhaps Aberline had even been caught in the riot she had left behind. While that was acceptable, she sighed at the thought of just whom Commissioner Waring might inflict upon her as a replacement. Furthermore, if Aberline was in Whitchapel, it was likely Clare was caught in the riot as well.

He is as safe as I can make him. Do pay attention, Emma.

The hansom-driver's whipcrack as he guided his sorry nag away jolted her into stinging awareness. Tideturn was approaching; it would give her fresh strength to follow her course. For the moment, though—

"*Priiiiima.*" A long, slow exhalation, backed by a draining hiss.

Mikal, a knife laid along his forearm, was between her and the alley-mouth. Emma shook her fingers, a cascade of sparks dying as she realised there was little threat.

Her dark-adapted eyes discerned a skeletal shape, wrapped in tattered oddments. The head seemed too big for its scrawny neck, and the hair was scanty. It leaned against the alley wall, and its pupils were full of green phosphorescence.

Scab-eyes, full of an alien intelligence. Bare feet, horribly battered. The starveling had been driven far from

Chapelease, and it coughed weakly and croaked again. "*Priiima.*"

"I listen," Emma said, cautiously setting a gloved hand on Mikal's shoulder, easing him aside. He did not resist, though the stiffness in him told her it was a very near thing.

His nerves were on edge as well, it seemed.

"*It feasstsss on flesssssssh.*" The starveling's reedy little piping strengthened slightly. Impossible to tell if it had been female or male, or what its station in life had been. "*A new thing, under the sssssssun.*"

Questioning the starveling would only confuse it. So she waited, and it did indeed have more to say.

"*Where the beggar burned, where the dial ssspun, there you will find the road to your quarry.*" For an instant, the thing's skeletal face stretched, becoming broader, the mouth becoming a V. Sharp white teeth flashed, as Thin Meg spoke through one of her hapless, consumed slaves. "*If you find him, he will kill you.*"

Interesting indeed. Mikal was almost quivering, leashed violence ready to explode. She kept her hand on his shoulder, fingers biting in. Emma nodded slightly. "I hear." Brief and noncommittal.

"*You hear, but do not hear. You sssssee but do not sssssee. Find the dial again, ssssssparrow-witch.*" A trill of burbling laughter, and the starveling's body crumpled, twitching. Its eyes collapsed, thin green tendrils racing outwards from the corpseglow sheen they had been filled with, and the body settled into a twisting, jerking dance as Scab consumed it. It would not last long, here outside Whitchapel.

Or perhaps some vestige of it would, and Thin Meg's reach would eventually extend even this far.

That is a problem for another day. She unclenched her fingers, and patted Mikal's black-clad shoulder soothingly as the starveling's bones crackled, foul steam rising. Flesh liquefied, the ragged material clinging to it unravelling under caustic sludge, and soon very little was left.

Emma, however, forced herself to watch. She did not look away until there was merely a verdant patch of Scab, gently sending up thin curls of black steam. There were lumps in it – whatever fragments of rotted teeth the starveling had possessed would be last to dissolve.

"Very interesting," she said, finally. "What do you make of that, Shield?"

"A riddle?" A single shrug, lifting and dropping her hand. "Couched in a threat?"

"And wrapped in Scab." A cool finger of dread touched her nape, she shook it away with an unphysical flinch. "Come, let us see what has the Yard roiling like an anthi—"

Wait. The cool fingertip against her nape returned, and Emma spun, ætheric force gathered into a tight hurtful fist. She did not strike, though, for that end of Whitehell Road was deserted. Yellow Londinium fog was a blank canvas, and the streetlamps had begun to sputter, their carefully applied wick-charms fading as dawn approached.

Mikal stepped away, to give himself room in the event

of attack – and a chill throatless chuckle bounced up from the cobbles and the side-paving.

"Emma, Emma." The voice was faintly familiar, for all the simple, elegant sorcery used to disguise its location and waft it to her ears. "You are a wonder."

She opened her mouth to reply, but the brass thunder of Tideturn rose from the Themis, filling Londinium's crooked streets and teeming warrens. It descended upon her, stinging as she fought the sudden helplessness, and she could only hope the other Prime would not recover from the flood before she did.

And that the other Prime's Shields had not been given orders to strike at Mikal.

She surfaced in a rush, ætheric force filling her and staving off physical weariness for a short while longer. The world wheeled underneath her, and she found Mikal's fingers bruising-hard about her arm again as he held her on her feet. She exhaled sharply, setting her feet on solid ground, and spoke a Word.

"D'sk—zt!"

Ripples spread, ætheric force disturbed in concentric rings about her. They broke and refracted, her attention sweeping vigorously through, rather as her gaze would slide down a page of text searching for a wrong penstroke or figure. Or a dress, searching for inadequate stitching, a badly pinned fold, a—

There you are. Her heart leapt, sought to hammer behind her ribs, was ruthlessly repressed. Sorcerous force became

a clamp, a vice, but he slid aside. A knight's move on a
chessboard, but she batted the distracting thought aside. It
was a clever feint, but her instincts were still sharp from
years of hunting treachery at Victrix's behest. A clatter and
a ringing sound – his Shields would be Mikal's to deal
with now that she had full control of her senses again.

"Not so fast," came the directionless whisper again. "I
am merely visiting, dear one."

She found her voice. "Do not be so familiar, sir."

"Most harsh."

There were more clatters, breaking sounds, and Mikal's
tone was passionless, crisp authority ringing in every
syllable. "Come closer and die."

"No need." The voice shifted direction again. "I simply
wish to speak to your mistress. Hear me, Prima. There is
a new spirit rising."

She marked the words in memory, set them aside. Hot
water leaked from under her lashes, dawn's strengthening
scoring her tender eyes. The more force she expended now,
the worse they would smart. It mattered little. "I take it
you are the one unseaming frails in Whitchapel, sir."

"Necessary."

"Are you mad?" She allowed her voice to rise, as if she
had become distracted by his gruesome calmness. She was
close, so *close*, a few more moments and she would find
him. He had to be physically nearby, possibly within sight
of her.

Once she located the source of the sorcery distorting
his voice, she could strike.

"Not mad. Merely ambitious. Help me, Emma."

He is most familiar with me, this masked Prime. "I find you rather presumptuous, sir."

"Do you like bowing and scraping to that magical whore? Does it please you to be held in contempt for your power and pride? I know what moves you, Prima, and I offer you alliance. And more."

She remembered the nosegay left on another sorcerer's narrow bed, a bloodstain upon the floor, and the same trick used to distort a voice in a filthy Whitchapel yard.

This was most likely the same Prime who had mysteriously moved to aid her during the Red affair, and she had thought it quite likely he was another in Victrix's service.

Now, she wondered.

Did he know his sorceries weakened Britannia? What was his aim?

A new spirit rising.

"Do you think," she began, choosing her words with care, "that a new spirit will be more amenable than the old?"

"Amenable?" The laugh was chilling, and another sound of breakage intruded. What was he *doing*? "Perhaps not. But certainly weak, for a long while. And grateful."

It was one thing to privately compass such a thing, but quite another to hear her adversary speak of it so blithely. She relaxed, abruptly, all her considerable attention brought to bear. "You know little of royalty and rule, sir, if you expect gratitude from either to be of any duration."

"And you know far too much to be allowed to become my enemy."

Another shattering sound, Mikal's exhale of effort. What on *earth* was occurring? She did not open her eyes, every inward sense twisting through a labyrinth, following shifting ripples as they doubled back upon each other, circling ever closer to the artfully camouflaged well of disturbance that would be her opponent.

"Think upon it, Emma. Would you rather serve, or be served?"

I would rather be left to my own devices, thank you very much. But she did not reply, for her attention snagged on a single flaw in the pattern, a break in the ripples, and she *pounced* without moving, plunging through the matrices of ringing æther. Snake-quick, but he was quicker, and sorcerous threads snapped as he cast his coat of camouflage aside. More shattering sounds, and she was driven to her knees by the expended force of her own blow, reflected back at her.

Oh, how very droll. A great ringing in her head, she shook to clear it, her skirts ground against something sharp and powdery.

"Prima?" Mikal, longing to give chase.

"No." She could not find the breath for more. *If he has laid his plans so thoroughly, he will have an ambush waiting, and I shall not lose you to such idiocy.* She fumbled for her veil with fingers that felt swollen-clumsy. Blinking furiously, she found herself kneeling before a heap of . . . shattered tiles?

Yes, they were roof tiles, of the old red clay in use on the sloped top of the stable opposite, which was ringing with the sounds of clockhorse distress.

The equines did not like this Prime, or his works.

Mikal crouched easily at her side, his hands covered in vicious, shallow slices, bright beads of blood against thick pink dust coating his skin. "Good practice," he said, tilting his head as he deciphered her expression behind the veil. "Simple locometry, I should think. And triggered from afar." He pointed to another rooftop, with a half-shrug that told her it was his best guess. "Crude. But effective."

Had she possessed another Shield, she might have also possessed a chance of catching the mad Prime while one stayed to protect her from the assault of flung tiles. But now was not the time for guilt or remonstrance. Her stays cut, her dress was covered with dust; her skirts were torn and stiff with blood. Mikal was a sight too, rolled in Scab and covered with various substances. His coat was shredded, and the glimpse of his muscled belly crisscrossed with angry red scarring – perhaps irritated by his exertions in the last few minutes – caused her a pang she did not care to examine more closely.

"Your hands," she managed. Her throat was very dry. She coughed, delicately, and reacquired her customary tone. "And . . . oh, h—lfire blast it *all*. This rather changes things."

"They are already healing." He held up his palms, and the sight of his flesh closing, sealing itself under the not-quite-ætheric glow of a Shield's peculiar healing sorcery, sent another bolt through her. "See?" Very gently, as if she were a still a student at the Schola, unfamiliar with a Shield.

"Yes. Help me up." She was glad of the veil, and doubly

glad of his strength as he steadied her. Her legs were not quite as strong as she would like, and her left thigh trembled, on the verge of turning in its resignation due to savage overwork. She swore, vilely, in an exceedingly low voice, and was further grateful Mikal was accustomed to her somewhat unladylike language upon certain occasions. She finished with a few scathing terms directed at whoever had thought to tile-roof a *stable*, though she knew such a thing was perfectly admissible, and when she ran out of breath, she inhaled sharply and fully, shaking her head, feeling the quivering all through her. She had expended a great deal of the force Tideturn had flushed her with.

It was small comfort that her opponent had, as well.

Mikal paused, making certain the storm was past, then turned to glance down Whitehell Road. There was a great deal of to-ing and fro-ing: clockhorse hooves and excited voices through the rapidly greying fog. "What next?"

She took stock. She simply *hated* to be so dishevelled, but there was no help for it, and a few cleansing-charms would waste what limited strength of hers remained.

"Next," she said grimly, "we find Clare. And Aberline." She took advantage of the moment to tuck a few more curls away under her veil, and blinked away fresh, welling hot salt water.

"That sounds too easy."

Indeed it does. "It is only a first step, Mikal."

"And then?"

"Then," she continued, setting her chin and taking an experimental step, her heeled boot catching and grinding on broken tiles, "we return home to repair ourselves. Afterwards, I avail myself of every means necessary to track down this mad Prime and halt his insanity. I must confess, Shield, that I am more than peeved." She took another step, leaning on his arm, and found she could walk. "I am downright *vexed*."

"Heaven save us all," he muttered, and she let it pass, leashing her temper tightly.

This mad Prime, whoever he was, had finally managed to anger her. She would teach him the error of such provocation soon enough.

Chapter Thirty-Three

In Sorcery, As In Science

Clare wrapped his hands around the thick, glazed mug of fragrant tea. It was not a mannerly attitude to take, but he found he required the heat *and* the support to brace his shaking fingers. The ripples in the surface of the liquid could be blamed on the tension outside – and inside – Inspector Aberline's office.

Young Pico had settled himself, one hip on Aberline's desk, and was glowering fiercely at him. "She'll have my hide," he kept muttering, between inspecting the sleeves of his torn jacket and his similarly injured waistcoat, at great length.

Clare affected not to hear him, though he had been immensely glad to be found by the rufous lad, who bore all the marks of a rough passage through Whitchapel's burning riots. The entire Eastron End was still heaving with unrest, the Metropoleans simply standing at every major ingress and egress to keep the disorder from spilling out. As soon as dawn was fully risen, no doubt the Crown would send Guard and sorcerers to quell whatever unrest remained, no doubt with a bludgeon or two to sweetly kiss the pates of anyone whose excitable nerves failed to settle.

Fortunately, the riots did not seem to have been directed at the Yudics, despite the simmering in the more irresponsible dreadfuls and broadsheets. Clare was of the opinion that such uncivilised things as "pogroms" did not belong upon the Isle; however, uncivilised behaviours were piling upon his Englene with distressing regularity at the moment.

It was probably best not to engage upon *that* line of thought, though.

Inspector Aberline had left them to their own devices after calling for tea, and Clare was glad to be so neglected. For one thing, once Clare gave his report, he rather doubted Aberline would still be attached to the investigation of this affair, between Miss Bannon's dislike of his person *and* the rather dangerous complexion Clare's experience put on the whole chain of events. For another, Clare was bearing in mind – cowardly as it was to have such a consideration – that Miss Bannon, despite their differences, was far from the worst ally to have when faced with something of this nature.

He all but shuddered, thinking of the wet, crunching sounds and the creature's horrid, uncanny speed. Its . . . *irrationality*.

Aberline had been gone more than a quarter of an hour, yet the trembling in Clare's hands refused to settle. The Yard was alive with hurrying and excitement, but it was oddly peaceful in this half-buried room.

A mannerly knock, and the door was flung open with quite unnecessary force. In stalked an incredibly dishevelled Miss Bannon. Her colour was dreadful, her skirts were tattered and crusted with blood, ombre petticoats underneath likewise rudely treated, and her veil torn. Her hair was a tumble-mess of dark curls, and despite Tideturn's recent occurrence, her jewellery did not spark as it usually did when she cared to appear in high dudgeon. She was also coated with a peculiar pink dust Clare's faculties identified as from broken roof tiles.

Mikal, at her shoulder, was hardly in better form. His velvet coat was sadly misused, and the sight of flushed, newly healed knife-marks on his belly might have fascinated Clare had he not seen the knife and extra-jointed appendages responsible for such damage very recently. The Shield was coated in roof-tile dust as well, but underneath it was a layer of straw, dirt, and foul-smelling remainders of the organic sludge coating Whitchapel's floor.

Another shudder worked through Clare. His gaze held Miss Bannon's for a short while that conversely seemed an eternity, and he was comforted to find he did not have to speak for her expression to change, as she instantly compassed – or deduced – some measure of events befalling him since his leaving Mayefair.

She swayed, and Clare might have thought his own

appearance was such as to discommode her. Mikal stepped forward, she took his arm with alacrity, and Clare realised the blood on her skirts had to be her own.

He had already gained his feet. So had Pico, who was first off the mark.

"It ent as bad as it looks, mum." Did the lad actually sound *abashed*?

"I certainly hope not." Her tone was dry, and an immense relief. "Whitchapel?"

"Limhoss first." Pico shrugged when Clare glanced at him. "Not like she wouldn't guess, squire."

"Ah." She leaned heavily on Mikal's arm. The Shield swept the door closed with a curious hooking motion of his foot, and the slam reverberated. "Aberline's habits have not changed. Is that tea?"

Pico hurried to the service, and her gaze returned to Clare's. They studied each other for a long moment, again.

"Good morning, Clare. Your arm . . .?" Even her lips were pale, and her childish mouth had lost its usual determined set.

"Yes, ah – good morning, yes. A whip." Another shudder worked through him, he denied it. "The creature is deuced unnatural."

"Ah." She nodded, slightly, and Clare remembered his manners. He motioned her towards the huge leather chair. "It has been rather a trying night for both of us, it seems. Please, take the chair."

She chose instead the overstuffed hassock, and sank down with a slight grimace. Iron-straight, as usual – but something in the set of her shoulders told Clare she remained upright through will alone. He had rarely seen her in such a state before.

Pico brought her another thick glazed mug of tea. "No cream, mum."

"It shall suffice, thank you. Have you had breakfast, Philip?"

"No mum. Wasn't time. Shall I?"

"See what you can find us; I declare I could eat an entire barrowful of pasty, no matter how rancid." She nodded, then turned her attention to Clare as Mikal handed the lad the requisite funds. "Did you find Aberline's method of seeking connexions between crime and criminal enlightening?"

"Was that what he was about?" The faint, poppy-hazed memory of Aberline's lips moving, quite strangely, rose before him. "I confess I was rather busy with my own reflections at the time."

The door closed behind Pico, and Miss Bannon shut her eyes, inhaling the steam from her cup. She really was quite awfully pallid. Yet her dark gaze was as disconcertingly direct as ever when she reopened her lids. "I am about to tell you something which cannot leave this room, Archibald."

"I shall be discreet," he returned, a trifle stiffly.

"I do trust you shall, and yet I must make absolutely certain you understand the gravity of what I am about to say." She inhaled deeply, for all the world as if steeling herself. "I believe we are facing a mad sorcerer."

"Again?" He could not help himself.

She acknowledged the sally with a tiny, wan smile. "Who has managed to find a means of creating a new genius of rule, draining the resources of Britannia in order to do so. He means to supplant the ruling spirit of Englene, Archibald."

He dropped into the chair. Its stuffing groaned in protest, and lukewarm tea slopped out of the rather rustic mug. He frankly *stared*, and Miss Bannon was too busy gazing into her own mug to notice.

Mikal, near the door, was a statue with burning yellow irises.

"And I very much think," she continued, after taking a prim sip and grimacing slightly at the harshness of the reboiled tea, "that he has quite a chance of succeeding."

Whatever reply Clare might have uttered was lost in Mikal's murmured warning. The Shield moved aside, the door opened with far less force this time, and Inspector Aberline hurried through, his jacket as torn as Pico's but his sturdy shoes in much better order than they should have been.

He noticed the two new occupants of his office and stopped short, his greeting dying somewhere in the region of his throat.

"Dear God," the inspector said. "You two look *dreadful*."

Clare expected Miss Bannon to give the inspector short shrift. Instead, she surprised both of them by giving Aberline the same news, preceded by the same dire warning of secrecy.

His reaction was no less marked than Clare's own. The man actually staggered; Mikal was at his shoulder in a heartbeat, holding him up.

Miss Bannon took another sip of tea. "Take him to his desk, Mikal. The inspector thinks better in familiar surroundings."

It was, Clare supposed, rather a mark of Aberline's intelligence that he did not waste time on superfluous questions or doubt. Instead, he settled himself behind his desk rather creakily, as if afflicted by old age. Mikal glided to the tea service, and poured two more mugs.

Apparently the Shield required a cuppa for bracing as well.

"This is extremely grave," Miss Bannon continued. "If it becomes public knowledge – or even not-so-public knowledge – every sorcerer with enough ambition and corresponding lack of scruple shall attempt such a thing."

"How many, precisely, would that be?" Clare's hands had steadied. "I am not attempting any merriment," he added hurriedly. "I am very curious."

Miss Bannon's weary shrug made her ripped veil tremble. She had tucked it aside, and her red-rimmed eyes seemed to be troubling her as they often did. "All it takes is one among sorcery's children, in any country possessing a spirit of rule, to cause chaos. Strife will inevitably follow, and competing spirits may well tear the map of Europa asunder. Who knows what may happen in Chinois or the Indus? The New World may be safe enough, but the method of creating such a spirit can no doubt be adapted. In sorcery, as in science, the mere knowledge that such a thing is *possible* means sufficient determination will find a way."

"Bloody sorcerers," Aberline muttered.

"Quite." Miss Bannon's soft tone did not alter. "No doubt you are lucky to not be among their number, Inspector."

Aberline's response was even more interesting. His throat and cheeks turned an ugly brick red. "And curse you too, you foul-skirted little—"

"Inspector!" Clare had not meant to say it loudly. Nor had he meant to leap to his feet, whereupon he slopped lukewarm tea out of its mug again. "*Mind* yourself, sir!"

Silence filled the office. Miss Bannon sighed, and slumped wearily. To see her posture crumble was shocking enough, but to see Mikal's reaction – he dug his fingers into her delicate shoulder cruelly, hawk's talons on a small soft piece of prey – was simply dreadful.

She straightened, and took another mannerly sip of tea. "Much as I would dearly like to hold an accounting with you, Aberline, it serves much better to use your particular talents – including those you wish you possessed more than a pittance of – otherwise."

"And who are *you* serving?" Aberline's colour had not faded. "*Any* sorcerer could do this, you say—"

"It requires a Prime, not that such a distinction matters to *you*. Nevertheless, I shall overlook your rather base and certainly groundless accusation. I could retreat behind my walls and let this affair take its course. Indeed, I am rather tempted to. It *does not matter to me*, sir. To be perfectly frank, neither do you."

"Likewise," Aberline managed, in a choked whisper.

"Then we understand each other." Miss Bannon did not look at him. She studied her tea as if it held a secret, and Clare began to feel faintly ridiculous, but unwilling to sink back into the chair. His foot had stopped throbbing, and he realised with a certain relief that he was finally free of the poppy's effects.

Make a note, Clare. It lingers for hours. Acceptable in some cases, but not in all. His faculties shivered inside his skull, and the irrationality of the creature in Mytre Square receded into a mental drawer for further study later, if necessary.

His straightening and throat-clearing focused every gaze in the room upon him. "Such discussions do nothing to impede this madman," he observed. "Miss Bannon, it appears you have a plan, or at least the glimmerings of one. Be so kind as to tell us our parts."

"And you will perform them without question or qualm?" The words quite lacked her accustomed crispness. She sounded rather as if she doubted the notion.

"Yes," Clare said, immediately. "And so will the good inspector, and I do not even have to wonder upon your Shield's willingness. Each of us in this room is a loyal subject of Britannia. Besides, this affair is an affront to public order. One simply cannot have this . . . *thing* . . . running about, murdering as it pleases."

"And yet women die every night, in the Eastron End

and elsewhere, under the lash and the knife." Miss Bannon shook her head. "Forgive me, Clare. I am weary enough to be unnecessarily philosophical."

A curious tightness had built in his chest, as if he were suffering the angina again. "That is beyond my purview." Stiffly, as if he were in the courtroom again, Valentinelli a silent presence in the crowd. "But at least we may halt this *particular* killer. I saw it – this spirit, I presume, that would replace Britannia – feasting upon the body of its victim, rather as would an animal."

A peculiar look drifted over Miss Bannon's dirt-smudged, childlike, tear-streaked face. "Not so surprising . . . do sit, Archibald, and tell me everything."

"Glove, or Recall?" It was an old jest, and her shadow of a smile rewarded him. "I suggest we repair to our homes, Miss Bannon, and that you lift your ban upon Inspector Aberline at your dinner table. This rather has the earmarks of an extraordinary situation, and I assure you, for the moment Mr Finch is the last thing on Inspector Aberline's capacious mind."

Aberline made a strangled sound, but his assent was clear.

Miss Bannon studied Clare, over the rim of her mug.

He suppressed the urge to cajole, settled instead for bare, dry fact. "We could all certainly use a spot of rest; we shall no doubt perform our parts better for it." He paused, but she still wore that extraordinary expression. Thoughtful, certainly, her eyebrows arched and her head tilted slightly, bright interest in her gaze and her weariness put aside for the moment. "And we may discuss our next moves at your excellent table, where we are unlikely to be overheard or disturbed. It is the logical path to take."

"I am convinced, sir." She handed her mug to Mikal, who had turned loose her shoulder and hooded his yellow eyes, whether from exhaustion or displeasure was difficult to measure. "Inspector. Present yourself at my door at half past five; I dine early and I believe we should discuss some aspects of this affair privately before we do so. The moment you treat Geoffrey Finch with *anything* less than complete courtesy, I shall learn the look of your blood." She rose, arranging her torn skirts as smartly as possible. "Mikal? Two hansoms, please, engage one to wait upon Clare and Philip. Good morning, Inspector, and I wish you luck with clearing up this mess. Should you need to, invoke my name with Waring and he will prove slightly more amenable; I have already prepared the ground for you in that regard."

Her timing, as usual, was impeccable, for at that moment Philip Pico flung the door wide without bothering to knock.

He was loaded down with a burlap sack full of bulges Clare's fastidious nose identified as sausage and cheese, filched from Heaven alone knew where. "Had a spot of luck, I did. You'll have to use your own knife on the bangers, sir and madam – ah. We're leaving, then?"

"Quite." She had retreated into her shell of calm precision, and swept towards Pico in the manner of a frigate swooping upon its prey. "Half past five, Inspector."

The lad hurried aside, Mikal shut the door behind his

mistress, and Aberline let loose an oath Clare chose to ignore as Philip Pico's eyebrows nested in his hairline.

"And you feel emboldened to make a promise upon my behaviour, sir?" The good inspector was outright fuming, and had gained his feet with a speed that was, considering the night's events, quite astonishing. "Why, I've a mind to—"

"You use the poppy in the manner the Grecque oracles used laurel fumes, to amplify your small sorcerous talent in some manner." Clare nodded. "Quite interesting. I must confess I was not taking notes, but Memory will serve me when I have a few moments to gather myself. Such a thing is not quite legal, sir."

The strength visibly left Aberline's legs. He sat down again, heavily, and the choler had fled his cheeks.

"I have," Clare continued, "been acquainted with Miss Bannon for a very long time, despite certain . . . variances . . . in our natures. On one point, however, we are emphatically *not* at variance, and that is in our service to what I would once have called Crown and Empire, but am now forced to name a very odd brand of Justice." He realised he was pontificating, cleared his throat again. The tea was dreadful, and cold now to boot. "I have noted that the lady in question does not, as a matter of habit, overstate her case. Quite the opposite. I believe we are facing a threat to the very foundations of Britannia, and you, sir, are a loyal son of the Isle. It is your *duty* to be pleasant and forthcoming while pursuing this matter under Miss Bannon's direction, and should it become necessary, sir, we shall settle like gentlemen after its conclusion." He fixed the inspector with what he hoped was a steely, quelling look. "I would be quite happy to meet you."

"Likewise." Aberline exhaled sharply. "And if I am not pleasant and forthcoming, you may go to Waring and drop a word in his ear about my dissolute methods. Using such substances to artificially strengthen sorcery is quite scandalous."

"There are laws against such things, no doubt Miss Bannon would know them with a fair degree of precision." Clare gave up seeking to straighten his jacket. It was hopeless. "I would not stoop to blackmail, sir. Instead, I would appeal to your better nature."

"Funny, that." A sour, pained grin. "I am here, Mr Clare, because I have precious little *better nature* left. Now do leave my office."

"Gladly," Clare said stiffly, and suited actions to words.

Pico, his eyes suspiciously round, said not a word. He merely clutched his burlap burden and hurried in Clare's wake.

Chapter Thirty-Four

Very Precise Conditions

The broadsheets screamed, their ink acid-fresh. *Double Murder In Whitchapel*. *"Leather Apron"* – *Two More Victims!* Speculations of the most vivid nature shared the columns with sober warnings against Vice and breathless tales of the want and violence flourishing just as the Scab did. *On the Recent Events in Whitchapel*. Drawings of the discovery of the bodies – Clare was not mentioned. Naturally, his discretion would have been easy to secure.

Waring's discretion had required no little amount of threat and blandishment in equal proportion. The commissioner was in an insufferable position, and it matched his temperament roundly. Still, he was useful, and she was fairly certain he would be the public face for whatever triumph or tragedy this affair would end with.

Emma glanced over the headlines, directed Horace to

deposit the broadsheets in her library, and fixed Finch with a steady gaze. Her head throbbed and her filthy dress was likely to give her a rash, she *ached* to be clean. Duty demanded she deal with Finch's nerves first. "You are perfectly safe, Geoffrey."

"Oh, I know that, mum." He had only paled slightly upon hearing the news of their dinner guest.

"Do you?" She made a slight movement, checked herself. Finch regarded her steadily, and she searched his features quite closely.

Madame Noyon appeared at the head of the stairs and bustled down, clucking over the state of her mistress's dress.

Finch nodded, slowly. "Yesmum. I do." There was a hint of a smile about his thin mouth now. "Rather pity the man, mum."

Relief filled her; she turned to the next order of business. "Then you are a kinder soul than I. I shall leave dinner in your – and Cook's – capable hands. They shall be in the smoking room afterwards; *do* make certain there are the cigars Clare prefers. And your nephew as well. He has rendered very tolerable service indeed so far."

"Glad to hear it, mum." He waited, but she had nothing further, and he consequently glided away.

"A *mess*," Severine Noyon fussed, her plump hands waving as she arrived at Emma's side. "Good heavens, *madame*, what did you do to yourself? A bath, and quickly. *Chocolat*."

I could eat a hanging side of beef and ask for more.

"And something substantial for breakfast, Madame, I have a quite unladylike appetite."

"*Mais oui, madame.*" The round little woman in her customary black wool ushered Emma toward the stairs. "Catherine! *Chocolat*, and much breakfast for *Madame* in the solarium. Sunshine, *oui*, to make her strong. Isobel! *Attendez!*"

The house filled with efficient bustling, a bath was filled, and Emma sighed with contentment as she sank into hot rose-scented water. There was no time for soaking, however. In short order she was drawn forth, chafed dry, laced loosely into fresh stays and a morning gown. Fresh jewellery was selected, her hair arranged by Isobel's quick fingers, and *chocolat* was there to greet her in the solarium. A hearty platter of bangers, scones, fruit, and a bowl of porridge were arranged in her favoured morning spot, and there was a bottle of nerve tonic set conspicuously to one side of the *chocolat*-pot.

Emma suppressed a grimace. Cook must have glimpsed her in the hall, to be so worried about her condition. Her servants did sometimes make small gestures.

The solarium was full of strengthening morning light, filtered grey through Londinium's fog. Spatters of rain touched glass, puffing into thin traceries of steam when they touched the golden charter symbols scrolling lazily through the transparent panes, reinforcing and defending the fragility. The charm-globes over those of her plants more tender or needing training tinkled softly, each one a different note in the soothing symphony of morning.

Unfortunately, Emma's nerves were not soothed.

Hard on breakfast's heels Mikal also arrived, freshly scrubbed and only a little pale from the night's excitement.

Emma had settled herself, let him stand for a few moments, filling her plate with measured greed. Fortunately her domestics were accustomed to her sometimes-unladylike appetite, and she needed to replace a great deal of physical energy if she was to carry out her plans.

She had reached a number of conclusions in the past half-hour. Arranging one's person was often sufficient to grant one solutions to certain other problems – the physical actions of proper dress and accoutrement tidied the mental faculties as well.

When she finally deigned to notice Mikal, he wore a faintly troubled expression. Perhaps he expected what was about to occur, or at least the nature of her mood.

Emma took a small, delicate bite of scone. Crumbly, dripping with melting butter, *delicious*. "Attend, Shield."

His unease deepened, a low umber glow to Sight. "I attend."

She was, truth be told, a trifle relieved to sense his discomfiture. Perhaps she was not viewed as *predictable* just yet.

Good. "There is a conversation we must have, and I have decided this is the proper moment."

"Have you." It was not a question, and his flat tone warned her.

Her own measured softness was a similar warning. "Indeed. You performed some feat while I lay dying of Her Majesty's thrice-damned Plague."

"Prima—"

"*Silence*." Her weariness did most emphatically *not* mean he was given leave to interrupt her, and she was a little gratified to hear the resultant ringing quiet in the sunroom. Even the climate-globes had hushed themselves. "You were aware of the Philosopher's Stone, and my gift of it to Mr Clare."

"Yes. Prima—"

"Confine yourself to answering my questions, Shield. If I wish further detail, I shall *tell* you so. Now, you performed some manner of feat while I lay upon my deathbed. Correct?"

"Yes."

"Does that feat have any lingering effects?"

"Yes."

"On you, or on me?"

"Both."

"Ah." She absorbed this. Whatever effects they were, they had not affected her sorcery. The only evidence she had to build assumptions or guesses upon was her feeling of quite-uncalled-for physical well-being. And, let it not be forgotten, a certain resistance to injury that she had grown quite accustomed to with the Stone married to her flesh. It was not as complete as a Stone's protection. Her left thigh twitched, reminding her. "It would seem I am somewhat more physically durable than a Prime usually is."

"Yes."

"How extensive is this durability?"

He was silent for a long moment. "There is very little I may not heal you from."

Ah. That he *may not heal.* "Dismemberment and death, I presume."

"I have an hour's time after your death. Less, if your . . . body is not . . . whole."

Fascinating. "I presume this has somewhat to do with your ancestry."

A shrug.

She restrained her temper yet again, but her purpose had been served, so she changed direction. "How did you evade detection at the Collegia?"

"I passed their Tests." His chin lifted, and she decided his defiance was not yet of the punishable variety.

"Of course you did, or you would not have been . . ." An odd thought occurred to her. She set her implements down, poured herself a cup of *chocolat*, and settled into the chair with it. "You are rather wayward, as Shields go. One might almost say, headstrong."

"Disobedient."

Quite the word I would choose. "Are you?"

"No."

"Hm." She took another sip. The almost-bitterness coating her tongue had two sources, now. "This places rather a different complexion on our . . . relations."

"Have I given you cause for complaint?"

Ætheric force jabbed, a sudden hurtful compression. She had precious little of Tideturn's force available to her now, but her sorcerous Will clamped about him. He was driven to his knees, not slowly, but not as quickly as she could have otherwise.

"Do not," Emma said, very softly, "*presume*, Shield. I did not give you leave to ask questions."

Perhaps he would have made a reply, but she lifted a fingertip delicately from her cup. A short Word, and his mouth was stoppered as well.

The solarium's glass walls had misted with condensation, for a feral heat now moved through the small room. She loathed this display, but her plans now depended upon a few very precise conditions, and she was determined to arrange them to her liking.

"Mikal." She felt the struggle in him; he sought to rise but was held immobile. "You displease me, and as a consequence, you are Confined. *C—x'b*."

The Word drained her, savage exhaustion running through her marrow. Tiny nips of pain in her fingers and toes, but training held her still and apparently unmoved by the expenditure of force. The house shivered once, sealing itself against the egress of one of its inhabitants.

Until she decided otherwise.

Mikal's irises flamed yellow. He ceased struggling, and instead, watched her.

She returned her attention to her *chocolat*. "You are dismissed to your quarters, Shield."

Woodenly, his body rose, a marionette's jerking motion. Turning inward, she sought for any indication that he was merely acquiescing instead of compelled. None was to be found, and her jaw tightened as he disappeared.

His progress through the house was slow and stilted, and it was only when he was within his dark, narrow room

– she had left it to be modified according to his whim, and rarely entered it – that she relaxed her grip even slightly. The slam of his door flung closed with sorcerous force was the snap of a wineglass's stem in clenched fingers.

Emma blinked, her eyes watering. Surely it was only her Discipline. Tears would be a weakness.

She settled to her breakfast, eating with mechanical good manners. She needed the fuel. Her cheeks were wet, and her morning dress, black watered silk as wasp-waisted Prima Grinaud had always worn, was dotted with tiny splashes of hot salt water.

Now, many years after her graduation from under the grand magistrix's thumb, she wondered who – or what – Prima Grinaud had been mourning. Or if the redoubtable lady had entombed herself at the Collegia alive to escape the world outside.

How long would it be before Emma herself was tempted to do the same?

Chapter Thirty-Five

Quite Confident Indeed

Falling into bed, Clare decided, had done him a world of good. His Baker Street flat was indeed dusty, and full of the ghost of a Neapolitan assassin, but he had not cared. His narrow bed smelled rather vile, but he burrowed into its familiarity and was lost to darkness. Pico could have breakfast; Clare wished surcease.

He woke at early teatime when the lad nudged him, and made his toilet with the focused inattention bred of habit and familiarity. Pico exhibited the instincts of a good valet, fussing over Clare's clothing in a manner that was almost familiar. He also charmed the redoubtable Mrs Ginn, sweetening the landlady much more than Valentinelli had ever cared to. The tea tray was not up to Miss Bannon's standards, but Clare welcomed it nonetheless, and Pico confined himself to remarking upon the weather and asking Clare's opinion of this or that waistcoat.

It was not until their arrival at Miss Bannon's gate that Pico betrayed a certain nervousness, rubbing at his freshly shaven cheek. "*She* might not be happy."

"That is exceedingly likely," Clare allowed, straightening his cuffs. They were a trifle late – a hansom, he thought irritably, was *never* about when one needed it. "She does prefer punctuality."

"Well, at least you're alive, right? And in one piece. My heart fair gave out when you vanished in the riot, sir. Never been so glad to find someone in my life." Pico blinked sleepily, his sharp foxface pale as milk.

"No fear on that account," Clare murmured. The thought no longer sent a sharp pang through him. Quiet and familiar, Brooke Street nonetheless had the appearance of a foreign country. Perhaps he was simply seeing it with fresh eyes.

The cadaverous Finch took Clare's hat, and he was imperturbable as usual. "The drawing room, sir."

"Thank you." There was an odd sensation just under his breastbone. "Has, ahem, the inspector arrived?" *And were you prepared to face him?*

"Yes, sir." Finch's manner betrayed no discomfiture.

"He, erm . . . he did not upset you, Finch?" Enquiring in this manner was so bloody *awkward*. Finch gave him a rather curious look, and Pico coughed.

"No, sir." And that, apparently, was that. Finch motioned for Pico to follow him, and the lad went without question or qualm.

Miss Bannon had taken steps to reassure him, apparently. It was entirely like her.

The drawing room was full of clear, serene light, its mirrors dancing and the fancy of waterlilies and birch stems never more marked. There was even a subtle freshness in the air, but perhaps that was Miss Bannon's perfume – for the lady in question had settled herself on the blue velvet settee, and Inspector Aberline, his hands clasped behind his back, stood gazing into the fireplace, where burning coal had developed a thick white cover.

Miss Bannon's dark eyes had crescents of bruise-darkness underneath them, yet her posture was as straight as ever. She was markedly pale, though, and her mien was of careful thoughtfulness. Only her hands, lying prettily in her lap and bedecked with four plain silver rings on the left and a large yellow tourmaline on her right middle finger, betrayed any tension.

Inspector Aberline's colour was high, and his coat and shoes had been given a thorough brushing. He had obviously repaired to his home at some point, much as Clare had.

He was long to remember this moment: the peculiar brightness of the light, Miss Bannon's exhausted face, and Aberline's clenched jaw.

Clare braced himself, and shut the door.

Dinner was superb, of course, but Miss Bannon ate very little. Nor did she take anything but water. "It used its whip upon you?"

"Yes." Clare set his implements down properly, indicated the length of the slash along his forearm. "It seemed quite put out at being disturbed."

"What on earth *is* it?" Aberline wondered aloud. "What method was used in its construction?"

"I believe it may be similar to a Charington's Familiar." Miss Bannon took a mannerly sip of water from a restrained crystal goblet. The gryphon-carved table legs were not restless, as they sometimes were when her mood was unsettled. "At first the Prime would have to kill on his own account – Tebrem, for example, he chose to cut in a relatively sheltered location. Afterward the spirit could commit its own foul acts – but only at night, I should think. There is some physical focus for this spirit, some piece of it that held it to the fleshly world while sorcerous force was poured into it, and until it may walk in daylight that focus is vulnerable. Additionally, each location has become a taproot driven deeply into Londinium to gather force from the city's essence, if you will . . . I do wonder, why a coachman?"

"It seems rather . . . plebeian . . . for a ruling spirit," Aberline observed.

"The spirit of our time *is* rather plebeian." Clare savoured a bite of roast; the sauce held a flavour he had not yet defined. "One only has to take the train to ascertain as much, or a turn about Picksdowne."

"Some hold that Britannia was once the local spirit of Colchestre, a humble minder of pottery." Miss Bannon regarded her plate with a serious, thoughtful expression.

"Books which speak of such a possibility are difficult to procure, for obvious reasons."

"That's all well and good." Aberline had a remarkably hearty appetite, for a man sitting at table with a woman he regarded as a viper. "How do we stop this bas— ah, this mad sorcerer?"

Miss Bannon glanced at the dining-room door. Not for Mikal, certainly, for he did not attend dinner. Nor for Valentinelli. Pico would dine with the servants tonight; Miss Bannon had given orders.

Clare found his busy faculties turning these few facts about and around, seeking to make them fit together. There was a missing piece.

"There is . . . well, there is fair news, and foul." Miss Bannon ceased to even pretend to consume her dinner, pushing her plate back slightly with a fingertip. The tourmaline ring flashed. "Much was decided with the first murder. Every death since then has narrowed the possibilities, so to speak. Such is the way of such Works of sorcery. I believe this mad Prime is very close to achieving his purpose."

"That's foul enough news." Aberline took another mouthful of roast, and Clare, troubled, set his fork and knife down.

Miss Bannon's small smile held no amusement. "That was actually the fair news, Inspector. He requires a very specific victim for the culmination of his last series of murders, and I believe he has settled on one."

"Then how do we find her? Whitchapel teems with drabs."

"Finding her is my task," Miss Bannon returned, equably enough. "*Do* enjoy your dinner now, Inspector. Afterwards I shall inform you of your part in the plan."

Aberline's gaze darted to Clare, who began to have a very odd sensation in his middle. The inspector looked ready to object, and visibly thought better of it. "You are confident in your ability to find, out of all the unfortunates in Whitchapel, the one our Leather Apron has settled on?"

"Quite confident." Miss Bannon's faint smile bore a remarkable resemblance to a grimace of pain. She took another sip of water. "Quite confident indeed. I would explain, but sometimes a Work must not be spoken of." She pushed her chair back, and both men leapt to their feet as she rose. "My apologies, sirs. My digestion is somewhat disarranged. Please, enjoy the remainder of dinner, I implore you. The smoking room is ready for you afterwards."

Her black skirts rustled as she swept past Clare, and he discovered that she was not, as he had thought earlier, wearing perfume.

How peculiar. He settled once more into his chair, and Aberline applied himself to the roast in earnest. Finch was not serving tonight; Horace and Gilburn would bring the next course in due time. It was, Clare reflected, almost as if the house were *his*, and this a quiet dinner with a colleague or a fascinating resource.

"Have I been pleasant enough?" Aberline did not wait for a reply. "What do you make of that?"

"I am quite puzzled, I confess." *It is not like Miss Bannon to have a troubled digestion. Where is Mikal?*

"No need to let it ruin one's appetite. She dines well, if early."

Clare almost replied, but another thought struck him.

It will be growing dark, and Tideturn is soon.

His faculties woke further, seeking to weave together disparate bits of information and deduction. Some critical piece was missing, and had he not been so . . . uneven . . . lately, he might already have it. Feeling did its best to blur Logic and Reason, and he had indulged himself too far in its whirling.

Did it matter, what irrational act Miss Bannon had committed upon him? It did not, and with the clarity of Logic he could even see why she had not told him. She had been . . . right, it seemed.

The vegetables arrived, and the sorbet. Dessert, and the savouries were savoured. Clare grew quieter and quieter, and Aberline saw no reason to draw him out. It might have been quite a companionable meal, had Miss Bannon been there – and the inspector absent.

It was not until he had entered the smoking room afterwards, its familiarity somehow smaller and more confining, that Clare realised he had been quite a buffoon, and Miss Bannon . . .

. . . was gone.

Oh, bloody hell.

❊ *Chapter Thirty-Six*

Where The Dial Spun

Under a thick woollen blanket of vile buttery fog, Whitchapel seethed. The great hazy bowl of Londinium's sky had darkened rapidly, yet the Scab had not come creeping out. There was oddness about, of late. From Kensington to the Dock, Caledonia to the Oval – and beyond each of those landmarks – the great smoky-backed beast was curiously . . . hushed.

As if it dozed.

Yet the shadows in Whitchapel were darker than ever. Ink-dark, knife-sharp, and even those who spent their brief violent lives using every scrap of shade to pursue survival felt a cold breath upon their napes. The Scab always came out at dark; it was like Tideturn or bad luck. Since there was no escaping, one made merry in the face of the reek, downed what passed for gin to soothe the sting, and snatched what one could.

To feel the absence of that familiar terror was to feel worse than uneasy.

She kept to those cold, sharp shadows; a short slim woman with a shawl over her head. Oddly, she passed unmolested through the darkness. The flashboys never bothered to catcall or demand a toll for passage; the young, unAltered blades seemed not to notice her. Once in a while an unfortunate glanced at her, taking her for one of the sisterhood braving the thoroughfares and alley-ways early to earn a few pence for doss or gin, or more likely, gin and more gin, and one last customer before staggering to a narrow bed if one was lucky.

If not, well.

Leather Apron, they whispered to each other, and each time they did, the shadows deepened. As if the fear and trepidation, the passage of rumour, somehow . . . *fed* that darkness.

The glamour should not have been so difficult to maintain. Emma was weary, disciplined Will alone kept her upright. Tideturn would be soon, she could already almost-hear the approaching, brassy thunder. The dozing beast of Whitchapel drew her in, a tiny particle in its vast pulsing, and she was *quite* content to pass unremarked.

Finding and engaging a hansom had been the difficult part. Now that she was here, a minnow in deep waters, it was . . .

Well, it was as if she had never left.

It was marvellous, how the intervening years fell away. Struggle, striving, experience, all of it so many shed garments, dropping away from the nakedness of memory.

The starveling's words, of course, had made a mad manner of sense. *Where the dial spun, where the beggar burned*. How did Marimat know?

More importantly, who might have paid her enough – and in what coin – to divulge such things? Of course, the Scab witnessed black acts every night in Whitchapel. What might it whisper to the fallen creature in her pit?

Was her opponent Diabolic after all?

Emma put her head down. Tideturn grew closer, and she moved slowly because the rushing had filled her ears. Without Mikal, she would be blind and vulnerable when the golden flood from the Themis filled the city.

A sorceress, even a Prime, could vanish into the sinks of the Eastron End; but once, long ago, she had not feared these streets. Did a fish fear the water it breathed? The danger was simply air or rain, and when she had been plucked from it by the Collegia childcatchers she had suffered the gasping every fish performed when torn from its habitat.

Where the beggar burned.

She remembered, oh yes. A sweet-roasting stink, the crowd's laughter, flames. After that, her mother – was it correct to call that poor creature a mother? She had fallen far, the woman who birthed Emma Bannon; her respectable husband's death in a fire started by a drunken brawl meant poverty, shame, hopelessness. The men she gave herself to, while her youth lasted, had perhaps been kind enough. Some of them even spoke of marriage again, but it all came to naught.

Emma, grown weedlike and stunted in the Scab's blight, learning to scurry and steal. Learning the cant and argot of the flashboys and the unfortunates, cuffed when she was noticed and learning to be watchful. Inside her, a spark of ruined pride, and the deeper flame of sorcerous talent.

The last man – one of many, she thought perhaps he might have been a carter or even a flashboy, though she could not remember any Alteration on his gin-thickened frame – had announced his intention to sell Emma into a bawdyhouse if one could be found that would take a skinny brat, and the mother had turned on him with drunken fury. Whether it was because some spark of natural feeling for her burdensome child remained, or simply that said burden represented a shilling or two the raddled woman felt should not go to the broad-faced, rotten-toothed *monsieur* who had paid for their doss that long-ago night was unclear.

What was perfectly clear was the blade as it flicked, unseaming the mother's neck. A horrid scarlet necklace, a spray of crimson, and the burning in a thin child's chest had ignited.

The man had dropped the knife and screamed, beating at leprous-green flames erupting suddenly, sorcerously, from his skin and clothes.

A second beggar's burning, there in the reek and the dark. The child had run away, and been caught in a net other than the one she had feared.

Emma halted in a pool of darkest shadow, the glamour held close. Brass thunder unheard by most filled the air, and from one end of the street, a flood of ætheric force roared from the direction of the Themis's cold, deep lapping.

Tideturn.

Golden charter symbols crawled over Emma's skin. The shadows did not hide their flashing, but the malodorous passageway she stood swaying in was luckily empty of any witness. When the flood receded, she blinked and shook her shawl-covered head, expecting at any moment to feel Mikal's hand upon her arm and his quiet word of orientation.

Instead, she heard the scraping of tiny paws, a muffled squeak. Her skin sought to crawl, training clamped upon the waste of energy and it passed. She knew that sound, of course – grey whip-tailed rats with beady dark eyes, sensing in her stillness a possible weakness. The scuffing sounds retreated, and her nose wrinkled slightly, fresh strength filling her limbs.

She took careful stock of her surroundings again. Dorsitt Street was not strictly as she remembered it. Emma was uncertain whether this was a comfort or a danger, and took another few moments to study what she could.

Of course even squalor would change over time. It was still cramped and clotted with refuse, but the carts that had crouched here selling all manner of items were gone. The public houses thumped with the sounds of drunken revelry, but the flashboys did not congregate in their doors here, as was their usual wont.

Even a fast, murderous, well-Altered flashboy might well fear the creature hunting in Whitchapel.

A door slammed, raucous laughter and yellow gleams of gaslight spilled onto the street, and Emma drew further back into shadow. Three women, shapes very much like her own, with bonnets instead of shawls, hurried tipsily down Dorsitt toward the other ginhouse; the one in the middle had evidently been their first stop.

"Lea' *off*, Nan," one slurred petulantly, and her companions laughed.

"Black Mary, Black Mary," one chanted, with a lisp that spoke of missing teeth. "High-mighty *Jinnit*."

"I'us in France ons't," Black Mary retorted, hotly. She sounded young, and would be successful while that youth lasted. "I'en spek Westend dravvy, I may."

A small smile touched Emma's lips. The slurring song of Whitchapel cant was strangely soothing. *I was in France once. I even speak proper Englene, I may.* Perhaps her sad little story was told to draw custom. Or perhaps she *had* been to France, such a thing was not impossible.

Emma's slight smile faded as she turned away from Dorsitt, picking her way with care further down the passage. The smell, oh, it was familiar. Coal and grease, rotting vegetables, spoiled meat. Rancid, unwashed bodies crammed into tiny rooms, the sooty trembling flames of rag wicks in fat.

The only thing missing was the thick greenness of Scab.

She caught herself placing each foot carefully, a slip-sliding movement because the resilient ooze underneath should have been thick in this darkness.

She could feel ancient crumbling bricks, cobbles in some places. Her throat was so dry. The walls of the passage were only hinted at by some sense that extended around her, invisible fingertips brushing. Even her sensitive vision could not pierce this gloom.

Her skin chilled. Her skirts dragged; the quality of the cloth would outweigh the slight value of her life in this slice of Londinium. Yet she let the glamour unravel as she stepped carefully, shedding one more garment between herself and the past.

There, on the left, was the door. A window with a broken pane – it had been whole once. Another door had been cut further down the passage, but there was no true exit to the street save the one she had entered.

She remembered running, bare child's feet slipping in thick Scab, bursting out into the whirl of Dorsitt Street on a late-summer evening, gold in the air and the rank ripe heat simmering all of Londinium on a plate.

The child-catchers had felt the ætheric disturbance, a powerful burst of untrained sorcery. Given chase, and finally brought her to bay in a blind court not far from here. How she had struggled, and bit, wild with terror, thinking only *He has come to kill me too*.

The door was locked. Emma cast a glance over her shoulder, then regarded the broken window for a few moments. A whispered charm, a breath of sorcery, and the lock yielded. She felt a twinge at her trespassing, set it aside. Foxfire light glimmered from her necklace, just an edge of illumination to show the dimensions of the sad little hole.

Where the dial spun, the starveling whispered again, and to Emma's relief, the room was changed. A different bed was placed in an opposite corner, and the shabby hob had a cheapmetal kettle on it and nothing more. The floor-boards were familiar, though a dark stain had been scrubbed away in one rotting corner.

She went unerringly to that corner. Knelt, her fingers just as deft as they had been in childhood. *Perhaps*, she thought, and her lips shaped a different word.

Please. Let it be gone, and me a fool.

If what she sought had vanished, she could call Marimat the Fallen's whispers a feint, and retreat into her house's safety. Let Clare think what he would, let Aberline go his merry way, and make to Mikal some manner of restitution for the display she had forced him to endure.

Leave Victrix – and Britannia – to her fate. At this juncture, such a thing would please her, and if she felt another murder within her frame, she would view it as a last unpleasant reminder that she had once served one who secretly despised her.

Magical whore, the mad sorcerer's disguised voice sneered, and the term was so familiar. It teased at memory, but she set it aside. That was not the slice of the past she wished to consider at the moment.

It took a special pressure to lift the edge of the

floorboard, and her hand wormed into the space underneath. Her fingers touched rotting cloth; she shut her eyes and fished the small thing out, settling back on her heels.

It was still wrapped in a scrap of cambric, the threads so rotted they fell apart at her gentle touch. Her skirts would no doubt collect all manner of dust and unwholesome things from the boards, but she did not care. Her fingers trembled as she brushed thin fabric aside, and the pocket-watch, its casing grimed with the passage of years under the boards, gave a slight gleam.

Its chain was short, and it was no doubt a corpsepicker's bargain, but it had seemed so flash and fine to a young girl, once.

They had both been in a stupor when Emma's fingers had relieved the man of his watch. She had slid it into the hiding place, intending to pawn it for perhaps enough pence for a pasty, or even a flower for her weeping mother.

But when *he* woke, he had noticed the theft, and threatened to beat them both to a pulp. The mother wailed that she had been next to him the whole time and her daughter said nothing, despite being prodded and her child's shift searched thoroughly. Shivering, she had heard the man pronounce his doom: he'd get his pence back from a bawdyhouse, if they would take such a stick of a thing.

Then the cries, the red necklace, the fire.

Emma rose, a trifle unsteadily. The watch hung from its short chain, and she twisted her fingers to spin it, feeling the old childish fascination with its motion. If she wound it, would it work?

Who could tell?

Where the dial spun.

Old guilt rose, its edges sharp, and it was almost a relief to hear the soughing of air moving as the door drifted open.

She stood, very still, watching the spinning. Who cared how Thin Meg had known this secret? What mattered was that Emma had been brought to exactly the right place, and of her own will.

He approached, softly. Did he think her unaware?

When he was close enough, she drew in a sharp breath. "All in, all in," she said softly, as if they were children playing the perpetual game of tag in the alley.

He halted for the barest moment. Approached, step by step. "Why have you ventured here, Emma?"

His voice, familiar, teased at her memory. She held very still. *Come now. Stop speaking. I am offering myself; let it be quick.*

"You are so clever, my love," a dead man breathed in her ear, and he clamped a foul-smelling rag over her face. "Too clever by half."

Emma's body slipped her control for a moment, but any struggle was useless. The clot-thick vaporous substance on the rag filled her lungs, and the effect, purely physical, was perhaps the only one that would deprive a wary sorceress of her senses.

She felt, after it all, a certain relief.

Then, darkness.

Chapter Thirty-Seven

And If Not, Vengeance

Aberline hammered at the interior of the front door of 34½ Brooke Street, using quite colourful language, while Clare made himself comfortable on the stairs and, in defiance of all good manners, puffed at his pipe. No servant hurried to find the source of the noise; Miss Bannon had no doubt given orders.

There was no use in seeking to escape until the mistress of the house released them. Little good would be done by exhausting oneself as the good inspector was currently doing, but at least if the man was shouting and hammering he was exactly where Clare could see him.

It was the other man who gave Clare some pause.

Mikal had appeared in the smoking room just after dinner, looking grey and drawn as he did on those rare occasions when Miss Bannon left him to cool his heels.

Just behind him had drifted the cadaverous Finch, who did not even deign to glance at the glowering inspector. Instead, he had presented Clare with a folded missive of familiar creamy paper, a delicate, feminine hand – also familiar – on its outer flap, his own name traced with her usual care.

The note inside the folds was extremely simple.

Come and find me.

Which was all very well, Clare thought, but locking them inside her house so deliberately was rather a bar to her stated wish.

The inescapable conclusion, since it was unfathomable that Miss Bannon had not planned this to a fare-thee-well, was that she intended them to issue forth . . . but not quite yet.

So, he smoked. He had taken the precaution of changing from dinner-dress into something a fraction more suitable to chasing a sorceress across night-time Londinium. Philip Pico, having apparently arrived at the same conclusion, had done the same. Or perhaps he had not dressed for dinner at all.

The rufous youth had settled himself easily on the stairs below Clare, and gone still as a stone. He eyed the inspector's display with an air of faint condescension, but when his gaze drifted across the silent, haggard Mikal, it became troubled indeed.

Tabac smoke, fragrant, drifted up and was sorcerously compressed near the ceiling into neat spheres that bumbled off in search of a chimney. Clare had arrived at a number of conclusions, but the nagging sense of a missing piece would simply not cease.

Aberline finally left off hammering at the door. He whirled, and fixed Mikal with a baleful glare. "*You*. Where is she? Why, I've a mind to—"

"Cease your chatter," Mikal returned, amiably enough. "Or I shall *make* you."

Clare puffed again, thoughtfully. Quite a riddle the lady had posed. Quite.

Aberline clearly thought better of provoking the Shield any further; he cast about for a new target. "Where's that knife-throwing son of a whore? *Finch!*"

"Do be quiet," Clare remarked. "And *do* leave Mr Finch be. In any case, he will not answer your summons. There is only one being who commands that man, and she is not at home." He puffed again. "When you have calmed, sir, we shall proceed."

"Proceed? We are sitting here while . . . what on earth can she be doing? What could have *possessed* the bit—"

It was, strangely enough, Pico who interrupted. "*Watch* your tongue, guv." He actually bounced to his feet as well, and his hands were fists. "I've had about enough of your high'n mighty."

Clare sighed. "This solves nothing."

Whatever Aberline might have replied was lost in a soughing sound.

Clare tilted his head, and the massive clock at the end of the entry hall spoke. In the midst of its chiming, a subtle pressure drained away, and Clare gained his feet with another weary sigh.

Midnight, precisely, and the crackle of live sorcery could only mean one thing. "I believe the door will open now," he observed. "And our murderer will strike again tonight. I further believe Miss Bannon rather desperately requires our aid."

Mikal nodded. "Yes." The word was chilling in its flatness. "The house is no longer sealed. I am no longer Confined. Yet I cannot sense my Prima."

"Bother." Archibald jammed his hat firmly onto his head. "I had hoped you could find her in some sorcerous manner."

The Shield looked positively sick under his dark colouring. "If she is . . . alive, I could. But *I cannot sense her.*"

Clare stared for a moment. Aberline's mouth hung open, and the inspector blinked several times. Mercifully, he remained silent.

"She could have set the house and my Confinement to release at this moment," Mikal continued. "Or . . . not. It would release if she . . ."

Clare cleared his throat. *Down, Feeling! Logic. Logic must serve here.*

But . . . *Emma.* She had been so pale, and taking only water. So certain she would have no trouble finding the next victim.

She betrayed a certain familiarity with Whitchapel. The listening look she wore, when inside its environs. Her origins, however obscure, were no doubt of a sort to make her familiar with Want, Vice, Crime, and other unsavouries. She was also connected to Victrix, and hence Britannia, in numerous ways. Not to mention her rather incredible ability to find a treasonous criminal once she set herself seriously about it.

It would make quite a bit of sense for this lunatic sorcerer to see her too great a threat to continue breathing.

It would *further* make quite a bit of sense for Miss Bannon to wave herself before such a man in the manner of a rag waved before a bull to engage its fury.

She had such a distressing habit of disregarding her personal safety.

Emma. For God's sake. Do not . . . do not be . . .

He forced himself to think upon it, the cold tearing in his vitals savagely repressed. "She is not dead," he said, finally, conscious of the lie. He told himself it was necessary, that the Shield would be of more use if he held to faint hope. "She is most likely incapacitated in some manner. Pico, my pistol." He accepted the weapon with a nod. "Now, gentlemen, I trust everyone here sees the course we must take."

"I am afraid I most certainly do *not* see—" Aberline began.

Clare fixed him with a steady gaze. "Your knowledge of the worst sinks in Whitchapel, where I have deduced this monster is no doubt hiding, is very valuable. We may even, should we be forced to, find a poppy den and hope your small talent at sorcery will help. I am *quite* prepared to be ungentlemanly about this, sir, and furthermore, Mr Mikal will take it badly should you give anything less than your full effort to finding our sorceress."

Aberline had gone the colour of milk. He glanced at Mikal, opened his mouth, shut it, and nodded. There was a fire in the back of his dark gaze that promised much trouble later.

At the moment, Clare did not care one whit.

Emma. He had to examine his pistol, critically, as if assuring himself of its readiness.

Bulldog. Made by Webley, very fine. Gift from Emma, to replace the pepperbox. Fully loaded. His faculties replayed the loading procedure, but just to be certain, he checked the chambers. Five shots, .450 Addams cartridges, and there were more in his pockets, should he need them. *For emergencies,* the sorceress had said with a smile, presenting him with the walnut box.

He swallowed, very hard, and slid the weapon into its holster. A moment's work had it buckled to his belt, and the familiar weight was not nearly soothing enough.

Archibald Clare drew himself up to his full, if somewhat lean, height. "Pico, lad, go and tell your uncle we shall be taking the carriage, if Miss Bannon left it for us. On the shelf in my workroom you will find a decent purse for just such occasions as this. Mr Aberline, come with me; you shall be clothed properly for our descent. Mr Mikal—"

"I know my part," the Shield replied, and turned on his heel.

"If you feel any inkling of Miss Bannon's, er, location—"

"You shall know. And if not . . . vengeance." He disappeared to the far side of the stairs, no doubt heading for the stable to rouse the coachman. "Hurry."

"Never fear," Aberline commented sourly. "The sooner this is finished, the better."

"I hope she's alive, Inspector." Clare paused. "For your sake."

The man actually bristled. "Do you mean you—"

"No, you need not worry about me. You do, however, need to worry about Mikal. Come, let us find you more suitable cloth."

"*Stop!*" Aberline cried, and almost threw himself from the carriage. He would have landed ignominiously face-first on cobbles if not for Pico's lightning-quick reflex to grab at his jacket; Harthell cursed roundly as he pulled the vehicle to a juddering halt. The clockhorses, unhappy at being roused at this hour and further unhappy at such treatment, let their displeasure be known.

"*Canning!*" Aberline hailed what Clare, blinking, perceived to be a hurrying shape on the pavement. "I say, man, halt!"

"What the devil – oh, it's *you*." The voice had an odd lilt, possibly Eirean. "Where have you been? Don't you know?"

"Obviously I do *not*, sir." Aberline motioned the man closer. "What news?"

Clare squinted, and made out what had to be a fellow inspector. The man's hat plainly shouted he was of the

Yard, and his serviceable shoes held steaming traces of Scab's kiss. He was bandy-legged and thick-necked, and when he stepped under a sputtering gaslamp, Clare could see bright blue eyes and a reddened nose. Fog-moisture clung to his jacket and hat, and the steaming from his shoes added vapour to the choking mist.

How very odd. He had not, in his small experience of the organic sludge coating Whitchapel's floor, seen it behave in just this way.

"Another murder. The worst yet. Dorsitt Street. And the Scab . . . well."

"The Scab? What of it?"

"It hasn't come out. And where it has, it behaves oddly."

"As if it ever behaves in a different manner." Yet Aberline looked troubled, and he did not pursue this fascinating tidbit. Instead, he turned the conversation in quite another direction. "Where are you bound?"

"I'm to the Yard to report to Waring. There was some chalk on a door – something about the Yudics. He ordered it rubbed out, but too late. The entire Eastron End is up in arms again. There's a Yudic church burning, mobs looking for Leather Apron all the way to the Leae. Even Soreditch is restless."

"The murder in Dorsitt?" Aberline prompted, as the horses stamped and champed.

"It's dire, Aberline. It's inside a doss, for once, but that meant he had time to do his work. A real artist, our ripping lad."

"How bad is it?"

A bitter laugh greeted this query. "I'd say, don't dine before you view it, sir. Everyone's been at six and seven trying to find you, sir. Shall I tell Waring you've been sighted?" His tone plainly said that he expected a refusal of this generous offer.

Surprisingly, though, Aberline nodded. "Do, there's a good fellow. Tell him I am at the scene already. Dorsitt Street, you say?"

"Aye, between the Bluecoat and the Britannia. The ginhouses are near to empty serving the thirst of every blighter in the Eastron End come to view the scene, and it will only get worse. I'd use a whip for the crowds, if I were you." A half-bitter sound of amusement, and Canning touched his hat. "I'll be off then. I'll tell Waring you were already there. Fine carriage, by the by."

"Do you think so? Many thanks, sir, and regards to the missus."

"You should perhaps think on your own, there's a letter on your desk from her."

Aberline winced visibly. "I see. Good evening, Canning."

"Good evening. You'll need one." The man took himself off at a trot again.

"Dorsitt Street, as fast as you may," Aberline called to Harthell, whose reply was a snort saying that *he had heard, thank you, and mind to shut the door*.

Clare eyed Mikal, who had not moved during the entire exchange. The man's eyes were downright unsettling, catching some flash of random illumination and glowing gold. His hands had been loose and easy on his knees, but they had slowly tightened over the duration of the conversation. Aberline settled back next to Clare as Pico shifted a trifle uncomfortably.

I would be uncomfortable too, next to that stillness. Clare cleared his throat. "That does not sound encouraging."

Aberline made as if to wring his hands, thought better of it, and sighed deeply. "I have never heard Canning refer to a crime in quite such terms before. No doubt our mad sorcerer has surpassed himself."

The whip cracked and the carriage jolted forward. Clare still examined Mikal closely. The Shield's gaze had fixed on a point over Aberline's head, and the only thing more disconcerting was the slow unclenching of his fists.

"You did not ask for particulars," Clare noted, finally. *A description of the victim might aid us at this moment.*

Or are you afraid?

"I did not think it wise." Aberline dusted an imaginary speck from his borrowed trousers; the carriage jolted them all most rudely. "We shall see what Leather Apron and his creature have left us soon enough."

Chapter Thirty-Eight

You Will Give Me The World

A chanting, low and sonorous, a faint brushing against her skin as ætheric force crawled over her. She lay perfectly still, returning to consciousness much as a trickle might fill a teacup.

She was not in her bed.

How odd. I cannot move. Sorcerous and physical constraints, certainly, and a Prime's displeasure at being held so would no doubt begin to fray her temper before long. The said fraying would loosen her control in short order, and she would quickly become a frantic struggling thing, robbed of much of her mental acuity.

Unless she resisted.

Do as Clare does. Observe. Deduce. Analyse. I am only temporarily helpless.

It did not help quite as much as she might have wished.

She slowly raised her eyelids, training twisting its sharp hold deeper into her physical frame as her pulse struggled to quicken and her breathing sought to become shallow sips. *None of that now. Look about you.*

Her eyelids were not paralysed, though she could not turn her head. At first there was only an umber glow, but as she blinked, testing the confines of the restraints for any weakness in a purely reflexive unphysical movement, shapes became visible.

There was movement, and the chanting came to a natural end, dying away.

A slight hiss. The movement became a gleam on a knife blade, and Emma studied the tableau before her.

A black-clad back, one shoulder hitched high with a heavy hump upon it, claw-like gloved fingers. He stood before a large, squared chunk of obsidian, the lighting from wicks floating in cuplike oil-lamps instead of proper witch- or gaslight.

The wall she could see was of rough stone, the masonry old enough to be the work of the Pax Latium. The sounds were odd – what reached her through the distortion of shimmering sorcerous restraints echoed as if they were underground. Of course, Londinium's first burning and rebuilding had been courtesy of the Latiums. Even Britannia had not resisted them completely, or forever.

The shape before the obsidian stone – it looked much like an altar, she realised – turned with a queer lurching motion.

At first she feared the sorcerous restraints were affecting

her vision, or the foul substance he had used upon the rag had lingering aftereffects. But no. Everything else was in its proper, if shabby and worn, dimensions.

She watched his painful movements. Above the black altar – light fell *into* the stone and died, no reflection marred its surface – was a shifting, smoky substance hanging, moving in time to a slow beat very much like a sleeping pulse. She studied it more closely, and caught flashes.

Coal-bright eyes, extra-jointed fingers. Dead-pale flesh peeking through shabby coat and worn, knitted gloves. Neatly coiled atop the obsidian was the whip, the sharp barbs at the end of its long fluid flow pulsing as well with sickly blue-white flashes. The knife, slightly curved by much whetting, stood, quivering upright, balanced on its point. Occasionally, the smokelike suggestion reached down to stroke the rough, leather-wrapped handle, and a bloody flush would slide down the gleaming blade.

Ah. I see. It was a marvellous thing, to bring a spirit from nothing in this manner. All it took was the will to do so, and enough ætheric and emotional force. The trouble was, most such spirits tended to be malformed things, working only in a very limited way, as a golem or a Huntington's Chaser or even a *necros vocalis*.

Sorcery's children were cautioned to never let such a spirit grow too strong, for the trembling border between slave to a sorcerer's will and sentience could be breached after enough time and force had become the creature's ally.

And then . . . well. Better to create a new slave than have one grow too powerful and turn against its Maker.

Yes, she decided. Quite interesting. It was most certainly a Promethean. Difficult to create, a thousand things could go awry during the process. Also, it approached sentience very quickly. Why had she not thought of this possibility?

Because a sorcerer would have to be mad to attempt such a thing. It had to be fed, frequently. When those of Disciplines blacker than the Diabolic, malformed but drawing breath just the same, had achieved the status of gods among some benighted primitive clans, the accepted food for such constructs was the most tender and innocent of all, plucked from grieving mothers' breasts. Without such regular nourishment, the spirit would turn on its creator and roam free, gathering strength from casual, wanton murder. The æther around it would tangle and grow clotted, and it would eventually collapse under the weight of that curdling. Some whispered that the sorcerer queen of Karthago had created such a spirit to wage her desperate war against the Pax Latium, and that the blight surrounding that fabled lost city was a result of her death before she could bring it to a second, monstrous birth.

For there was one thing that set a Promethean apart from other created spirits. It could, if certain conditions were met, merge with its creator, and become something . . . *other*. Emma strained her well-trained memory, for once ignoring her own pulse as it quickened. She had, of course, under careful Collegia tutelage, studied several pages of books those of Disciplines other than the Black could not open. Her own Discipline, deeply of the Black, twitched slightly inside her as it recognised something akin to it.

That is why, when I disturbed its feeding-site, it became attuned to me. How very interesting.

"She's awake." There was a harsh, grating laugh, and the hunched figure straightened, stretching. Creaks and crackling, bulging and rippling, and parchment-pale hair fell to his shoulders. A terrible raddled face slowly came forward into a circle of smoking lamplight, and she recognised him afresh. "And so prettily, too."

She knew him. How could she not? The questions that had nagged at her for so long now had an opportunity to be answered.

Broad shoulders, one hitched much higher than the other. The black-clad chest bulged obscenely on one side, the cloth cut away to show a latticework of Alteration: arched ribs of scrolled, delicate iron and the dull reddish glow of a stone, curved on one side and flat on the other.

She recognised that as well.

For before she had wrenched it free of her flesh and married it to Archibald Clare's, she had borne one just like it. A Philosopher's Stone, made from a wyrm's heart. Wyrms were held outside of Time's river by their very nature, and a youngling's heart was powerful proof against most ills.

So he *had* possessed two after all.

Llewellyn Gwynnfud, Lord Sellwyth, returned from the dead, creaked as he bent over her.

Now she could see the thin, fleshy filaments spinning out from the ruins of shattered ribs, the wet gleam of organs rebuilding themselves under a carapace of Alterative sorcery. His gloved fingers reached down, most of them broken stubs coming to small points as they regrew, and he reached through the blurring of sorcerous restraints to touch Emma's hair. It was an oddly gentle caress.

Had he ever bothered to remain so tender, he might have had Emma's loyalty, instead of a young queen who would eventually insult her past bearing.

She sought to speak. Nothing came out – of course, she was gagged and silenced. A trickle of saliva slid from the corner of her cruelly bound mouth, pooling under her cheek. She could feel splintered wood underneath her, a hard surface holding her up from the floor. From the wet sound he made when he moved, she supposed she should be grateful.

"And she recognises me," he croaked. No wonder he had gone about muffled up to solicit the Coachman's initial victims. "You should see your expression, darling one."

Her brain began to race, furiously. The beginning of the Plague affair; she had felt another Prime in Victrix's receiving room. She had assumed – oh, how Clare would chide her for that! – it was one of Victrix's creatures, as she herself had been. The sense afterwards she had of being watched, the unseen hand that had aided her in unravelling the whole affair . . . of course, he would have wanted her safe and whole for his own plans. How he must have laughed. Perhaps he knew she did not possess the *other* Stone at this moment. Did he guess? What could he know?

The most likely solution was that he had bargained

somewhat with Thin Meg. Or found some means to exert some pressure upon that unlovely creature.

What could such a Prime, who had been torn apart by his own sorcery after his erstwhile lover had literally stabbed him from behind, not accomplish, if he possessed the will to rebuild his shattered body?

The pain must have been incredible. She had found only bleached bones scattered about the tower in Wales where he had sought to bring one of the Timeless to the surface. Had some of them been his, twitching towards each other as he gathered strength?

What must he have *felt*?

"I have followed your career with much interest." His teeth had regrown, straight and pearly. His lips were scarred, but the scars would no doubt recede, given enough time. As his body regrew he would no doubt shed the Alterations. Had he performed them himself? The Transubstantive exercises would surely yield to his patience, if not his skill or Discipline. "You broke my heart, you know."

Oh, I doubt that. You were dallying with that French tart and later with Rudyard, while you amused yourself with me. Had you been honest, we might have made an agreement. And had you not accused me of a hand in said tart's death, I may have forgiven you. She calmed her pulse, drew in what air she could slowly and deeply. Thankfully the sorcerous restraints kept her nose clear; he did not wish her to suffocate.

Yet, she reminded herself.

"Do you wonder why I have not simply killed you outright?" His chin bobbed as he nodded, fat snakes of his matted hair brushing his shoulders with avid little whispers. "You have been well guarded for a very long time. That thing you keep as a Shield, oh, my dear. Quite resourceful, and quite dangerous." He smiled fully, a tear in his cheek widening before sealing itself with a wet sound. "But that is *not* the reason. I have plans for you, my love. Wonderful plans. I am going to give you a gift." The smile widened. "And then," Llewellyn Gwynnfud continued, "you will give me the *world*."

Chapter Thirty-Nine

Once The Temptation Is Large Enough

The tiny little court growing from Dorsitt Street was crammed with bluecoated bobbies and others, jostling and elbowing. It was better than the crush outside, where it seemed every criminal, unfortunate, or poor tradesman in Londinium had come to gawk. Aberline's authority carried them to a hacked-apart door guarded by a very pale young man in bluecloth. There was a large wet stain to one side of the door, and a broken window.

Clare's heart sank. He shook off sentiment, steeled himself, and peered into the darkness.

Beside him, Pico made a strangled noise. The lad turned, fumbled past the bobby, and heaved just where a similar viewer of the scene had, right onto the wet reeking splash that should have been covered by Scab.

The lad's eyes had been better than his. He took two

uncertain steps, lifting the lanthorn one of the Yard men outside had surrendered to Aberline.

There was a low punky glow from the fireplace. The kettle on the hob had melted, warped by unimaginable heat.

Beside him, Aberline cursed softly. There was a rancid burp rising in Clare's throat, he denied it.

Behind them, Mikal's step was soundless, but his presence pushed against Clare's back, along with prickles of gooseflesh.

The glimmers described . . .

Long dark curling hair, knocked free of its womanly confinement. Nakedness, indecent enough, but the gaping hole and shredded flesh . . . flayed thighs, the white gleaming of bone, the marks where a dexterous knife had dug in and the thing had feasted . . . feasted upon . . .

Control yourself, Clare. He realised, quite calmly, that he had handed the lanthorn to Aberline. Crazy shadows danced over the rotting walls. There was a hole in one corner of the room, the floorboard wrenched up.

He found his busy fingers working his left glove off.

There was very little that could shock or disgust a mentath. He realised, foggily, that he had perhaps found one way to do so. His faculties shivered under the assault, and he was very, very close to becoming a useless, porridge-brained idiot.

He brought his left hand to his mouth and bit in, savagely.

The pain of teeth in flesh was a bright arrow, striking the centre of his brain. It shocked him into some manner of rationality, and he found himself with a mouthful of bloody saliva, staring at the battered body on the bed.

Aberline had said something. Mikal's reply was a short, grating curse. The Shield had approached the bed, his shoulders rigid, and bent closer. How he could stand to have his face so near the . . .

Clare bit down again. It worked, but only just. He blinked, furiously, shutterclicks of dim, roseate light striking him as fists. The face had been stabbed, cheeks laid open, the teeth . . .

Wait.

Mikal's gaze met his. The Shield had turned from the bed, and the colourless sizzle around him was rage.

The teeth. They were not pearly little perfect white soldiers standing on their curved, rosebud-pink hills. They were discoloured, one or two under the opened flaps of cheekflesh decayed. The shape of the ear he could see was wrong as well, and it bore no hurtful little mark of piercing for bright earrings to dangle from.

The relief threatened to do what the sight of the body had not, and drive him to his knees. He swayed, the lanthorn swinging crazily again as Aberline caught his arm.

The hand that lay curiously unmarked to one side was small and delicate, but it was not soft, nor did it bear the indentation of rings. Chapped and reddened, it was a hand that had seen much weather and some measure of hard work.

His faculties, shocked, began functioning again. "Ah." He cleared his throat, again, and the smell struck him. The bowels had been opened . . . had the creature eaten them, too, and whatever offal they contained?

How very interesting.

Mikal read his expression, and the Shield actually staggered as well. When he regained his equilibrium, he strode across the room. He brushed past Clare like a burning wind, sparing Aberline only the briefest of glances, and halted in the doorway.

"Mentath?"

Clare found his voice. "It is . . . it is not. Her. It is not her."

Mikal nodded, once. "Work quickly." He stepped outside, and Clare wondered if he would lose whatever dinner he had partaken of as well. There was a murmur – Pico, and Mikal's toneless reply.

What work is to be done here? But he knew. There had to be some clew, some small detail that would lead them in the proper direction. Miss Bannon evidently had faith in his abilities, and was trusting her life to him.

Unfortunately, a mentath suffering irrational waves of Feeling would have even more difficulty untangling a sorcerous crime than one who was not so burdened by . . . relief? Hope? What *was* the dashed word for it?

It did not matter.

"Are you certain?" Aberline, curiously hushed. "Or did you tell him so because . . ."

"I am quite certain." Clare drew in a deep breath, wished he had not. He examined the kettle on the hob, melted and scarred. Scraps of charred cloth – had he burned her dress to give himself light? Or was it sorcerous in nature? "What do you make of this?"

Aberline drew the lanthorn closer. He cast an uneasy glance at the bed, with its hideous cargo. "Perhaps to delay her identification? Or some sorcerous reason . . . or perhaps he needed light to work by."

"The creature preferred darkness before. What sorcerous reason?"

"See the rings in the metal, there? And there? Chrysfire. Untraceable, unlike witchflame." Aberline dug in his pocket, wiped his forehead with a wilting handkerchief. "It bears little stamp of the kindler's personality. Sorcery is a distinctly *personal* art."

"Miss Bannon often remarked as much." Clare crouched, Aberline holding the lanthorn higher to shed some gleams upon the charred mess. "Quite a bit of cloth. None of it the quality that a lady might wear."

Aberline glanced back at the bed, struck by a thought. "Her teeth. Of course. It cannot be her. I am a fool. Well, what do we do now? I confess I am at a loss."

"You will not like the direction my thoughts are tending."

"I fancy I won't."

"Most poppy users reserve a small amount, rather in the manner of a talisman against want of the substance." *As do most users of coja.* Perhaps a fraction of that sweet white powder would help. Clare shut the thought away. "Do you?"

"You are correct." Aberline had gone pale. "You wish me to . . ."

A gleam caught Clare's eye. He leaned forward. *How odd*. "A button," he murmured. "A very familiar one, at that."

"What?" Mystified, Aberline nevertheless lowered the lanthorn a touch.

"Why on earth would the creature burn its own coat, too?" He settled on his heels. "Mikal. He might know." The ashes were still warm, but Clare's fingers had lost none of their deftness. He tossed the button from palm to palm, rather like a baked potato, and saw with some satisfaction that he was correct. It had the faint impress of a ship's anchor upon its false-brass face, and though deformed by heat it was indubitably the same button the Coachman-thing had worn upon its coat.

"In any case," he continued, "this is an item from the creature's coat. I believe a physical object can be of use in finding a certain person's location?"

"Sympathy? I have none of the power for such an operation." Aberline had gone quite pale.

"Let us hope Mikal does." Clare straightened, rising. "For he may compel you to attempt, power or no."

A few questions elicited the most likely name of the unfortunate upon the bed – Marie-Jinnete, surnamed Kelly, also called Black Mary. She had retired to her room after dark with a customer, and not been discovered until one of her other suitors or customers returned to batter at her door and make quite a scene, thinking her unfaithful.

Which of course she was, and had paid harshly for it.

She had been many shillings behind on the rent for the sad little corner she inhabited, which no doubt led to the decision to peer through the broken window, and consequently force the door.

The missing sorceress had most likely been nowhere near this corner of Whitchapel during the night.

The Shield's face was as white as Aberline's, and just as set. The Yard men in the small court – named after a miller, though there had likely never been one of that persuasion plying his trade here – were at the other end, doing their best to hold back the crowd. Mikal's long coppery fingers turned the small lump of metal over, thoughtfully. "He does not have the power," he said, finally, jutting his chin at Aberline. "And I may only use such a Sympathy in close proximity to my Prima."

"How close?" Clare all but hopped from foot to foot.

Mikal shrugged. "Within her very presence. I do not understand, though – if she is alive, I should *feel* her . . ." His pause was matched by a curious change in expression. "Unless . . ."

"Unless?" Clare prompted.

Was it hope, dawning on the Shield's features? Weary, disbelieving hope, perhaps. "Unless she is far underground, or behind certain defences. Hothin's water-wall, for example, or a muirglass."

"Underground?" A little colour had come back to Aberline's face. "Hm."

The silence that grew about them had all the crackling urgency of the breath before a storm's breaking.

Clare let them cogitate. Beside him, the lad Pico had tensed too, as a bloodhound scenting prey.

"Scare's Row." Pico sported feverish spots on both cheeks, and kept wiping his mouth nervously. His shoulder touched Aberline's, and neither moved away from the contact. The situation was rather beginning to paper over their personal differences, and it was high time, too. "Fan End, too."

"Crithen's Church." Aberline nodded. "That's where I'd go."

"*Do* speak clearly, sirs." Clare eyed the crowd at the end of the court. There was an air of carnivorous festival about the whole scene he did not quite like, even if he was heartened to find all four men upon whom Miss Bannon was now depending finally behaving reasonably

"Tunnels. From the Pax Latium, it's said. Sometimes they're rumoured to have beasts living in them, like near the Tower." Pico made as if to spit, reconsidered. "Bad business, all of them."

"Dark holes. Worst sinks in Whitchapel. Some of them host ginhouses; if the drink does not blind you, a knife may." A fey light was slowly dawning on the inspector's features. "Why did I not think on it before? A mad sorcerer, hiding there . . . sending his creature forth . . . using the tunnels as a means to move undetected . . . hm. Yes, Crithen's Church is where I would start. The deeper holes are all about that location, the ones even the flashboys and Thin Meg's starvelings don't venture into."

Clare jammed his hat more firmly upon his head. "Then

there we shall go. Mr Mikal, once we are underground, will you be able to sense Miss Bannon?"

"Perhaps." His hand flicked, and the button disappeared. "This may be useful, if we draw close enough."

Clare struggled with himself, and lost. "Can Inspector Aberline's powers, such as they are, be magnified in some manner?"

Mikal stilled, and so did Aberline. "There are ways," the Shield admitted, and viewed the inspector afresh. "Blood, for one."

"None of that." Aberline backed up two steps, his steps loud on the Scabless ground.

"We have other methods," Clare said, hastily. "You have a small amount of poppy, Aberline."

The man's reply was unrepeatable, but it satisfied Clare that he did, in fact, possess a small lump of said substance. Not that it mattered – any apothecary could be induced to part with enough laudanum to replicate the effect, should it come to such a thing.

Finding Miss Bannon outweighs any injury to his pride, Clare told himself. He did not care to think further upon the chain of logic – what else did it outweigh? His life? Clare's? Or, it could not, for Clare was made proof against such things.

Sacrificing another was so easy, was it not? Once the temptation was large enough. Once the Feeling outweighed pure logic. How did Emma bear such storms of emotion, without a mentath's skills to shield her? How had she borne his accusations? And Valentinelli's death – how could he have thought her unmoved?

Concentrate, Clare. "Very well. To the carriage. Pico, climb up with Harthell and direct him to this church. Mikal, do bring Inspector Aberline, and make certain no harm comes to him."

He set off for the mouth of the court, and his face crumpled for a moment before resmoothing itself. For he had realised something.

First, that he had sounded *exactly* like Miss Bannon. And second, he had no particular qualm about shedding the good inspector's blood.

Should it become necessary.

Chapter Forty

The Cap To His Ambition

The painful, twisted wreck of a Prime shuffled away, and Emma was left to her own devices, her gaze roving over what little she could see without moving her head. Her pulse struggled to rise, again, the fact of confinement looming, a Prime's will finding such a thing unbearable.

It is no different than a corset, she told herself. *It is no different than being a woman in a world that seeks to chain every woman it can find. It is no different than your entire life, Emma. Be still. Be logical. Plan.*

Did Clare feel this distress, when irrationality loomed? Perhaps they were the same – he was logic trapped in an illogical world, and she was a Prime's will trapped in a woman's flesh.

Enough to base a Sympathy on, I should think. Will they

guess where I have been taken? I am underground. Mikal . . . he may not . . .

It was immaterial. Whether they accepted her invitation to find her or not, she had a duty here. Not to Victrix, not even to Britannia. She had *chosen* to be confined in this manner, offering herself as a sacrifice.

He had taken the bait. It was now her aim to become poisonous.

And you shall give me the world. What did he *mean*? How many times had she thought him dead? The simulacrum in Bedlam, the tower at Dinas Emrys . . . it reminded her of certain novels, wherein a villain was a mad reflection of the hero, and escaped death through the most fantastic of means.

The Promethean, in its egg of smoke over the lightless obsidian block, moved sluggishly. Rather like a swelling spawn in an ungodly womb. Of course it had eaten and charred the organs of generation. They were incredible sources of ætheric force, both because of their biological purpose and the importance accorded them by custom and human instinct.

If Llewellyn sought to marry the Promethean to his own regrowing flesh, why would he need *her*? And why, oh why, would it have such an effect on Britannia?

For the ruling spirit had been afraid. And Thin Meg, in her pit, had neatly placed Emma in a trap – or had she?

I do not know enough. Logic, Emma. Imagine Clare is here. What would he say?

Perhaps it was the wrong question. Her body twitched, her will flexing against the bonds. They held fast.

Now she remembered, unwillingly, the last time she had been held fast so completely. Dripping water, her despairing, unconscious sounds of rage and pain, and the choking as Mikal strangled his former Prime, slowly, and the horrid sounds of him tearing flesh asunder, before freeing her from the bonds.

Miles Crawford. The name of her captor. All the rage, all the terror in the world held in those syllables. She had been outplayed by him, and her Shields had paid the price. If not for Mikal's disobedience—

Remember your purpose. Which is not to relive that moment.

Then why had she done this? Perhaps for no other reason than the one she had given a man who had not listened.

If not for luck, I could have been any one of them. All of them, or more. Or less, as the world would have it.

Perhaps he did not mean to marry the Promethean to his own flesh. And yet, marrying it to hers would be problematic as well. He could not tell, of course, that she had given the second wyrm's heart to another, or even if she had taken it for herself. The beauty of the Philosopher's Stone was its ability to pass undetected by even the finest unphysical senses. Just as a wyrm could lay undetected beneath a tower for aeons, as the world turned about it. Would the Stone bar another item's introduction into the body it protected from harm and decay?

You shall give me the world.

Perhaps . . .

The connection trembled just out of reach. Something,

some symmetry, was escaping her. Just as the nature of the Promethean had—

Wait.

If Llew had created a Promethean, and fed it on unfortunates in Whitchapel . . . no. That was wrong.

The only certainty was that a Promethean had been created. Perhaps it had chosen its own meat and drink, as it were.

You have more enemies than you know, sparrow-witch.

A Prime always did.

Ætheric force twitched restlessly. Come Tideturn, she might be able to find a crack or a chink in the restraints. They felt supple, slightly elastic, but any pressure against them would make the entire trap harden. Elegant, and just the thing to keep a Prime still and quiet.

If you did not mind said Prime losing her mind from the very fact of being trapped.

She might become just as mad as he was. Except he was not lunatic, really. Simply ambitious. He saw no reason to cap his ambition, any more than Emma did.

The only cap to my ambition is myself. What is the cap to his, I wonder?

The gleaming knife trembled upon the stone, turning on its tip rather like a ballerina *en pointe*. Its slight scraping would have sent a shiver down her back, if she could move.

She essayed a slight humming noise, deep in her throat. The gag would keep her from shaping Words, true. Much could be done with tone and—

Blackness devoured her vision. Panic, as her nose was stoppered as well as her mouth. Sorcerous training could not control the fear of strangulation, and she went limp. Air returned, as did consciousness.

There was a soft, mocking laugh. She could not *see* him, and the restraints made the sound echoing and unearthly.

"You think I'd leave you any opening, my darling? No." He scraped back into sight, moving a little more easily. More damp, splashing sounds.

Emma squeezed her eyelids shut. Hot water trickled between her lashes. Then she let them open just a fraction, disliking the dark.

"I *respect* you. Not like that magical whore. It took me by surprise, her luring you into the open. I had hoped to bring you out a different way." A shadow flickered between her and the yellow-rose glow of the lamps. "But here you are. And in such good time, too."

Think, Emma. Think.

Unfortunately, he straightened, metal and bone clicking as the ruins of his body shook about him. He reached out, and Emma's eyes opened wide.

His misshapen right hand closed about the knife, and he lifted it free of the stone with a physical and ætheric effort. He turned, and the tenderness on his features was almost worse than the glitter of insane calm in his dark eyes. Thin threads of yellow shone in the muddy irises, a reminder she did not need of Mikal.

Her Shield was most likely frantic by now. How much

time had passed? Was it midnight yet? Could Clare find her? They were underground, could Mikal sense her with any accuracy once he was close enough?

Do not worry upon them, Emma. You have more than enough to occupy you here.

Llew shuffled toward her. "$X-\dot{z}'t'ks'm$," he breathed, a sorcerous Word that bent strangely as it was uttered. The knife shimmered with ætheric force, and the smoky egg containing the Promethean convulsed afresh.

Her Discipline stirred, sleepily.

Too late, she began to understand what he meant to do, and how stupid she had been to use herself as a lure.

He began to chant, the language of Making and Naming alternating as he described what he wished the sorcerous force to shape itself as, how it would affect the tangled fleshly snarl of the physical and the gossamer of the unseen. Stone shivered uneasily as the taproots driven into Whitchapel stirred, only faint echoes where Emma had cleared them but driven deep in many other places. Many, many other victims had fallen – the creature found its own meat and drink, but its creator had been busy with murder, too.

Lines of force coalesced, becoming visible to Sight, and Llewellyn raised the knife. His mouth grinned and slavered over the consonants as he described her death, and what that ending would fuel.

The Promethean was nearing the end of its infancy. It needed a vessel, a mockery of birth. The knife lowered, and a faint piping reached Emma's ears – souls, straining for release, perhaps. Each of the victims crying out, a chorus of the damned.

The smoky egg over the obsidian – it *was* an unholy altar, she realised, another mockery, yet the form was completely appropriate to the Work Llew was attempting – drifted free of its moorings. The two live coals of the Coachman's eyes glared from a suggestion of a face, and Emma's entire body tensed, as if it could deny the coming violation.

The knifetip touched her throat.

Chapter Forty-One

To Crithen's Church

It was no use. Clare pushed the carriage door open as the clockhorses shrilled. If they went any further, the carriage would become well and truly mired in the crowd, and Harthell's steady cursing was already lost under the noise. Screams of frightened women, breaking bottles and tearing wood, the roiling of men's voices. From somewhere torches had arrived, for the gaslamps were guttering, their wickcharms dying. The throng ahead filled the main thoroughfare of High Whitchapel Road, and the press of the crowd even on this small tributary was becoming rather worrisome.

Leather Apron! Leather Apron!

The public, that great beast – or at least a healthy slice of it – had lost patience with the keepers of order.

In her very bed, he did, and they do nothing, all high

and mighty! Heard he opened her up, even her face. Welladay, the Metropoleans don't care as long as he kills poor frails. Our girls, they are, even if low.

Lining High Whitchapel were shops and better-to-do homes; the crowd pressed uneasily against them. The carriage had not yet become a target, but it was only a matter of time.

Aberline was beside him, casting an eye over the heaving mass. The fog had greyed as if dawn was incipient; Clare's pocket-watch told him that indeed, sunrise was very close, with Tideturn not far behind. More glass shattered, and Harthell cursed again.

"We shall not stir a foot in this," Clare observed. *Soon they may take a mind to upend the carriage.*

"Not without sorcery or a regiment." Aberline, sour-faced, had regained some of his colour. Mikal was silent, but his tension was clearly apparent.

"Ho! Pico, come down. Harthell, take the carriage home." Clare had to shout. "We shall proceed—"

A different sound pierced the seashell roar. High and chilling, a silverwhistle.

"Oh, *blast* it all." Aberline leapt from the carriage, landing heavily on blackened, broken cobbles. "Waring, you bloody *fool*. He's called in—"

"Headcrackers. And possibly a regiment," Clare said, grimly. "Or two. There will be blood shed this dawn."

"Other sorcerers will muddy the waters." Mikal had grasped Aberline's elbow as the crowd surged around them. A toothless beldame in red calico shrieked, falling against a sturdy flashboy with an Altered left hand, metal sharpened and gleaming as he thrust her away with a curse. "How close are we?"

"To Crithen's? A ten-minute walk, were this a fine morning. Today . . ." Aberline indicated the throng at the juncture of Bent and High Whitchapel.

Harthell evidently agreed with Clare's estimation of the situation, for he wheeled the carriage hard right and vanished down Tehning Cross; the crack of his whip sent a chill up Clare's spine. *Set it aside. What may be done? Think!*

Mikal glanced up, studying the rooftops. "I think—"

Whatever he had meant to say was lost in an angry roaring. Beneath it, drumbeats, and the clopping of hooves in unison. Yet it was not from that end of Whitchapel the flaming lucifer that set off a crowd's tinder dropped.

It was from the *other* end, and as soon as Clare heard the sound, his heart sank.

Ever afterwards, none could discern from the conflicting reports who had given the City Streamstruth Regiment the order to fire upon the crowd. The volley was enough to cause a few moments' worth of shocked silence.

There is a moment when a crowd ceases to be a mass of separate beings, when it becomes a single mind and turns upon its tormentor. Or simply, merely upon anything within reach. Once it becomes such an organism, it tramples, heaves, tosses, and smashes with no restraint.

Being caught in the jaws of that monster was not acceptable.

Mikal shoved Aberline to the side of the street, where an open dosshouse door showed a slice of yellow lamplight. "*Go!*" he cried, and pushed Clare for good measure. Pico hopped in their wake with youthful alacrity, and it was Mikal again, suddenly before them, who kicked at the door even as a burly just-awakened stout in braces and a thread-bare shirt sought to slam it against sudden danger.

A quick strike, Mikal's hand blurring, and the dosshouse doorman folded; Pico shoved the door closed and sought a means to bar it.

Clare found himself gasping for breath. *How annoying.* Still, they were out of danger for the moment, and Mikal evidently had some manner of plan.

"Up," the Shield said. "Find a staircase."

"And then what?" Pico enquired, shoving a flimsy chair against the dosshouse door. The entry hall was dingy and smelled overwhelmingly of cabbage and unwashed flesh; on the ground the doorman stirred slightly. Pico thought a moment, then grabbed both the supine man's wrists. Aberline helped him drag him for the door, and Clare's protest died unspoken. The wood cracked and heaved; outside, the sound of the crowd was now a wild howling of pain.

"Then," the Shield said, "we run. And you pray to what-ever god you choose that we find my Prima."

Clay tiles scratching underfoot; timber creaking uneasily when a man's weight touched it. Mikal, impatient with their slow progress, nevertheless shepherded them carefully.

The geography of Londinium appeared much altered when seen from this vantage. Ground became tile and sloped roofs, streets long channels separating thin island-fingers. Crossing the channels was either nerve-wracking – a slide and a leap, Mikal's hand flashing forwards to drag a man onto solid safety – or entirely irrational, a matter of clinging to the Shield and closing one's eyes while he leapt in some sorcerous fashion. Each time he did so, hopping across thoroughfares as if it was child's play, Clare's most excellent digestion threatened to unseat itself.

At least now he knew how the man kept up with Miss Bannon's carriage.

Clare peered at the sky as Pico slithered down the roof-slope behind him, boots scraping dry moss and accumulated soot. Even here, life clung to gullies and cracks; he saw hidden courts, walled off by the rapid building of slum-tenements, with the remains of old gardens gone to seed. Twisted trees no eye but the sky had viewed for years, and even grass and weeds clinging in rain-gutter sludge. Londinium's roofs were a country of mountainous desert, concealing throbbing life and violent motion beneath its crust.

Whitchapel was ablaze, figuratively and actually. Two fires had started, one near the border of Soreditch and another, from what Clare could tell, sending up a black plume from the slaughteryard near Fainmaker's Row. Yellowing fog swirled uneasily, and the virulent green of Scab held to mere fringes and dark alleys.

Cries and moans, the roaring of a maddened crowd, more sharp volleys of rifle fire. Had the Crown authorised such a deadly response? Was it the Old City, nervous at the proximity of the restless poor? Waring was merely a commissioner, he could not have taken the step without approval from the Lord Mayor *or* the Crown—

"Mind yourself," Pico said, grabbing his sleeve. "Look. Crithen's, just there."

Clare peered down. Mikal landed atop the slope with a slight exhalation of effort, and Aberline retched once, quietly.

"Enough power to feel the effects," the Shield said, soft and cold. "And should I need to, *Inspector*—"

"Cease your threats." Aberline sounded pale. "I told you I would do my best."

"Mr Mikal?" Clare's voice bounced against the rooftop. "A moment, if you please?"

"What?"

"It is past dawn."

Mikal was silent for a long moment. There was a flash of yellow as he checked the sky, and Pico moved along the edge of the roof.

Clare cleared his throat. "Do you have any idea why Londinium is still, well, subject to Night? Is this sorcery?"

"Perhaps." The Shield halted, still with a hand to Aberline's elbow. "A Work meant to replace a ruling spirit, or create a new one . . . perhaps this is an effect. My Prima would know. Are we close?"

"The place is there." Clare pointed, as Pico had. "Though I must say, it does not look in the least churchlike."

It was a slumping, blasted two-storey building, set between two ditches that served, if Clare's nose was correct, as nightsoil collectors. Also, if his vision was piercing the dimness correctly, a dustheap or two. "I cannot even tell . . . was it a house?"

"They call it church because Mad Crithen nailed his victims to the walls." Pico sounded dreadfully chipper. "He was popish, he was. Leastways, that's how I heard it."

"Mad Crithen?"

"A murderer." Breathless, Aberline shook free of Mikal. "*Lustmorden*, but with a religious . . . he crucified his victims. I read of it in Shropeton's analysis of—"

"There's a way down!" Pico shimmied lithely over the edge of the roof and vanished. "Here!"

Clare patted his pistol, secure in its holster. "It is extremely likely there will be unpleasantness within. I cannot think this sorcerer will not guard his lair."

"He may not need to." Mikal pointed. "Look."

A subtle wet gleam in the ditches, and stealthy movement in the shadows. Skeletal shapes, in ragged threadbare clothes, and under the sound of riot and mayhem, a queer sliding whisper.

"Scab. In the ditches." Aberline sucked in a sharp breath. "And . . . starvelings? Here?"

"Starvelings?"

"Marimat." Mikal's mouth turned the syllables into a curse. They made little sense to Clare, but he shivered anyway. "Of course. Come, quickly. We must reach the place before they can hold it."

"I don't suppose you—"

But Mikal had already embraced Aberline's stout waist with his arm, and flung them both from the roof with a rattle and a peculiar whooshing. Clare scrabbled for the place Pico had disappeared, and the lad's disgusted curse from below was lost in a rising, venomous hiss.

❀Chapter Forty-Two

No More

The prick of the knifetip made a vast stillness inside Emma Bannon. The world shrank, Time itself stretching and slowing.

And so I die.

It pressed further, and the smoke-egg floated free of the obsidian's tethering influence. As it did, it grew heavier, blacker, and the block of glassy stone crackled. Thin fissures threaded its surface, and the lamplight now reflected wetly from its shifting planes.

Ah. Much more of the inner workings of Llewellyn's creation became apparent to her. The insistent pressure at her throat mounted, and the following moments were, paradoxically, endless . . . and too quick to contain everything that occurred within them.

Emma turned inward, into that stillness, her eyes forgotten in that quick motion. It was not a physical movement, and her slackened muscles meant the restraints about her loosened.

Raw aching places inside her woke in a blinding sheet of pain, and she trembled on the thin edge of forcing her spirit free by an effort of will, stoppering her lungs and heart before the mad Prime she had once loved could cut her throat.

To do so would deny him his victory – where else would he find such an apt victim for this, the last murder to fuel an unholy transformation?

No.

They burst upon her, the murders she had felt and those she had not. Cleaving of flesh and bright copper fear, gin fumes and desperation. Their lives, colourless drudgery and danger, painful except when the gin soaked through and insulated against hunger, the men and their grasping, hurtful hands. A sweet word in the darkness, coaxing them to take one more customer. A faceless thing, and the blade so sharp it almost did not hurt as they were unseamed . . . hot blood, the merciful blackness swallowing them whole.

I could have been any one of them.

None knew from whence sorcerous talent sprang. A lucky chance, and she had been lifted from the mire – but her skirts were still draggled, and she would never be allowed to forget.

At the very floor of Emma's consciousness, a barred door.

He seeks to give life. I am of the Black, my Discipline is Endor . . . and there is no better way to cheat him of his prize.

Her throat swelled, a trickle of blood tracing white skin. The restraints, sensing a gathering, tightened. The constriction, sudden and unbearable, roused the same blind fury that had once caused sickly green flame to sprout from a drunken man's skin and clothes. The same will, fed and exercised, grown monstrous, able to endure temporary confinement only because she had suffered it, in one form or another, her entire life.

The door at the bottom of her soul creaked. *No more*.

A shattered hulk of a sorcerer, his rasping voice raised in a chant of a Discipline not his own, tensed. Next would come driving the knife home, and the creature – his only issue, a son who might be grateful – would feast upon this sacrifice. And she, *she*, would be given a gift of blackness and no more pain.

Black chartersymbols woke, racing along Emma Bannon's skin. Her eyelids snapped wide, and each pupil kindled with a bright, leprous-green flame. The charter symbols crawled up her legs, rushed over her torso in a wave, devoured her arms – still encased in shredded mourning cloth – and flowed under her hair, smearing across her slackened face in their hurrying.

They reached the knifepoint digging into her flesh, a cascade of pale green sparks fountaining from the contact.

Inside her, the hurtful flower of her Discipline bloomed.

Llewellyn Gwynnfud, still chanting, pushed down.

He dragged the razor-sharp blade across his former lover's throat.

Chapter Forty-Three

A Betrayal That Struck One

The starvelings were skeletal corpses, still animate through some feat of sorcery. There were so *many*, shuffling forward with the slowness of the damned, their hands held out. Those soft, insistent graspings could drag a man down, and then they would cluster him, pressing life and breath away with that soft, low, terrifying hissing. They had narrowly avoided losing Pico, and Clare tipped the empty cartridges out of his Bulldog as he sprinted for the door of Mad Crithin's Church.

Mikal wrenched the worm-holed, flimsy wooden door open. It had been chained with iron, and the cylinder-lock dangling from rusted metal links was new, though smeared with grease to disguise any shine. The chain snapped, broken links cascading in a chiming stream, and an exhalation of neglect and rot swallowed them all. Aberline's ankle, twisted just after the man wrenched starvelings from Pico's slim frame with a roaring fit for a lion, was already swollen.

Clare gained the dubious safety and Mikal slammed the door to. "Brace . . . it," the Shield managed, breathlessness the only indication of the efforts he had made so far. "*Hurry*."

Does he think we treating this as a Sunday amble? Clare did not waste his own breath on a sharp reply. Pico, his jacket in tatters and his fine waistcoat ripped, was already shoving a jumble of broken wood that had once been a secretary against the door. Mikal's boots slipped slightly on grime-caked wooden boards, and cords stood out on the Shield's neck as he sought to hold the entry against the soft, deadly pressure from outside.

Aberline hobbled, dragging a sprung-stuffing chair across the uneven boards. Clare's lungs protested, he whooped in a deep breath, reloading his Bulldog. When that operation was finished, he helped Pico drag another piece of shattered furniture against the door; next came a huge, shipwrecked chunk of masonry helpfully fallen from somewhere.

The soft scraping from outside did not lower in volume at all. *That* was quite chilling, Clare allowed, and proceeded to ignore it. He straightened, dusting his hands. "Where now?"

"Down-cellar." Aberline leaned heavily upon Pico. "Good God, is Thin Meg *mad*?"

"Has she ever been sane?" Mikal's laugh was a marvel of restrained rage. "My Prima visited her, she knew far more than she allowed."

"Ah. And Bannon *believed* what Meg said?" Aberline sounded as if he rather did not credit the notion.

"I should think not. She is too wise to believe many things." Mikal pointed at a far corner, between mounds of wrecked wood and marble. "There, I would say."

The walls had been torn through, and there were fittings – brass, copper, other materials – that could have been sold. Yet Clare did not think those who passed through, no matter what crypt below Londinium they aimed for, would take anything from this sad, ramshackle place. There was a faint chill exhalation from every surface, and the darkness seemed altogether too thick to be mere shadow.

"Been two years since I last," Pico breathed, once. "Hasn't changed a bit."

"It never does." Aberline, shortly.

They were making a great deal of noise, but Clare saw no point in quieting them. Mikal was a ghost, and he kept Aberline well within sight.

The cellar was reached through a hole hacked in the floor of what might have been a sitting room, once. There was a ladder made of what looked like nailed-together bits of lath, though it was surprisingly solid.

Aberline made a short pained sound when he landed, and would have toppled if not for Mikal's steadying.

Even here, things were not quite right. A drift of coal, worth good money, clustered against the closer end of the cellar, though the chute it would have been poured through seemed blocked.

Rather good thing, too, Clare thought, and shivered at the idea of hearing soft starveling hisses in the dark.

Aberline had struck a lucifer, and Clare saw a yawning hole in the ground opposite the coal-pile. It looked far too large for its own borders, one of Londinium's more irrational corners, and a familiar pain gripped his temples.

Mikal paused. His dark head came up, a stripe of blood and dirt on his cheek black in the lucifer's glare.

Aberline halted as well, quite amazingly pale under the muck and dust he was covered with. He grimaced as he shifted his weight. Pico's breathing was stertorous in the stillness, but the lad was holding up gamely. With his hair knocked out of its careful slick-back and his eyes wide, he looked rather young.

And fragile.

"Mikal?" Clare whispered.

"I think . . ." The Shield shook his head, as if tossing away said thought. "Come."

Clare, his faculties straining under the weight of what he might be about to witness, had a very rational thought. *We should have brought a lanthorn.*

As if in answer, a sound rose from the hole. Long, and loud, it stripped the hair from their fevered brows and brushed against their clothing.

Later, Clare could not think quite *what* the sound had been. A rumble, a moving of earth, the roar-breath of a massive fire, the sea suckling at its rocky confines? No, too much. Perhaps it was the internal shifting of a lie told or found out, or a betrayal that struck one to a heart's core

– but that was *ridiculous*. It was merely Feeling, and Clare should set it aside.

Aberline gasped, rocking back on his heels, but Mikal's reaction was even more marked.

"*Emma!*" he screamed, and leaped forwards into the dark, his footsteps, for once, heavy with reckless speed.

The massive sound did not echo, but it left some imprint on the space around the three left in Mikal's wake, broken only by a thin, light, unholy tapping Clare had heard before: footsteps of a creature that carried a sharp-ended whip. The healed slice along his forearm send a pang up to his shoulder.

Clare also heard, as if in a nightmare, a slow, soft, *draining* hiss.

Chapter Forty-Four

In The Final Weighing

*T*he first surprise was that it did not hurt. The knife cleaved flesh, yes, and there was a hot jet of salt-crimson blood.

Then . . . droplets hung in midair, and the blooming within her was a sweet pain. Her Discipline roared, needing no chant to shape it. No, when a Discipline spoke, the entire sorcerer was the throat it passed through.

It required only the strength to submit. As long as that strength lasted, wonders could be worked.

What had she done? Turned inward, yes, and found . . . what?

Not m'pence, *Marta Tebrem* whispered. Needs it for my doss, I do.

They spun around her, sad women and merry, dead on a knife or by a strangle, in childbed or by fever, by gin or misadventure, in hatred or in desperation, by folly or chance. She was of the Endor, but even more importantly, she was of their number, and the spark that rose within her was both negation and acceptance.

Some of them had wished for release from the miserable drudgery and endless pain. There was the acceptance.

Yet even louder, and containing the acceptance as a shell contains a nut, the denial.

No. I will not.

Should not, or could not, those were incorrect. The refusal was a hard shell, wrapped about the tender thing called a soul trapped in a fragile and perishable body.

Beat me, hurt me, kill me, I will not.

Or perhaps the refusal was merely her own, even her Discipline bending to a will grown strong by both feeding and confinement.

They streamed through her, the women of Whitchapel, and their cries were the same as the Warrior Queen Boudicca in her chariot – a vessel of Britannia dishonoured, slain in battle, but still remembered.

Still alive, if only in the vast storehouse of memory a ruling spirit could contain.

No. I live.

The heart struggled, the lungs collapsing with shock. Her murderer crowed with glee, his purpose achieved, his chant becoming the savagery of an attacker's, almost swallowing the sound of sorcery spilling through the bloody necklace of a cut throat.

I live.

They burst free of her not-quite-corpse – for the throat-cutting does not kill immediately, for a few crucial moments the sorceress, her Discipline invoked, was between living and dead. A threshold, a lintel, a doorway . . .

. . . and Death itself, the other face of the coin called Life, for a bare moment gave a fraction of the citizens of its dry uncharted country their mortal voices back.

The unsound was massive, felt behind eye and heart and throat . . .

. . . and it struck down the man who had sought to give a mockery of Life with a flood of leprous-green flame.

He squealed, beating at the fire that erupted from his slowly regrowing mortal flesh, but such is the nature of Death's burning that it consumes metal, red muscle, rock itself, the dry fires of stars and the tenderness of green shoots, all in their own time.

He fell against the obsidian altar, and the sound of its shattering was lost in another – the scream of a malformed soul given half-life, brushed with a feather of sorcery and set free.

The Promethean fled, shrieking, and on a wooden shelf in a stone womb underneath Londinium, a sorceress's mortality writhed.

For a dizzying moment she trembled between, neither alive nor dead, as the sisters of murder and confinement clamoured for her voice to be added to their number.

No.

In the end, the choice was hers alone. If she suffered under the lash of living in a world not made for her sex, it was the price extracted for protecting those upon whom her regard fell. Those she protected – did her arrogance extend so far as to think she was, in her own way, their final keeper?

To rule is lonely, and there was the last temptation.

The pieces of her erstwhile lover's spell curled about her. Her mortal death could fuel its completion, for she had taken from him, again, everything.

He had wrought too well, when he sought the perfect victim. In that perfection itself lay his undoing.

Oh yes, it was possible. To take the shards and knit them together, to drive the taproot deep into the shimmering field of pain and Empire, and to become what he had wished to create: a spirit of rule.

One last, painless lunge, and she would Become.

She could be what she had pledged to serve and turned against. She could drain the vital force of the ancient, weary being who charted Empire's course. She could wrap herself in its vestments and strike down the physical vessel of that being, choose a vessel of her own and arrange not merely her household but the world itself to her liking.

It would take so little. In the end, only the decision to do *mattered.*

And yet.

For the final time, the will holding the door open for Discipline spoke. The choice was made, had always been made, for she was as she had been created, and the pride she bore would not allow her to become an usurper.

Her answer was clear, if only in the shuttered halls of

a human heart – that country where sorcery and even Death are only guests. Tolerated, but, in the final weighing, negligible.

I live.

I live.

I live.

Chapter Forty-Five

A More Difficult Problem

"Curse the man," Aberline muttered. "Curse him, I say." Creaking, groaning sounds. "I am *not* venturing into that hole." He lit another lucifer. He was using them recklessly, having a pocketful of them – perhaps it was part of an inspector's duty, to have one when necessary? "Clare, your pistol—"

"Five shots." He lifted the Bulldog calmly. "Then they will swarm us as I seek to reload. Pico?"

"I've a blade or two." The youth spat aside, still bracing Aberline from the side. The whites of his eyes gleamed. "I don't fancy being suffocated by Thin Meg's children, mind you."

Who is this Meg? She sounds atrocious. Then again, Londinium was full of such creatures. Had he not seen a dragon in Southwark, once? The irrationality of the memory no longer bothered him overmuch, in the face of the current situation.

Clare tilted his head. They were drawing closer, those light, unholy, dancing footsteps. "We may have a more difficult problem in a few moments, gents. To the coal-pile, quickly!"

"What about *him*?" Pico's chin jutted toward the hole.

Perhaps he shall solve that problem for us. Or be solved himself. "He is well-equipped to handle himself, and he will find Miss Bannon. We are not so durable, and I can hear that *thing* coming. To the coal, now. Come, Aberline!"

Groaning sounds, scraping, from overhead. The starvelings had patiently, inch by inch, pushed the blockage at the door aside. Or they had found some other means of entry. Even the skeletons had some weight, and enough of them could work their way around every obstacle. Those fingers of theirs, dead-white and squirming . . .

A rustling, and a thump. A pale shape fell past the lath-ladder, hit the packed dirt of the cellar floor, and lay there twitching.

Tiptap. Tiptap. Tip tip tap tap tip tap tip tap—

They reached the coal. Aberline flung himself upon its hard pillow with a grunt, and Clare whirled, his Bulldog's stout nose coming up. He would at least sell their lives dearly. "Climb the coal," he hissed, fiercely, as the starveling made a convulsive, tired movement. It was insane, to think of anything so skeletal moving, a glitter of mad intelligence in its yellowed, sunken eyes. "*Climb, damn you!*"

Tiptap. Tiptaptiptaptiptap.

The Coachman burst from the dark hole Mikal had vanished into, its eyes red coals, and Clare bit back a cry. The thing was terribly solid now, and its face was no longer mercifully obscured. A ruin of runnelled flesh, broken glass-sharp teeth, wide sunken nostrils, hands of clawed monstrosity. It ran with a queer lurching grace, one shoulder occasionally hitching higher than the other as if it was a hunchback, and as it ran its bones crackled.

It paid no attention to the men on the hillock of cursed coal. Instead, it hurled itself on the single starveling that had fallen down – a pebble in the face of a larger avalanche – and buried its face in the skeletal creature's midriff. The howling that rose was a broken-glass scraping against sanity, but Clare, for once, did not look away.

He watched the irrationality unfolding before him as Aberline cursed, Pico let out a strangled noise, and several small soft plops sounded as more starvelings fell through the hole to swarm the unholy thing consuming one of their number.

Chapter Forty-Six

Pronounced Once Before

Choking. A clot of soft rock in her throat, forced free, she spat a wad of blood and phlegm aside and inhaled. Her breath died on a scream; the lamp-flames trembled. The altar was grinding itself to pieces, shards of obsidian piercing the body that had fallen across it, and her cry was matched by another – a rusty, horrific sound.

She landed in wet noisome filth, falling from the shelf that had kept her free of the squelching. This far below Londinium, the Themis's puddled feet were at the bottom of every hole. Her skirts and petticoats were flayed to ribbons, but her stays were still intact, and she was glad of their support as she screamed, throat afire with the memory of a scarlet necklace-wound.

A sobbing inhale, she fought the urge to scream again. It *hurt*, ætheric force bleeding through rips and rents, her *self* forced into a brutalised container. Her Discipline receded, the touch of sunheat on burned and blistered skin all along her internal pathways.

Retreating little tips and taps, she heard the Promethean fleeing. Tortured breathing that was not her own echoed as the obsidian shredded, thrusting its fragments heavenward with popping and sharp glass-singing noises.

What happened?

The memory of infinity receded, training forcing it aside. Black flowers bloomed at the corners of her vision, and the idea of just collapsing into the sludge beneath her was *wonderfully* enticing.

Get up. The Promethean is gone. Finish what you came for.

The question was, just what exactly *had* she endured this for? Certainly not Britannia.

Oh, d—n it all, Emma. Get UP.

She levered herself painfully to her feet. Her hair was a tangled mess, full of dirt and heaven alone knew what; her dress was all but gone. She used the wooden shelf she had been lain upon to finish the job of hauling herself upright, and saw with no real surprise that she had been sharing that hard narrow couch with an ancient skeleton. The skull was shattered, the brown bones traced with green – mildew, moss, perhaps even Scab.

A shudder wormed through her. She hunched her shoulders, like a child expecting a sharp corrective blow, and turned her head aside from the skull's grimace.

The second pair of lungs working in this small stone

cube were Llewellyn Gwynnfud's. The shattered block of glassy volcanic stone had turned to fanglike fragments, and speared through his body, regrowing flesh and metal Alterations pierced alike. Steaming crimson blood and thick black oil-ichor coated the larger shards. As she watched, the obsidian fractured again, and the wreck of a sorcerer made another wretched sound as fresh spears pierced him.

How does it feel, sir? Does it satisfy your hunger? She coughed again, a second blood-clot forced free of her lungs, and when she spat the hot nasty pellet aside she found she could breathe much more easily.

One thing left to do. She was so weary.

He had taken her shoes off. Barefoot as a Whitchapel drab, she tottered across the intervening space. "Llew." A harsh croak; she would never sing as a lady.

Oh, I pretend, and I put on a good show. But in the end, I suppose it's taken a Whitchapel girl to bring him down.

I wonder if it took one to build an Empire, too?

Immaterial. She found her voice again. "Llewellyn." What did she have to say?

His mad muddied gaze was a dumb animal's. What must it be like, for Will and Stone to scrape a body together from the wreckage of a Major Work gone wrong? *Had* the bleached bones at Dinas Emrys been host to his consciousness?

Had he watched her stand over them, expressionless, for a half-hour before she turned and walked away? Could he have seen that without eyes?

Amid the broken, metal-laced ribs of his chest, the Stone gleamed.

"*Emma*," he breathed, and his deformed hands twitched. One of them had kept the knife hilt clasped tight, and still knotted about it. The blade was no longer shining, but twisted and blackened. In its heart, a thin line of crimson.

The whip, and the knife. The Promethean is above, and will begin to murder. She set herself, and leaned drunkenly forward.

"*Emma!*" A cry from behind her.

Her fingers, blackened by dirt, soot, and her own blood, curled about a warm pulsing.

"Emma," Llew breathed. Had he remembered her name, and forgotten his own?

"Llewellyn Gwynnfud." A wetness on her cheeks, scalding, as the lamplight scoured her eyes. "I loved you, once."

The curled, useless knifeblade twitched. His mouth opened, perhaps to curse her, perhaps to plead.

Emma Bannon set her heels, gathered her strength, and *pulled*, with flesh and ætheric force combined.

A vast wrenching *crack*.

The lamps snuffed themselves as a moaning wind rose. She fell backwards, collapsing in filthy water, the second Philosopher's Stone clutched to her chest.

Very close now, a howling.

Mikal.

He screamed her name, but if he had followed her this far, he would be able to proceed in her direction without light.

She clasped the warm hardness of the Stone to her chest, and with the last scrap of ætheric force she possessed, breathed a Word she had pronounced once before.

In the dark, bones ground themselves to powder as the glassy broken altarstone shivered afresh.

Frantic splashing, and he blundered into the darkness, his irises yellow lamps and his hands a clutching relief as they bruised her, wrenched her upward and away.

As she had hoped, though perhaps not in the way she had planned, Mikal had found her.

Chapter Forty-Seven

An Echo Within Himself

A snowdrift of pale, emaciated bodies falling through the opening overhead, making very little sound as they dropped upon the Coachman's convulsing form. The starvelings' jaws worked restlessly, clicking and grinding small, discoloured teeth together as they smothered the creature.

It was deadly, and it ripped at their frail forms, but it could find nothing in them to eat. Rancid green dust slid from the rents torn in their stretched-tight flesh, the Coachman's slaver turning vilely luminescent as it mixed with that granular decay.

Clare kept the pistol trained. The scene before him was revolting, but even worse, it was *irrational,* and the throbbing in his temples was his faculties straining to make what he saw obey the dictates of Logic and Reason.

Do not look away.

The hissing became the soap-slathered gurgle of wash-water sliding down a pipe. The thing's struggles were weakening, and its whip was lost under an undulating mass of starvelings. Its long, spidery fingers kept seeking for the handle, blindly, but even had it found the braided leather it could not possibly have untangled it from the writhing.

Keep looking. The Bulldog's nose trembled. Behind him, Aberline was violently sick; he muttered something about the sorcery, and then wet, crunching noises began.

The Coachman screamed, a miserable baby-cry. It squirmed, and cloth ripped. The starvelings' clever, bony, insistent fingers peeled away scraps of muffler, of a different frock coat than the one the creature had worn before, of shirt. A button shone, describing an arc and catching a gleam from somewhere – where, Clare never discerned, for it was dark as sin, and his night-adapted eyes could only see suggestions lit by the Coachman's glowing slaver as the starvelings commenced their meal.

"Climb," Pico said, his voice breaking boyishly. "*Come on, Clare!*"

He kept the gun's snout level and steady. "Go on," he heard himself say, as if in a terrible dream. Was this, indeed, what dreaming felt like? "I shall hold them back."

For some of the starvelings had noticed, in their wandering, lethargic way, the living meat upon the pile of coal. They dragged each other upright with terrible blind insistence, shuffling across the cellar floor. Closer, and closer, and he had five bullets. They would have to count.

He could perhaps empty the chambers and reload as they retreated up the coal-hill, but there was the blockage in the chute to consider.

I believe we are all going to die here, even Mikal. I wonder, will they chew me to pieces? Am I proof against that? Or smothering?

And . . . Emma. They had brought the beast to bay, but what of the sorcerer?

A second faint green radiance bloomed, in the opposite corner. Clare kept the pistol trained. "Aberline?"

A retching cough, before the inspector's calm, hopeless voice. "Yes, Mr Clare?"

"I am sorry to have brought you here." *I am sorry for more, did you but know.*

At least the inspector was a gentleman *in extremis*. "Quite all right, old boy. Couldn't be helped." The words trembled, firmed. "We shan't get out this way, you know. It's blocked."

A series of alternatives clicked through Clare's faculties, discarded as they arose. A means could be found to ignite the coal, but the fumes and smoke would asphyxiate them before doing any good.

He was savagely weary, even though physically unharmed. Apparently, there were limits to even Miss Bannon's gifts.

Emma. Are you alive?

The Bulldog barked, and the flash destroyed his vision for a moment. The nearest starveling folded down, its head a battered mess, that green dust sliding out with its terrible, soft hissing sound.

The Coachman screamed again, a wailing infant under a steadily growing pile.

A woman's voice, freighted with terrible power. "*K—g'z't!*"

Slow grinding, the noise of mountains rubbing together.

Clare surfaced with a jolt. He found himself sprawled on coal, Pico's boot in his back, as starvelings cowered at the end of the cellar. The leprous-green radiance at the opposite end of the cellar had intensified, and under it, he could see a thin shape.

It was Miss Bannon, in the rags of her mourning dress and petticoats. The shadow behind her was Mikal, propping her up as her knees buckled. Clare squinted, and saw a glaring scar on her white throat, under a layer of filth. She had clapped one naked hand to her equally naked neck – her jewellery was gone, and it was queerly indecent to see her so. The pale glow, a different green than the starvelings' dust, but equally irrational, issued from about her, a corona of illogical illumination.

"Back," she husked, a dry croaking word. "*Back,* Marimat. They are *mine*, they are not for you."

The starvelings writhed. One final, weak little cry from the Coachman-creature, silenced with a last nasty crunching. A sigh rippled through the starvelings, a wet wind on dry grass.

"*Sssssparrow-witch.*" A thick, burping chuckle; it was one of the starvelings, but some other dark intelligence showed in its empty, rolling eyes. "*Did you enjoy your sssssssojourn?*"

"Quite diverting, twice-treacherous one." Miss Bannon's expression was just as empty, a terrible blank look upon her childlike features. "But I am at home again, Maharimat of the Third Host, and *they are not for you*."

"*Little ssssparrow*." The starveling twitched forward. "*You are flessssh, and you are weak. How will you ssssstop my children?*"

"How indeed." The sorceress's chin lifted. "I am *Prime*." Her tone had lost none of its terrible, queer atonality. "Set yourself against me, creature of filth, and *find out*."

The hush that descended seemed to last a very long while. But the starvelings, cloaked in their mumbling hiss, drew back in a wave. The ones that could not climb the lath-ladder fell and split open, the green dust spreading and rising in oddly angular curls on a breeze from nowhere.

He wondered what might grow from that dust. Was that how the Scab spread?

The starvelings left behind a curled, battered, unspeakably chewed and quickly rotting body curled in the ruins of a coachman's cloth, and a tangled whip shredding itself as it jerked and flopped, the bright metal at its ravelled end chiming before it blackened and twisted like paper in a fire. There was a creaking and a crack, a final obscene wet chuckle, and the lath-ladder plunged down, shivering into sticks.

The Coachman was indisputably dead. Its ruin fell apart with a wet sliding, and green smoke rose. It shredded, making for a moment the likeness of an anguished face, and the soughing that slid through the cellar lifted sweat-drenched hair and a pall of coal-dust.

Coughing, Clare lowered the pistol. Behind him, Aberline retched again, deeply and hopelessly. Pico breathed a term that was an anatomical impossibility, but nevertheless managed to express his profound, unbelieving relief at this turn of events.

Miss Bannon stayed upright for a long moment before crumpling, and Mikal caught her. His expression, before the green flame winked out, was full of the same devouring intensity Clare had witnessed only once before, in front of his mistress's bedroom door, in the dark, after he had worked a miracle to save her from the Red Plague.

What would he call such a twisting of a man's features? Was there a word for it? Did it matter?

It did not. For he found, to his dismay, that he recognised the look, though he could not name and quantify it. It found an echo within himself, one which could not be spoken of or even thought too deeply upon lest it break his overstrained faculties.

So Archibald Clare sagged back against the coal and closed his eyes. In a moment he would set his wits to the matter of bringing them out of this awful place.

For now, though, he simply lay there, and felt the breath moving in, and out, of his thankful, whole, undamaged, and quite possibly immortal frame.

Chapter Forty-Eight

To Sting, Or To Soothe

The fussing was not to be borne. "Tighter," Emma said, and the corset closed about her cruelly. "Enough, thank you. Severine, I am *quite* well."

"*Mais non, madame*." The round woman in her customary black was pale, but she forged onwards. "You can barely stand, and *monsieur le bouclier* said you were to sleep until—"

"Mikal does not dispose of me, Severine. *I* dispose of myself, thank you, and if you truly wish to help, *stop* this fretting and tell Mr Finch I am not receiving unless the widow calls." *He will know what that means.* "And make certain Mr Clare and Philip are properly attended to."

"Stubborn," Severine said, under her breath, and as she flounced from the dressing room Bridget and Isobel brought forth a dress from a tall birchwood wardrobe.

The housekeeper was met at the door by a silent Mikal, who held it courteously for her and slid into the dressing room without bothering to knock.

"She is quite worried." He halted, watching as the dress was lifted over Emma's head. Quick fingers put everything to rights, brushing black silk tenderly, and Emma told herself that the trembling in her knees would fade. This was no time to appear weakened.

"Worry is acceptable." Her breath came short. It was the corset, she told herself. "Ordering me about is not. Loosen the neck a trifle, Isobel. I rather dislike being throttled so."

Isobel hurried to obey. She did not remark upon the glaring scar ringing her mistress's throat. It would pale and shrink, as the Stone in her chest – a familiar, heavy, warm weight, how had she lived without it? – worked its slow wonder.

She had not needed whatever miracle Mikal had wrought – or had she? Would she have survived, even with the flood of her Discipline sustaining her?

Her plan had succeeded. They had indeed come to find her. Now, though, she wondered if she had been quite wise to treat Mikal so.

"Isobel, fetch a bit more *chocolat*, please. And Bridget, I have a mind to refill that perfume flask – no, the green one. Yes. Do hurry along to Madame Noyon and have her do so, then come back to attend to my hair. Yes, girls, off with you."

They exchanged a dire look, Bridget's freckles glaring

against her milky cheeks, but they obeyed. Familiarity could only be stretched so far, here at 34½ Brooke Street.

That left her alone with her Shield, with stockinged feet, her hair undone and not a scrap of jewellery to armour her.

He was just the same, except for the marks of exhaustion about his eyes. Tall and straight in olive-green velvet – he had, apparently, decided he no longer mourned. Or perhaps he wished her to insist.

She wet her lips with a nervous flicker of her tongue. Wished she had not, for his gaze fastened upon her mouth. Her legs were most unsteady, but her stays helped to bolster her, at least to some degree.

"It was necessary." She plunged ahead, for his expression was set and quiet, and she did not like the . . . what was it, that she felt? Uncertainty? "I could not have you following me too soon. And . . . whatever you performed upon me, Mikal, I could not—"

"You do not have to explain yourself to your Shield, Prima." He took two steps towards her, halted.

They regarded each other, Shield and sorceress, and the sounds of movement elsewhere in the house were very loud behind their silence.

Perhaps I wish to. Emma swallowed, dryly, acutely conscious of the movement of muscle in her vulnerable throat. "Mikal . . ."

He looked away, at the open wardrobe. Dresses peeked out, in the darker jewel-shades she preferred. She would mourn properly for Ludovico, now. When she shed the black, perhaps there were other things she would shed as well.

Except the names of her failures, the *rosario* she repeated to puncture her own arrogance. *Harry. Thrent. Namal. Jourdain. Eli.*

Ludovico.

She braced herself. Lifted her chin, aware that the scar would show. It was time, she decided, for Mikal to receive some measure of truth from her. "I would not care to lose you, Shield."

As if *she* were the Shield, and he, her charge.

A slight smile. "I would not care to be lost."

Did it mean he forgave her? Dare she ask? It was Mikal, why on earth should she feel this . . . was it fear? A Prime did not stoop to *fearing* a Shield. Or craving forgiveness from one of that brotherhood.

Then why were her palms a trifle moist, and her heart galloping along so?

She gathered herself, again. Chose each word carefully, enunciated it clearly. "One day, Mikal, I shall ask precisely what feat you performed while I suffered the Plague. I shall further ask why Clare knew of it, and I did not."

He still examined her dresses. "On that day I shall answer, Prima."

It was not satisfying at all. "Are you . . . distressed? By . . . recent events?"

He finally turned to face her again. The smile had broadened, and become genuine. He closed the remaining distance between them with a Shield's quiet step, and his fingers were warm on her cheeks.

His mouth was warm too; she did not realise he had driven her back until her skirts brushed the dressing table and her shoulders met the wall to its side, her own fingers tangling in his hair and her body suddenly enclosed in a different confinement, one that robbed her of breath and the need to brace her knees.

He held her there, tongue and lips dancing their own Language of fleshly desire, and when she broke away to breathe he printed a kiss on her cheek, another on her jaw, a third behind her ear where the hollow of flesh was so exquisitely vulnerable.

"A heart is a heart," he breathed, against the side of her scarred throat. "And a stone is a stone."

What on earth does that mean? She stored the question away, stroked his dark hair. He was shaking, or was it that her own trembling had communicated to him?

"You are my Shield," she whispered, and drew her hands away. Laid her head upon his shoulder, for once, and allowed the will that kept her upright to slacken for a few moments.

He held her, rested his chin atop her tangled curls. His reply was almost inaudible.

"You are my heart."

Like any reprieve, it did not last very long. In short order she had descended to the solarium, her hair finally set to rights, silver chalcedony rings upon three of her fingers, her ear-drops of marcasite and jet comforting weights, and a twisted golden brooch bearing a teardrop of green amber pinned to her bosom.

Finch cleared his throat.

Emma glanced up from the hellebore, which was springing back quite nicely under its charm-globe. "Ah. Finch. Is Mr Clare awake?"

"Yesmum. He is in the drawing room." Finch blinked once, rather like a lizard. He looked grave, but no more than usual. "With a certain personage, mum. *Two* certain personages."

"Ah." She studied the hellebore for a few more moments. "I am . . . sorry that you must endure the inspector's presence."

"Quite all right, mum." Did he sound slightly shocked? "I . . . have every confidence, thank you. In your, erm, protection."

At least someone does. She was hard-pressed not to smile. "Good. I take it the second personage is a widow?"

"Quite right, mum. Waiting on your pleasure."

How that must gall her. "How very polite. I shall take luncheon in my study, Finch, and we shall go over the household accounts with Madame Noyon afterwards."

"Yesmum." There was a certain spring in his step as he left, and she allowed herself one more moment of studying the hellebore's wide leaves and juicy, thriving green before she made her way to the drawing room.

Mikal was at the door, sweeping it open at her nod.

Clare was at the mantel, studying the mirror over it with

an air of bemused worriment. Inspector Aberline, his wounded ankle securely wrapped, leaned heavily on a brass-headed Malacca cane, but he did not dare sit in the presence of the stout, heavily veiled woman on the blue velvet settee.

Mikal closed the door, and Emma surveyed them, clasping her hands in ladylike fashion. She did not pay the woman a courtesy, instead regarding Aberline with a lifted eyebrow.

"Good morning, Inspector. I take it you're well?"

He glowered. "Fires. Property damage, loss of life. Waring swears he'll have my head, the public is calling for my dismissal."

"How very uncomfortable." *Given your usual methods, I cannot say I mind.* Still, he had aided Clare. "Do you wish to keep your position? Should you not, I am certain those present may be of aid in finding a better one."

"I'm to go on holiday until the fuss dies down." His gaze turned to the veiled woman. "With your permission, Your Majesty, I shall be about my duties."

"We are grateful for your services, during these troubled times." The Widow of Windsor offered a plump, gloved, beringed paw, and he bent over it. "You have Our thanks, and Our blessing."

Much good may it do you. Emma held her tongue.

Aberline limped past her, pausing at the door. "My regards to Mr Finch, Miss Bannon. Good day."

I shall not pass along any of your regard, sir. "Good day, Inspector. Pleasant dreams."

He restrained a curse, but only barely, and she waited until she heard the front door close behind him before her attention turned elsewhere.

The silence quickly became uncomfortable. Clare appeared to take no notice, until, with a sigh, Victrix pushed her veil aside and regarded the sorceress.

Her eyes were shockingly, humanly dark, the constellations of Britannia's gaze dim and faraway in pupils that had not been visible for years. "Sorceress."

"Your Majesty."

"They tell me it is . . . finished."

For me, yes. "It appears so."

Her reply apparently did not satisfy. Colour began below the high neckline of the Widow of Windsor's stiff black gown, mounted in her cheeks. Died away. The tiny points of light flickering in her pupils sought to strengthen. Emma observed this with great interest.

Finally, Victrix spoke again. "We are weakened. No doubt this pleases you."

"It does not." *I wish you every joy of it, though.* "The sorcerer responsible for the recent . . . unpleasantness . . . suffered a hideous fate, Your Majesty. Perhaps that may comfort you."

The Queen hefted herself to her feet. Clare stepped away from the mantel, as if to assist, but she merely stalked to within a few feet of Emma. Their skirts almost brushed, and the sorceress banished the smile seeking to rise to her mouth.

It would not do.

"We are not comforted, witchling." There was no cold weight of power behind the words, but the echo of Britannia's frigid, heavy voice underlay Victrix's words. "We suspect . . ."

Have you learned nothing, my Queen? Emma did not blink.

Two women, studying each other, the only thing separating them a wall of trembling air. And, of course, a measure of pride on either side.

Victrix's shoulders sagged. Her hand twitched, slightly, as if she wished to reach out.

If she did, what would I do? She is not the queen I served.

The memory of vast weight, the temptation to step aside from her human self and become *more*, rose inside her in a dark wave.

Emma Bannon found, much to her relief, that her decision was still the same, and that she suffered no regret.

"You are the Queen," she murmured, and lowered her gaze. She stared at Victrix's reticule – and what use did royalty have for such a thing, really? She certainly never went marketing. Perhaps it was a touch of the domesticity she had craved with her Consort.

What dreams had been put aside when the spirit of rule descended upon Victrix? Did she curse the weight and cherish it at once, as a Prime might well both curse and cherish the burden of a Will that would not allow rest or submission?

"We are." But Victrix only sounded weary. "We shall not trouble thee again, sorceress."

Is that meant to sting, or to soothe me? Emma merely nodded, and Her Majesty swept past, her veil whispering as she lowered it again. The door opened, and Emma turned her head, staring at the velvet-cloaked window. "Your Majesty."

A pause, a listening silence.

"I shall not trouble *you*, either."

There was no answer.

Chapter Forty-Nine

You Have Caused Her Grief

Most intriguing. Clare cleared his throat. "Emma."

Her head rose, and Clare discerned a redness rimming her dark eyes, a trace of moisture upon her cheek.

The front door opened, closed again, and he was alone with the sorceress.

"Archibald." The high neck of her gown failed to disguise the livid scar about her neck. What had she suffered at the hands of the mad, faceless Prime?

"How . . ." *How do you feel?* The ridiculousness of the question kindled a fierce heat in his cheeks. Was he *blushing*? Irrational. Illogical. "You look . . . well. Quite well."

"Thank you." A colourless reply. She studied him, her chin set, her hands clasped – he did not miss the tension in those knotted fingers. It must pain her, to clench them so. "You do, as well."

"Ah, thank you." He took a deep breath. "I . . . Emma, I must ask. The . . . stone. The thing you . . . can you, *will* you, take it from me? It is . . . irrational. It causes . . . Feeling."

"How interesting." She studied him, dark eyes moving slowly, her earrings swaying a trifle. "That is generally not among its effects. And no, Clare. I will not." She halted, and answering colour burned high on her soft, childlike cheeks. "Not even if you . . . if you hate me."

What must it have cost her, to say such a thing? Hate? He was a *mentath*. He did not . . .

And yet. Was it the thing she had done to him that created these storms of Feeling?

Was it the woman herself?

Or, most unsettling of all, were these tempests somehow . . . his own?

"Emma." Hoarsely. There was something caught in his throat. "I do not . . . I *cannot* hate you."

She nodded. "Thank you." What was her expression? Did he dare to name it? Could he?

"But I am . . . I am leaving. I must learn how to . . . moderate my reaction to this . . ." This was not how he had thought such an interview would go. What had he expected – tears? Cries of remorse? From her? From himself? "To this . . . gift. Of yours. This very fine . . . gift."

Another nod, the crimson in her cheeks retreating. "Very well."

"I cannot . . . I do not wish to cause you . . . pain." How on earth did others bear this illogical, irrational agony?

"Do as you must, Clare." Her fingers were white, clasped so tightly. "Should you ever need my aid, all you must do is send me word."

His throat was alarmingly dry, he forced himself to swallow. "Thank you. I . . . I shall." He could delay no longer, yet the urge to do so rose. He denied it. "Pico has a hansom waiting; I shall pay his wages myself. He is a very useful young man."

She said nothing.

There was nothing more for him to say, either, so he forced his legs to perform their accustomed function. He paused at the door, studying its crystal knob. Slowly, as an old man might, he twisted it, opened the door and stepped outside.

When it closed, he turned and made for the front. In the entry hall, though, was the last gauntlet to run.

Mikal tilted his dark head. His hair was slightly disarranged, and his hand rested upon a hilt – one of the knives at his hips, wicked blades Clare had a healthy respect for his facility in handling.

Clare drew his gloves on, slowly. Settled his hat.

"Mentath." The Shield's words were a bare murmur, but Clare's quick ears caught them. "You have caused her grief."

It was his turn to nod. There was no denial, no excuse he could offer.

There was, however, an answer to the charge. "So have you, sir."

Mikal's hand fell away from the hilt. Clare expected

more, but the Shield was simply silent as the mentath brushed past. Just before the front door, he paused.

Once I leave, will I ever return?

There was no answer. He took a deep breath, adjusted his hat, and stepped out into a foggy Londinium midmorning. A spatter of rain touched the small, exquisite garden, and Miss Bannon's gates were merely ajar instead of fully open.

He sallied down the stone path, and when he exited the gate it closed behind him, with a small, definite click. There was a hansom waiting, the driver's face half-hidden by a striped muffler, and a chill touched Clare's back.

It was irrational, so he discarded it, and clambered into the hansom.

Pico, cleaning his fingernails with a thin, flexible knife, greeted him with a nod. "All's well?"

No. "Yes. Quite." He settled himself, and tapped the roof. "Baker Street, please, number 200."

"Sir!" The whip cracked. Clare suppressed a shiver.

What came next? If he thought only of what must be done next, he could, he thought, perhaps navigate this situation properly. "Mr Pico. Miss Bannon has released you into my service. I trust you have no objection?"

"Course not, guv." The lad grinned. "Interesting indeed. Still want to learn from her grim one, though."

I am certain you do, he is most dangerous. "When your duties permit. You are a bright lad, and shall be of great help. Tell me, are you fond of travel?"

"Can't say as I've ever tried it, guv."

"Well." Clare settled himself, steepled his fingers, and gazed past them at the faded fabric curtains swaying as the hansom rocked over cobbles. "You shall, and very soon." *Very soon indeed*. "There are experiments to be done."

He lapsed into a profound silence, which did not discommode Pico in the least. As the conveyance bore them away from Brooke Street, the lad even began to whistle.

Note

A string of brutal killings in London in 1888 are still a subject of unholy fascination to this day. I make no apology for the allusions to said murders within this work of fiction, for indeed it is difficult to write of Victorian London without tripping over a mention or two of the fear that gripped the city in that awful autumn. I do, however, wish to state that there are a number of excellent books and interesting theories about the murders, and that I availed myself of several.

I wish to further state that though I may allude, I deliberately do not address the killer by the name he might have given himself, or the name the nascent "popular media" christened him with and that he is known by today. Instead, I shall list other names:

Emma Elizabeth Smith
Martha Tabram
Mary Ann Nichols
Annie Chapman
Elizabeth Stride
Catherine Eddowes
Mary Jane Kelly

There are a multitude of others who also met untimely ends, by violence or poverty.

If they cannot be avenged, may they all, at least, be at peace.

extras

orbit

www.orbitbooks.net

about the author

Lilith Saintcrow was born in New Mexico, bounced around the world as an Air Force brat, and fell in love with writing when she was ten years old. She currently lives in Vancouver, Washington. Visit her website at www.lilithsaintcrow.com.

Find out more about Lilith Saintcrow and other Orbit authors by registering for the free monthly newsletter at www.orbitbooks.net.

if you enjoyed

THE RIPPER AFFAIR

look out for

FULL BLOODED

Jessica McClain: Book One

by

Amanda Carlson

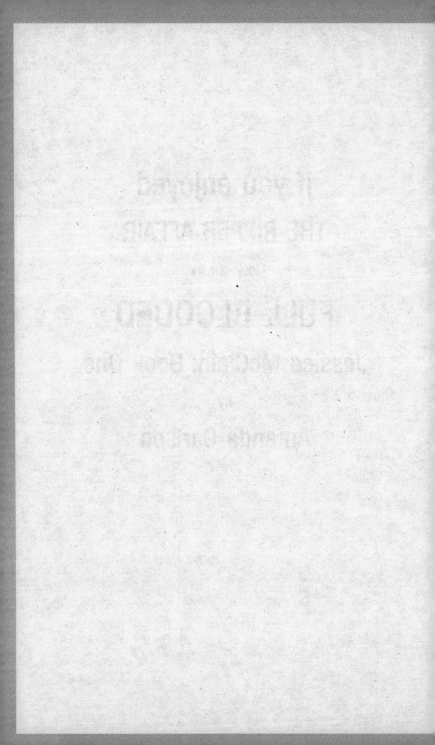

CHAPTER ONE

I drew in a ragged breath and tried hard to surface from one hell of a nightmare. "*Jesus*," I moaned. Sweat slid down my face. My head was fuzzy. Was I dreaming? If I was, this dream hurt like a bitch.

Wait, dreams aren't supposed to hurt.

Without warning my body seized again. Pain scorched through my veins like a bad sunburn, igniting every cell in its path. I clenched my teeth, trying hard to block the rush.

Then, as quickly as it struck, the pain disappeared.

The sudden loss of sensation jolted my brain awake and my eyes snapped open in the dark. This wasn't a damn dream. I took a quick internal inventory of all my body parts. Everything tingled, but thankfully my limbs could move freely again. The weak green halo of my digital clock read 2:07 a.m. I'd only been asleep for a few hours. I rolled onto my side and swiped my sticky hair off my face. When my fingers came in contact with my skin, I gasped and snapped them away like a child who'd just touched a hot stove.

Holy shit, I'm on fire.

That couldn't be right.

Don't panic, Jess. Think logically.

I pressed the back of my hand against my forehead to get a better read on how badly I was burning up. Hot coals would've felt cooler than my skin.

I must be really sick.

Sickness was a rare event in my life, but it did happen. I wasn't prone to illness, but I wasn't immune to it either. My twin brother never got sick, but if the virus was strong enough I was susceptible.

I sat up, allowing my mind to linger for a brief moment on a very different explanation of my symptoms. *That scenario would be impossible. Get a grip. You're a twenty-six-year-old female. It's never going to happen. It's probably just the flu. There's no need to—*

Without so much as a breath of warning, another spasm of pain hit clear and bright. My body jerked backward as the force of it plowed through me, sending my head slamming into the bedframe, snapping the wooden slats like matchsticks. My back bowed and my arms lashed out, knocking my bedside table and everything on it to the ground. The explosion of my lamp as it struck the floor was lost beneath my bona fide girl scream. "*Shiiiit!*"

Another tremor hit, erupting its vile ash into my psyche like a volcano. But this time instead of being lost in the pale haze of sleep, I was wide awake. I *had* to fight this.

I wasn't sick.

I was *changing*.

Jesus Christ! You've spent your whole life thinking about this very moment and you try to convince yourself you have the flu? What's the matter with you? If you want to live, you have to get to the dose before it's too late!

The pain buried me, my arms and legs locked beside me. I was unable to move as the continuous force of spasms hit me one after another. The memory of my father's voice rang clearly in my mind. I'd been foolish and too stubborn for my own good and now I was paying the price. "*Jessica, don't argue with me. This is a necessary precaution. You must keep this by you at all times.*" The new leather case, containing a primed syringe of an exclusively engineered cocktail of drugs, would be entrusted to me for safekeeping. The contents of which were supposed to render me unconscious if need be. "*You may never need it, but as you well know, this is one of the stipulations of your living alone.*"

I'm so sorry, Dad.

This wasn't supposed to happen. My genetic markers weren't coded for this. This was an impossibility. In a world of impossibilities.

I'd been so stupid.

My body continued to twist in on itself, my muscles moving and shifting in tandem. I was locked in a dance I had no chance of freeing myself from. The pain rushed up, finally reaching a crushing crescendo. As it hit its last note, my mind shattered apart under its impact.

Everything went blissfully black.

Too soon, pinpoints of light danced behind my eyelids. I eased them open. The pain was gone. Only a low throbbing current remained. It took me a moment to realize I was on all fours on the floor beside my bed, my knees and palms bloodied from the shards of my broken lamp. My small bedside table was scattered in pieces around me. It looked like a small hurricane had ripped apart my bedroom. I had no time to waste.

The dose is your only chance now. Go!

The bathroom door was five feet from me. I propelled myself forward, tugging myself on shaky arms, dragging my body behind me. *Come on, we can do this. It's right there.* I'd only made it a few thin paces when the pain struck again, hard and fast. I collapsed on my side, the muscles under my skin roiling in earnest. *Jesuschrist!* The pain was straight out of a fairy tale, wicked and unrelenting.

I moaned, convulsing as the agony washed over me, crying out in my head, searching for the only possible thing that could help me now. My brother was my only chance. *Tyler, it's happening! Ty, Ty . . . please! Tyler, can you hear me? Tyyy . . .*

Another cloud of darkness tugged at the edges of my

consciousness and I welcomed it. Anything to make all this horror disappear. Right before it claimed me, at that thin line between real and unreal, something very faint brushed against my senses. A tingle of recognition prickled me. But that wasn't right. That wasn't my brother's voice.

Dad?

Nothing but empty air filled my mind. I chastised myself. *You're just hoping for a miracle now.* Females weren't meant to change. I'd heard that line my entire life. How could they change when they weren't supposed to *exist*? I was a mistake, I'd always been a mistake, and there was nothing my father could do to help me now.

Pain rushed up, exploding my mind. Its fury breaking me apart once again.

Jessica, Jessica, can you hear me? We're on our way. Stay with us. Just a few more minutes! Jessica . . . . Hang in there, honey. Jess!

I can't, Dad. I just can't.

Blood.

Fear shot through me like a cold spear. I lifted my nose and scented the air. Coolness ran along my back, forcing my hair to rise, prickling my skin. I shivered. My labored breaths echoed too loudly in my sensitive ears. I peered into the darkness, inhaling deeply again.

Blood.

A rumble of sounds bubbled up from beneath me and I inched back into the corner and whined. The thrumming from my chest surrounded me, enveloping me in my own fear.

Out.

I leapt forward. My claws slid out in front of me, sending me tumbling as I scrabbled for purchase on the smooth surface. I picked myself up, plunging down a dark tunnel into a bigger space. All around me things shattered and exploded, scaring me. I vaulted onto something big, my claws slicing through it easily. I sailed off, landing inches from the sliver of light.

Out.

My ears pricked. I lowered my nose to the ground, inhaling as the sounds hit me. Images shifted in my brain. *Humans, fear, noise . . . harm.* A low mewing sound came from the back of my throat. A loud noise rattled above my head. I jumped back, swiveling away, searching.

Then I saw it.

Out.

I leapt toward the moonlight, striking the barrier hard. It gave way instantly, shattering. I extended myself, power coursed through my body. The ground rushed up quickly, my front paws crashing onto something solid, my jaws snapping together fiercely with the force of the impact. The thing beneath me collapsed with a loud, grating noise. Without hesitation I hit the ground.

Run.

I surged across hard surfaces, finding a narrow stretch of woods. I followed it until the few trees yielded to more land. I ran and ran. I ran until the smells no longer confused me, until the noises stopped their assault on my sensitive ears.

Hide.

I veered toward a deep thicket of trees. Once inside their safe enclave, I dove into the undergrowth. The scent pleased me as I wiggled beneath the low branches, concealing myself completely. Once I was settled, I stilled, perking my ears. I opened my mouth, drawing the damp air over my tongue, sampling it, my nostrils flared. The scents of the area came quickly, my brain categorizing them efficiently. The strong acidic stench of fresh leavings hung in the air.

Prey.

I cocked my head and listened. The faint sounds of rustling and grunting were almost undetectable. My ears twitched with interest. My stomach gave a long, low growl.

Eat.

I sampled the air again, testing it for the confusing smells, the smells I didn't like. I laid my head down and whimpered, the hunger gnawing at my insides, cramping me.

Eat, eat, eat.

I couldn't ignore it, the hunger consumed me, making me hurt. I crept slowly from my shelter beneath the trees to the clearing where the tall grass began. I lifted my head above the gently waving stalks and inhaled. They were near. I trotted through the darkness, soundless and strong. I slid into their enclosure, under the rough wooden obstacle with ease. I edged farther into the darkness of the big den, my paws brushing against the old, stale grass, disturbing nothing more.

Prey.

The wind shifted across my back. They scented me for the first time. Bleating their outrage, they stamped their hooves, angry at the intrusion. I slipped under another weak barrier, my body lithe and agile as I edged along the splintered wood. I spotted my prey.

Eat.

I lunged, my jaws shifting, my canines finding its neck, sinking in deeply. Sweet blood flowed into my mouth. My hunger blazed like an insatiable fire, and my eyes rolled back in my head in ecstasy. The animal tipped over, dying instantly as it landed in the dirty hay. I set upon it, tearing fiercely at its flesh, grabbing long hunks of meat and swallowing them whole.

"Goddamn wolves!"

My head jerked up at the noise, my eyes flickering with recognition.

Human.

"I'll teach you to come in here and mess around in my barn, you mangy piece of shit!"

Sound exploded and pain registered as I flew backward, crashing into the side of the enclosure. I tried to get up, but my claws slipped and skidded in the slippery mess. *Blood.* I readjusted, gaining traction, and launched myself in the air. The pungent smell of fear hit me, making my insides quiver with need.

Kill.

A deep growl erupted from inside my throat, my fangs lashing. My paws hit their target, bringing us both down with a crash.

Mine.

I tore into flesh, blood pooled on my tongue.

"Please . . . don't . . ."

No!

I stopped.

No!

I backed away.

"Bob, you all right out there?"

Danger.

Out.

I loped forward, limping along in the shadows. I spotted a small opening, jumped, and landed with a painful hiss. My back leg buckled beneath me, but I had to keep moving

Run.

I ran, scooting under the barrier. A scream of alarm rent the air behind me. I ran and ran until I saw only darkness.

Rest.

I crawled beneath a thick canopy of leaves, my body curling in on itself. I licked my wound. There was too much damage. I closed my eyes. Instantly images flashed through my mind one by one.

Man, boy . . . woman.

I focused on her.

I *needed* her.

Jessica.

I called her back to me.

She came willingly.

Jessica! Jessica! Honey, can you hear me? Answer me!

Jess, it's Ty. You have to listen to Dad and wake the hell up!

My brain felt foggy, like a thick layer of moss coated it from the inside.

Jessica, you answer me right now! Jessica. Jessica!

"Dad?"

I squinted into the sunlight filtering through a canopy of branches a few feet above my head. I was human again. I had no idea how that had happened, but I was relieved. I tried to move, but pain snapped me back to reality the instant my leg twitched.

With the pain came everything else.

The change, the escape, the poor farmer. I shuddered as the memories hit me like a flickering film reel, a snippet of my life one sordid frame at a time. I'd been there, I'd seen it, but I hadn't been in control for any of it – except at the very end. I hoped like hell the farmer was still alive. Saying no had taken so much effort, I couldn't remember anything at all after that. I had no idea where I was.

From everything I knew about wolves, not being in control was an extremely bad sign. If I couldn't subdue my wolf – couldn't master my Dominion over the new beast inside me – I wouldn't be allowed to live.

Holy shit, I'm a wolf.

I lifted my head and glanced down the length of my very exposed, very naked body. I focused on my injury and watched as my skin slowly knit back together. *Incredible*. I'd seen it happen before on others, but until now I'd never been in the super healing category myself. Young male wolves gained their abilities after their first shift. My body must still be adjusting, because my hip was still one big mash of ugly muscle. Dried blood stained my entire right side, and the heart of the gunshot wound resembled a plate of raw hamburger.

Thankfully there was no bone showing. If there'd been bone, there would've been bile. Now that I was awake and moving, the pain had increased. I closed my eyes and laid my head back on the ground. My encounter last night better not have been a normal night out for a new werewolf. If it was, I was so screwed.

Jessica!

My head shot up so fast it slammed into a pointy twig. *Ow.* "Dad?" So it hadn't been my imagination after all. I knew the Alpha could communicate with his wolves internally, but hearing his voice was new to me. I concentrated on listening. Nothing. I projected a tentative thought outward like I used to do with my brother.

Dad?

Oh my God, Jessica! Are you all right? Answer me!

Yes! I can hear you! I'm fine, er . . . at least I think I am. I'm in pain, and I can't really move very well, but I'm alive. My hip looks like it went through a meat grinder, but it's mending itself slowly.

Stay where you are. We'll be right there. I lost your scent for a time, but we're back on your trail now.

Okay. I'm under some thick brush, but I have no idea where. I can't get out because of my leg.

Snort. *You're not healed yet?*

Tyler?

Who else would it be?

Hearing my brother's voice in my head released a flood of emotion. I hadn't realized how much I'd missed it until right this second. *It's safe to say I wasn't expecting you back in my brain. We haven't been able to do this since we were kids, but it's good to hear you now.*

Tyler's thoughts shifted then, becoming heavier, like a low, thick whisper tugging along the folds of my mind. *Jess, I heard you calling me last night. You know, when it first happened. It sounded awful, like you were dying or something. I'm so sorry I didn't make it there in time. I tried. I was too late.*

It's okay, Tyler. We haven't been able to communicate like this in so long, I really wasn't expecting it to work. It was a last-ditch effort on my part to take my mind off the brutal, scary, painful transition process. Don't worry about it. There wasn't anything you could've done anyway. It happened mind-bogglingly fast. Almost too fast to process. My heart caught for a second remembering it.

I heard, or maybe felt, a stumble and a grunted oath. *You'll get used to it,* Tyler said. *The change gets easier after you do it a few more times. Hold on, I think we're almost to you. We lost your scent back at the barn. Jesus, you ripped that place apart. There was blood everywhere.*

An ugly replay started in my mind before I could shut it down. *I hope the farmer survived.* I shifted my body slightly and winced as a bolt of pain shot up my spine. My injuries would've killed a regular human. I was clearly going to survive, but it still hurt like hell.

My dad's anxiety settled in sharp tones in my mind. *We're close, Jessica. By the time we picked up your scent on the other side of the barn, we had to wait for the human police and ambulance to leave. It shouldn't be long now. Stay right where you are and don't move. Your scent grows stronger every moment.*

Yeah, you smell like a girl. It's weird.

Maybe that's because I am one. Or have you forgotten because you haven't seen me in so long?

Nope, I haven't forgotten, but you don't smell like a regular wolf, Tyler said. *Wolves smell, I don't know, kind of rustic and earthy. You smell too female, almost like perfume. It sort of makes me gag.* I could feel him give a small cough in the center of my mind, which was totally bizarre.

Then I should be easy for you to find.

Snort.

We'll be right there, my dad assured me. *Don't worry. We've got a car not too far from here waiting to take you back to the Compound.*

All this effort to communicate was taking its toll, and

my head began to ache in earnest. The pain in my hip flared and a whooshing noise started in my ears. *I'm feeling a little woozy all of a sudden . . .*

Hang on—